W9-CFQ-317

THE KING'S SPIES

THE KING'S SPIES

Simon Beaufort

This first world edition published in Great Britain 2003 by
SEVERN HOUSE PUBLISHERS LTD of
9–15 High Street, Sutton, Surrey SM1 1DF.
This first world edition published in the USA 2004 by
SEVERN HOUSE PUBLISHERS INC of
595 Madison Avenue, New York, N.Y. 10022.

British Library Cataloguing in Publication Data

Beaufort,   Simon
    The king's spies. - (A Sir Geoffrey Mappestone mystery)
    1.   Mappestone, Geoffrey, Sir (Fictitious character) - Fiction
    2.   Great Britain - History - Henry I, 1100-1135 - Fiction
    3.   Detective and mystery stories
    I.   Title
    823.9'14 [F]

    ISBN 0-7278-6039-9

Typeset by Palimpsest Book Production Ltd.,
Polmont, Stirlingshire, Scotland.
Printed and bound in Great Britain by
MPG Books Ltd., Bodmin, Cornwall.

To Richard Reynolds

Prologue

Antioch, February 1098

It was winter, so the searing heat of the desert was not as terrible as in the summer months. What *was* terrible, however, was that the Christian army laying siege to the heavily fortified town of Antioch had not had a proper meal in weeks. The Crusaders had soon exhausted the supplies plundered from nearby villages, and had been obliged to send foragers in ever-widening circles to hunt, steal or beg. But recently, even the best scavengers had come back empty-handed. Morale was low: the soldiers were weakened by disease and lack of food, and longed to be home, away from the flies that plagued them by day and the dismal rains that drenched them by night.

Philip the Grammarian was angry. Although he had his own supply of victuals, carefully hidden so he would not be obliged to share, he was furious that he – a son of the great Earl of Shrewsbury and a member of the powerful House of Montgomery-Bellême – should be reduced to grovelling in the mud like a peasant. He had not wanted to take part in the Crusade in the first place, but he had been banished from England and his estates confiscated, so obeying the Pope's call for brave men to travel East had seemed the only way to recoup his losses.

As the Earl's fourth child, Philip had been destined for the Church, and the nickname 'Grammarian' denoted the learning he was supposed to have acquired. However, there was more irony than truth in it: he disliked scholarly activities, and did not want to make a paltry living as a cleric. Philip had a different plan for his future: he was going to save the Holy City from the infidel with a weapon so powerful

1

and terrifying that he knew Jerusalem's defenders would surrender the moment it appeared. His glorious success would bring the riches and fame he felt he deserved.

His stomach rumbled, because the dried meat he had eaten that evening had not been enough to satisfy him, even though it was more than most men had had. Food was now so scarce that a loaf of bread cost a gold coin, and a scrawny chicken cost three. Ordinary soldiers could not afford such prices, and it seemed the Crusade would flounder long before it reached Jerusalem, brought to its knees by empty stomachs. Meanwhile, safe in their fortress, Antioch's Turks looked down on the hungry, sick and disheartened Crusaders, and jeered.

Philip disapproved of the siege, and did not see why they had to capture Antioch before marching on Jerusalem. He had told his fellow commanders again and again that they were wasting time and could be attacking the Holy City itself, but most leaders argued that leaving Antioch in the hands of hostile forces would be to place themselves between two enemy armies. Philip thought they were wrong: he just wanted to rescue Jerusalem and go home in glory.

He glanced at the box under his bed that held his secret. It contained a small amount of a deadly substance called Greek Fire, along with instructions explaining how to make it. Greek Fire had been used against the Crusaders often enough, but they had been unable to reproduce it themselves, because there was a mystery ingredient their alchemists could not identify. Philip had learned the secret from a dying soldier in Constantinople, whose wits had been rambling and who had not been in a position to understand the ramifications of his fevered revelations. Philip had written down the formula for the potion that burned like magic, and that water could not quench, and knew it was the key to his future.

It had occurred to him to use his weapon against Antioch, but he knew it would not work there: the only way *that* city would fall would be for someone to betray it from within. Since he did not want to squander his secret needlessly, he had determined to save it for Jerusalem alone – then no man would mention the liberation of the Holy City without also praising the name of Philip the Grammarian.

Philip yearned to join the powerful Lord Bohemond, one of a few sensible men who had abandoned Antioch to march on Jerusalem instead. However, Lord Tancred, among the army's most able of leaders, mounted nightly patrols, not only to protect his encampment from Turkish raids, but to stem the steady trickle of deserters. To escape, Philip would need to slip past these guards, and that would not be easy with horses, squire and food – and he certainly did not intend to leave empty-handed.

Another growl from his stomach helped Philip to reach a decision. Not for him a grim death from starvation when his food ran out, or from the bowel sickness that killed more men than any battle. He was going to leave Antioch, and then he and Bohemond would attack Jerusalem and achieve immortality.

He felt better once he had made up his mind, but he knew he would have to make enquiries about the nightly patrols before embarking on his bid for freedom. Some guards were better than others, and he did not want to be dragged back in disgrace. He left his tent with his squire in tow, and started to walk through the camp, hearing the low moans of men whose dreams were plagued by visions of bread and meat, and the feeble, wrenching cries of those who would be dead by the morning.

He was not pleased to learn the commander on duty that night was a knight called Sir Geoffrey Mappestone, one of Tancred's most trusted officers. Geoffrey's patrols were thorough and well planned, and Philip knew he would never slip past him undetected. He was heartened, though, when he learned that the Lorrainers would be in charge the following day. These were an unruly, disobedient rabble, who preferred dozing behind rocks to prowling a desert where they might meet bands of marauding infidel. Philip knew he would have no trouble evading *their* watch.

Feeling hopeful for the first time in weeks, he informed his squire that they would be leaving the following evening. The man nodded in relief, because it was only a matter of time before Philip learned he was not the only one living off the hidden supplies: the squire did not see why he should starve, and had not been looking forward to the day when Philip discovered the truth. If they escaped, Philip would never know what had been happening.

Philip watched Geoffrey brief his men and then climb on to his warhorse to study Antioch's four hundred towers and twenty-five miles of walls. Philip snorted in disdain. Did the knight really believe his painstaking inspections would make any difference? Antioch had deep wells that were awash with fresh water, and its storehouses were full of grain. Philip knew the besiegers could wait until Judgement Day and the city would not fall.

He was about to return to his tent and rest, when he heard a yell. Near the camp was a narrow bridge that had linked Antioch to the plains around it in happier times. Now it was only used when raiders slipped along it under cover of darkness to cause chaos among the besiegers, or when brave and determined men like Geoffrey attempted to storm the fortress. In horror, Philip saw torches flicker and leap, and tents in flames. His stomach clenched in fear. The camp was under attack! Men rolled from their sleeping blankets in a daze, many too weak even to hold a sword, let alone repel an invasion by well-armed and healthy enemies.

Sick with terror, Philip dashed to his tent and wriggled under the bed, to hide with his precious box. His squire watched his cowardice in appalled disbelief, then made an unpleasant, strangled sound as something hissed through the roof and landed in his chest. It was a fire arrow.

While the squire died in writhing agony, Philip scrambled away, knowing he would be burned to a cinder if he remained where he was. Still clutching his box, he rushed outside, careful to leave his shield behind, so it would not identify him as someone high-ranking and worthy of an infidel's blade. He looked around wildly, trying to determine where the fighting was thickest, so he could run in the other direction. By now, the whole camp was bathed in an unsteady, orange glow as fires blazed out of control. He felt like crying. His food would be destroyed, and he would be obliged to sleep without a tent, like a common soldier.

'There!' he heard Geoffrey shout. 'Stop them!'

4

He turned to where the knight pointed, and saw a line of Turkish soldiers running towards the huts where valuable items like maps and spies' reports were kept. They held torches, and it was obvious what they intended to do. With a shock, Philip saw Geoffrey expected him to act. The knight held a heavy broadsword in one hand and a dagger in the other, and was yelling for Philip to follow him. With a battle cry that made Philip's blood run cold, Geoffrey plunged into the line of Turks, and began laying about him. He was soon surrounded and outnumbered. Philip shrank back into the shadows, declining to become embroiled in a skirmish that would surely see him hacked to pieces.

He turned to run again, but there was a sudden burning pain between his shoulders and he found himself unable to breathe. He dropped the box and scrabbled behind him, to free himself from the searing ache in his spine. When he looked at his hands, they glistened darkly with blood. He had been stabbed in the back! A shadow eased its way past him, and he saw his assailant was no Turk. With mute dismay, Philip saw he was not going to die in glorious battle, where his soul would be flown directly to Heaven, but had been viciously murdered like a beggar in an alleyway. He sank to his knees and watched helplessly as his killer snatched up the box and melted away into the night.

One

London, March 1102

S ir Geoffrey Mappestone and Sir Roger of Durham were experienced and heavily armed Norman knights, yet both felt uneasy as they made their way through the streets of Southwark towards the London Bridge. It was nearing dusk, and the narrow alleys were alive with characters who were never seen in daylight hours – robbers who stalked their prey in the darkness, sharp-faced prostitutes who enticed men into dimly lit taverns for the contents of their purses, and fallen priests who had prospered in the lax reign of William Rufus with their black arts. Rufus's successor, King Henry, was not so tolerant, and peccant priests were obliged to hide, to emerge only when the sun had set and they would not be recognized and pointed out to the King's spies.

Geoffrey knew the London Bridge closed at dusk, sealing Southwark and its shadowy activities from the more prosperous city of London, which sprawled along the opposite side of the River Thames. He pressed his knees into the sides of his great warhorse to urge it to walk faster, reluctant to linger in a place where he, Roger and their three men would not be welcome. It was not long since the Conqueror had invaded England and made Saxons inferior subjects in their own country, and the defeat still rankled. Geoffrey sensed there were many Southwark night-folk who would relish an opportunity to kill a Norman knight, steal his horses and plunder his saddlebags. His black and white dog whimpered uneasily, and Geoffrey knew how it felt.

The daylight was fading fast, showing how short a March day could be. It was not yet five o'clock, but shadows lay thick and black across the streets, and lights burned in the

6

houses of those wealthy enough to afford a lamp and fuel. It began to rain, too, and the mottled clouds that slouched overhead played their own part in bringing an early dusk. Gradually, the occasional drop became a pattering downpour, blown in spiteful, sleety flurries by a chill north wind.

'We should find an inn,' said Roger, running a thick finger around the neckline of his cloak, sodden from where water had run in rivulets from his conical helmet. He glanced around him. 'It is not pretty here, but I have slept in worse places. We can cross the bridge tomorrow at dawn and still be in time to obey your summons from the King.'

'No,' said Geoffrey, thinking that if Roger had stayed in worse than Southwark, then he must have graced some very insalubrious towns with his presence. 'We cannot stay here. It is not safe.'

'Not safe?' scoffed Roger. 'We are knights, armed with the finest steel gold can buy, and with Crusaders' crosses on our surcoats that tell people we are *Jerosolimitani* – those who freed Jerusalem from the infidel two years ago. Who do you think will harm us?'

'This is different,' argued Geoffrey, who knew that while the residents of Southwark were unlikely to engage them in open battle, they might well fire arrows from dark alleys or abandoned houses.

'Rubbish!' declared Roger uncompromisingly. 'No one would dare.'

A slithering sound made Geoffrey tense, hand on the hilt of his sword as he scanned the street for danger. But there was nothing to see. He looked up to where thatched roofs formed a jagged margin to the thin strip of grey sky above, and thought Roger a fool to be complacent. Neither they nor their servants carried much of value, but their cloaks and armour were of good quality, and their warhorses expensive and well trained. They were certainly not beyond the ambitions of an opportunistic thief who was handy with a bow.

Ahead lay an inn, which illuminated the dirty street with slivers of light escaping through cracks in its window shutters. A sign above the door swung back and forth, creaking loudly enough to be audible over the hiss of sleet and

7

the sounds of drunken conversation coming from inside the tavern.

'The Holy Hero,' said Roger squinting at the sign. It depicted an unhappy-looking Crusader, whose head appeared to be coming away from his body. Words were scrawled underneath, which meant nothing to the illiterate Roger. 'I have had enough of traipsing in the wet for tonight, and we are too late to cross the bridge anyway. We will stay here.'

'We will not,' said Geoffrey, whose ability to read made most of his fellow knights regard him with rank suspicion, Roger included. 'It is called the Crusader's Head and the sign shows your "hero" being decapitated by a Southwark whore. It is not the kind of place that would welcome us.'

'I agree,' said Geoffrey's sergeant, Will Helbye, edging his horse forward so he could speak. 'I do not like the look of it, either.'

Helbye, a grizzled veteran in his late fifties, had been in Geoffrey's service for many years, and it was well past the time when he should have retired to his home on the Welsh borders. But Helbye did not want to be a farmer, and Geoffrey supposed he intended to remain a soldier until he either was killed in battle or dropped dead in his saddle.

Geoffrey's squire, Durand, nodded agreement, but Durand was fussy and cowardly, and Geoffrey seldom took any notice of his opinions. Durand was old for a squire, older than Geoffrey himself, and was a neat, slender man with a head of long, golden hair. Geoffrey had been amused at first when Durand had been mistaken for a maiden from behind, but one or two misunderstandings over his sex had turned violent, and he quickly learned that his squire's appearance was more of a liability than a source of humour.

'It not only smells, but I just saw a whore go inside,' said Durand with a shudder that had his companions regarding him warily. Durand's disapproval of prostitutes extended to women in general, which the others found difficult to understand.

'It is perfectly respectable,' argued Roger. 'My horse is lame and it is time we stopped. Geoffrey does not have to

8

meet the King until noon tomorrow, so we do not have to cross the river tonight.'

Geoffrey understood his friend's reluctance to continue travelling when the prospect of a warm bed beckoned. They had been in the saddle since dawn, and Roger was ready for a rest, particularly in a tavern well supplied with prostitutes and ale. A man with a full purse and a strong thirst could ask for little more.

Roger was a large, frank man, whose father – the sly Bishop Flambard of Durham – was one of the most hated men in England, although Roger and his devious parent were nothing alike. Like Geoffrey, Roger wore his hair short and was clean-shaven, and his face was ruddy from a life spent out of doors. Geoffrey was smaller and cleaner, with light brown hair and green eyes, and was intelligent enough to enjoy the challenge of occasional subterfuge, although he disliked it on too regular a basis.

Geoffrey surveyed the Crusader's Head warily, considering his options. It was one of the largest taverns on the south bank, and comprised wattle-and-daub walls and a thickly thatched roof. It had been extended and rebuilt more than once, because the different parts of it did not sit well together and formed a complex jumble of windows and walls. Stains seeped from the oils that protected its timbers, and its roof was covered in moss and rot.

As he hesitated, Geoffrey became aware of a strange smell lurking below the stench of sewage and filth that coated the street. It was acrid and somehow dangerous, and vague memories clawed at the back of his mind. It was an aroma he had encountered before, but could not place where or when. He identified the warm, rotten stink of sulphur and the sharper scent of something alkaline, and wondered what sort of ale the landlord served to his patrons.

It did not take many moments for him to conclude that Roger was wrong, and that the Crusader's Head was not the sort of place he and his companions should patronize. He was about to ride on when there was a yell from one of the building's upper windows. He glanced up just in time to see something large drop out, almost directly above him. He raised one arm instinctively to ward off the plummeting mass, but it never reached him. Instead, it stopped just above his head, accompanied by an unpleasant snapping sound.

Durand gave a shrill screech of fright and promptly lost control of his pony, while Geoffrey's dog barked furiously and began to dart in tight circles around the horses' legs.

'God's teeth!' exclaimed Geoffrey irritably, because Durand's scream had startled him more than the sudden and unexpected descent of the object from above.

'It is a man!' Durand babbled, pointing at the bundle that swung back and forth with rhythmic creaking sounds. 'And he is dead!'

'Someone has hanged him,' said Geoffrey, who had realized as much as soon as he heard the sickening crack of a neck breaking as it came to the end of the rope. He stood in his saddle to grab the dead man's feet, slowing their macabre dance. 'You have seen this before, surely?'

'I have not!' said Durand in an unsteady voice. 'I was destined for the Church before that incident with the butcher's son. You know that. The only other corpse that has sullied my eyes before today was that of my grandmother, who choked on a slipper last Easter.'

Geoffrey knew better than to ask for details, intriguing though the story might sound. Durand had been expelled from the Church for 'perverse practices', and then foisted on Geoffrey by his liege lord, Tancred, because Tancred had owed Durand's father a favour. Tancred had quickly realized there was nothing *he* could do to convert Durand from monk to soldier, but when a summons had arrived from King Henry of England, demanding Geoffrey's presence at Westminster Palace by noon the day before Palm Sunday, Tancred had agreed to let his knight go on condition that he took Durand with him – and made him a warrior into the bargain. Geoffrey soon learned the task was beyond him, too. Durand wanted to spend his time in churches, railing against the circumstances that had snatched away his chosen career. It was not a happy state of affairs, and Geoffrey felt Tancred had secured the better half of the bargain.

'What shall we do?' asked Roger, seizing one of the dead

10

man's ankles and turning the body to look at his face. It was too dark to make out more than a grossly angled head.

'There is nothing we can do,' said Geoffrey practically. 'He is dead and we should go before someone thinks we had something to do with it.'

'We cannot just abandon him,' said Durand, appalled by the notion. 'We are not Saracens, to leave our dead for the birds to peck at. We should tell someone to cut him down.'

'Someone will discover him soon enough,' said Geoffrey. 'And it is none of our affair. We can tell a priest to come and give him last rites, if leaving him troubles your conscience.'

'A priest will not give him last rites,' said Roger. 'He is a suicide.'

Geoffrey turned the body, so Roger could see its hands tied crudely but firmly behind its back. 'He was murdered. Did you not hear the scuffle and the yell he gave?'

He heard Durand give a whimper of fright, and wished the man would get a grip on himself. It did Geoffrey's own reputation no good to have a retainer snivelling in terror behind him. His dog was no better, and stood with its tail between its legs, looking up at the body with haunted eyes. He envied Roger, whose squire was a sturdy Saxon called Ulfrith. Ulfrith was not Durand's intellectual equal, but he rarely expressed fear, and always did exactly what Roger ordered, no matter how inane the task.

'You mean someone *threw* him from the window with a rope around his neck?' asked Ulfrith. 'And bound his hands so he could not free himself?'

Geoffrey nodded. 'These are poor knots, but they only needed to work for a few moments – until his neck broke or the rope strangled him.'

'Murder!' wailed Durand in a voice loud enough to make the others start in alarm.

'Control yourself!' snapped Helbye sharply. 'Do you want to summon half the robbers and vagabonds of Southwark to see why you are screeching?'

'I do not,' said Durand fearfully, turning his horse in the direction of the bridge.

But it was too late. The inn door opened, and several

11

people tumbled out to see who was making the noise. Two leaned on each other, laughing helplessly at a joke humorous only to ale-soaked minds, while a brown-robed cleric with bad teeth clutched a half-naked whore, ignoring her protestations that she did not want to be outside *sans* clothes. Another woman stared blearily at the travellers for a moment, then her eyes were drawn upwards. When she saw the still-twisting body, she opened her mouth and released the shrillest scream Geoffrey had ever heard. It went on and on, and other patrons began to swarm from the tavern like wasps from a nest. Within moments, the two knights and their three men were surrounded by a hostile crowd that clearly thought the murder was their doing.

Geoffrey did not feel particularly intimidated by the throng. Although many possessed knives and cudgels, they would succeed in inflicting little damage through his mail tunic, conical helmet and padded surcoat. Also, he knew he needed only to draw his sword to see most of them scuttle for their lives. His horse, trained for battle, was inured to such situations, and waited patiently for a command to plunge forward or kick out with its hoofs.

He looked for someone in the crowd who might act as spokesman, but saw only pinched and impoverished faces that looked about as likely to possess leadership qualities as sheep. Several people at the back wore hoods to conceal their faces, and Geoffrey assumed they were merchants or nobles who did not want to become involved in trouble at a Southwark tavern. He caught the glitter of silver thread in the garments of one, while another sported a fur-lined cloak, expensive and well made. The man was careful to keep his face in shadow, but Geoffrey could see the distinct shape of a head with hair cut very short on top, so it stood up in spikes.

At the very back of the gathered onlookers, Geoffrey saw two figures hurrying away with a long box. One person was large and moved easily and purposefully, while the other was slight and not so strong, so the chest jiggled and bounced as they went. Geoffrey supposed they were a merchant and his apprentice, trading illegally acquired goods that they wanted to conceal now a murder might attract the King's guards.

Eventually, a burly man with a bushy yellow beard pushed through the crowd to take charge. His clothes were stained and he wore a filthy apron that identified him as the landlord. He glanced up at the body, then back to Geoffrey and Roger, taking in the Crusader's crosses on their surcoats.

'Why have you done this?' he demanded. 'Did you not have enough slaughter in the Holy Land?'

'No, actually,' replied Roger, taking the question literally. He enjoyed nothing more than a tough skirmish in which he could practise his fighting skills, and he and Geoffrey had argued about this more than once, when Geoffrey had opted for a peaceful solution and he had yearned to use force. 'I have not slain anyone since—'

He stopped when Geoffrey shot him a warning glance. He did not always know why his friend prevented him from saying what he wanted, but he had learned to ask why later, when they were alone. In this case, Geoffrey had decided that Roger declaring a fondness for killing would not win them any friends.

'This was not our doing,' Geoffrey said. 'We were passing when he toppled out of the window.'

The taverner was astonished. 'You expect us to believe that? A pair of Normans "pass", and one of my patrons just happens to be hanged at the same time?'

'It does not matter whether you believe it or not,' said Geoffrey shortly. 'It is what happened.'

The landlord regarded him through narrowed eyes, reassessing knights who did not ride away after they had had their murderous fun, but remained to explain themselves. Geoffrey began to feel hopeful that an unpleasant situation might be averted after all.

'I am Oswin.' The man indicated the Crusader's Head with considerable pride. 'I am the landlord of Southwark's finest tavern, so you had better tell *me* the truth.'

Geoffrey shrugged. 'We have no reason to lie to you, Master Oswin. We are witnesses to this death, not its instigators.'

Oswin took a flickering torch from one of his patrons and elbowed people out of the way to inspect the body that still dangled above them, clearly relishing his position of authority and the way folk accepted his right to act as their spokesman. He moved the unsteady flame upwards until he could see the face of the dead man, then released a horrified gasp that was echoed in several of his patrons. Geoffrey saw one or two immediately slink away.

'But this is poor Hugh!' cried Oswin, turning accusingly to Geoffrey. 'What could *he* have done to warrant this? He is witless and not nearly the man his father was. How could you do such a thing?'

'We do not know "poor Hugh",' replied Geoffrey. 'And how could we be responsible, when he was hanged from inside the tavern and we are on the outside?'

Oswin looked sceptical. 'So you say, but the tavern is busy tonight, and we only have your word you have not been in.'

'We do not lie!' objected Roger indignantly. 'Nor do we hang folk for no reason.'

Geoffrey ignored them as they began to argue, more interested in the fact that the wavering torchlight allowed him to see the body properly for the first time. He saw it was not a pauper as he had first assumed – perhaps someone caught stealing and rewarded with instant justice – but a man who had been able to afford good clothes. Gold glittered at his throat, where an expensive brooch was pinned, and the boots were clean. Hugh had been a man of consequence, who had ridden to the inn, not waded through the muck of the roads. Geoffrey also noticed that Hugh had been in his early twenties and was the owner of a mane of long black hair.

'This is dreadful,' muttered Oswin. More spectators left the crowd, shaking their heads and muttering that they wanted nothing to do with it, while several of the hooded figures who lingered at the rear exchanged uneasy glances. One pushed forward for a better view, and then hurried back to his companions, where Geoffrey saw them conferring.

'Who would want to kill Hugh?' mused a thin-faced man

14

with massive ears. He wore a dirty apron that was similar to Oswin's, and Geoffrey supposed he was a pot boy. 'He was harmless.'

'He was a child, Wulfric,' replied Oswin coldly, although his comment was directed at Roger, whom he eyed with unconcealed dislike. 'No one needs to harm a child.'

'Well, we do not know him, child or not,' said Roger impatiently. Geoffrey saw his friend had had enough of Oswin and was itching to be away, so he could relax with a jug of ale and company that was more conducive than that of the accusing landlord.

'You will,' said Oswin with a nasty smile. 'You see, Hugh is the illegitimate son of Hugh.' He folded his arms and regarded Roger in a way that indicated he should be impressed. The big knight stared at him warily, as if told a joke he did not understand.

'Then you must send our condolences,' said Geoffrey, before they could be regaled with lengthy explanations they did not need to hear. 'But we have business in London, and cannot linger—'

'It is past dusk,' said Wulfric, maliciously satisfied. 'You cannot cross the bridge now. It is closed at night, to prevent London merchants from invading us and making off with our worldly goods.'

Geoffrey tried not to show his amusement at this interpretation of the curfew, suspecting that while rich merchants might well slip across the river to the insalubrious lanes of the south-bank settlement, it would not be for plunder. It would be for business that could not be negotiated by day, or to sample the prostitutes known as Winchester Geese, who worked in buildings rented from the Bishop of Winchester.

'The guards will allow *us* to pass,' said Roger with grim determination. 'If they will not accept a silver coin, they will obey steel.' His hand dropped and, with a ringing sound, he hauled his broadsword from his belt. More people melted away like snow under a hot sun, and others began to mutter resentfully. Geoffrey sighed, wishing his friend would let him do the talking. It would not be the first time Roger had instigated a brawl with his unwise habit of whipping out his weapons.

'You are too late,' said Oswin, unperturbed by the knight's display of force. He saw Roger look speculatively at the Crusader's Head. 'And do not think you can persuade *me* with your silver and swords, either. I have no rooms for foreigners.' He spat on the ground.

'I am not foreign,' said Roger indignantly. Geoffrey coughed loudly, because he had an awful feeling Roger was about to say he was an illegitimate son of the Bishop of Durham, an unpopular man because of the ruthless taxes he had imposed. England was full of folk who would be more than happy to kill a kinsman of the detested prelate.

'And you *will* be needing the safety of a tavern tonight,' added Wulfric spitefully. 'No one kills Hugh and gets away with it. You should find yourselves somewhere secure.'

'I suppose this Hugh will come for revenge,' said Durand, wide-eyed with fear. 'The father, not the son, obviously. The son is beyond avenging himself on anyone.'

'Why?' sneered Oswin disdainfully. 'Are you afraid?'

'Of course I am,' said Durand, surprised that such a question should be asked. Geoffrey closed his eyes in exasperation. Between Roger's aggression and Durand's transparent terror they were likely to end up with some serious problems. 'I abhor arguments, especially ones that end in violence.'

'You are a funny Norman,' said Oswin, eyeing Durand doubtfully and taking in the pretty golden hair, neat clothes and soft leather boots. 'Normans usually love violence.'

'We do,' said Roger, glaring at Durand. But it was too dark to see and Durand was blithely unaware of Roger's ire.

'I do not want to be a knight,' Durand confessed to the crowd. Many exchanged bemused glances at this unexpected confidence. 'I was to be a monk, you see, but I met the son of a butcher, and the next thing I knew was that I was forced to take up arms. My father wants me to go to the Holy Land and honour the family by obtaining the title of *Jerosolimitanus*. But, frankly, I do not like flies—'

'I am sorry about Hugh,' interrupted Geoffrey. 'But we should be on our way.' He started to move forward, but the remaining onlookers pressed around him and he did not want to use force, aware that it would take very little to ignite the situation into something ugly.

'You have no idea who Hugh was,' remarked Oswin, peering into Geoffrey's face in the torchlight and trying to gauge his expression. 'Do you?'

'None at all,' said Geoffrey, who did not much care.

'But you have heard of Robert de Bellême, the Earl of Shrewsbury?'

Geoffrey had indeed, and was aware of the fear that rippled through the crowd at the mere mention of that dreaded name. Bellême was widely regarded as the most barbaric and dangerous man in the world. He had attempted to overthrow King Henry the previous year, hurling his forces behind the claim of Henry's older brother, the Duke of Normandy. Bellême and the Duke had been routed, but Bellême was not a man who took defeat well, and he had vented his fury on his own people, initiating a reign of terror that shocked even the most hardened of warriors. Geoffrey had met the Earl once, and had experienced for himself the man's raw menace and power.

'Everyone knows Bellême,' said Durand, when Geoffrey did not reply. 'What of him?'

'Bellême is fond of Hugh,' said Oswin. 'He will want to know who killed him.'

'Oh, no!' whispered Durand in horror. 'The Black Earl of Shrewsbury will think *we* did it! He will kill us first, and ask his questions later.'

'Yes,' agreed Oswin with a sly grin. 'That summarizes your situation very well.'

Geoffrey was indifferent to the news that Bellême had a liking for the hanged Hugh. Bellême had spies everywhere – it was how he kept his considerable empire intact – and the loss of one would not affect him unduly. Moreover, Geoffrey was under the impression that Bellême had not dared to set foot in England since his defeat by King Henry the previous year. He was aware that people glanced uneasily at each other every time the Earl's name was mentioned, and became impatient with them.

'For God's sake! He is miles away in Normandy and not in a position to harm any of you.'

17

'He is here,' countered Wulfric, surprised that Geoffrey should not know. 'He is in London, for an audience with the King. Hugh is his nephew – the illegitimate son of his brother.'

'Hugh the Elder died four years ago, and Bellême stole the Earldom from his rightful heirs and kept it for himself,' supplied Roger helpfully, even though Geoffrey knew this perfectly well. Everyone was familiar with the complex machinations of the House of Montgomery-Bellême, and the family's manoeuvrings were a scandal that both shocked and entertained, and were a common topic of gossip.

'Bellême and his family have been ordered to appear before the King's Easter Court and explain why they sided against him last year,' added Oswin.

'They are not pleased,' said Wulfric gleefully. 'Have you not heard? It has been the talk of London for weeks. It is said that Henry intends to confiscate *all* their estates.'

A good many people looked around uncomfortably, and Geoffrey saw that the loyalties of most were with neither the King nor his rebellious vassal. He could understand why: Henry was hard on criminals, such as the ones who thrived in Southwark, while Bellême was generally regarded as the epitome of evil. It would not be an easy choice for those who lived at the edges of the law.

'Bellême loved his nephew,' said Oswin nastily. 'So you can be sure he will come looking for his murderers.'

Geoffrey supposed he should be on his guard if Bellême were to pay him a visit – they had not parted on the best of terms when they had last met, and Geoffrey had antagonized the man to the point where he was regarded as an enemy.

'How do you know Hugh was murdered?' he asked, aware that Oswin had not seen the dead man's tied hands, so could not know whether he was pushed or had jumped.

'A man does not order a jug of wine and three goblets only to hurl himself out of a window moments later,' said Oswin scornfully. 'He was murdered, all right.'

'But not by us,' said Geoffrey, now tired of the conversation and wanting to find somewhere quiet, where he could consider what Bellême's presence in England might mean for his own family, who were legally the Earl's vassals. 'You can see the noose is attached to something inside your tavern. Therefore someone *inside* tied the rope around his neck and threw him out of the window, not men who happened to be riding along the street outside.'

'But, as Master Oswin said, folk have been coming and going all night—' began Wulfric.

'But not us,' interrupted Geoffrey firmly. He gestured to the dark streets behind him. 'Dozens of people saw us riding towards the London Bridge as dusk fell. We cannot be your culprits, so you must look among your customers for the killer.'

'Oh, no!' exclaimed Oswin, jumping into Geoffrey's path to prevent him from riding away. 'I want to know your names. The Earl will ask questions about his nephew's death, and I intend to tell him about *you*. I do not want him setting my inn alight when others are to blame.'

'I know the Earl,' said Geoffrey. 'I will tell him myself.'

'You do?' asked Oswin, backing away in alarm. His demeanour changed immediately, and he became obsequious. 'You should have said so, sir. I suppose he ordered you to kill the lad himself?'

'To keep his followers on their toes,' added Wulfric, nodding in understanding. 'He likes even his most loyal henchmen terrified of him. His siblings are afraid, too – his brothers Roger and Arnulf, and their three sisters.'

Geoffrey was about to try to leave again, when he saw that two of the inn's patrons had gone to Hugh's chamber, and were sawing through the rope that held him. He decided to wait, to see whether the body might yield clues about the killer that would permanently exonerate him and his companions. The body jigged as they hacked, and then fell with a thump into the ordure of the street.

People pressed closer when the body dropped. Even the hooded figures who lurked at the back surged forward, and one reached Hugh and huddled over him for a few moments before moving away. Geoffrey wondered if he was a friend or a servant.

'Look!' exclaimed Wulfric, who was unashamedly rummaging through Hugh's clothes in the hope of finding a purse. He had discovered the tied hands instead, and stood back so people could see. Geoffrey studied the knots that held noose and bonds in place. They were unlike any others he had seen – clumsy and untidy – although they had done their work well enough.

'There is something in his mouth,' said Oswin. He held the torch near Hugh's face and pointed at something pale that was thrust between the dead man's teeth. 'What is it?'

'That is odd,' said Geoffrey to Roger. 'I thought I heard him yell before he dropped from the window. How could he shout with a full mouth?'

'Perhaps it was the killer we heard,' suggested Roger. 'That is a large mouthful, and I am not sure he could have shouted around it. Mind you, it was just a scream: there were no words.'

Geoffrey supposed that was true. A gagged man might still be able to express his final terror, even if he could not howl the name of his killer or holler a prayer to save his soul. Meanwhile, Wulfric had retrieved the item, and was regarding it suspiciously. It was a piece of parchment. Oswin took it from him and unravelled it with great care, turning it this way and that in evident disappointment.

'It is nothing but writing,' he said, holding the torch so close that he threatened to incinerate it. Geoffrey eased behind him. 'I thought there might be a picture, but there are just words.'

'Were you expecting a picture?' asked Geoffrey, suddenly suspecting that Oswin knew more about why Hugh had died than he had led them to believe.

Oswin shrugged, and Geoffrey could tell he was lying. 'Not really.'

'Why was Hugh here in the first place?' asked Geoffrey, wondering why a wealthy relative of Bellême's would frequent a sordid tavern in Southwark at all.

'He was meeting friends,' replied Oswin vaguely. 'He came often. The Crusader's Head is more honest than the taverns in London, and he liked the company of men he could trust.'

Geoffrey refrained from pointing out that someone in the inn had just murdered him, so it seemed he could not trust the patrons of the Crusader's Head any more than he could the taverns across the river. He wondered whether the men Hugh had been meeting – two of them, since Oswin said he had ordered wine for three – were among the shadows at the back of the crowd. He looked around for them, but they had gone, apparently realizing they were too visible in the rapidly dwindling onlookers.

'I do not think Hugh could read,' said Oswin, continuing to jerk the parchment this way and that, as if he imagined movement might induce it to reveal its secrets. 'So I suppose this was forced into his mouth to stop him making a noise.' He registered his disgust by screwing the document into a ball and tossing it in the gutter, where it bobbed for a moment, then sank from sight.

Once Hugh had been carried to a nearby church, and there was nothing left to see, the last of the crowd dissipated. Geoffrey and Roger found themselves alone with Oswin.

'I meant what I said,' repeated the landlord. 'I have no spare rooms, even if you are in the service of the Earl. These are dangerous times, and my tavern is already involved in things I wish it were not.'

'What do you mean?' asked Geoffrey.

'Meetings,' said Oswin in a low voice, glancing around to ensure they were not overheard. 'People coming in the middle of the night, demanding rooms for their business. I do not like it, but what can I do? Only a fool says no to the Earl.'

'Bellême's people use your inn?' asked Geoffrey, intrigued, despite the alarm bells that warned him to ride away and have nothing more to do with the matter.

'Yes,' said Oswin unhappily. 'They keep their livery hidden under their cloaks, but I know who they are. I hope the Earl is not planning another rebellion before the Easter Court – or rather, that he does not intend to use my inn as his headquarters. The King would hang me for certain.'

'Probably,' agreed Geoffrey. 'He does not tolerate traitors.

21

But what about that parchment? What did you expect to see there?'

'A weapon,' replied Oswin miserably. 'I expected to see a picture of a great weapon that will win wars and throw an enemy into confusion.'

'Whose enemies?' asked Geoffrey uneasily. 'The King's?'

'Bellême's.'

Geoffrey fought to understand what the man was telling him. 'Are you saying Bellême has devised some new weapon to use against King Henry?'

'Yes,' said Oswin in a strangled whisper. 'And Henry will hang me for a traitor because its design came from my poor tavern.'

Geoffrey and Roger left the Crusader's Head and its agitated landlord, with Durand, Helbye and Ulfrith riding in a tight knot behind them, all on their guard. Although the attitude of the crowd had changed after Geoffrey had professed to be personally acquainted with the dreaded Earl, he still did not trust them. Southwark was a place full of hidden dangers, and he disliked being in a position where he could not see the enemy he was to fight. He glanced behind him for the third or fourth time since leaving the tavern.

'I wonder what this weapon is,' mused Roger, intrigued. 'Oswin said it can win wars and throw an enemy into confusion. As a knight, I should like to know more about it.'

'You may not be the only one,' said Geoffrey, assuming this was why Hugh had been murdered. If the device was as devastating as Oswin believed, then men might well be killed for it.

'I wonder who has this secret,' Roger went on. 'Is it the King's weapon, and the Bellême clan are trying to get it? Or have the Bellêmes invented it?'

'The latter,' said Geoffrey. 'The King is fairly secure on his throne now, and developing new weapons would be useful, but not essential. However, it is entirely possible that Bellême has devised one because he knows he will be expelled from England soon – unless he can defeat Henry in open battle. A new weapon may well tip the balance in his favour.'

'So, Oswin was right,' said Roger admiringly. 'Bellême and his followers *have* invented some deadly device under his roof.'

'I am not so sure,' said Geoffrey, considering the matter carefully. 'It would be very difficult to create such a thing without the King's spies knowing or seeing, and I think it more likely that Bellême has managed to get hold of something used by our enemies on the Crusade, rather than inventing something original. We know from personal experience that we have a lot to learn about the war machines of other civilizations.'

'Turks or Arabs,' mused Roger, recalling the various battles he had fought in the East. 'Do you think they mean to equip their troops with curved scimitars, then? Like the Saracens?'

'No. If this weapon were just a different kind of sword, it would be very difficult to keep secret.'

'Why?'

'Because it would involve cartloads of iron being ferried to forges, blacksmiths labouring day and night, and men practising with whatever they produce. The King's spies would ferret them out in a moment, and it would be a secret no longer.'

'What then?'

'Think, Roger. What weapon did the Arabs use during our siege of Jerusalem? What did they throw that burned so fiercely we could not put it out, and that smouldered through flesh and bone?'

'Greek Fire?' asked Roger in an awed whisper. 'That was a terrible weapon, right enough! Some landed on my helmet, and it burned for hours before I was able to scrape it off. And it killed Ancellus of Méry, if you recall.'

Geoffrey remembered very vividly what had happened to the French knight when a mass of Greek Fire had caught him full in the chest. Geoffrey had tried to smother the flames with his cloak, but they re-ignited as soon as he thought they were out. He had poured the last of his drinking water over them, but the fire had hissed and spluttered and burned more fiercely than ever. He had scraped handfuls of sand over his comrade, but the fire continued to rage. Even urine – rumoured to douse most blazes – had not worked. By the time it had extinguished itself, Ancellus was long dead.

'We tried to learn what Greek Fire was made of,' he said. 'Some alchemists believed it was quicklime and sulphur, but their own experiments could not reproduce the same effects. We concluded the Arabs added a secret ingredient, but we never discovered what.'

'It would be a fabulous weapon for either Bellême or Henry,' said Roger soberly. 'Oswin is right: it might well win one of them a war. But what makes you think someone has brought it to England?'

'Did you not notice the smell? When we first arrived, the stink of sulphur and quicklime lingered in the street. Someone had ignited Greek Fire near the Crusader's Head.'

'But Hugh was hanged, not incinerated,' said Roger, bewildered.

'Yes,' agreed Geoffrey. 'And I looked at his hands and clothes for signs of burning, but saw none. Perhaps he had simply witnessed a demonstration to which he had not been invited, and was hanged to ensure his silence.'

'Was the secret written on the parchment in his mouth, then? I know you read it, because I saw you peering over Oswin's shoulder like an old monk.' He shot his friend a disapproving glare.

'No, that was a message from the King. It stated he had no wish to negotiate with anyone from the House of Montgomery-Bellême behind the Earl of Shrewsbury's back.'

'You see?' asked Roger, his voice thick with disgust. '*Words* brought Hugh to his end. He tried to cheat his uncle by dealing with the King – probably wanting to save himself when his family's estates are forfeit. And Bellême found out what he was doing and had him killed.'

'Possibly. Or perhaps Bellême knows nothing about Hugh's attempted treachery, and the murder was the King's doing.'

Roger gazed at him. 'But then why would Henry leave the message in Hugh's mouth? That basically tells anyone who sees it that Henry is responsible for his death.'

'Right,' said Geoffrey, glancing at his friend askance. He tended to forget at times that Roger was a straightforward

24

man, and subversive doings were largely beyond his comprehension. Roger was not honest – he was too much a Norman for that, with a Norman's love of gold – but he would never indulge himself in the kind of treachery and intrigue that marked the courts of powerful men. 'That traitors can expect to be hanged may well be the message the King wanted the Bellême clan to receive. Or, alternatively, the message may be to warn Bellême that one of his kin is negotiating with the King.'

Roger sighed gustily. 'I should have known not to expect a simple answer from you. You always see far too many sides in every situation. So, just tell me in one word whether you think Hugh's death is related to this Greek Fire business.'

'Yes,' said Geoffrey. 'But I do not know how. He may have been murdered trying to steal the secret from Bellême to give to the King. If that is true, then it is possible the King did not appreciate what Hugh was offering him.'

'You mean Hugh stole the secret from Bellême and offered it to Henry, but Henry, not being a Crusader, had never heard of Greek Fire? He did not know to grab the secret while he could, and instead sent that message? When Bellême found out what his nephew had done he had him killed?'

'Basically,' said Geoffrey. 'Although I am sure Henry knows all about Greek Fire. Perhaps Hugh gave the King the wrong formula. If he really was dim-witted, as we have been told, then he might have believed he could cheat Henry by providing him with false information and still be paid.'

'It is all very confusing,' said Roger disapprovingly. His voice became loud as he triumphed that a plot relying on the written word had failed. 'But whoever wrote that message intended it to be found by someone, and *you* are the only one who read it before it was thrown away.'

There was a soft rattle behind them, and Geoffrey saw someone dart out from the shadows and race away into the darkness. Whoever it was had gone in an instant, and his footsteps quickly faded into nothing.

'I am not sure it was a good idea to bellow that,' said Geoffrey reproachfully. 'Now someone else knows we are party to a secret.'

Two

By the time Geoffrey and Roger arrived at the London Bridge, its gates were closed and the guards were locked in their gatehouse. Roger hammered on the door and demanded an audience with their captain, but the guards merely called back that it was more than their lives were worth to allow anyone – no matter how heavy their purses – to cross outside the curfew. One added that if they looked above the gate they would see a severed hand. Geoffrey stepped back in disgust when a maggot dropped from the hideous thing on to his shoulder.

'That was Norbert's,' called the guard soberly. 'He took a silver penny from a monk who wanted to cross. The monk was one of the King's spies, and Norbert lost his hand. You can keep your gold. Better men than you have tried to persuade us to break the law tonight, but we will not do it.'

'Damn that Oswin,' growled Roger. 'It is *his* fault we arrived too late to cross.' He looked up and down the road as he tried to decide which direction to take. Neither appeared promising, with hovels lining each side and huge rats foraging among heaps of stinking rubbish. 'He was probably delaying us on purpose, so we would be forced to stay in his miserable inn.'

'I do not think so.' Geoffrey shivered. Night had brought a chill northerly wind, and the rain had turned to sleet; water seeped through his cloak to form a clammy cocoon around his body. 'He clearly disapproves of Crusaders. And who can blame him if it has resulted in dangerous weapons being discharged under his roof?'

'You think he is actually *manufacturing* Greek Fire there?' asked Roger, startled. 'Within a stone's throw of London?'

'No. The stink from large amounts of the stuff would alert the King's spies and it would be investigated. I imagine tonight was just a small demonstration of what it can do, while the bulk of it will be hidden elsewhere. Of course, just because someone has the formula does not mean all the ingredients are readily available. We know from our own experiments that it is not easy to make.'

'Will you tell the King tomorrow that Bellême has Greek Fire and will use it against him?'

'We do not know for certain it is true,' hedged Geoffrey, reluctant to become embroiled in a political struggle. 'It is just what we have concluded ourselves, and we have no real evidence – other than an odd smell and the confession of a frightened landlord who may recant his story tomorrow. I think we would be wiser to say nothing to anyone. It is none of our affair.'

'I would not mind laying my hands on a bit for myself, though,' said Roger fondly. 'I can think of a number of times when it would have come in useful.'

'Which way do you want to go?' asked Geoffrey, to change the subject. Greek Fire was not a substance he wanted in his saddlebags, and he was not sure he would travel with Roger if his friend stored some in his. It was far too dangerous to be carried so close.

The dog grew tired of standing in the bitter weather and slunk away to stand in the cover of a wall, trying to escape the driving wind. Meanwhile, Durand looked thoroughly miserable, and Helbye's stiff old joints were in desperate need of a fire. Ulfrith cared nothing for weather of any kind, and merely looked around with the eager fascination he always displayed when visiting new places.

Roger was about to reply when two women lurched by, already the worse for drink. One wore an orange wig, which kept slipping from her shaven head, while the other had lank, greasy hair and ears that stuck through it as though they were trying to escape. Geoffrey assumed they were Winchester

27

Geese. Roger, never fussy where prostitutes were concerned, gave them one of his leering grins.

'Good evening, ladies. Where can we sleep tonight? Do you have a mattress on which a man can lay a weary head, perhaps in company with a warm woman?'

'We know a quiet wall,' suggested the bewigged lady, coming closer so that Geoffrey could see she was missing teeth, as well as hair. He wondered what she had done to allow them to become so sadly depleted, and supposed it was due to disease. It did not encourage him to want to lie with her.

'A wall?' asked Roger distastefully. Even he had standards.

'It faces away from the wind,' added the bewigged woman enticingly. Roger appeared to reconsider.

'I do not want a wall,' said Geoffrey firmly. 'I want a clean tavern.'

'Oh, a *clean* tavern,' mocked the greasy-haired slattern with an unpleasant sneer. 'Well, you are in the wrong part of town for that, good sir. Give me a penny. I have not eaten all day.'

'Liar,' said the other. 'You had a bit of cat just this morning.'

'Only the skin,' replied Greasy Hair indignantly. 'That does not count.'

'Find us a dirty tavern, then,' suggested Roger, still leering. 'And then I shall treat you to something a little tastier than cat.'

'Actually,' said Red Wig seriously, 'there *is* nothing tastier than cat. It is a flavoursome meat, and not like hare or ferret, which are full of bones and lack good texture.'

'But cat is so chewy,' argued Greasy Hair. 'Now badger is a meat for—'

'The inn,' prompted Geoffrey, unwilling to sit around while they discussed the culinary virtues of every hapless beast that inhabited Southwark.

'If we show you, will you share your chamber with us?' asked Red Wig slyly. 'Then we will not have to pay the Bishop. He already earns more than he should from our honest labours.'

'No,' said Geoffrey, thinking that they would probably snore and keep him awake half the night. Red Wig scowled, while Helbye looked appalled that Geoffrey's fastidious principles were about to lose him a comfortable night. 'But I will buy you a place in the stable loft and a dish of cat.'

'And I will pay you for something else,' said Roger, making an obscene gesture with his hand, lest they should not understand what he meant.

The women shrieked with laughter, and Roger beamed at them, clearly seeing himself a regular wit. Geoffrey sighed, not wanting to linger in the sleet while Roger honed his brutal courtship skills. He headed his horse along the riverside, hoping the tavern was not too far. He wanted nothing more than a fire and a jug of warmed ale, and would not even be too particular over the state of the bed, as long as it had nothing too large crawling in it.

'Not there, dearie,' called Red Wig, waggling her hips at him. 'Come this way.'

Geoffrey wheeled his horse around, aware as he did so that someone darted quickly into the shadows of a ramshackle warehouse nearby. He cantered over and peered into the darkness, but could see nothing. He hoped it was just an optimistic thief, and not a spy following them after the incident at the Crusader's Head. He did not like to think that either Bellême's agents or the King's were on his trail.

The two women led the way along a narrow alley until they reached a tavern that was smaller than the Crusader's Head, but that looked just as disreputable. Ulfrith, who was fond of the horses, muttered that he was not leaving them unattended, and elected to remain with them for the night. After a quick glance at the inn's main chamber, Helbye decided to do the same, and Geoffrey had grave misgivings when even the dog hesitated, one paw raised as it sniffed with wary disdain. It had an unerring eye for what was good for it, and seldom made mistakes where its well-being was concerned. It entered the tavern so slowly, and with such reluctance, that Geoffrey seriously considered going elsewhere. But Roger pushed past him, bellowing for the landlord, and that was that.

29

Geoffrey expected objections from Durand, who was fussy over where he slept, but the squire was cold, wet and prepared to risk a good deal for a seat near a fire. He alighted daintily from his nag, and made for the door, taking a scented pomander from his scrip to place over his nose in anticipation of the welter of smells all travellers knew to expect from seedy taverns. He did not walk as much as mince, and Geoffrey thought he would have done very well in a monastery, had he managed to control himself with butchers' sons.

The Heron Inn's drinking chamber was shadowy and cramped, and Geoffrey saw several clients leave through a rear door when two Norman knights entered their domain. Resentful glances followed them as they walked towards the fire, although Roger either did not care or did not notice. He bawled to the innkeeper to bring ale and a platter of meat, and stood over two men who sat near the hearth until they left, intimidated by the clanking armoury that adorned his large person. Geoffrey sat, thinking it was small wonder Saxons considered Normans bullies, if they all behaved like Roger.

'Ale,' snapped the landlord, slapping jug and goblets on to a table next to them. It was freezing cold, and Geoffrey surmised that either the Heron did not bother to take the chill from its ale on cold winter nights, like most taverns, or the landlord had decided the best way to rid himself of his unwelcome guests was to provide them with poor service.

A dirty pot boy brought a tray of gristly meat, wiping his running nose on his hand as he did so. Another servant carried a basket containing bread long past its best. Roger fell on the food as though it was the most delicious thing he had ever eaten, breaking the congealed mass of cold flesh into more or less even quarters and handing one to Geoffrey. The women grabbed a piece each, although Red Wig had problems in biting off portions small enough to gum.

'It is Lent,' said Durand disapprovingly, using his monastic vocation to hide the fact that he had been too slow to claim a piece and was left with bread. 'You are not supposed to eat meat during Lent.'

'Religious horse shit,' said Roger contemptuously. 'A man needs flesh to keep up his strength. Do not be prissy, man, and eat what the good Lord has seen fit to give you. That is what my father always says, and he must be right, because he is a bishop.'

Geoffrey shared his portion with Durand, who picked distastefully at the offering before the dog hurried forward to slather at his knees. Durand was frightened of the dog, and nearly always gave it what it wanted, just to make it go away. He took one look at its dripping fangs and unfriendly expression, and flung most of the meat into a corner. The dog reached up and snatched the remainder from his fingers before joining the rest to consume at its leisure.

'You should not have done that,' said Greasy Hair. 'It is not right for dog to eat dog.'

Geoffrey threw his portion to the animal, too. 'He is not fussy.'

'Unlike you,' said Red Wig in disgust, as the dog finished its repast and slunk away, presumably to join Helbye and Ulfrith in the more conducive surroundings of the stables. 'Throwing away good meat as though it grows on trees. *We* cannot afford such luxuries.' She looked pointedly at the purse that hung from Geoffrey's belt.

'We would like a room,' said Geoffrey, when the landlord returned with more ale and several wizened apples. He wondered why the man assumed they wanted more of his nasty cold beer, but Roger made no objection, and downed the jug in one, smacking his lips in appreciation and showing he was not a man of discerning taste. Geoffrey drank more slowly, aware that murky ales past their best could bring a man low the following day with gripes in the bowels.

'And cakes,' added Roger, as the landlord started to leave. He winked at Red Wig, who grinned back at him in delight.

'Cakes?' asked the landlord dubiously, making them sound like something obscene. 'We do not sell that kind of thing here. There is not much call for them.'

'*I* am calling for them,' said Roger, as though that should be sufficient for the landlord to change his culinary practices on the spot. 'Ones with figs,' he added unreasonably.

'What are figs?' asked the landlord warily. 'Witches' food?'

'We will just take the room,' said Geoffrey, not wanting to become involved in a detailed discussion about exotic fruits and their availability in wintertime London. He also did not want the landlord to complain to the authorities that there were men in his tavern demanding foods more usually consumed by the Devil's familiars. He had enough to worry about with meeting the King the next day, and did not want to be obliged to defend himself against accusations of sorcery.

'This is not a whorehouse,' said the landlord stiffly, eyeing the women meaningfully. 'The Bishop of Winchester has one of those next door, so go—'

'I only want to sleep,' said Geoffrey, disassociating himself from Roger's antics. It was not that he disapproved of dalliances with women – he was actually quite fond of them, and had enjoyed many pleasantly memorable occasions in the past – but he had standards, and bald, toothless women tended not to meet them unless he was really desperate. He pushed a silver coin across the table.

The landlord snatched it up and secreted it in his clothing so quickly that Geoffrey wondered whether it had actually happened. 'In that case, you can have my own chamber. I will tell my wife to stoke up the fire and tether the cow. She will not bother you during the night; she just lies near the window and chews the cud.'

'I assume you mean the cow,' said Geoffrey, hoping he was not going to be obliged to share the room with some ancient crone who would mutter and snore all night.

'My wife never sleeps near the window,' declared the landlord huffily. 'She does not like draughts.'

The chamber was surprisingly clean, given that it was home to a large brindled bovine, and Geoffrey supposed the landlord and his wife wanted better conditions for themselves than for their patrons, because the rest of the inn was filthy. He ordered Roger to do his courting in the corridor, settled on to a soft straw mattress, and was asleep within moments, with Durand lying at right angles to him at the bottom of the bed. He snapped awake when Roger flopped next to him, and stirred when the cow lowed softly, but nothing else disturbed him until just before dawn. And then he awoke to feel cold steel against his throat.

The blade dug into Geoffrey when he tried to sit up, so he raised his hands to show his captor he was at his mercy. He assumed the man did not want to kill him immediately, or he would have done so already. Meanwhile, Roger snored on, oblivious to the drama that was unfolding at his side, and Durand lay on his back with his mouth open.

Geoffrey was appalled that someone could have crept up on him unawares – something that had not happened since he was twelve years old, and had left the austere comfort of his father's castle to begin his knightly training. Any such laxness on the Crusade would have seen his throat slit in an instant, and he usually prided himself on his vigilance. The cow shuffled restlessly, and he supposed the sound of its chewing must have masked any odd sounds. Also, his dog was not in there, to bark warnings at uninvited guests.

'Where is it?' hissed a voice in his ear, and the knife nicked him again. Geoffrey felt sluggish and thick-headed as though he had consumed too much ale, although he had actually drunk very little. He wondered what was wrong with him.

'Where is what?' he asked loudly, hoping to wake Roger or Durand. His assailant was not amused, and the dagger waggled about menacingly.

'Do not think you can rouse your friends.' The voice was hoarse, as though its owner was trying to disguise himself. 'Your ale contained poppy juice. The big one resisted its effects long enough to cavort with his women, although you and your squire succumbed easily enough. But do not play games with me. Tell me where it is or I will kill you.'

Geoffrey supposed he should be more careful about what he ate and drank in strange places in the future. He recalled a second jug of ale following hard on the heels of the first, and realized he should have been suspicious at the time. The landlord was unlikely to have provided another drink quite so quickly without first seeing their money, and Geoffrey should have guessed something was amiss instead of swallowing it without question.

33

'It is over there,' he said, making a vague gesture in the darkness with his hand.

His captor eased his grip a fraction as he leaned forward to see where Geoffrey was pointing. It was enough. With one rapid movement, Geoffrey reached up and twisted. He grabbed his assailant's arm, jerked it away from his throat, and used the momentum to haul the man off his feet and on to the bed. Then he dropped on top of him with considerable force. Geoffrey was tall and strong, and had not bothered to divest himself of his armour before he went to sleep. He was heavy, and the man gasped for breath as the knife slipped from his fingers and clattered to the floor. Roger and Durand stirred restlessly as the bed heaved and bucked around them, but did not wake.

'How much of that soporific did you give them?' demanded Geoffrey angrily, once he was sure he had the man subdued. Roger had also acquired the knack of resting with one ear alert to potential danger, and the fact that he was slumbering through a wrestling match did not bode well.

'More than I wanted to waste,' snapped his would-be assailant, sounding more irritable than afraid. 'I was beginning to think it would never work. I should have been away from here long before now, and instead it is almost dawn.'

'You followed us,' said Geoffrey, recalling the skulking figure he had spotted the previous evening.

'I am not very good at that sort of thing. I imagine you saw me at least twice.'

'What do you want?' asked Geoffrey, bemused by the man's attitude. Most people would have been a little more conciliatory under the circumstances.

The man fell silent, so Geoffrey jerked him upright and dragged him to where a tinder lay next to a candle stub, indicating that he was to light it. Reluctantly, the fellow obeyed, and the chamber soon filled with a low, flickering light. The cow watched with disinterest, chewing purposefully with its legs tucked underneath it. Geoffrey glanced at Roger and was relieved to see his chest rise and fall rhythmically, while Durand smiled in his sleep. Satisfied his companions were as well as could be expected, he

34

turned his attention to the intruder, whom he still kept at knifepoint.

He was almost as tall as Geoffrey, but slimmer. His face was hidden by the hood of his cloak, so Geoffrey yanked it away. He was proud of himself when he betrayed no surprise at the discovery that it was not a man but a woman, who had taken the unusual precaution of wearing a man's leather leggings and short tunic under her cloak. She glowered at him with a face as black as thunder. Her dark hair was wrapped into a coil at the back of her head, and he saw from her worldly-wise eyes and the laughter lines around her mouth that she was well past youth – perhaps middle forties. Her accent was cultured, so he assumed she was not one of the Winchester Geese he had heard coarsely advertising their wares in the street the night before.

'What do you want?' he repeated, stepping closer with his knife at the ready.

'You already know,' she retorted angrily. 'And incidentally, there are armed men outside who will come for me when I do not return, so you had better rethink your position.'

Geoffrey doubted there were any such guards, or they would not have allowed her to sneak into the chambers of sleeping knights alone, but he admired her audacity and resourcefulness.

'I have no idea what you are talking about,' he said, wishing he felt more alert. He recalled Roger bellowing out the fact that Geoffrey had read Hugh's parchment before the landlord tossed it into the gutter, and suspected his nocturnal visitor had something to do with that, although he was not going to make matters easy for her by guessing.

'You *do* know,' she flashed furiously. 'I want the parchment you stole from Hugh.'

'What makes you think I took it?'

'You were seen.' Geoffrey supposed one of the shadowy, wealthy-looking figures at the back of the crowd had told her. 'Do not play games with me. Where is it?'

'The landlord found it, not me, but he threw it away when he could not read what was written. You can try hunting for

35

it outside his inn, but I doubt you will find it. It is probably in the river by now.'

She cursed colourfully in a way that indicated no matter how cultured her Norman-French, she had nonetheless spent time in less exulted circles. 'Are you sure? It contained valuable information.'

'What sort of information?'

'Nothing to interest you. Now put up your weapon. I do not like knives waved at me.'

'What sort of information?' He forced her up against the wall with the blade near her throat.

She sighed irritably and tried to push him away. 'You are better off not knowing. You should have kept riding and not become involved.'

'I am *not* involved,' said Geoffrey firmly. 'But now you have piqued my interest. Tell me what you expected to find in that parchment and I will let you go.'

She gave a half-laugh of disbelief. 'And how do I know that I can trust you?'

'You do not. Trust is something earned over long periods of time, not exchanged carelessly in the depths of the night between people who do not know each other.'

'A soldier's answer,' she said, sounding amused. 'Well, perhaps we should introduce ourselves, then. I am Matilda de Mortain. Who are you?'

'Geoffrey Mappestone.' Her name rang a distant bell in Geoffrey's memory, and he tried to recall where he had heard the name Mortain before. He was certain the answer would have sprung more readily to mind had his wits not been pickled in poppy juice. 'So, now we know each other, you can tell me what you think was on that parchment. And then I will release you.'

'A map or some directions,' Matilda replied. 'There is something I need to find, and I think Hugh knew where it was.'

'Where what was?'

'No more questions,' she snapped. 'I have kept my part of the bargain, so let me go.'

'You replied so vaguely that it is no answer at all.' Geoffrey was not so sluggish that he did not see she was attempting to mislead him. 'What were you hoping to find?'

'Something belonging to my mother,' she replied shortly. 'Something personal.'

Geoffrey frowned in puzzlement, wondering how the terse letter from the King could possibly reveal the location of lost property. It did not make sense, and he realized that either the letter was not what she expected, or she was lying.

'It said nothing about property,' he said. 'It informed the recipient that King Henry declines to negotiate with anyone from the House of Montgomery-Bellême without the knowledge of the Earl of Shrewsbury.'

As soon as the words were out of his mouth he regretted them. He took a deep breath, trying to clear his wits, and wondered what other stupid things he might say before the soporific wore off.

'You said it went into the river,' said Matilda accusingly. 'How do you know what it said?'

'I read it.' There was no point in being coy now, he thought.

'Reading is an odd skill for a Crusader knight.'

He said nothing.

'And it was from the King?' she asked, sounding bemused. 'Are you sure?'

'It was signed with his name.'

She was silent for a moment. 'And there was nothing about where a particular object might be located? Perhaps a drawing or a set of directions?'

'If there had been a drawing, then Oswin would have kept it,' Geoffrey pointed out. 'He threw it away because what he saw made no sense to him.'

'You are telling the truth about that,' conceded Matilda. 'Oswin *would* have kept the parchment had he understood it. He would think he could sell it.'

'The parchment I saw gave no details about any property,' said Geoffrey, supposing there must have been more than one missive concealed on Hugh's corpse. 'Unless it was in code.'

'It would not have been in code,' she said. 'Damn! What

sort of game was Hugh playing? Are you sure you do not still have it?'

'You are welcome to search my bags, but you will find I am telling the truth.'

Matilda thought for a moment, then pushed away the hand that held the dagger. 'I believe you. Now you can return to your slumbers, and I will be about my own business.'

Geoffrey considered his options. There were two: he could release her or kill her. She no longer sounded hostile, and he had always disliked cold-blooded slaughter, so moved away and sheathed his dagger – although he kept his hand on its hilt just in case he had misjudged the situation. She would not ambush him a second time and live to tell the tale.

'Go, then,' he said, gesturing to the door.

Matilda did not leave, but studied him intently in the candlelight. 'You are a strange fellow, Geoffrey Mappestone. What is stopping you from cutting my throat to repay me for invading your chamber?'

'Because I have an audience with the King tomorrow, and I do not want it to begin with a discussion about a murder in the tavern where I spent the night. So go, and continue your search elsewhere.'

'Hugh was my nephew,' said Matilda softly. She went, uninvited, to sit on the side of the fur-strewn bed, where Roger did not so much as flicker an eyelid. Geoffrey knew he would be sorely disappointed to learn there had been a woman on his bed and he had slept through the invasion. Matilda frowned in thought for a moment, then continued. 'He was running an errand for me when he was killed. I should not have used him, because he was short of wits.'

Geoffrey opened the door for her to leave. There was a corridor outside, and he was startled to see Roger's two women there, lying in a jumble of limbs and discarded wigs. He wondered again how much soporific had been used to reduce them to such a state.

'You do not understand,' said Matilda, gesturing he was to close the door and sit next to her. 'My brother will not be pleased when he hears what happened to Hugh – and he will not be amused when he learns we still do not know the location of our mother's . . . property.'

Geoffrey tried to force his mind to work, and hoped his wits would clear before his audience with the King, because he was certain he would need them. King Henry would detect any such weakness, and would be sure to turn it to his advantage.

'Did Henry send you?' he asked, wondering whether the poppy juice was his idea.

'Henry?' she asked, startled. 'The King? Of course not! I imagine he has armies of agents to perform *his* dirty work, while I am obliged to do my own. Do you think I enjoy this kind of thing? Dosing strange men with sleeping potions and breaking into their chambers in the dead of night?'

'I have no idea,' he replied, thinking that he had met plenty of women who would relish such an idea.

'Well, I do not,' she said. 'My brother would not approve, and it is always wise not to offend him.'

'Your brother?' said Geoffrey, sensing this information was important, but unable to see why.

'My brother,' she said impatiently. 'Surely you know the man who is uncle to Hugh, son of Hugh?'

'Robert de Bellême? You are the Earl of Shrewsbury's sister?' He stepped away in horror, appalled one of Bellême's female kin was lounging on his bed at such an hour. He could imagine what the Earl would make of that, and was certain he would not believe they had been talking about missing documents. Gradually, it also occurred to him that if Matilda was Bellême's sister, then she was a formidable character in her own right. Bellême had five living siblings, all of whom were powerful and wealthy, especially his three sisters: Emma, Matilda and Sybilla. Then he knew why the name Matilda de Mortain had been familiar. The wealthy Count of Mortain, dead twelve years, had been Matilda's husband, and had left her with a lot of property.

'You *have* heard of my family.' She smiled faintly, acknowledging that there were few who had not. Mothers used the spectre of the Bellêmes to frighten children into obedience, and, since arriving in England five days earlier, Geoffrey had heard several brats being informed that, if they did not behave, the Earl of Shrewsbury would get them.

'I know your brother,' said Geoffrey, wanting her gone from his room. 'He tried to cheat my family with a forged will two years ago, and we did not see eye to eye over the matter.'

'I imagine not. Robert does have a weakness for other people's belongings.'

But it was not just Robert, Geoffrey thought. The rest of the family had an equally dubious reputation, and their mother – whose property Matilda was determined to locate – was regarded as the worst of them all. Although the terrifying Mabel de Bellême was long dead, she was still feared. During her violent lifetime she had amassed vast riches by murder, deception, threats and war. She had not been pleasant, and her death was generally considered to have been a very good thing.

'Will you help me?' she asked, somewhat abruptly.

'Help you do what?' he asked uneasily. 'I have already told you that the message in Hugh's mouth is gone. I doubt we will find it – and even if we did, it would be illegible. The ink will have run.'

'His mouth?' she echoed in disgust. 'You did not mention that before. What was it doing there?'

'Perhaps Hugh's killer wanted people to know what happens to those who try to betray your brother. Or perhaps he wanted to show what Henry will do to any Bellême who expects leniency. Who can say?'

'The note is irrelevant,' she said, after a moment of considering its implications. 'I am more concerned with my mother's property than messages purporting to be from Henry. Robert will not be pleased when he hears we have lost our legacy again.'

'He has more to worry about than missing property at the moment. His attention should be focussed on saving his wealth from confiscation by the King. The matter of a dead nephew and a peculiar message will pale into insignificance compared to his other problems.'

40

Her eyes flashed, and Geoffrey saw the family resemblance. Like the Earl, she possessed thick black hair, coal-dark eyes and a strong, determined face. He knew she was telling the truth about her heritage, because the similarity between her and her brother was uncanny.

'You do not know Robert,' she snapped. 'He is an intelligent man, and details *are* important to him. He wants this property very badly.'

'Well, I am sorry,' said Geoffrey, who had little sympathy for a family that possessed unimaginable riches and yet was determined to have more. 'I cannot help you find your wealth.'

'It is not *wealth*,' she said impatiently. 'But I want you to help me with something else, as it happens. It concerns the message you *did* read—'

'No,' said Geoffrey firmly. 'I do not want to become embroiled in anything that places me between your brother and the King, thank you very much.'

She ignored him. 'There were two tasks Hugh agreed to complete on my behalf. The first – and most important – was to gather information about the whereabouts of my mother's legacy. And the second was to act as messenger between me and King Henry. I wanted the King to know that not all members of my family are set against him, and that some of us are willing to negotiate a truce.'

'Then you have had your answer,' said Geoffrey. 'It was Henry's reply to your offer that Oswin threw into the gutter.' And the message had been short and to the point: Henry was not interested in dealing with any of the Bellême clan, even ones who offered to deal secretly without the Earl knowing. The letter had been genuine after all.

'I am not so sure,' said Matilda, leaning back on Roger. He snored on, oblivious that he was being used as a cushion. 'Henry is a wise man, and does not close doors before he has fully examined the contents of their rooms. He would not dismiss me so abruptly: he would listen and then make his decision. I do not believe the message was from him.'

From what he knew of the King, Geoffrey was inclined to agree. Henry was prudent and clever, and would certainly be

41

intrigued by a falling out within a rebellious clan. Geoffrey imagined he would have arranged a meeting with the disaffected sister, not dismissed her out of hand. However, the House of Montgomery-Bellême had been a thorn in his side for so long that perhaps Henry had tired of them all, and wanted no exceptions when he banished them from his realm.

'I am confused,' he said. 'Oswin believes Hugh's death had something to do with a new weapon. Then you come up with two more theories: that it was connected with your mother's lost property *or* because Hugh carried a message purporting to be from Henry, which is not from Henry.'

'Yes,' she said with an enigmatic smile. 'Things are always complex in our family, and we seldom have one plot on the boil when several will do. My three brothers are intent on acquiring some Greek Fire, in case Henry is unreasonable when we appear at his Easter Court and we are forced to fight. Meanwhile, all five of my siblings are interested in regaining our mother's property. And finally, I have been attempting to reach Henry on behalf of myself and my two sisters, just in case the Greek Fire does not work and my mother's property remains undiscovered.'

'I do not understand why this property is so important,' said Geoffrey, bemused. 'You are all so wealthy that you cannot need more treasure.'

'I have told you already that it is not treasure, so do pay attention. It is something else.'

'What?' asked Geoffrey, intrigued. He wracked his brains, but could think of nothing the Bellêmes would want other than gold, silver or jewels – unless it was Greek Fire, of course. 'A new weapon?'

'Men put far too much faith in instruments of force. However, I know from personal experience that there are easier and cheaper ways of convincing folk of a point of view. My mother's property is nothing to do with weapons, and I am unwilling to discuss it further until I know you better.'

'Very well,' said Geoffrey, abruptly deciding that she never would. Even his muddled wits told him that he did not want to know what was so valuable to the Bellême siblings they

42

would send their sister to raid bedchambers in the depths of the night. He wondered whether their mother had invented her own version of Greek Fire. From what he had heard of that lady, it was not inconceivable.

Matilda gave a sudden smile and Geoffrey saw she was a lovely woman, with her dark features and glossy black hair. 'But I am always willing to make new friends, and this is as good a time as any. And then you can do me a small favour . . .'

'Are you sure this actually happened?' asked Roger the following morning, as they broke their fast in the Heron Inn's main room with bread and a pudding of peas. It was a gloriously bright day; the sky was a clear, brilliant blue, and frost glittered on the rooftops opposite. He glanced around as though their mysterious nocturnal visitor might still be nearby and lowered his voice. 'You did not dream it?'

'You were the one who snored all night,' said Geoffrey, who had fought to stay awake after his visitor had left, afraid there might be more invasions. 'God alone knows how much poppy juice she used in our ale. Those two women are still asleep in the corridor, and I am still light-headed.'

'Aye,' agreed Roger, rubbing his temples. It had taken a bucket of cold water to rouse him that morning. 'The tavern was busy last night, and it would have been easy for someone to slip us doctored ale. I do not take kindly to that sort of thing, and want nothing to do with her kind.'

'Her kind?'

'Witches,' said Roger primly. 'They say the Bellême stock is populated by warlocks and witches, and this proves it. She made me sleep like a baby while she tried to slit your throat. Do not tell me that is not the way of a sorcerer. I cannot believe you said you would help her.'

They walked into the inn's yard where Ulfrith and Helbye were waiting and the horses were saddled and ready to go. Sergeant and squire looked refreshed, and Geoffrey supposed they had slept better in the stables than he had in his chamber. Durand's eyes kept closing, however, and Geoffrey was sure he would fall asleep and tumble from his pony before the day was out. The man was usually full of complaints in the mornings, but had barely uttered a word that day. Geoffrey wondered whether Matilda would give him more of the stuff, so he could dose him every night.

'I agreed to tell Henry she wants to parley,' said Geoffrey, climbing into the saddle. 'But only if the occasion arises. If I think Henry will not be receptive, then she will have to find someone else.'

'But you do not *know* her, lad!' protested Roger, aggrieved. 'She is playing you for a fool – sending you into the King's presence with a message from the family he is determined to crush. He may assume you are on their side and crush you, too. What would I tell Tancred? He will not be pleased to hear his favourite knight has been executed.'

'I am sure he will survive the news,' said Geoffrey mildly. Tancred would be furious if Geoffrey was killed, but not particularly grief-stricken. The Holy Land prince was a hard and practical man, and would not waste his energy on anything as pointless as mourning.

'I told you not to come here,' grumbled Roger self-righteously. 'You have not even met the King yet, and you are embroiled in a plot that has seen one man hanged and us poisoned. You are normally so cautious. Was she pretty, this maid?'

Geoffrey shrugged. 'She looked like her brother.'

'Moustache and beard, then,' said Roger, nodding seriously. 'And eyes that glitter like a snake's. She can probably read, too, which would certainly make her attractive to you.'

Geoffrey laughed, amused by the disdain in his voice and his strange idea of what he thought his friend admired in a woman.

Roger eyed him coolly. He had not meant to be funny. 'I did not come all the way from the Holy Land to see you thrown into a dungeon. You should not have agreed to assist her.'

Geoffrey sighed, and wished he had undertaken the long journey from Antioch alone, although he acknowledged that his friend's broadsword had come in useful more than once since they had left the baked, sunny lands of the East. He had not wanted to travel to England at all, because he had

44

only just returned to Antioch after an eventful visit to his family near Wales and to Roger's home in Durham. But King Henry's summons had contained a veiled threat. Although most of Geoffrey's life had been spent overseas, his brother and sister owned Goodrich Castle and managed his own little manor of Rwirdin. He had no great love for his brother, who was argumentative and sly, but he was fond of his sister, and Henry's letter intimated that Joan's protection from Welsh raids could not be guaranteed if Geoffrey did not come. Since Geoffrey did not want Joan to suffer, he had no alternative but to head westwards. But he wished he had not involved Roger in the escapade, too.

'It is usually the other way around,' nagged Roger. 'I am the one fooled by a sweet smile and a promising tongue, and it is you telling me she is not safe. I cannot believe I am obliged to warn you about strange women who appear in your bedchamber armed with steel.'

'There was no harm done,' said Geoffrey, ignoring the fact that he, Roger and Durand were still out of sorts from her generous doses of poppy. 'And, as I said, I will not deliver her message if I feel it is the wrong thing to do.'

'But the problem is that you will not *know* it is the wrong thing to do until you have already done it,' grumbled Roger. 'Then it will be too late. I am telling you, Geoff, no good will come of this. What is she called, anyway?'

'Matilda,' said Geoffrey, who had always liked the name. 'Shrewsbury has three sisters, and she is the middle one. Emma, who is the eldest of the trio, is said to be the witch.'

'Well, that is all right, then,' said Roger, heavily sarcastic. 'We have not been enlisted by the one everyone *knows* is the witch, just one of the ones who is more discreet with her craft. So, tell me again what she wants from us.'

'Nothing from *us*,' said Geoffrey, who had already decided to keep his friend away from the whole business, just in case it misfired. 'She would like *me* to tell the King that she and her sisters are prepared to swear an oath of allegiance, vowing not to add their forces to their brothers'. I do not see why the King should object to hearing that someone wants to be loyal to him.'

'But someone has already died trying to deliver such a message or its reply. For all you know, Matilda may have offered the King her loyalty on a previous occasion and he found her lacking.'

'I know,' said Geoffrey. 'I am not stupid, Roger. I will be careful.'

Roger shot him a resentful glance to indicate he was deeply unhappy with the situation, but Geoffrey had had enough of Roger and his gloom. The rain of the previous night had dissipated, the sun had risen and the shabby buildings of Southwark were transformed from browns and blacks to orange-gold. The air was cool, and only just beginning to stink of the night soil tossed from upstairs windows into the streets below. Geoffrey inhaled deeply, detecting the scent of the river, foul and salty, among other familiar odours – the smell of fresh fish and horse manure, and a mixture of tar and wood from a shipwright's yard.

They reached the London Bridge and lined up to pay the toll with others who wanted to cross. From his reading, Geoffrey knew there had been a bridge across the River Thames since the Romans had built one many centuries before. He glanced uneasily at the rickety structure, and thought a little more money should have been invested in something so important to the city's commercial success. It was wood, when it would have been more sensible to use stone – not just because stone would be less affected by the fires that regularly plagued London, but because it would have been safer for the hundreds of folk who wanted to use it: he could feel the thing swaying under his feet as he walked.

He glanced over the side to the water below, where boatmen were doing a brisk trade, ferrying customers and their goods from one side to the other. The river was muddy brown and smelled foul, like bad eggs. All manner of filth swept past: discarded rags, pieces of wood, offal from the butchers' stalls and even a dead cow, bloated by water and death and floating with its legs stretched grotesquely skyward. Geoffrey was glad when he reached the other side.

And then he was in the city of London itself. The air rang with noise as barges and boats laden with cloth, wool, coal, timber, peat and grain crowded and nudged each other to reach the seething wharves. Traders weaved in and out of the crowd, trying to sell their wares, shouting at the tops of their voices that theirs was the finest ribbon, the cleanest candles, the freshest bread. Dogs barked, geese honked and cattle lowed miserably as they were herded towards the slaughterhouses. Geoffrey had visited many places in his years of travel, but none had been as noisy, smelly, rough or confusing as London. It was amid all this chaos that he knew for certain they were being followed again.

'I know about this bit of the city,' said Roger with mounting excitement, as he looked around him. 'It is called Ethelredshythe, and there is a public lavatory here that I would dearly like to see. You do not find those just anywhere, and it is the only one of its kind in the country.'

'Another time,' said Geoffrey, thinking that Roger must be wrong. There were many public latrines in Normandy and the Holy Land, and he did not imagine the country of his birth was so backward as to discover their virtues only now. Then he glanced at the foul gutters that ran along each side of the road and the murky waters of the Thames and supposed Roger might be right.

'Do you know there is someone following us?' asked Roger, glancing casually behind him. 'I have seen you looking around often enough, so I suppose you do. I am of a mind to run him through. I do not take kindly to folk watching my every move.'

'Neither do I,' said Geoffrey. 'But we should not kill him until we know who he is. I do not want the King asking why we killed one of his best spies.'

'You think Henry is having us followed?' Roger was not impressed.

'He is the only one who expects us to be here.'

'There is your woman,' said Roger disapprovingly. 'Matilda. She knows what you intend to do.'

'She does not,' said Geoffrey. 'I do not make a habit of telling strangers our plans, as you know perfectly well. But it is possible that she has set one of her retainers after us. She need not have bothered. He will not come close enough to

47

hear what I say to Henry, so will not know whether I have carried out her request or not.'

'He may be a robber,' said Roger, fingering his sword. 'Or perhaps he has something to do with Greek Fire. Or Bellême may have hired him, because we discovered his nephew and you defiled his sister. There are many reasons why he represents a danger. We *should* kill him.'

'Here? With all these people to say it was an unprovoked attack? And what if he is an agent of the King's? How will you explain why you murdered him? Say you dislike being followed?'

'We could separate, and I could shove a dagger in his ribs. That would be the simplest solution.'

'But not the wisest,' replied Geoffrey, wishing Roger was not always so ready to use violence.

They stood aside to allow a funeral procession to pass. At the front was a priest, who rang a small handbell to warn people to pay their respects. Behind were four men carrying a bier, bearing it like a stretcher, as though the corpse were still alive. Geoffrey thought they looked familiar, but knew that was impossible. Their clothes indicated they were local, earning a living by fishing on the river, and Geoffrey had certainly not mingled with fishermen on his previous fleeting visits to the city. He glanced at the bier as it passed and saw the dead man's face. Geoffrey felt his stomach lurch. It was Oswin, landlord of the Crusader's Head.

Three

A crowd of mourners followed Oswin's bier. His family were first – a heavily built wife and a gaggle of children – while behind were some of the patrons Geoffrey had seen the previous night, although none were the wealthy folk who had kept themselves hidden at the back. Among them was Wulfric, whose eyes were red from crying. He looked more frightened than griefstricken, and Geoffrey supposed his tears were for himself, and what would happen to him now his employer was dead.

'What happened?' Geoffrey asked him.

Wulfric dropped out of the procession, and his eyes lit hopefully on Geoffrey's purse. 'Oswin died. His widow says she will sell the inn, and I do not see the new owners wanting to keep me on.'

'Why not?' asked Roger. 'Are you a thief? Do you spit in the ale?'

'Yes,' replied Wulfric unhappily. 'Oswin did not mind, as long as I kept to Crusaders and religious types, and left his other patrons alone.'

'Why?' demanded Roger indignantly. Helbye and Ulfrith exchanged startled glances, while Durand sniggered nastily. 'What did he have against men who risked their lives to liberate the Holy City?'

'His son took Holy Orders to go on the Crusade,' replied Wulfric with a sloppy sniff. 'Oswin was proud of him. But the lad got so drunk celebrating his courage that he fell overboard while his ship was still in port. He drowned, and Oswin blamed the Crusade for the tragedy.'

'I see,' said Geoffrey, understanding why the man had been

49

so hostile the previous evening and why he had chosen such an odd name for his tavern. He changed the subject. 'How did Oswin die?'

'Stabbed,' said Wulfric, wiping his nose on his filthy apron. 'We all went to bed as usual – at about eight o'clock – but when we awoke this morning he was lying in his bed with a knife in his heart.'

'Someone killed him while he slept?' asked Geoffrey, astonished. 'But surely a large, busy tavern like that must have been full of people who would notice murderous intruders.'

'I sleep in the next chamber, and I heard nothing. Nor did his wife, and she was in the same bed!' Wulfric watched the procession round a corner and lowered his voice, so Geoffrey and Roger had to lean close to hear what he was saying. 'Personally, I believe demons came for his soul and snatched it, while all us good folk slept.'

'Demons do not kill with daggers,' said Geoffrey, amused by the notion.

'How do you know?' asked Wulfric fearfully. 'Are you familiar with their ways?'

Geoffrey sensed he was on dangerous ground, and saw he would be condemned whichever way he answered. Roger did not care whether or not folk thought he consorted with witches and warlocks, however, and was ready to offer an opinion.

'Demons kill with claws,' he announced authoritatively. 'Or by wrapping long tails around their victims' throats. They never use human weapons. My father told me that, and he is a bishop.'

Wulfric looked suitably impressed, and Geoffrey did not bother to ask why bishops should be so much better acquainted with the Devil's creatures than lay folk. 'So, you heard and saw nothing during the night?' he asked instead.

Wulfric shook his head. 'We slept heavily, because of the shock regarding Hugh. We had been busy, because we had to make sure the body was covered nicely, and that a priest was hired to say masses. We do not want the Earl to think his nephew's corpse was treated disrespectfully.'

'Indeed not,' said Geoffrey, although what he knew of

Bellême suggested that he would not care one way or the other. Still, Oswin and Wulfric were wise not to risk offending the man.

'You said you know the Earl,' Wulfric went on. 'So, you do not need *me* to tell you that he might have tired of his stupid nephew and had him dispatched. But we thought we had better be careful nonetheless. You never know with the Earl.'

'He *is* that kind of man,' agreed Roger. 'You would not want him at your side in a battle. You would never know who he might decide to fight for.'

'He consorts with the Devil,' said Wulfric matter-of-factly. 'Everyone knows that, so he probably ordered his familiars to make an end of Oswin as well as Hugh.'

'Why would he harm Oswin?' asked Geoffrey, who could see the Earl killing a weak-witted nephew by hurling him out of a window with a rope around his neck, but not stabbing a landlord in the dead of night. Bellême's murders tended to be more flamboyant and grisly than a knife in the heart. 'Oswin allowed him to use his inn as a meeting place. There are not many who would take that risk, when everyone knows his family are not friends of the King.'

'I do not think the *King* had Oswin killed,' said Wulfric, although Geoffrey had not meant to imply the murder was royally inspired. 'But it is possible, I suppose. Who knows in these troubled times?'

'When you woke this morning, did you feel thick-headed?' asked Geoffrey, as a thought struck him. 'Did you sleep longer than usual?'

'How do you know that?' asked Wulfric suspiciously. 'We all slept like the dead, which is odd for me, because I usually need to rise in the night to visit the latrine.'

Geoffrey did not reply. He knew from personal experience that it was difficult to relax after witnessing unsettling incidents like violent deaths, and thought that Oswin, Wulfric and the others would have been restless and fitful, as their minds played back the event and prevented them from sleeping. It seemed obvious to him that poppy juice had been added to more ale than his and Roger's.

'Did you ever witness the meetings Bellême held in

51

Oswin's tavern?' he asked. 'What was discussed and who attended?'

Wulfric paled and backed away. 'I cannot tell you that! The Earl's demons would come for certain, and it would not matter whether they use daggers, claws or tails to kill, because I will be dead regardless.'

Geoffrey reached into his pouch and removed a silver coin. Wulfric regarded it thoughtfully, assessing whether such a large sum was worth risking his life over. He decided it was.

'I did not see much. Men came in dark cloaks, but they wore hoods and I never saw their faces.'

'Were there women, too?' asked Geoffrey, aware of the sharp look Roger threw in his direction. His friend had just made the connection that there were two cases of heavy sleeping the previous night.

'I do not think so,' said Wulfric, glancing around in a way that indicated he was frightened. 'I told you: they took pains to hide their faces. And I do not know what they discussed, either.'

'I do not believe you,' said Geoffrey, replacing the coin in his scrip. 'Oswin knew what the meetings were about, and I think he told you – his best and most loyal employee.'

'He did mention a few things,' admitted Wulfric, flattered to hear himself so described and determined to have Geoffrey's coin. 'There was something about a weapon. And they talked a lot about the head of the family: Mabel de Bellême, who is the Earl's mother.'

Geoffrey was confused. 'She was killed twenty-five years ago. She is not head of their clan.'

'She had been bathing in the river,' added Roger, who was fond of this particular story, because it contained a little of everything he held dear: violent death, unclad women and a healthy dose of superstition. 'She went back to the castle and lay naked on her bed to dry off. It was then that some knights burst in and murdered her with their swords. They cut off her head and took it with them when they left. She died cursing them, and they all died hideous deaths soon after.'

'Her killers were never apprehended,' corrected Geoffrey,

knowing the last part was pure fabrication on Roger's part, although the rest was true enough. 'Despite a massive hunt by the Earl.'

'Well, one of the two stories is true,' said Roger carelessly, not concerned by the fact that they represented very different outcomes. 'Suffice to say she was a demon, and the world is a better place without her in it.'

'But she might be,' said Wulfric, looking around him nervously again. 'In it, I mean. They talked about her as though she was still alive. Perhaps she did not die, but lives on, horribly disfigured. Or perhaps the Earl's sister, Emma the Witch, has summoned her from the dead.'

'Mabel was decapitated,' said Geoffrey shortly. 'And the men who killed her stole her head when they escaped. I doubt even the most powerful sorceress could bring life to someone with no head.'

Roger and Wulfric exchanged unhappy glances to indicate that the lack of a head merely made the spectre all the more terrifying, and its absence would make little difference to someone like Mabel. Geoffrey heard Helbye inform Ulfrith and Durand that he had heard of many cases where the dead walked with missing body parts, and that such details would not represent a serious obstacle to a powerful sorceress like Emma. Ulfrith nodded sagely, agreeing with every word, while Durand added that it was possible to use parts from other corpses, if the originals could not be found.

Geoffrey ignored them. 'What did the family say about Mabel, exactly?'

'That she is the head of their family,' Wulfric repeated. 'Everyone thinks it is the Earl, but it is her. She must be a powerful demon, to exist without a head.' He gazed defiantly at Geoffrey, daring him to contradict.

'Is that all?' asked Geoffrey. 'They talked about a weapon and Mabel de Bellême?'

'And about the King,' said Wulfric, his voice wheedling as he fixed his gaze on Geoffrey's purse. 'About how unfair it is that Henry should order them to his Easter Court in Winchester next week.'

'Did Oswin lend his tavern to anyone outside the Bellême household?' asked Geoffrey.

'Maurice, the Bishop of London, comes occasionally,' said Wulfric. 'He tries to disguise himself, too, but he is fat and has a distinctive waddle, so he is impossible to mistake for anyone else. Besides, he always has a Winchester Goose afterwards, and she sees him naked, so we know who he is.'

'He attends the same gatherings as the Bellêmes?' asked Geoffrey. 'Or business of his own?'

Wulfric told him that Maurice joined the Bellêmes, then listed men Geoffrey did not know: a soldier named William Pantulf and someone called Beaumais, both men desperate for power and wealth. They professed loyalty to Bellême, but had also sworn an oath of allegiance to the King.

Geoffrey wondered how many other nobles were plotting against the King, throwing in their lot with the rebellious Earl. Not everyone agreed that Henry had a right to the English throne, and there were many – secretly, Geoffrey was among them – who believed the crown should have passed to the Duke of Normandy, Henry's older brother. A perfectly legal document signed by their dead brother King William Rufus designated the Duke as his heir, and Geoffrey did not approve of legal documents being casually ignored.

He gave Wulfric the coin and advised him to leave Southwark as soon as Oswin's requiem mass was over. The Crusader's Head was no longer safe, and Geoffrey imagined it was only a matter of time before whoever killed Oswin realized he needed to silence others, too. He wondered how long it would be before that same person reached the conclusion that he and Roger might be in possession of information that could prove dangerous, and tried to kill them, too. He dropped his hand to the hilt of his sword and determined to be ready for them when they came.

Once Wulfric had scuttled away with his treasure – running not after the funeral procession, but in the opposite direction, obviously intending to follow Geoffrey's advice immediately – the two knights and their servants made their way through the narrow streets that ranged along the northern bank of the

River Thames. Their destination was Westminster, which stood outside London and apart from its chaotic, noisome bustle. Westminster was where King Henry resided when he was in his realm's largest city, and where Geoffrey had been ordered to appear no later than noon that day.

'I do not like any of this,' grumbled Durand, as he rode at Geoffrey's side. 'A man is hanged and we are blamed for the death. Then it transpires that the dead man is a kinsman of the Earl of Shrewsbury, but might also be a spy for the King. Meanwhile, his aunt has been using him as a messenger to organize a secret treaty behind her brother's back, and is the kind of woman to drug men and clamber into their beds in the dead of night. And now a second man is murdered.'

'I agree,' said Roger, shooting Geoffrey a baleful look. 'Wearing men's clothes and climbing through windows is hardly the behaviour of a gentlewoman, is it? And now we learn that she drugged Oswin and stabbed him before coming to you.'

Geoffrey supposed this was possible. Matilda had invaded his chamber not long before dawn, and Wulfric had said that the folk at the Crusader's Head had retired at the comparatively early hour of eight o'clock. Geoffrey saw she might well have slipped the doctored ale to him and Roger, then gone on to dispatch Oswin. When she returned, expecting Geoffrey and Roger to be deep in their slumbers, she found Roger cavorting with his prostitutes, and was obliged to dose more of his ale and wait until she was certain he was insensible. He rubbed his head wearily, wondering how he had become embroiled in such a mess. He decided to quit the country as soon as he had had his audience with Henry.

Durand was still complaining about their dire misfortune. 'And if the murders of Hugh and Oswin are not enough, we discover that the Bellêmes are making Greek Fire to hurl at Henry and learn that Mabel de Bellême has been brought back to life using witchcraft. She is probably the one who told Matilda to double-cross the others by attempting to arrange a treaty with King Henry.'

'Why would she do that?' asked Geoffrey, bemused by his squire's logic. 'If she really has been brought back to lead the family, she is hardly likely to weaken her clan by sending one of them to treat with the enemy. She will want them united and strong.'

'But she is no longer human,' said Durand earnestly. 'She became something else when her grave was disturbed. She will not see the world in the same way as you or me, not any more.'

Helbye and Roger looked alarmed, and Geoffrey wondered how two such bold and courageous soldiers – both practical men who were afraid of very little – could be unnerved by such tales.

'Do not be ridiculous,' he said firmly. 'Mabel is no demon. She is nothing but a pile of dusty bones that are doubtless lying peacefully in some corner of Normandy.'

'She is here,' said Durand with a dramatic shudder, drawing the hood of his cloak over his luxurious mane of yellow curls, as if he imagined it might protect him. 'I can *feel* it.'

'No wonder the House of Montgomery-Bellême is so powerful and evil,' said Roger, more willing to believe Durand's flights of fancy than Geoffrey's common sense. 'They are taking orders from a woman who has been in her grave these last twenty-five years, but who has emerged to help them in their hour of need.'

'Lord!' sighed Geoffrey, not sure how to convince them that corpses did not stand up and take charge of tactical operations after a quarter of a century in the ground. 'Oswin misheard or misunderstood what they were saying. And anyway, raising folk from the dead is impossible.'

'Jesus did it,' argued Helbye. 'I know the story of Lazarus. It is in the Bible, so it must be true.'

'But the Bellêmes are not Jesus,' Geoffrey pointed out. 'And Mabel died years ago, whereas Lazarus had only been dead a few hours and was not missing his head. The two cases are not comparable.'

'I have already informed you that demons do not need a *whole* corpse,' said Durand crisply. 'I read about these things in my abbey. There are many ways of calling a soul back from the dead, and a complete corpse is not a prerequisite of any of them. I hear the infidel are good at that sort of thing, which is why the Crusaders took so long to liberate Jerusalem.'

Geoffrey did not bother to reply, seeing his companions had already made up their minds about Mabel de Bellême's headless return. There was no point trying to convince them otherwise, and he would only become angry with them if they discussed the matter further. He was not surprised Roger and Helbye had chosen to accept such superstitious nonsense, but he had hoped Durand would be more discriminating. The squire had enjoyed an abbey education, and should have known better.

As they rode through the city, Roger started to grumble again about what Geoffrey had agreed to do for Matilda. He had a point: courts were dangerous places, and alliances were made and broken with mind-boggling rapidity. Geoffrey knew little of current courtly affairs and might well end up in danger by meddling in matters he did not understand. But there was something about Matilda that Geoffrey had liked. She was far more interesting than the simpering whores Roger favoured, or the prim nunnery ladies his sister sometimes recommended as suitable wives. He had been intrigued by Matilda, despite the fact that she had come close to cutting his throat.

They rode along a bustling thoroughfare called Athelyn-gestrate and eventually met the towering walls that marked the edge of London, built many years ago to defend the city against Norse invaders. They were still formidable, and it seemed London's burgesses spared no expense in keeping them in good repair. Geoffrey could see why. London was a rich jewel of commerce in a country that relied heavily on agriculture. If an enemy attacked England, then London would be a magnet for looters.

There were a number of gates set into the walls, but they were small, and only one cart could pass through at a time. Since those wanting access to the city were being granted priority over those who wanted to leave – the burgesses were more interested in pleasing folk who brought money into their city than those who took it out – Geoffrey and his companions were obliged to wait. Westminster was only a mile or so outside the city, and it was still relatively early in the morning, but Geoffrey chafed at the delay, hoping it would not make him late for his audience with Henry.

He scanned the heaving throng that pressed about him for signs that they were still being pursued, but saw no one acting suspiciously. A number of people eyed them, but it was unusual to see *Jerosolimitani* in England, and Geoffrey was used to being regarded as something exotic.

While they waited, a fat Benedictine sidled up to them and asked if they intended to travel to Westminster. Durand had invited him to ride with them before Geoffrey could object. Geoffrey assessed the monk carefully, but decided he was too fat and soft to present a danger, and did not blame the fellow for seeking safety in numbers outside the city gates. England's roads had a bad reputation, and even a monastic habit was no protection from some robbers.

'I have messages to deliver there,' said the man, happy to pass the time in idle chatter while they waited to be allowed out. 'Westminster is not far from London, but I dislike travelling alone.'

'Quite right,' said Durand. 'Few roads are safe these days.'

'King Henry has eliminated many of the outlaws that plague our highways,' the fat monk chattered on. 'But there are still too many for comfort.'

'Who are your messages for?' asked Durand nosily.

'Maurice,' replied the cleric. He saw Durand's blank look and elaborated. 'The Bishop of London. I have letters for him from Ralph d'Escures, Abbot of Sées. Sées is the mother house of the Benedictine monastery at Shrewsbury, and Ralph is there at the moment, assessing the value of our holy relics, while Maurice can usually be found at Westminster.'

'Maurice is a good friend of my father's,' said Roger to Geoffrey. 'I meant to tell you when that pot boy said Maurice sometimes attends the Bellêmes' illicit gatherings in the Crusader's Head. Nice man, Maurice. I would not have imagined *him* throwing in his lot with the Earl.'

As far as Geoffrey was concerned, the fact that Maurice

was an associate of the disgraced Bishop of Durham automatically implied that his morals and character were in question. He shook his head in disgust, thinking that the Court must seethe with corruption and intrigue if it welcomed men who enjoyed that particular bishop's company, and was even more determined to leave as soon as possible.

'Have you come from Shrewsbury Abbey, then?' Durand asked the fat monk. 'I would like to live there, enjoying a cloistered life away from the filth and degradation of the world.'

'There is nothing wrong with filth and degradation,' said the monk cheerfully, sounding as though he preferred that to a sterile and probably dull life inside a convent's stalwart walls. 'And, yes, Shrewsbury is my home abbey. My name is Brother Petronus.'

'What do your messages contain?' probed Durand. Geoffrey smiled at his audacity. Letters sent by abbots to bishops tended to be private, and not for casual discussion with strangers *en route*.

Petronus's smile slipped a little, startled to be asked such a blunt question. 'Abbey business,' he replied vaguely. 'Shrewsbury is under the lordship of Robert de Bellême, and the monks are afraid it might suffer when he answers for his treachery at the King's Easter Court.'

'So, Abbot Ralph is asking Bishop Maurice to intervene on his monastery's behalf,' surmised Durand. 'That is wise. I have heard that the King plans to strip Bellême of all his estates, and Shrewsbury Abbey may well suffer. It will serve Bellême right, though. He is a godless man, and it will do him good to reflect on his sins when he is banished and has his English lands confiscated.'

'I know nothing of that,' said Petronus uncomfortably, obviously unwilling to speak openly against the man who ultimately controlled his abbey. 'But I need to be at Westminster soon – Bishop Maurice is expecting me – and we should not waste time here when we could be on the road.'

Before Geoffrey could stop him, he had marched to the head of the patiently waiting queue, and demanded that he and his companions be allowed through the gate immediately, on

59

the grounds that they had important business with the King. There were mutterings and groans from the onlookers, but no one was overly vocal in his disapproval.

Geoffrey paid yet another toll, and he and his companions emerged in a vile little shanty town of lean-to shacks inhabited by folk who watched them with dull, flat expressions. He mounted his horse and rode through their camp, appalled by its desperate poverty. He had encountered destitution before, but he had never seen it when there was luxury and plenty so near by. He spurred his horse into a trot, wanting to be away from the shabby, mean little hovels as quickly as possible.

When the stench of open latrines was left behind, he slowed and allowed his horse to choose its own pace along a pleasant track that followed the glistening mudflats lining the northern bank of the Thames. The others caught up with him, with Petronus careful to place himself between the two knights for security. They passed strip fields, where peasants laboured with hoes and spades. Small children gathered stones in piles around the fields' edges, so they could be hurled at marauding birds later in the year, when the crops were vulnerable.

The cultivated land gave way to a kind of seascape, where the scent of the river dominated, and small streams meandered across flat, boggy wasteland. Herons fished in the shallows, and Geoffrey saw fat brown trout in the rills they crossed. He glanced behind him from time to time, but the road was empty, and whoever had been following them earlier seemed to have given up. He assumed Roger had been right: the fellow had been a hopeful thief. However, he understood why Petronus had wanted company for the last leg of his journey from Shrewsbury. It would have been a lonely ride alone.

To the right was a belt of trees, which swept down to meet the water's edge. Sunlight filtered through the budding branches and made dappled patterns on the ground. Geoffrey listened intently, thinking it odd that the copse should be so silent when March was a time for courting birds, but the trees that pressed in on them from both sides were still and quiet.

Durand, riding last in the little procession, suddenly released a piercing cry and toppled from his horse. Geoffrey swung around, tugging his shield from its fastenings on the saddle. He raised it not a moment too soon, because an arrow immediately thudded into it. There was a sharp howl, and Petronus fell to the ground with a bolt protruding from his shoulder. Geoffrey wheeled around, and saw a cluster of oaks to his left. He drew his sword and galloped towards it, seeing there was no other place from which an ambush could be mounted.

Another arrow slapped into his shield, and the metal barb sliced through the wood and came through the other side, narrowly missing his arm. As he crashed into the trees, he saw someone scramble from beneath a bush. He slashed with the flat of his blade, knocking the man from his feet. The archer staggered, then fell and lay still. A second man darted from the scrub, and when he saw Geoffrey in pursuit he abandoned his bow and began to zigzag through the trees, desperation in his every move.

Geoffrey yelled to Roger to stay with the man he had felled, and bent low to avoid being knocked from his saddle as branches tore past his head. He was gaining, and could see terrified eyes as the archer glanced back at him. Geoffrey drove his horse harder, and the bowman made a critical mistake: instead of staying in the copse, where bushes and branches afforded him protection, he set off across an open glade. Geoffrey was on him in a trice, and had just snatched up a handful of his hood, when he made a hiccuping sound and crumpled. An arrow was embedded in his throat, and there was nothing Geoffrey could do to help him as he gurgled his last. Geoffrey raised his shield and gazed around wildly, trying to determine the direction from which the shot had been fired.

He heard other hoofs pounding the ground, and it was not many moments before a tightly packed group of horsemen emerged from the opposite side of the wood. Geoffrey braced himself, taking a tighter grip on his sword and adjusting his shield. He wheeled his horse around, and went on the offensive, seeing he was outnumbered by at least six to one and determined to strike as hard as he could before he was overwhelmed. He headed for the leading

61

horseman, who fumbled for his sword to parry the hacking swipe Geoffrey aimed at his head. At the very last moment Geoffrey recognized the face and the colours of the rider, and managed to avoid what might well have been a killing blow. His horse thundered on, unable to stop, and Geoffrey was tempted to keep going. But he reined it in and trotted back to face the man he had almost decapitated.

'Sir Geoffrey Mappestone,' said the horseman, trying to appear nonchalant, although his white face and unsteady hands indicated he had been seriously shaken.

Sheepishly, Geoffrey bowed in his saddle. 'Your Majesty.'

The knights who had ridden out hunting that day were furious that their monarch had come so close to death while he was under their protection, and Geoffrey saw they would dearly have loved to express their outrage by striking him down. He did not try to explain that men who fired arrows at Crusader knights should expect a sword first and questions later, because he hoped the King had not taken his instinctive reaction personally. However, because Henry's brother, King William Rufus, had been shot in a forest two years earlier, woodland 'accidents' were a delicate subject in the royal household. No one knew what had really happened to Rufus, and, although he would not have bloodied his hands personally, Henry had certainly acted promptly when he had heard the news, and had had himself crowned before most of the country knew Rufus was dead.

However, almost killing Henry was not the way Geoffrey had intended to obey his summons to Westminster. He apologized profusely, and did what was expected of him by dismounting and kneeling, offering his sword as a sign that he acknowledged Henry's sovereignty and that he knew he had transgressed. He also knew Henry was not a man to forget such an incident, and suspected it would cost him dear at some point, when Henry would claim he had witnesses that Geoffrey had tried to decapitate him.

Henry declared the hunting was not good that day and ordered the party to abandon their sport and return home. Although several knights, spoiling for a kill, exchanged glances to indicate they disagreed, no one dared argue, and the riders began to move towards Westminster. All carried bows for the stags and boar they had hoped to slaughter, and Geoffrey had no way of telling whether it was the monarch's own arrow that had killed the renegade archer or one of his courtiers'.

Geoffrey had no choice but to go with the King. He glanced surreptitiously behind him, but Roger was nowhere to be seen, so he assumed he had recognized the King's standard and prudently declined to identify himself with a man who had attacked him. Geoffrey also assumed Roger would question the first archer and find out why he had opened fire on innocent men, before turning him over to the local sheriff and making his own way to Westminster.

'I am sorry, sire,' he said yet again, spurring his horse so he rode next to Henry, and ignoring the resentful mutters of those courtiers who had been looking forward to a morning of bloody sport. 'You took me by surprise.'

Henry grimaced. He was in his early thirties, and was of middle height with black hair and dark grey eyes that were full of expression and could flash with anger as easily as they could dance with delight. They could also be unreadable, and it was certainly impossible to know what he was thinking that day.

'It has taught me a valuable lesson. In future, I shall allow one of my knights to ride first into that sort of situation, and not attempt to do so myself. I was overly eager to greet you; I have been waiting weeks for you to obey my summons. I said *no later* than noon the day before Palm Sunday, and you have left it until the very last moment.'

'I came as soon as I could.' It was true, and Geoffrey had been hard pressed to meet the monarch's deadline, since he had not been in Antioch when the summons had been delivered.

'Prince Tancred was happy to let you come? He trusts you to return to him, and does not think you might prefer to settle amid the cool green hills of home?'

'He knows I am aware of my duty,' said Geoffrey, anticipating what was coming next. He was not mistaken.

Henry jerked his dark curls at the knights who rode in a

63

protective circle around him. 'You saw for yourself that the men who guard me are less than adequate. Can I persuade you to leave Tancred and join me? There are very few *Jerosolimitani* who are English born, and it seems a pity to see them in the service of foreign princes.'

'You have good men here,' said Geoffrey, aware that they were listening. 'They will serve you better than I could.'

'An ambiguous reply,' said Henry, smiling at the implication that Geoffrey's services would be found lacking if he was forced to abandon Tancred. 'But consider my offer well, Geoffrey. I would like the prestige of a *Jerosolimitanus* in my court, and would pay handsomely for it. I know you own Rwirdin manor, but it is a paltry place and too close to the rebellious Welsh. There are better estates in my power to give loyal retainers.'

'Thank you,' said Geoffrey, wishing the King would accept that he had already vowed allegiance to Tancred, and was not in the habit of breaking his word because he was offered a few farmhouses and a field of sheep. 'But I cannot break my oath.'

'Geoffrey the Loyal,' said the King, a little too caustically for Geoffrey's liking. 'Still, you cannot blame me for trying. I like the way you remain faithful to Tancred, even though you have better offers elsewhere. Good knights are not easy to find, especially ones with your talents. There are not many soldiers who are literate, and since I read myself, I know how useful it can be. Now, what of this archer? Who was he and why were you chasing him?'

'Just a brigand, sire,' replied Geoffrey. He was relieved to discuss something else until it occurred to him that Henry should not have known the man was an archer, because bow and arrows had been abandoned in the woods. All Henry saw was someone running and Geoffrey in pursuit. The knight's heart sank when he realized there was already some plot in operation that saw Henry planting bowmen on the London-to-Westminster road with orders to shoot. He wondered whether they had been instructed to fire at anyone, or at Crusader knights in particular.

'I have striven to eradicate robbers from my highways,'

said Henry. 'Particularly this one, which I use myself. Are you sure you do not know what he wanted?'

Geoffrey regarded him warily, uncertain what the King was asking. Had he heard about the trouble at the Crusader's Head, and thought the attack might be connected to the murder of Hugh? Or did he know that Matilda had invaded his bedchamber and suspected he had been recruited to serve the House of Montgomery-Bellême? Or was the attack nothing to do with Geoffrey, and Petronus was the target? The monk had been hit, after all, although the arrow had taken him high in the shoulder, so he should have survived. Geoffrey recalled Durand falling from his saddle, and wondered whether his squire had been killed, or whether he had an injury that would heal, too.

'I suppose the robber saw our saddlebags and decided to take his chances,' he replied cautiously.

'No sane brigand attacks a knight.' Henry's face was unreadable again. 'Even one who is alone.'

'I was not alone,' said Geoffrey, suspecting that the King knew all about Roger, Helbye, Durand and Ulfrith, and was probing his honesty. Again, he discovered he had read the King correctly.

Henry smiled. 'You came with Sir Roger of Durham and three servants. My spies saw you disembark at Dover, and have been watching you ever since. Perhaps Roger would like to enter my service, if you will not. Where is he?'

'Chasing the other robber, I expect,' said Geoffrey, not wanting a clever man like Henry to get at someone so openly trusting as Roger. The bluff northerner might well find himself sworn into Henry's service without even knowing what he had done. 'The archer you killed shot a monk called Petronus, who delivers messages from Abbot Ralph of Sées to Bishop Maurice of London.'

'I see,' said Henry flatly, and Geoffrey could not tell whether he already knew Petronus's business, or whether he was merely uninterested in such details. 'Did Roger stay with this Petronus, then?'

'I could ride back and find out.' Geoffrey started to move

away from Henry, but the King reached out and grabbed his bridle.

'It does not matter. Ride with me. It is always pleasant to converse with an old friend.'

Geoffrey was not sure that was how *he* would describe his relationship with the King. He did not know how to respond, so said what was on his mind, aware that Matilda's ale was still in his system, because he still did not feel as sharp-witted as he would have liked.

'It is a pity the archer is dead, because I wanted to question him.'

'Why?' demanded Henry. 'A peasant would have nothing to say to you, and his death means one fewer outlaw breaking my peace.'

Geoffrey's thoughts were in turmoil. Was the robbery a chance attack by peasants desperate with hunger and need? But it would have to be a very desperate and needy man who would ambush fully armoured knights from such an indefensible place, and he could not imagine any sane robber taking such a risk. He pondered again whether Henry had deliberately prevented the archer from speaking. There had been no need to shoot the man, and Geoffrey had an uncomfortable feeling that there was a reason for his death, and that the King knew what it was. It was not a pleasant thought, and he wondered uneasily what new dangers he was about to face.

'The attack was odd,' he said cautiously, not sure how far he could take the subject. 'The man was not a dedicated outlaw, or he would have chosen his quarry and his position with more care. I think he wanted to kill someone in my party.'

'Who?' asked Henry. 'Roger, because he is a son of the outlawed Bishop of Durham? Petronus because he carries messages from Abbot Ralph – a vassal of my enemy Robert de Bellême – to Bishop Maurice, whose loyalty to me may also be in question? Your squire Durand, for attempting to seduce any man he meets with his golden curls? Or you, because you are here to do me a favour?'

Geoffrey did not like the sound of the word 'favour'. He was confused, but could only conclude that if the bowmen had been hired by Henry, then Geoffrey had not been their target. He did not think the King would bother to murder Roger, because Roger had inherited none of Flambard's cunning intelligence, and was no threat. So, was the intended victim Petronus, because he carried messages between two enemies? Or had the archers been hired by someone else – the Bellêmes for example – to prevent Geoffrey from carrying out whatever 'favour' the King intended to demand?

'Let us discuss this peasant no more,' declared the King. 'We should talk about happier matters. You are doubtless wondering why I have asked you here?'

'Yes, sire,' said Geoffrey, hoping that the King would state his request, accept his reasons for refusing, and let him return to Tancred.

Henry laughed when he saw Geoffrey's wary expression. 'You are already thinking of excuses to refuse me, and you have not even heard me out.'

'I will do your bidding if I can – assuming it does not interfere with my oath to Tancred.'

'It will not affect Tancred one way or another,' said Henry. 'I want you to help win a battle for me. It will be against the Earl of Shrewsbury at his fortress at Arundel.'

The sun was at its zenith by the time the King and his hunters arrived at Westminster. The palace and abbey stood on the island of Thorney, formed where the Tyburn Stream split into two encircling arms before flowing into the Thames. Neat strip fields surrounded the settlement, but did not extend far into the marshes, which were the domain of sedge, alder scrub and honking waterfowl. Wooden bridges spanned the streams in several places, giving access to a complex of chapels and halls that made Geoffrey slow his horse to admire them.

Dominating all was the Benedictine church, built by the saintly Edward the Confessor. It was a grand affair boasting three towers that were full of bells, all ringing in a discordant jangle to announce the monks' offices. On its south side ranged a cloister, halls for sleeping and eating, chapter house, administrative quarters, gatehouse, kitchens, brewery, bakery and storerooms.

Nearby was the palatial hall built by Rufus. It was by far the largest Geoffrey had ever seen, and walking through its main door was akin to entering a cathedral. Great timber posts divided it into nave and parallel aisles, and every available patch of wall had been painted, mostly with hunting scenes. He stood for a moment, King forgotten, as he admired the clever design of the roof and the gallery below the upper-floor windows.

'My brother was disappointed with this,' said Henry, bemused by the knight's obvious admiration. 'He said he wanted a great hall and instead was given a bedchamber.'

'Then he must have owned a very large bed,' replied Geoffrey, thinking that Rufus had been unfair.

'I do not like it personally,' said Henry, gazing around disparagingly as he removed his hat and flung it at a waiting squire, who fumbled and dropped it in his nervousness. 'It is too big for most purposes, and too small for others.'

He strode to the far end of the hall, where clerks and scribes filed piles of documents: the affairs of state were being carried out, even while the King hunted. He stopped randomly to inspect the work, an unsettling practice that Geoffrey was sure would encourage high standards.

While his knights stacked their weapons and went towards a table laden with food, Henry led Geoffrey to the hearth. He snapped his fingers at the anxious squire, a thin man in his early twenties, with dark curling hair and pale skin that made him look unhealthy. The young man regarded his monarch uncertainly, as though he had no idea what he was expected to do. He advanced warily, holding the hat in front of him, as if he anticipated the King might like it back again. Geoffrey felt sorry for him – he had been a squire himself once. He made a drinking gesture, to tell him Henry wanted wine. Sighing with relief, the fellow shot away.

Henry watched in exasperation – Geoffrey's help had not gone unnoticed. 'He will never make a squire or a knight. I do not know why I persist with him.'

'I have one of those, too,' said Geoffrey, thinking of Durand and his monkish habits. He considered asking Henry

68

if he would like to swap, because he thought he could do a lot more with the clumsy lad than he would ever be able to achieve with Durand.

'Your squire is the son of a man who saved Tancred's life,' said Henry, to show Geoffrey that his spies were efficient information gatherers. 'But mine – Philip – is a hostage to good behaviour.'

Geoffrey was familiar with the practice of disgraced nobles leaving their children in the care of enemies as security for friendly relations. He supposed the King had a number of them, all doing their best to please him, so they might be spared should their relatives breach any agreements.

'That is Philip the Grammarian's bastard,' Henry went on, watching the squire reach a table and gaze helplessly at the array of wine jugs on it. 'He should have followed his father and become a priest, because he is good for nothing else. You must have known Philip; he was a Crusader.'

Geoffrey had indeed encountered Philip the Grammarian on the Crusade. He was one of Bellême's brothers, and it was rumoured that his family had forced him to leave home because he was so dissolute and dangerous that they did not know what else to do with him. Geoffrey recalled that Philip usually wore the robes of a monk in the hope that they might save him in the event of an attack. He had drunk, looted and raped his way to Antioch, and had died during the siege there more than a year before Jerusalem had fallen. Many had heaved a sigh of relief when he had been killed, and Philip had been neither missed nor mourned.

'We seldom spoke,' said Geoffrey, declining to admit any acquaintance with a man who had possessed not one redeeming feature.

'But you met him?' asked Henry, regarding the knight with interest. 'His family is proud of his contribution to the Crusade. They say he died protecting vital supplies from Turkish bandits, and claim he was successful, because the raid was thwarted and Antioch eventually fell.'

'Is that what they believe?' asked Geoffrey, startled.

Geoffrey had been detailed to oversee the burial of the dead after that particular fight. The skirmish had been one of many

69

during the nine months that the Crusader army had camped outside Antioch, and he found his memories of individual attacks blurred. But he recalled the one in which Philip had been killed for two reasons. First, the man had slunk away to save his own skin, leaving Geoffrey fighting alone. And second, Geoffrey had seen Philip's body, and knew that the fatal wound in his back had not come from a Turk's curved blade, but from a Crusader's straight one: Philip had been murdered by someone on his own side.

'Do you know otherwise?' asked Henry. He was an astute man, and Geoffrey supposed that no matter how short and uninformative his answers, the King would always read more in them than he was comfortable revealing.

'I barely recall that particular battle,' Geoffrey lied, thinking that the safest option was to deny all knowledge of Philip. 'I was not with him when he died, and I have no idea how he comported himself during the attack.'

'He had the reputation of a man who preferred lying with women to fighting,' said Henry, which Geoffrey thought was rich coming from a man who had no mean reputation among the ladies himself.

'I never saw him fighting,' said Geoffrey, trying to be noncommittal.

'I thought as much,' said Henry in satisfaction. 'The man was a coward, and probably burned to death inside his tent when he should have been standing with his comrades. Philip was no hero – not if his son is anything to go by.'

'How did he come to be with you?' asked Geoffrey, trying to shift the emphasis of the discussion.

'Bellême gave him to me when his invasion of England failed last year. Philip the father was obviously not in a position to object, and young Philip is an acknowledged member of the House of Montgomery-Bellême. However, the illegitimate son of a dissolute priest is not someone of any great value, and I think I was cheated.' Henry gave a wry smile.

Geoffrey agreed. The Bellême clan seemed to have a number of illegitimate sons wandering around, so the bastard child of a fourth brother would be no great loss. Geoffrey doubted whether the prospect of young Philip hanged would prevent his uncle from rebelling if the mood took him.

'Philip is in no danger from me,' said Henry, reading Geoffrey's thoughts. 'Look at him! He is all fingers, elbows and bewildered eyes. It would be like slaughtering a kitten. However, I would dearly love to turn him into a warrior. That would teach Bellême a lesson.'

'I think you have a lot of work ahead, sire,' said Geoffrey doubtfully, watching the squire walk towards the King carrying a brimming cup in both hands, tongue thrust between his lips as he concentrated. He had not even learned that wine was to be brought in a jug on a tray with more than one goblet, so the King would not be obliged to drink alone.

Henry gave a gusty sigh. 'He cannot remember how to perform even the most basic of tasks. If he cannot be taught how to serve wine, then how will he deal with a sword?'

'With great difficulty, I imagine,' said Geoffrey, amused.

'I do not suppose you would oblige?' asked Henry, taking the goblet and sipping its contents. He winced, and thrust the goblet back, so it slopped over Philip's tunic. 'This is servants' wine! You cannot serve your monarch the nastiest brew from the kitchen! Fetch me something decent.'

'I already have Durand, thank you,' said Geoffrey, watching the lad trip over a loose flagstone and fall to his knees in his haste to be away. 'But he is worse, because he would rather be a monk.'

'They are the worst,' agreed Henry. 'Well, I expect you are wondering when we will come to the crux of the matter: why I want you to fight Bellême? You want to know what I have in mind.'

Geoffrey nodded.

'It is quite simple,' said Henry. 'You will inveigle yourself into the Earl's service when he appears at my Easter Court at Winchester next Saturday. He will then return to his castle at Arundel to lick his wounds and you will accompany him. And then I want you to make an end of him for me.'

Four

Geoffrey fought not to gape as the implications of the King's words sunk in. He wondered whether he had heard him correctly, but saw from the amused expression on Henry's face that he had. Henry was laughing, knowing that such a request would result in exactly the kind of reaction he was seeing. Geoffrey wondered how he could decline the King's generous offer and still leave Westminster alive, and cursed himself for a fool for allowing himself to be put in such a position.

'You wish you had not obeyed my summons,' said Henry, reading his mind again. 'You want to be in the Holy Land, among the flies and the dust. However, you owe me your allegiance, Geoffrey. Your little manor is in my realm, and you would not want me angry with you.'

Geoffrey shrugged, affecting a nonchalance he did not feel. 'I seldom visit Rwirdin, so it would not distress me greatly to know you had seized it.' That was true, at least. He had only ever visited it once and he was not especially attached to it.

'But it would distress your sister to lose it,' said Henry maliciously. 'You dislike your brother, but you are fond of Joan, and she needs Rwirdin's income to support her castle at Goodrich.'

'She can look after herself,' said Geoffrey. Joan was a formidable lady, who took after their warrior mother, and Henry would have bitten off more than he could chew if he attempted to play games with her.

'The Welsh are rebelling again,' said Henry softly and in a way that was vaguely threatening. 'Prince Iorwerth's men mass all along the Marches, ready to attack English manors on the other side. Joan's estates are on that border, and the rivalry between your family and the Welsh goes back many years. You would not like me to be tardy in offering assistance when the Welsh strike, would you?'

Geoffrey regarded the King with dislike. It was true that the truce between his family and their Celtic neighbours was an uneasy one, and it would take little to provoke outright warfare. The Mappestones had few trained troops of their own and, although they could withstand a local invasion, they would certainly be overwhelmed if their neighbours recruited the Welsh princes who were ripe for rebellion. Men like the fiery Iorwerth were able and cunning fighters, who would swoop down on Goodrich like a hawk on a rabbit, burning fields and villages, stealing livestock and killing the inhabitants. It would be over before the English knew it had begun, and Geoffrey did not like to think of Joan lying with her throat cut, just because Henry had dallied over sending reinforcements.

'I cannot kill Bellême on your behalf,' said Geoffrey, not even trying to hide his distaste at the suggestion. 'If he was murdered, everyone would know it was your doing.'

He wondered whether Henry planned to have him killed, too, after he had carried out his sinister duties, and glanced around him. No one else had heard what the King had said, so he assumed Henry had already decided there were to be no witnesses to the discussion.

'Why, Geoffrey!' exclaimed Henry, his eyes widening in shock. 'I did not tell you to *kill* him! I said I wanted you to *make an end* of him, which is not the same thing at all. I meant I want an end of him here, in England. I want you to help me have him exiled.'

Geoffrey did not believe him for an instant, and assumed the wily monarch had been testing the waters. If Geoffrey had agreed to resolve the problem that the powerful Earl had become, then he was sure Henry would not have demurred. But Geoffrey was no cold-blooded killer, and his services for that kind of business were not for hire.

'You have been too long in foreign places,' said Henry,

gesturing that Geoffrey was to sit with him near the fire. 'You think like an infidel, rather than a civilized man.'

Geoffrey refrained from pointing out that most infidel were a good deal more civilized than the brutal louts – such as Bellême and his clan – who haunted the western courts. Henry settled himself on a pile of cushions near the hearth, while Geoffrey selected a bench. Then Philip's son reappeared. Someone had obviously taken pity on him and told him what to do, because this time he carried the proper tray with jug and goblets. He stumbled as he walked, and some of the wine splattered across the floor.

Henry glared in disapproval. 'Have a care, Philip. That is expensive and not for dogs to lick up.'

'Shall I scrape it up for you, then, sire?' asked the squire with open-eyed innocence. 'I can fetch another cup to put it in, and you can enjoy it later.'

Geoffrey regarded him in astonishment, wondering whether the lad was using his guileless expression to insult the monarch, or whether he genuinely believed that Henry wanted him to retrieve the lost wine for future consumption. He started to laugh, because he thought either option was amusing. Henry scowled, while Philip's expression changed from eager innocence to dismay.

'I cannot drink it after it has been on the floor, boy!' snapped Henry irritably. 'That is not what I meant when I told you to be careful.'

'Yes, sire,' muttered Philip, blushing furiously. 'No, sire.'

'Just pour the wine and be gone,' said Henry crossly, while Geoffrey fought to control his mirth. 'And I shall have mine in a goblet, please – not on the floor and not in my lap. God's blood! What have I done to deserve you?'

His furious glare made Philip more nervous than ever, and another generous splash of claret made its acquaintance with the floor. Henry sighed gustily, then jerked his feet out of the way when the squire accidentally kicked the table, spraying more wine towards the hearth. When Philip eventually finished, one cup was overflowing and the other was only half full. He beat a hasty and prudent retreat before he could be criticized, leaving Henry shaking his head and Geoffrey struggling not to smile.

'Are there no others who can act as your squire?' Geoffrey imagined there were many nobles who would dearly love their children to be given such a chance, and he was surprised that the awkward Philip should be tolerated.

'Plenty,' said Henry, politely passing his guest the fuller of the two goblets. 'But it pleases me to know I have a Bellême under my control. You should not have laughed at him, Geoffrey. He was not making a joke, you know. He is wholly devoid of humour, and meant what he said quite literally.'

'I am sorry, sire,' said Geoffrey. 'He took me unawares.'

'He does that,' agreed Henry dryly. 'You are not the first to be shocked into laughter at his gross ineptitude.' He drained what little claret there was in his cup, then gestured for Geoffrey to pour him more. 'Did you know that all four of Bellême's brothers named their bastard children after themselves? Hugh has an illegitimate brat called Hugh; Philip the Grammarian called his boy Philip; Roger the Count of Marche has at least four baptized Rogers; and Arnulf the Earl of Pembroke has three Arnulfs. Still, at least that practice makes their offspring easy to keep track of.'

'And their legitimate children?' asked Geoffrey, glad to be discussing something other than how to murder the Earl of Shrewsbury. 'Do they name those after themselves, too?'

'Hugh and Philip had none before they died,' replied Henry. 'And Bellême, Roger and Arnulf all named their rightful heirs William. They are a simple family.' He roared with laughter, despite the fact that he had populated his Court with a number of Henrys himself.

Geoffrey heard breathing behind him, and turned to see Philip had not moved away as far as he had first thought, and was listening to the discussion between King and knight with undisguised interest. Henry waved him away, but he did not go much farther. Geoffrey suspected he could hear only disjointed fragments of the conversation, but he considered it unwise to be plotting the downfall of the lad's uncle when he was in earshot regardless. The Earl may have abandoned him to an uncertain fate as a hostage, but family ties were important, and Geoffrey did not like to imagine the kind of messages Philip might secretly send the Bellêmes.

'My brother, the Duke of Normandy, invaded my kingdom in July last year,' said Henry, casually changing the subject. Geoffrey nodded warily, wondering what was coming next. 'Among his troops were Bellême, his two surviving brothers and the disgraced Bishop of Durham – Roger's father.'

Geoffrey tried to conceal his anxiety. He did not want Henry to exploit Roger for his connection to the outlawed bishop. Henry smiled.

'Do not worry about Roger: my quarrel is with his father, not him. But when my army and my brother's met in Hampshire, I was able to negotiate a truce before any blood was spilled.'

'The Duke renounced his claim to the English throne and it was agreed no barons who had taken part in the campaign on either side would be punished,' said Geoffrey, to let the King know he was not totally out of touch with what was happening in England. He did not add that Henry had already started to break the terms of the treaty. The rebel Earl of Surrey had lost his English lands on trumped-up charges, and Bellême was about to suffer a similar fate.

'I am tired of the House of Montgomery-Bellême,' said Henry bitterly. 'They have rebelled three times now: twice against my brother Rufus, and once against me. I am weary of them all – Bellême, his brothers, and his three meddlesome sisters, Emma, Matilda and Sybilla.'

'I see,' said Geoffrey, supposing this was not a good time to act as Matilda's ambassador. 'How have the sisters offended you? They played no part in the rebellions.'

Or had they? He reconsidered, recalling the fact that Matilda had broken into his bedchamber and held him at knifepoint. She was probably perfectly capable of revolt.

'They did their part,' said Henry curtly. 'They are formidable women, like your sister Joan. And Matilda is the most cunning of them all.'

'Oh,' said Geoffrey, supposing that Roger had been right to be sceptical of her. 'In what way?'

76

Henry narrowed his eyes. 'You seem unnaturally interested in my affairs all of a sudden. Normally, you detest hearing about the strife in my kingdom, and cannot wait to escape. Have you met any of the Bellême sisters? I know Sybilla is in London, trying to rally support for her brother.'

'I have not met Sybilla,' replied Geoffrey evenly.

'She may contact you, to ask you to speak in her defence,' Henry went on, and Geoffrey was glad the King was watching Philip's clumsy attempts at polishing a pair of spurs and not studying Geoffrey's own reactions. 'She is determined that her family should keep their lands. But I cannot afford them in my realm. If I want a stable, peaceful kingdom, they have to go – the whole clan.'

'Including the sisters?'

'Most certainly the sisters. They will all answer to me next week at my Easter Court. My agents tell me that Emma is due to arrive in London today, but I do not know what has happened to Matilda. I am told she is not yet here, but she is a slippery woman, and may well have insinuated herself inside the city without my spies knowing.'

'You have summoned the whole family?' asked Geoffrey, wondering why Matilda had not made her presence known to the King. If she wanted to ensure she kept her lands while her brothers lost theirs, she had no reason to hide, but plenty for presenting herself to Henry in person.

'All six siblings,' said Henry with satisfaction. 'And then I shall exile them. Of course, they are squirming like maggots in a dead pig, claiming they are innocent, but I am not interested in excuses.'

'They have contacted you?' asked Geoffrey, wondering whether Henry would admit to sending the letter of rejection to Matilda, rebuffing her attempts to reach a settlement.

'No,' said Henry. 'Although I anticipate it will not be long before they do.'

Geoffrey could not tell whether he was telling the truth. The letter Geoffrey had seen had borne no seal, so it was possible the King had had nothing to do with it. Or had he deliberately kept his official mark away from documents that might later prove to be problematic? Geoffrey had no idea, and the contorted affairs of state began to be too much for him. He longed to be away from the sordid dealings of the monarch and his rebellious subjects.

'Hugh is dead,' he said, afraid that Henry might hear about him being in Southwark when the young man was hanged, and accuse him of deceit if he was not open about it. 'The son of Hugh,' he added when Henry looked startled at what he evidently considered a non sequitur.

'Well, that clears things up,' drawled the King facetiously. 'What are you burbling about, man?'

'Bellême's nephew,' elaborated Geoffrey, wondering if the King was pretending not to know, so *he* could not be accused of playing a role in the murder. 'You mentioned him just a moment ago.'

'The halfwit?' asked Henry. 'The one who is even less capable of wielding a sword than that pitiful specimen?' He waved a hand in Philip's direction. 'The Bellêmes should be more careful with whom they couple, because their bastards are not children to be proud of. Not like mine.' He smirked smugly, evidently pleased with his success in that particular direction.

'Hugh was murdered in Southwark last night,' explained Geoffrey. 'I happened to be passing.'

Henry sighed. 'What was he doing there? After the Winchester Geese, no doubt. Well, it is a shame, because Bellême was fond of the lad. I hope he does not accuse *me* of this murder. It would be most tiresome.'

'Did Hugh come to you with messages from Bellême's sisters?' asked Geoffrey, trying to make his question sound like a casual enquiry and not an accusation.

Henry gave a short bark of laughter. 'Of course not! The boy would not have known what to do with an important message if it came to life and issued him orders.' He tapped his temple significantly, then glanced at Geoffrey. 'You did not kill him, did you?'

'No.' Geoffrey shifted uncomfortably and decided Matilda could petition the King herself. He had liked her, but acting as her ambassador was simply not worth the risk.

'Very well,' said Henry. 'Now, hear what I want you to

do. Bellême and his siblings will appear before my Easter Court in Winchester next week – on the sixth day of April. They will hear the charges against them – that they built an unlicensed castle at Bridgnorth, collected illegally imposed taxes, and other serious offences – then I expect them to withdraw, so they can prepare their defence.'

'You think they will leave the country?'

'I wish they would. Then I would pronounce them outlaws, seize their lands and that would be an end to the whole unsavoury matter. But Bellême believes he can defeat me. I predict that he and his siblings will dash to his castle at Arundel, where they will lock themselves inside and dare me to attack. Arundel is a powerful fortress, and I do not want to waste my troops on a siege that might last months. I want you to inveigle yourself into Bellême's confidence and end the siege by stealth.'

Geoffrey was deeply unhappy with what Henry had charged him to do. He pointed out that he was the wrong man to undertake such a venture, because the last time he and Bellême had met they had parted on bad terms, and there was no earthly way the Earl would invite him to join his household. Henry overrode his objections, informing him that these were unimportant details, and that a man of Geoffrey's intelligence should be able to find a way around them. When Geoffrey indicated the busy hall, which was crammed to the gills with men desperate to win the King's favour, and asked why another person could not be entrusted with the mission, Henry's smile became enigmatic, and he wagged a finger at Geoffrey as though he had said something cheeky. Then the King walked away to speak to his clerks and the interview was at an end.

Geoffrey gazed after him in agitation, seeing he had been issued with a royal command, and that he would have no choice but to try to see it through to the best of his ability. However, he had a feeling the task might prove to be beyond him, and that it could well bring about his death at Bellême's hands. Bellême was not a man to tolerate treachery, and Geoffrey felt as though he had been offered a choice of drowning or remaining on a burning ship. If it had not been for Joan, he would have fled to Normandy before the King realized he was missing.

While he stood thinking out his options, he became aware that one of the clerks had disengaged himself from his scribing and had come to stand next to him. He was a tall, elderly man wearing a simple monastic habit, and Geoffrey could see a hair shirt underneath, indicating he was someone who took his religious vocation seriously. He smiled without humour or friendliness.

'I know what the King has ordered, and I am here to answer any questions you have. However, since this is a dangerous task, I recommend you keep your plans to yourself. It is safer that way.'

'Thank you,' said Geoffrey shortly, wondering whether this was the fellow's way of informing him that *he* could not be trusted, either. 'Who are you?'

'My apologies,' said the monk, bowing. 'I am William Giffard, Bishop of Winchester.'

'The man with the Geese,' said Geoffrey before he could stop himself. He closed his eyes and rubbed the bridge of his nose, thinking he should be more tactful with his greetings if he did not want a blade slipped between his ribs before he even left Westminster. It was probably unwise to comment about how the bishop filled his coffers with revenues from prostitutes.

Giffard shrugged. 'It is a sordid business, and I abstain from the sin of fornication myself, but someone must organize these women and make buildings available for them to use.' Geoffrey was taken aback, and wondered whether Giffard's fellow prelates were equally pragmatic about brothels. 'But we should discuss you, not me. You are Sir Geoffrey Mappestone, who has family estates on the Welsh border. The King has threatened to isolate them if you do not do as he asks.'

'That summarizes my position very neatly,' said Geoffrey bitterly. 'My sister will suffer if I do not agree to this ridiculous plan.'

'She will,' agreed Giffard gravely. 'Bellême has allies among the Welsh, and they are preparing to rise up in his name. Your family cannot hold off an attack alone, and they will be destroyed if they are not relieved by royal troops. King Henry is a man of his word – well, most of the time – and I think he will carry out his threat if you do not do as he orders.'

'A man worthy of loyalty,' muttered Geoffrey, angry enough to speak imprudently. 'No wonder he cannot trust his own retinue to do his will, if he uses blackmail as a means to secure them. He wants me to leave Tancred and enter his service, but Henry is not a man I am inclined to follow.'

'You should consider lowering your voice,' suggested Giffard mildly. 'If you must abuse the King, then at least do it quietly – especially in his own court.'

'Why can he not ask someone else?' demanded Geoffrey, not caring who heard. 'How can I make Arundel fall by stealth? Even if I do manage to inveigle a place in Bellême's retinue – which is unlikely – I will not be trusted to a point where I can achieve anything useful. It amounts to suicide.'

'The King devised this plan because of Antioch,' explained Giffard in his serious manner. 'We all heard how it was an impregnable fortress, and how the Crusader army sat outside it for nine months without making a scratch in its defences. And then it fell, not through military tactics, but by treachery from within. Without that treachery you would still be there.'

'True,' said Geoffrey. 'But I did not arrange the treachery myself. All I did was help storm the city when the traitors arranged for the gates to be opened.'

'But you know how it was done,' insisted Giffard. 'You have details most of us do not understand, and will be able to apply the same plan a second time.'

'Is that what Henry imagines will happen?' asked Geoffrey, appalled. 'Is that why he dragged me all the way from the Holy Land? Because he thinks I can re-enact the fall of Antioch for him?'

'All he did was dictate a letter and hire a messenger. You may have endured all manner of adventures to travel here, but Henry cares nothing for that. You are the only England-born *Jerosolimitanus* he knows, and it made sense for him to order you to arrange the fall of Arundel. He does not want a siege to last months. He wants the Bellêmes out of England before Yuletide.'

'But there are differences between Arundel and Antioch,' objected Geoffrey, horrified that the King expected him to repeat military history at the snap of his fingers. 'Arundel may not be the kind of castle that *can* be lost to treachery. Do not forget that Antioch contained Greek and Armenian Christians, who took up arms against the Turks: we would not have won without their help. But there will be no army willing to fight against Bellême inside Arundel, even if I do manage to open a gate.'

'You will not be alone,' said Giffard softly. 'You may not have an army of Greeks and Armenians, but there will be one or two others who have the King's interests at heart. Of course, none of you will know each other, lest one is caught. It would not do for one to reveal the names of the others, and for none of the King's contingency plans to work.'

'But that means we will be effectively alone. If we do not know who is on our side, then we cannot enlist help in case we approach the wrong person.'

'You must pray for divine help, then,' said Giffard, and Geoffrey saw he was perfectly serious. 'God brought about the fall of Jerusalem, so you must petition Him about Arundel.'

'But He might not hear,' objected Geoffrey, thinking it was an uncertain way to ensure assistance, because the Heavenly Host did not always answer even the most fervent prayers – and might even decide to support Bellême. 'I really do not think I can help the King in this matter.'

'You have no choice,' said Giffard. 'Only a fool would refuse Henry, and you are not a fool.' He regarded Geoffrey intently, then asked a question that made Geoffrey even more reluctant to become involved. 'When you were in the Holy Land did you ever encounter something called Greek Fire?'

'Why?' asked Geoffrey warily.

'Do you know how to make it? If you do, then I might be able to persuade the King to release you from your other obligations and produce him a vat of that instead. I think he

82

would rather have Greek Fire than another spy in Arundel Castle.'

'I do not know the formula,' said Geoffrey. He returned Giffard's scrutiny, and decided to be honest. It would not do for Henry to learn that Geoffrey had listened to Oswin's claims about a new and deadly weapon, but had not bothered to mention it. 'Bellême might, though.'

'We suspect as much,' said Giffard. 'There is a rumour that Philip the Grammarian secured the recipe on the Crusade, and sent it home to his kinsmen. Do you think it is true?'

Geoffrey nodded slowly. Matilda had said her brothers *wanted* Greek Fire, not that they had already secured some, but the distinctive stench Geoffrey had noticed outside the Crusader's Head indicated they had access to at least a little. If Bellême did not have the genuine article, then he had developed something very similar. And Oswin certainly thought the weapon was already in Bellême hands.

'We know it contained sulphur and quicklime, but we never discovered the identity of the other ingredients,' he said. 'I believe at least one was something found only in the East, so it would need to be imported if Bellême planned to make Greek Fire in any quantity. But it *is* possible Philip met someone who told him the secret.'

'Then why did he not produce it while you sat outside Antioch? He was there for several months before he was killed. Why did he not use it to end the siege?'

'I do not think Greek Fire would have helped there,' said Geoffrey. 'It was not the sort of fortress that could be easily breached by weapons of any kind.'

'Well, it is a pity you do not know the formula,' said Giffard, disappointed. 'The King is deeply concerned that his enemy has a military advantage, especially now we are so close to what might end up as a pitched battle.'

Geoffrey thought Henry was right to be worried. Not only was Greek Fire a devastating weapon, but its use by the enemy had made a serious dent on the morale of the Crusaders. Henry's troops would be unwilling to attack any castle if they thought they were going to be pelted with a material that caused such horrific injuries.

'Bellême's mother,' said Geoffrey thoughtfully, trying to tie several mysteries together in the hope that they might make sense. 'She would not have had the recipe, would she?'

'If she did, then I am certain she would have used it in her lifetime. Mabel was an evil woman, who preferred the company of the Devil to praying in a church. Why do you ask?'

'There is a rumour that she is still alive,' said Geoffrey. He considered Matilda's confidences, too: that she wanted some property of her mother's. Perhaps it *was* the secret of Greek Fire, and that had been what she had hoped was written on the parchment discovered in Hugh's mouth.

'She is not,' said Giffard brusquely. 'Unless she rose from the dead and wanders the earth headless and slashed to pieces.'

Geoffrey recalled that Roger and his men believed she might have done exactly that.

Once Geoffrey's interview was over, Henry had ordered him to eat in the hall and, although Geoffrey was not hungry, he felt he had no choice but to linger a while. The King would not tolerate him disregarding a command too brazenly, and he had learned to accept food when offered anyway, on the grounds that soldiers rarely knew when the next opportunity to eat might come. It was a habit he knew he would have to break when he came to live a more sedentary life, or he would grow fat.

After his discussion with Bishop Giffard, Geoffrey wandered among the dignitaries and nobles, recognizing some from the liveries worn by their retainers, but not most. At a table bearing fruit, two men argued furiously, standing so close that Geoffrey imagined they must both be drenched in spit. They spoke in low, hissing voices, and their row was sufficiently absorbing that they were oblivious to all else. One was fat and wore the robes of a cleric, while the other appeared to be a soldier, although Geoffrey thought his sword was more for show than for serious fighting. It had a shiny, unused look about it, and Geoffrey imagined its jewelled hilt would probably interfere with the balance of its blade. He edged away, not wanting to hear what they were snapping at each other.

'*I* want that,' came an aggrieved voice as Geoffrey reached for a piece of bread a short time later. He saw that the man who addressed him was the quarrelling soldier; the cleric was nowhere to be seen.

The man was tall, with smooth, shoulder-length hair held in place by more oil than Geoffrey had ever seen on a single head. The whole mane shone greasily, and a peculiar smell emanated from it. His face was what caught Geoffrey's attention, however. It was sardonic, and the expression could only be described as a sneer. Geoffrey immediately surmised that he was vindictive, and since he had no wish to be detained at Westminster while the King decided the outcome of a squabble over a lump of bread, he overlooked the remark and moved to a different platter.

'I want that, too,' said the man, as Geoffrey took an egg instead.

'You must be hungry,' said Geoffrey with a tight smile, heading to where wine and ale stood on a separate table. He was about to pour a goblet of claret when he became aware that the man had followed him, and since he did not want to be informed a third time that he was about to select something he could not have, he abandoned the wine and decided on ale instead.

'That is *my* cup,' hissed the voice in his ear.

Geoffrey suppressed a sigh. He backed away with his hands in the air to indicate that he wanted no trouble and started to walk outside.

'Will you strut away from me while I am talking?'

Geoffrey was losing patience. He felt he had acted with admirable restraint, but there was only so long he was prepared to tolerate the fellow.

'What do you want?' he asked coldly.

'To talk.' The man took his arm and ushered him to one side, where a number of arches afforded privacy. Geoffrey tried to pull away, but saw he could only free himself by using force and he did not want to draw attention to himself. 'I am Richard Beaumais, a vassal of the Earl of Shrewsbury.'

'Then you are in the wrong place,' said Geoffrey, thinking

85

him a fool to mention such a fact to a stranger. 'The King will not welcome Shrewsbury's minions here.'

'I am no minion,' said Beaumais haughtily. 'I am a trusted advisor. But do not look alarmed. The King knows of my allegiance, and does not mind my presence here, so why should you?'

'I see,' said Geoffrey, wondering whether Beaumais might help him worm his way into Bellême's presence. Was he one of the other unfortunates Giffard had mentioned, who had also been forced to act as spy? Geoffrey decided not to leave without hearing what Beaumais had to say.

'The Earl's fortunes are on the wane in England,' said Beaumais. 'You and I are in the same boat, my friend. We have both followed a man we should not have done.'

'Meaning what?' Geoffrey asked warily, wanting more clarification before he committed himself.

'The King intends to kill you,' said Beaumais, glancing around furtively. 'Do not ask how I know, but I assure you it is true. I started that row over the bread and eggs so you would walk away and I could speak to you without wagging ears overhearing. I am telling you what I know, because we are in the same position and you may be able to help me one day.'

Geoffrey doubted it, but he smiled his thanks. It crossed his mind that the King might well stage an attack, just to make Geoffrey appear more attractive to Bellême. He wondered again whether the archer who had shot at him in the woods – and who was then conveniently dispatched – had been hired by Henry. He supposed he would have his answer when he met Roger, who would have questioned the man's accomplice.

'How do you know who I am?' he asked.

'Young Philip told me.'

Geoffrey nodded, then wondered whether Philip had also informed Beaumais that the King had ordered Geoffrey to bring about Bellême's downfall. Philip might be in a dangerous position, but Geoffrey did not much like his own, either. He felt he was being crushed and manipulated between powerful forces, who did not care whether their plotting killed him. He was tempted to ride hard for the nearest port and seek sanctuary with the Duke of Normandy, who had no love for Henry and who would help Geoffrey if he asked. But then what would happen to Joan?

'Be careful,' said Beaumais, with another glance around him. Geoffrey had no way of knowing whether the agitation was genuine. 'The King's spies are everywhere. Do not trust anyone unless you are absolutely certain of his loyalties.'

Geoffrey watched Beaumais walk to the far end of the hall, where he was waylaid by Bishop Giffard. Geoffrey frowned as he watched them together. Why had Giffard intercepted Beaumais? Was it because he thought the man who openly professed loyalty to Bellême might be plotting treason in the King's own Court? Was it because Giffard and Beaumais were in league, and were both involved in some plan that would see someone fall – be it the King or Bellême? Or was Giffard waylaying anyone he thought might be a spy at Arundel? No matter how much Geoffrey stared at them, he could not decide from their gesticulations whether their discussion was friendly or otherwise.

He was still watching them when he found his arm encased in a vice-like grip from another quarter. It was the cleric with whom Beaumais had been arguing. He was enormously fat, and when he moved, the limp jowls under his chin quivered and bounced. There was food on the front of his habit, and the man wheezed and gasped as though he had just engaged in a mile-long run, rather than a short walk across a hall. A large gap between his two front teeth completed the unappealing picture.

'What did he tell you?' he demanded of Geoffrey. 'And who are you, anyway?'

'I could ask you the same question,' said Geoffrey tartly.

'I,' said the cleric, drawing himself up to his full portly glory, 'am Maurice.'

'Good day, Maurice,' said Geoffrey, trying to recall whether one of Bellême's many siblings had been called Maurice. He did not think so, and the man was too old to be a brother of the Earl, anyway. He was nearing sixty, although as a serving wench passed, he gave her a slavering leer that indicated he did not allow age to interfere with his carnal pleasures.

Maurice sighed when he saw Geoffrey was none the wiser after his grand proclamation. 'I am the Bishop of London, man. Where have you been living, if you do not recognize me? The moon?'

'The Holy Land,' said Geoffrey, immediately on his guard. Wulfric had told him that the bishop was one of those who met with the Bellêmes in the Crusader's Head.

'I am the one who has been building London's Cathedral of St Paul,' Maurice went on, clearly thinking his fame revolved around his architectural achievements rather than his sinister assignations with the Bellême clan. 'You have doubtless admired its glories?'

'Not yet,' said Geoffrey, interested, despite his antipathy towards the obese prelate. He loved grand buildings, and was hopelessly fascinated by the clever engineering that allowed them to be raised. A discussion about architecture invariably led him to forgive the most appalling wrongs, and he was certainly prepared to overlook Maurice's dalliance with the Earl of Shrewsbury in exchange for learning more about the cathedral that was the talk of London. 'I hear it is to be the largest in England – even greater than Durham.'

'You have seen Durham?' asked Maurice, raising his eyebrows curiously.

Geoffrey nodded, unable to hide his enthusiasm. 'It is one of the most glorious buildings I have ever seen. Unusually, its Lady chapel is at the west end, because—'

'We will discuss it another time,' interrupted Maurice, smiling faintly. 'And you must allow me to guide you around St Paul's before you leave: it is rare to find a knight who admires a building he is not at liberty to loot. But first, you will tell me what horrible untruths Beaumais uttered. What did you say your name was?'

'I did not, but I am only Godric de Mappestone's youngest son, and no one confides in me. Beaumais merely said that the King fires an arrow first and asks his questions later.'

'That is true,' said Maurice. He gave a sudden grin. His eyes twinkled, and Geoffrey saw he had a pleasant face when he smiled. 'I knew your father. I was the Conqueror's chaplain, and Godric was a good and loyal subject. Your mother was the same. Now there was a fine, hot-blooded lass.' He rubbed his hands together and issued a salacious snigger.

Geoffrey regarded him uneasily, hoping the man was not about to confess to seducing his mother – although from what he recalled of that redoubtable lady, Maurice would not necessarily have been the one who had made all the moves.

'Your messenger was shot today,' he said, changing the subject before he heard something that would unsettle him, and thinking instead about the cheery-faced Petronus of Shrewsbury. 'The wound was not fatal, so you should still see your missives from the Abbot of Sées.'

'I have them here,' said Maurice, patting a pouch at his side. Another passing serving wench squealed in shock as the bishop's hand snaked out and made a grab for her ample rump. She darted away without looking around, and Geoffrey suspected that only the careless or the uninitiated wandered too close to the deft-handed Bishop of London. 'But Petronus is dead.'

'Dead?' echoed Geoffrey in astonishment. 'But it was a flesh wound. He cannot be dead!'

'I saw his body myself. Perhaps the shock of an arrow in his shoulder made his heart stop and he died of natural causes. But he is dead, regardless.'

Geoffrey gazed at him, not sure what to believe. 'But you received the messages he carried?'

Maurice nodded. 'When the King's chief huntsman brought the body to the chapel.'

'Was Petronus killed for them?' asked Geoffrey, more to himself than to Maurice.

The prelate shook his head. 'They contain nothing that warrants the taking of a man's life. However, it is a sad world where men kill just to steal a plain wooden cross from a monk.'

'His body was stripped?'

'Not stripped,' said Maurice. 'But the cross he always wore was gone.'

'Was anyone else brought in?' asked Geoffrey nervously, hoping that his confidence in Roger's abilities to look after himself was not misplaced. There was also Durand to think about, and Geoffrey recalled how he had cried out as he fell from his saddle.

'Just Petronus. I warned him that robbers haunt the road between London and Westminster, but he must have ignored me and decided to travel alone.'

Geoffrey rubbed his chin. Had Petronus died of heart failure, as Maurice claimed, and Roger had abandoned the body because he could do nothing else? And had Maurice received *all* the missives Petronus carried, or had some been delivered into other hands? Geoffrey sighed, wondering why everything that revolved around Henry always transpired to be so complicated.

'Beaumais did not mention that business with Matilda, did he?' asked Maurice, obviously more concerned with his reputation than the dead messenger. He made an apologetic moue. 'I have an excuse. My physician informs me that if I do not relieve myself regularly and often with women, my humours will become fatally unbalanced.'

'I know a lot of men like that,' said Geoffrey, thinking he could do with a physician who fabricated that sort of nonsense. 'Which Matilda are we talking about?' A sudden horrible thought struck him. 'Not King Henry's wife?'

'Lord, no!' said the Bishop in genuine horror. 'My condition regarding women may mean I am ill, but I am not insane! No, I mean Bellême's sister. She offered herself to me, and I am not usually a man to repel the desperate.'

Geoffrey imagined she must be desperate indeed, and found he was disappointed in her. She was an attractive woman, and need not stoop to entertaining an unattractive man like Maurice. He supposed she had had her reasons, and that they were doubtless something to do with the political turmoil surrounding her family's looming expulsion, but that did not absolve her in his mind.

'Did you talk much?' he asked, not very subtly, in an attempt to find out what she thought she had been doing.

The bishop sniggered and nudged him in the ribs. 'I am

not a man for chatting when there is a woman awaiting my services, if you know what I mean, but we did gossip a little afterwards. She wanted to know whether I had ever been to Arundel. Then she bounced off the bed, thanked me for my exertions, and was gone into the night.'

'Is that all?' Geoffrey was bemused.

'Well, I *have* been to Arundel, as it happens, and she wanted to discuss my visit – to the point of tedium actually. But then, abruptly, she tired of the subject and was gone. I have not seen her since. But I am sure you understand that I do not want Beaumais telling just *anyone* that I have been bedding female members of the House of Montgomery-Bellême. The King would not like that at all.'

'No,' agreed Geoffrey, wondering why Matilda had wanted to know about the bishop's knowledge of Arundel badly enough to sleep with the man. 'He would not.'

Maurice took Geoffrey to the abbey church, where the monks had accepted the murdered body of one of their own order and promised to prepare it for burial. Two brothers knelt near where Petronus had been dressed in a clean habit, hands roped loosely together as though he was praying. Someone had washed his face and brushed his hair, and the cross Maurice said had been stolen was replaced with another. While the two monks and Maurice chanted psalms, and seemed oblivious to his presence, Geoffrey went and stood over the body of the man he had barely known.

There was a rip in Petronus's habit, at the top of his shoulder. Geoffrey crouched down and touched it gently. Below, he could see the arrow wound, which some caring brother had already washed clean of blood. It was not a serious injury, and should not have brought about the man's death. Then he saw Petronus's throat, marred by dark smudges. It took a moment for Geoffrey to recognize what they were: bruises caused by fingers. He put his own hands over Petronus's neck, and saw they matched the marks his hands might make, had he strangled the man. There were two large ones at the front, where thumbs had pressed on the windpipe, and four smaller patches on each side caused by fingers. Petronus had not been killed by the arrow after all. He had been throttled.

Geoffrey wandered out of the church, wondering what had happened after he had dashed off in pursuit of the archer. Petronus had fallen to the ground, and may have been stunned. It would have taken little effort for someone to straddle an inert body and choke away the life. But who? And why? And where had Roger been? Geoffrey felt coils of unease begin to twist in his stomach, and wished he had never allowed his friends to accompany him to England. He hoped they were not lying dead somewhere, murdered by ambushers he had not seen.

He collected his horse, and rode to the copse where they had been attacked, moving slowly and cautiously, and with his shield held ready to fend off new attacks. He found the place where Petronus had fallen, and saw spots of blood and scuffed leaves. He could not tell whether the mess had been made by the strangler, Roger or the men who had carried the corpse to the abbey. He also located the spot where Durand had fallen, but there was nothing to tell him what had happened to his squire. There was no blood, so he began to hope the man had simply toppled from his saddle in fright when the first arrow had been fired. It was certainly something he had done before.

Geoffrey spent some time exploring the wood before realizing he would find no answers there, and that he needed to locate Roger. He knew his friend had not gone to Westminster, because he had checked the stables, and Roger's horse was not there. The only other place Roger would have gone was back to London. All Geoffrey needed to do was to decide where he should begin his search in the nation's largest city.

Five

It took Geoffrey the rest of the day to locate Roger. The big knight had remained in the wood for some time after the attack, because the archer Geoffrey had struck with the flat of his sword had recovered and sprinted off in the opposite direction just as Roger had dismounted to inspect him. It took years to train warhorses, and Roger was not prepared to risk his as Geoffrey had done, by haring off through the undergrowth. He had followed at a less reckless pace, which still allowed him to close the distance between him and the archer, while Helbye and Ulfrith had remained with Petronus. Meanwhile, Durand, unharmed other than a grazed elbow, reluctantly accompanied Roger.

When they eventually found the archer, it was to discover someone else had reached him first. The man lay on the ground with a crossbow quarrel through his chest. Durand noticed that the man was not quite dead, so knelt next to him and offered final absolution. Although expelled from his order, old habits died hard, and Durand liked dispensing pardons and blessings when he had the chance, despite being forbidden to do so. The archer had breathed his last, muttering something about a map.

Roger and Durand made their way back to the others. Petronus wanted Roger to escort him to Westminster immediately, but Roger had wanted to look for Geoffrey. Unwilling to wait, Petronus had continued his journey alone – on foot, because his horse had fled – and that was the last they saw of him. Roger and the squires had split up to search for Geoffrey, but when they discovered the body of the first archer – the one Henry and his men had shot – they guessed something was seriously amiss, and that further searching was pointless.

Helbye wanted to wait in the copse, claiming it would be where Geoffrey would look for them. He was right, and the knight spent some time hunting for signs of his companions among the leaf litter near the site of the attack. Durand insisted on stopping at the nearest tavern, arguing that *it* was an obvious place to wait. He was right, too, and the inn was the first building Geoffrey visited after his futile foray through the undergrowth. But Roger suspected his colleague might be some time, and wanted to do more with his afternoon than drink cloudy ale. He ordered the party back to the city, where he intended to see for himself the sight about which he had heard so much: the settlement's first public lavatory.

Near the lavatories was a tavern, and when Roger had fully satisfied his curiosity with the lines of wooden seats and the deep trenches below them, he declared himself in need of a drink. Helbye and Durand had no choice but to obey, although Helbye insisted on waiting outside.

It was dark by the time Geoffrey remembered Roger's earnest desire to inspect the new latrine and ventured towards it. He smiled in relief when Helbye came to greet him. The old sergeant looked cold and out of sorts, and informed Geoffrey he had not enjoyed his hours out in the cool spring air just because Roger had some peculiar interests. Geoffrey agreed, oblivious to the fact that he often subjected the elderly soldier to equally frigid expeditions when he became entranced by a building's architectural complexities. He gave the grumbling Helbye the reins of his horse and entered the humid, smelly atmosphere of the inn.

The room was filled with smoke from a puffing fire, and was warm to the point of discomfort. Most men had removed jerkins and tunics, and the person nearest the fire was bare-chested. The tavern smelled of spilled ale, unwashed human bodies and cat urine.

Roger sat by the door, sweating profusely in his mail, but unwilling to remove it in a place where he was a stranger. His face was red, partly from the heat and partly from the large quantities of ale he had imbibed. Because the inn was rough, no women were foolish enough to enter its shady confines, and he was bored. Durand was sullen, while Ulfrith was in the stables with the horses and was probably happier than any of his companions. Geoffrey's dog, which had hidden at the first sign of trouble in the woods, lay at Roger's feet. It lifted its head and wagged its feathery tail when it saw Geoffrey. Its welcome was friendlier than the one he received from his friends.

'There you are,' said Roger, irritably. 'I thought you were never coming.'

'We have been here all afternoon,' whined Durand, who had placed a piece of clean linen on the bench so he would not have to touch its grimy surface with his pristine posterior. 'Where have you been?'

'Looking for you most of the time,' replied Geoffrey tartly.

'Well?' demanded Roger, when Geoffrey was seated and had taken a tentative sip of Roger's ale. It was past its best and acidic, but he drank it anyway. 'What did the King want?'

'He wants you to go home,' said Geoffrey, lying easily. 'And I must remain a week or two longer.'

'Horse shit!' declared Roger immediately. 'He probably does not know I am here, and you cannot get rid of me that easily. We have travelled hundreds of miles together, and I am not about to leave now. Whatever Henry wants, you can trust me to help.'

'Although he has a point,' hedged Durand timidly. 'Perhaps we should go—'

'I know I can trust you,' said Geoffrey, touched by Roger's unswerving loyalty. Durand was ignored. 'But you cannot help, and I will be happier knowing you are as far away as possible.'

Roger was wary. 'I do not like the sound of this. Did he threaten to harm Joan? I would not worry about her. She is a powerful lady from all accounts, and can look after herself.'

'If I do not do as he asks, he will refuse to help her when the Welsh attack. And he says it is only a matter of time before they do, because he believes the Earl is preparing another rebellion.'

95

'Another?' asked Durand in awe. 'Bellême cannot learn when he is defeated! He has already made three attempts to overthrow the King, and has been thwarted each time. What does he want now? Is he still hoping to install the Duke of Normandy in Henry's place?'

'Henry plans to exile him and take his estates. Bellême has nothing to lose by plotting an uprising.'

'His final fling,' mused Roger.

'Exactly,' said Geoffrey. 'So, I cannot risk having Joan invaded by the Welsh.'

'But she is powerful and aggressive,' said Durand. 'Why risk yourself for her?'

'She is my sister,' said Geoffrey shortly, thinking that compassion and familial loyalty were not virtues Durand possessed in abundance. 'And besides, she and her husband have written to me almost every month for the last twenty years. I am fond of them.'

'*We* could defend her,' said Roger. 'We will put any rebels to rout.' Then he glanced at Durand, and his expressive face made it clear that he thought the golden-headed squire would be of no help.

'I doubt Henry would let me go to Wales when he has ordered me to work for him.'

'We will be *here*?' asked Durand, pleased. 'Good! I do not mind staying in London. There are plenty of churches to pray in, and it is a good city for a man of my talents.'

'You are too old to be a boy whore,' said Roger bluntly, automatically assuming the worst.

Durand flushed furiously. 'I was referring to my clerkly skills. I have been trained—'

'Henry wants me to offer my services to Bellême,' interrupted Geoffrey, unwilling to listen to what would be a tedious account of everything the man had learned. 'So, you cannot help me this time, Roger. You must return to the Holy Land and tell Tancred I will not be long.'

Roger gazed at him in disbelief. 'God's blood, man! Are you insane? You know Bellême detests you. Do you not recall what happened when he visited Goodrich and demanded that your family pay fealty to him? He almost killed you. You will not meet him a second time without blood being spilled – and it is unlikely to be his.'

'I know,' said Geoffrey wearily. 'I tried to tell the King the task was impossible, but he would not listen. He thinks Bellême will go to Arundel as soon as he hears the charges against him. The castle will come under siege, and Henry wants me inside, to bring about its fall by deception.'

'Like Antioch,' said Roger, nodding. 'Guards were bribed to get the Turkish soldiers drunk, then let us in. What does Henry have in mind? You throwing me the keys to the main gate one night?'

'I doubt keys will help,' said Geoffrey, thinking about what Bishop Maurice had told him of the place. 'Arundel is a strong fortress, and you will not take it by unlocking doors. Bellême will have archers on the walls and there are ramparts to fight through before you reach the inner bailey.'

'What, then?' demanded Roger. 'Does he want you to buy ale and make Bellême's soldiers drunk, so we can take them by surprise?'

'He did not say,' replied Geoffrey, knowing that once the castle was surrounded by hostile forces it would be impossible to buy ale in the kind of quantities Roger was talking about. The castellan would have it and the food locked away. 'He said that was for me to work out.'

Roger's eyes were huge. 'This is bad news, Geoff! Henry is a clever man, who anticipates the moves of his enemies, and the fact that he sent for you so long ago indicates that he has been planning this for ages. I wonder how many other plans he has in play at the moment, in case yours fails.'

Geoffrey thought about what Giffard had said: that there would be other agents working inside the castle to weaken Bellême. It occurred to him that by sending a man who was obviously a spy, Henry would draw attention away from the real ones. Geoffrey would be more of a tethered goat than a friend within. And how was he supposed to bring about the fall of a castle without help? He would not be trusted by Bellême's knights – and rightly so – so could hardly recruit any of them to his cause. He sighed and rubbed his head, aware that he had no idea how he was to proceed.

'You are a fool to become embroiled in this,' said Roger angrily. 'Ride to Dover tonight, and let me warn Joan that she can expect no help in the event of a Welsh invasion. Then, she can either come with us to Normandy, or she can stay and fight for herself.'

'You would not leave London alive,' said Geoffrey. He nodded to where a cloaked man appeared to be asleep as he leaned against a wall. 'He has been following me ever since I left Westminster and will stop us.'

'So, we must obey this ridiculous plan?' demanded Roger, aggrieved. 'But it will see us hanged!'

'Not necessarily. I cannot force Bellême to take me to Arundel, so I anticipate he will decline my generous and traitorous offer. The King will know I tried to obey him, but will accept that I have failed. And that will be that.'

'Then we will go east?' asked Durand hopefully.

'Yes,' said Geoffrey firmly. 'And probably never see these shores again.'

He was not sure whether that was as attractive as he had made it sound. England was cold and wet for much of the year, but he loved the brilliant greens of spring, and the air that smelled of grass warming under a summer sun. England was home, and he had recently come to realize it meant more to him than he had known. He wondered whether he would have time to visit Joan before he left for the last time.

'I have had too much ale and my bladder is fit to explode,' announced Roger in a booming voice. 'Come with me to the lavatories, Geoff. You will not be disappointed, I promise.'

'It is a tempting offer,' said Geoffrey dryly. 'But I think I shall decline.'

'Come on, lad,' said Roger, grabbing a handful of his surcoat to make him stand. 'You will have seen nothing like it. The King's wife built them for the citizens of London, and they are considering changing the name of the whole quayside in her honour – to Queenhythe. It goes to show how popular you can make yourself with a latrine.'

'I shall remember that,' said Geoffrey, shrugging him off. 'Perhaps I should build one to bring about the fall of Arundel Castle.'

'No,' said Roger, after a moment of serious contemplation. 'That would not work. Castles have garderobes, and its residents will have no need of a grand lavatory.'

While Roger went to drool in delight over the line of wooden seats and neatly constructed stalls of London's first public lavatory, Durand sidled up the bench to sit closer to Geoffrey. He, too, had noticed the sinister presence of the man in the cloak, and it had not escaped his attention that the man's eyes opened whenever anyone at Geoffrey's table stood or moved. He suggested Geoffrey should order him to leave them alone.

'There is no point,' said Geoffrey. 'He would deny following us, and I have no wish to engage in a brawl in this kind of place. I am surprised you let Roger come here.'

'He insisted,' said Durand sulkily. 'And you know what he is like. It is all right for him, encased in all that armour. But what about me? I have only boiled leather to protect *me* from an attack.'

'But you never fight,' Geoffrey pointed out. 'So you do not need armour.'

'Of course I do not fight!' said Durand vehemently. 'I might get hurt.'

'What do you know about the dead archer?' asked Geoffrey, to change the subject. He found Durand's brazen cowardice distasteful, but did not want to argue, knowing a debate would be pointless when each held such different views on the line between poltroonery and self-preservation. 'Did you see who shot him?'

'No,' replied Durand. 'And I assure you that I had a good look around before I went to his aid. Perhaps he was part of a band of robbers who had a falling out, and he and the other were killed for trying to attack the wrong kind of victim. Or perhaps there is someone who wanted to protect you – the King possibly. He would not have been pleased to hear you had travelled all the way from the Holy Land only to be slain in sight of Westminster Palace.'

Geoffrey wondered whether Durand was right. Matilda had confessed to following him the previous night, while Henry claimed his agents had been watching him since disembarking at Dover. He frowned thoughtfully. Someone in the King's hunting party – possibly Henry himself – had shot the archer. At that point, the man had represented no threat, with his weapons abandoned and Geoffrey's hand around his neck. So, why was it necessary to kill him? Because Henry did not want him telling anyone who had hired him? Was that why the second archer had been murdered, too?

'I gave him final absolution,' said Durand defiantly, knowing Geoffrey would disapprove of what was a gross deception on a dying man. 'There was no one else around, and it was better he had it from me than to go to Purgatory weighted down by sin.'

'Did he confess anything interesting?' asked Geoffrey, too weary to be angry. 'Such as who employed him or why he attacked us?'

'He muttered something about a "map", but I could not be sure what. I think he may have been trying to say your name – Mappestone.'

Geoffrey considered. If Durand was right, then it meant the archers had not been opportunistic robbers after all. But why would anyone want Geoffrey dead? At that point he had not agreed to do Henry's dirty work, and no one should have known about the royal plan to trick Bellême. Even if word *had* seeped out, Geoffrey was a long way from inveigling himself into the Earl's favour, and all Bellême had to do to thwart him was refuse to grant him an audience.

'Did Petronus say anything pertinent?' he asked, thinking that Durand might have noticed something Roger had ignored. Durand was more observant and certainly more intelligent than Roger.

'You mean did he think the attack was aimed at him?' asked Durand astutely. 'He did. He said his messages to Bishop Maurice were important, and it was imperative we saw him safely to the palace.'

'Did you believe him?'

Durand reviewed the question carefully, then nodded. 'He really *did* imagine he was significant enough to warrant the hire of ambushers. But that is not to say he was correct. No man likes to think he is expendable and his duties irrelevant.'

Geoffrey supposed he was right. The fact that Petronus alone had been hit must have made him assume he was the quarry, and it was not unreasonable for him to ask Roger to see him to safety. Geoffrey thought about the monk's death. He had been walking to the palace, because his horse had bolted, and it would not be difficult to approach a fat, unarmed priest and choke him. Such a method of execution was virtually silent, with no noisy fighting to bring Roger to his aid. So, was Petronus carried to the abbey by the men who had killed him? Or was he really just found by chance, as Maurice claimed? Geoffrey supposed he would never know.

'Do you think the attack had something to do with Hanged Hugh?' asked Durand worriedly. 'Or with the fact that Matilda came and asked you for a favour?'

'Matilda is not responsible,' said Geoffrey with more confidence than he felt. 'She wanted me to speak to the King for her, and would hardly have shot at me while I was on my way to meet him.'

'Was it someone who did not want you to deliver her message then?' pressed Durand. 'Someone like Bellême himself, or one of his brothers? I hear they are all at each others' throats and would sell their grandmother if it served their purposes.'

This made sense to Geoffrey. Bellême or his siblings might well have decided they did not want Matilda to have an advantage over the rest of them, so had made plans to deprive her of her messenger, just as she may have been deprived of Hugh.

'Did you do it?' asked Durand in a whisper, glancing around to ensure he could not be overheard. 'Did you tell the King that Matilda wants to negotiate without her brothers knowing?'

'No,' said Geoffrey shortly.

Durand's large blue eyes settled on the man who watched them. 'Then perhaps *he* is working for *her*, and she is angry you did not do as she asked.'

'She cannot know yet,' said Geoffrey, 'unless she has some very good spies – and if she is that well placed in

101

the King's Court, she would not have needed my help in the first place.'

'You have an eye for her,' said Durand accusingly. 'She has turned your head.'

'Roger is a long time,' said Geoffrey, not wanting to pursue that particular subject. He had taken a fancy to Matilda, but he was not going to admit it to Durand, especially now he knew she also dispensed favours to men like the obese Bishop Maurice.

He stood, and saw the cloaked man open a watchful eye. His dog came to its feet and shook itself. 'I am going to make sure Roger is all right. Stay here and finish your ale.'

'He can manage *that* by himself, surely,' said Durand disapprovingly. 'And you cannot leave me here alone. That fellow is looking at me.'

'Come with me, then,' said Geoffrey. He did not like the way everyone was pretending to ignore him. It was odd not being the recipient of hostile Saxon glowers, and that in itself was enough to put him on his guard. He opened the door and stepped outside, then stepped back in again just in time to see the cloaked man start to follow. The man knew he had been outwitted, and tried to hide his mistake by going to speak to a group of tinkers. The tinkers refused to acknowledge him, unwilling to become involved in business not their own.

Geoffrey walked briskly from the inn, dragging Durand with him. He darted down an alley and took cover in a shadowy doorway, aware of running footsteps as someone followed, desperately trying to find him. There were two of them – he glimpsed the King's colours in their tunics, which answered one question, at least – and he wondered where the other had been hiding. It was a clever ploy, using one obvious spy to draw attention from another. Geoffrey saw he would have to be more careful.

When he was sure they had gone, he abandoned the alleys and made for the dark mass that comprised the public lavatory. It was so sturdily constructed that the city burgesses felt it was safe to illuminate its wooden interior with a lantern. A dull orange glow came through the windows, and Geoffrey could hear Roger singing. He hesitated. There were places

102

where a man was entitled to his privacy, and a latrine was definitely one of them. Roger was bellowing the words to one of the bawdy ballads he had learned on the Crusade, all about eastern ladies and their improbably exotic ways. Then he stopped. Geoffrey tensed and his dog released a low whine of unease.

'He never misses out the next bit,' whispered Durand at his side. 'It is his favourite part.'

'Wait here,' ordered Geoffrey, beginning to ease along the wall towards the Queen's fine new building. 'Do not move until I get back.'

'What if you do not come back?' demanded Durand in a frightened voice. 'Then what shall I do?'

'Find a monastery and lie about your past,' suggested Geoffrey, clicking his fingers to indicate that his dog was to go with him. It regarded him malevolently, but followed readily enough, intrigued by the tempting smells that emanated from within.

Geoffrey reached the door, and opened it. Suddenly, the lamp was doused and the inside plunged into darkness. The dog yelped and ran for its life, while Geoffrey strained his eyes and tried to see. It was as well he had brought his shield, because the hacking blow aimed at his shoulder would have deprived him of an arm had it met its target. As it was, the force of the attack threw him off balance, and he only just managed to raise his sword to parry the next blow, which was towards his face. He recovered quickly, and went on the offensive, striking out at a shadow he could barely see. Then he became aware that someone was behind him, too. He turned, so he had the wall at his back, and looked from one to the other as they began to advance.

'That was a good fight,' said Roger the following morning, rubbing his hands as the landlord brought bread, fish, oatmeal and watered ale to their room. 'I would have managed alone, but it was good to see you. You distracted them, and allowed me to show off the full extent of my knightly skills.'

'But we do not know who they were or what they wanted,' said Geoffrey, taking some oatmeal. Durand nibbled fussily

103

on salted fish, and Geoffrey thought it was no surprise that the man was of such a fragile build when his appetite was so feeble.

'Who cares?' asked Roger airily. 'They were just after our gold. Everyone thinks *Jerosolimitani* are loaded down with treasure from the sack of Jerusalem and Antioch, so are worth robbing.'

'But I do not think these were robbers. Like yesterday's archers, they came for a specific purpose, and it had nothing to do with the contents of our saddlebags.'

'There were four of them against us two,' said Roger gleefully. 'And they went tumbling from the latrines as though the Devil himself was on their tails once I went at them. It was an amusing sight.'

After the fracas of the previous evening, during which Geoffrey felt he had embarrassed himself by his mediocre performance, he and his companions abandoned the lavatory and headed to a major thoroughfare called Eastceape, where there were a number of taverns that were a cut above the ones Roger usually favoured. Geoffrey had elected to stay at the Mermaid Inn, which promised clean beds and a good meal. They awoke with the dawn, and threw open the window shutters to see a street lined with beautiful houses, some even built in stone.

'It was definitely an ambush,' said Durand with conviction. 'They distracted Roger with a whore before he began his business in the lavatory, so you would worry about the length of time he was gone and would go to investigate. They thought they could dispatch you both at the same time.'

'I was not in the mood for a whore last night,' explained Roger. 'So I finished with her quickly. They were lucky you came so soon, Geoff, or their efforts would have been for nothing.'

'This is becoming ridiculous,' said Geoffrey resentfully. 'We are attacked wherever we go, and we do not even know why. Perhaps we will be safer in Bellême's fortress after all.'

'You will not,' warned Durand. Geoffrey noted that he did not say 'we' and wondered whether the squire planned on deserting. It would be a blessed relief to be rid of him, although he would have some explaining to do to Tancred.

'Did *you* recognize any of the four men last night?' he asked of his squire.

'It was too dark to see properly,' said Durand. 'Besides, I did not want to stray too far away from the shadows in case one of them spotted me. I cannot die outside a public lavatory. What would my father say? He would assume I had been soliciting.'

'We should not have let them escape so easily,' said Geoffrey, bitterly frustrated. 'Not without answering our questions.'

'And whose fault is that?' asked Roger. 'I was about to slit one's throat, but you told me to stop.'

'How could he speak to us if his head was all but severed from his body?' Geoffrey had seen the way Roger slit throats.

Roger began to laugh. 'You should have seen your face when they gave you that shove. I thought you were going into that latrine pit, and so did you.'

'It was that which allowed them to escape,' said Durand, who had watched from a safe distance. 'While you struggled to regain your balance, three of them ran away. And Roger abandoned the one he was fighting to rescue you.'

'I would have drowned,' said Geoffrey stiffly. 'That pit was deep and full, and my armour would have dragged me under. Then what would you have told Joan?'

'I would have thought of something,' said Roger with a nasty snigger. 'But you cannot blame me for not giving chase when I came to save you from an ignoble death in a latrine.'

'Public latrines are not a phenomenon that will last long,' said Helbye, arriving with Ulfrith from the stables and catching Roger's last comment. 'I prefer the convenience of "human lavatories", where you hire a man with a pail, and he uses his cloak to screen you from passers by.'

'But they can be expensive,' argued Roger, his mouth full of oatmeal. 'They seem to know when you need them most and raise their prices accordingly. And you cannot trust them not to lower the cloak at awkward moments, either, in order to demand a higher fee for raising it again.'

'The notion of the sponge on a stick in the public lavatories is clever, though,' said Ulfrith, reaching for a manly sized piece of bread that would have lasted Durand a week. 'It is a great improvement on the piles of stones, shells or bunches of herbs that are usually provided for cleaning yourself.'

'But only as long as the salt water in the bucket is regularly changed,' argued Durand with a fastidious shudder. 'And the ones I saw yesterday had not. They were afloat with —'

'The ambush,' said Geoffrey firmly. 'I want to talk about the ambush, not about London's sanitary arrangements, no matter how fascinating you all seem to find them.'

'Do not fret, lad,' said Roger comfortably. 'All is not lost. I got this from one of them before he fled for his life. I doubt *he* will be attacking folk in lavatories again very soon, given that I sliced him with my knife before he fled.'

Geoffrey took the item from him. It was a piece of silk, like the sort of token women offered knights before they went into combat. He had several himself, given by various ladies he had taken a fancy to and who had allowed him to act as their champion.

'Blue silk,' said Durand, regarding it admiringly. 'Pretty, too. I wonder who gave him that? It means he is not just a peasant, but someone important.'

'Why?' demanded Roger. 'They fought like peasants – all brute force and no skill.'

'Because peasants do not pass each other fine silk tokens,' Durand explained in a tone of voice that bordered on the insolent. Geoffrey would not have blamed Roger if he had taught the squire a lesson with his fists, but Roger was intrigued and Durand continued. 'You will find there is a *lady* who favours this colour, perhaps some noblewoman from the King's Court.'

'So, one of our attackers is a man with a lofty lover,' mused Roger. 'We shall have to visit the Court, and see if we can spot a damsel wearing clothes of this unusual blue.'

'We will not,' said Durand, pointing through the open window. 'Because there she is.'

*   *   *

Roger and his companions gazed out of the window, following the direction of Durand's finger. From their room on the inn's upper floor they had an excellent view of the street. Among the seething mass of people that scurried along it was a woman wearing a cloak that was almost the exact same colour as the piece of silk in Roger's ham-sized hand. He studied it carefully.

'Identical,' he declared. 'And an unusual hue at that. But what shall we do? Waylay her and ask whether her champions are in the habit of attacking innocent men in lavatories?'

Geoffrey reached for his cloak. 'Why not? That is the question we want answered.'

'No,' said Roger, gesturing to the remains of his breakfast. 'We have not finished, and I do not like questioning ladies on an empty stomach – and that is what she is: a lady. She is no peasant.'

'Stay here, then,' said Geoffrey. 'We do not want to tear after her in a mob, anyway. She will think she is being attacked. But do not wander off to inspect more latrines until I return, or we might never find each other again. This is a big city.'

'I will stay here,' promised Durand, whom Geoffrey thought might have offered to go with him. He did not want Roger, Helbye or Ulfrith, armed and ruffianly as they were, but Durand presented no threat to a lady. But Geoffrey was afraid she would be gone by the time Durand had donned his cloak and primped himself for the outside world, so he left his companions to the remains of their meal and ran lightly down the stairs.

By the time he reached the street, the woman was out of sight and Geoffrey found himself among a heaving throng of people that moved in all directions, pushing and shoving in their impatience to be about their business. There were gaudily clad merchants, doing their best to keep grubby fingers from their fine attire. There were serfs from the surrounding villages, come to display their wares on dirty blankets; they snatched at the ankles of passers-by to draw attention to squat purple turnips and silky-skinned onions. There were traders selling ribbons, pins, oily cakes, spices, candles and ropes. There were moneylenders, distinctive with black curling beards, and there were dark-robed clerics, some walking piously with hands tucked inside wide sleeves, but most striding as briskly as the merchants, minds full of the business of the day.

A herd of sheep was being driven to market by men with sticks, and small flocks of geese were shepherded haphazardly by children. Cows were being taken outside the city for daily grazing, and moved in unhurried gangs along the centre of the road, adding their own contributions to the mess of manure on the street. It stank so much that Geoffrey's eyes watered, and he could not think of anywhere he had ever been where there were so many people, so much noise and so many stenches. It was impossible to move with any speed, so he found it difficult to catch up with his quarry. He glimpsed her mantle now and then, and hoped he would not lose her if she entered one of the many houses that lined the street or turned up a lane.

As befitted a noblewoman, she was guarded by four soldiers. One limped and another held his arm stiffly, and Geoffrey assumed they were the four who had attacked him and Roger the previous evening. He wondered whether they were her permanent bodyguard, and grimaced, thinking she needed to choose some who were more proficient if she intended to use them as killers.

As they neared the eastern end of the thoroughfare, the crowd began to thin, which meant that Geoffrey was able to move closer to his quarry, but also that he was more likely to be seen. He had already decided to see where she went before making his approach, so he hung back, pulling his hat over his eyes and keeping his hands in his sleeves in the hope that a casual glance would mistake him for something other than a knight following a lady along an increasingly deserted road.

The houses along Eastceape became smaller and less grand farther away from the centre, and Geoffrey began to wonder whether she planned to leave the city altogether: he could already see the wall that protected the east side of London. But eventually she entered a church. The knights waited outside, scanning the street as they did so. Geoffrey kept walking to avoid catching their attention, then ducked up an alley.

He broke into a trot, moving through a maze of lanes until he was able to reach the back of the chapel without being seen by the men at the front. He arrived at a graveyard that, judging by the number of grass-covered mounds, was depressingly full, and slipped through it, holding his sword so it did not clank against his mail and give him away. He looked for a rear door, so he could speak to the woman without fighting through her guards. He did not want her to escape while he engaged them, since he imagined he was unlikely to spot her by chance a second time.

He was lucky. Although the Saxon church was a simple affair, there was a little priests' gate leading to the chancel in addition to the main door the woman had used. The gate was unlocked, and Geoffrey saw smoke rising from a house at the end of the cemetery. The resident cleric was evidently cooking himself some breakfast.

Geoffrey saw Eastceape was clear, with the exception of a cluster of figures in the distance, too far away to see what he was doing. They comprised a cloaked figure leading two others, who were carrying a long box. Geoffrey watched them until he was satisfied their attention was on their goods and not on him, then he opened the door and slipped inside the building. He found himself in a tiny vestry, which contained a couple of dirty robes hanging on pegs and a wooden chest. A second door led to the chancel. He opened it cautiously.

The woman in blue knelt in front of the altar with her hands pressed together and her eyes closed. Geoffrey was surprised, having imagined her brisk walk would have a more urgent purpose than saying prayers in some ancient and unremarkable church. They had passed several other chapels along the way, and he wondered why she had ignored them in favour of this one. He took the opportunity to study her. Although her hair was bundled behind a veil, he could see from the odd escaping strand that it was dark. Her face was olive-coloured, and attractively shaped, like a heart. She was a beautiful woman, and he was not surprised one of her knights carried her token.

109

He considered his options. He wanted to know why her men had been to such trouble to lure him and Roger into the lavatories in an attempt to kill them. He had never seen her before, and had no idea why she would order her officers to carry out such an attack. Or had she? Perhaps she was innocent, and her men had nocturnal operations of their own that she knew nothing about.

He rubbed his chin, trying to decide whether to approach her or to see where she went next. He was loath to spend his day stalking a woman while she shopped for baubles in London's many markets or spent hours in prayer, because he had hoped to begin the journey to Winchester that morning.

He was still debating, when the front door opened and someone else entered. It was the person he had seen leading the small procession along Eastceape. He was cloaked and hooded, so Geoffrey could make out nothing of his face or other features. He immediately went to one of the windows, and there was a splintering sound as something was broken. Geoffrey frowned in puzzlement. The woman in blue did nothing, and eventually the man came to kneel next to her. Geoffrey strained his ears to hear the conversation that followed.

'Well?' asked the man. 'What happened?'

'First,' snapped the woman, 'you can tell me where you have been. You said ten o'clock and it is far later than that.'

'You have only just arrived yourself,' sneered the man. 'Do not try to make me feel guilty. I had mother to take care of anyway, and she is more important than being prompt for you.'

'Where is she?' asked the woman, looking around as if she imagined someone else might be lurking in the shadows.

'Outside. But she is not pleased about last night, Sybilla.'

Sybilla! thought Geoffrey, suddenly aware of the similarity between the attractive, elegant woman who knelt at the altar and the alluring Matilda de Mortain: Matilda's younger sister was called Sybilla. He recalled Matilda's determination to have their mother's property, and wondered whether the man was one of their brothers, or whether the 'mother' to whom he referred was some other matriarch.

Intrigued, Geoffrey opened the door a little further, so he could hear better.

'What happened?' asked the man. 'Why did the attack on the Crusaders fail?'

'It went wrong,' replied Sybilla. 'They were ready for us, and my children were lucky to escape with their lives.'

At least one of Geoffrey's questions was answered. It was indeed Sybilla who had ordered the attack, although he could not imagine why, unless it was because of his arrangement with Matilda. He wondered who she meant by 'children'. Did she mean they were literally her offspring, which meant youth and inexperience would account for their dismal performance of the previous night? Or was it a term she used for devoted followers? For some reason, he shuddered.

'How could they be ready for you? No one knew what you planned to do except you, me and your children. Did one of them betray us?'

'Of course not! They would die before betraying me – or you – and two of them were injured fighting for our cause. I will see those meddlers die for that.' Her voice was sharp with malice.

'You cannot blame them for protecting themselves. Your children should not have engaged them in open combat, but slit their throats as they slept, as I suggested. Now they will be on their guard and we shall never remove them before they do us harm. I told you we should not avenge Hugh this way.'

'What shall we do?' asked Sybilla, ignoring his censure. 'Our options are beginning to run out, and I do not want to lose everything now, not when we are so close to a solution that will see us rich and more powerful than ever.'

'None of us do. Hugh should have been more careful. But I will be missed if I stay here any longer. Goodbye, sister. I will contact you again soon.'

He removed his hood to give her a parting kiss, and Geoffrey saw he was no man, but another woman, whose deep voice had misled him. He immediately noticed the resemblance between them, with their olive complexions and coal-black eyes, although the cloaked woman's hair was more grey than black. Geoffrey supposed this was the last of Bellême's sisters: Emma the Witch.

'Take care, Emma,' said Sybilla. 'Do not tackle Geoffrey Mappestone yourself. Leave him to me, and if I need help, mother will oblige.'

Emma gave what sounded like a snort of disgust, but said nothing more, and made off down the short nave to the main door. There was a clank as it opened then shut, and the church was silent once again. Geoffrey watched Sybilla thoughtfully, trying to recall if he had ever met her before and injured her in some way, without realizing that it was a member of the House of Montgomery-Bellême he had hurt.

Sybilla went back to her religious pose, hands together and eyes closed, evidently to give Emma time to leave and reduce the risk of them being seen together. Geoffrey had just made the decision to follow Sybilla after all, thinking he would have better answers in pursuit than in direct confrontation, when footsteps sounded outside the vestry door and the latch began to rise. It was either the priest returning from his breakfast or one of Sybilla's 'children' coming to make sure all was well. Geoffrey saw he was going to be caught in either case, so he opened the door to the nave and walked quickly to the altar. Sybilla jumped in alarm when she saw him and opened her mouth to scream, but he stopped her by kneeling close and pressing his dagger into her side.

'One sound and your children will be motherless,' he whispered, pulling his cloak over his arm to conceal the fact that he held her at knifepoint. He felt her tense next to him as the vestry door opened and a portly Benedictine bustled in, humming to himself. He was clearly Saxon, with fair hair and faded, kindly eyes. He hesitated when he saw Geoffrey and Sybilla and Geoffrey smiled at him, knowing that they appeared innocent enough – two people kneeling side by side in front of an altar.

'Do not mind me,' said the monk, unwilling to drive them from their meditations in case they forgot to leave a donation. Saxon churches were poor, and needed all the funds they

112

could lay their hands on. 'I will be at the back polishing the pewter. Stay as long as you like.'

Geoffrey sensed Sybilla drawing breath to shout for help, and dug the dagger more securely into her side. She gasped and turned to look at him.

'You would not slay me in a church!' she whispered, making it sound like a dare.

'Better than in a public lavatory,' retorted Geoffrey.

'Your soul would be damned for all eternity,' she hissed.

'How do you know it is not damned already?'

'What do you want?' Her voice was confident and sharp, and he sensed she was not afraid of him or his dagger. 'What kind of man bursts in on a woman at her prayers and thrusts steel in her side?'

'One who wants answers. And one who did not enjoy the attentions of your "children" last night. Why did you send them to kill us?'

'I have my reasons,' she spat.

'Then explain them.'

She sensed his growing anger and gave a heavy sigh. 'All right. Put away your dagger and we will speak like civilized people. My children will come for me in a moment, and they will certainly kill you if they see us like this.'

'I will take my chances,' said Geoffrey, keeping the blade pressed against her ribs. He suspected that as soon as she was free she would screech for help and he would find himself facing the four knights. 'Will you tell me what is going on or do I have to cut you first?'

She was silent for a moment, as though gathering her thoughts, and then began to speak. 'You have made an arrangement with King Henry to bring down the House of Montgomery-Bellême. Philip overheard it all. You intend to supply the King with Greek Fire. And you killed Hugh.'

'You are wrong,' said Geoffrey shortly. 'Philip was too far away to hear what the King said to me, and I could not supply Henry with Greek Fire, because I have no idea how to make it – although it sounds as though your family does. Nor did I kill Hugh. You could have asked Oswin to verify my story, but someone made sure he would never talk again.'

113

'I heard about his murder. It was a pity, because he was useful and relatively discreet.'

'Until yesterday,' said Geoffrey, suspecting that Oswin may have been killed because he had broken his tradition of silence. 'He was terrified that your family was using his tavern to devise an evil, devastating weapon that will destroy the King.'

'You make us sound sinister,' she said accusingly. 'We are not. We will soon be at war with Henry, and we must do all we can to ensure victory. It is not wicked or corrupt, but simple survival, and any soldier would do the same.'

'Not with a weapon like Greek Fire.'

She sighed again. 'You do not understand. My brother Robert is desperate: he knows he has rebelled once too often, and that he is about to pay with his English estates. We *need* Greek Fire to defeat Henry and his tyrannical ways.'

'But this is nothing to do with me,' he pointed out. 'How can my death make your situation easier?'

'Philip said you were going to ease yourself into Matilda's affections, and destroy us from within. Matilda is not as sensible as Emma and me, and would be flattered by attentions from a handsome man. You had to be stopped.'

'Philip has a wild imagination,' said Geoffrey coolly. 'I am not in the habit of wooing women to bring about their downfall.' He did not add that he had been charged by Henry to woo Bellême and bring about *his* downfall, however.

'You deny entertaining her in your bedchamber in Southwark?' Sybilla clearly did not believe him.

'I did not invite her. She asked me to tell the King she wanted to parley on your behalf – a message I did not deliver, I am afraid – then she left. There were no expressions of affection on either side.'

'But you admire her,' said Sybilla, nodding when she saw the expression on his face. 'Men do. And she mistakes their lust for loyalty and trusts those she should not. Like the killer of poor Hugh.'

'I did not kill Hugh,' said Geoffrey again, thinking what incredibly bad luck it had been that he had been passing when the young man had died. Had it happened a few moments

114

earlier or later, he would not have been involved. A thought occurred to him. 'Your mother was Mabel de Bellême, was she not? She died in Normandy.'

'She was murdered,' corrected Sybilla. 'As she lay naked and unprotected on her bed.'

He voiced what was on his mind. 'But Emma the Witch just talked about her as though she is still alive. She said she was outside.'

'Our mother will always be with us,' replied Sybilla simply. 'You must have lost loved ones, and later felt their presence, giving you strength?'

'Not that I recall,' said Geoffrey. He reconsidered. 'Although I had a friend called John de Sourvedal, who was murdered in Jerusalem two years ago. I felt sometimes his tortured soul was driving me to solve the crime.'

'Well, there you are, then,' said Sybilla. 'You know what it is like.'

'But Emma implied she was here literally,' he pressed. 'She said she was outside.'

Sybilla smiled enigmatically. 'Our mother was a witch in life, and she remains a witch after death. Therefore, she would not be comfortable in a place like this.' She gestured at the chapel.

Geoffrey stood. He had had enough of the Bellême family, and wanted to know no more about Sybilla's mother and the sinister notion she was everywhere except holy places.

'I did not kill Hugh and I do not know the secret of Greek Fire,' he said with finality. 'So, from now on, you will leave me alone and keep your "children" away—'

Suddenly, the door opened, and the four knights saw that their lady was not alone. Drawing their swords, they piled into the church, readying themselves for an attack. Geoffrey pushed Sybilla away from him and drew his sword reluctantly, not wanting to brawl in a church. The monk gave a shriek, and darted towards the main door, intending to escape while he could. One knight flicked a wrist, and he fell to the ground with a cry, blood spurting from his arm. Geoffrey was appalled.

'That was unnecessary,' he shouted angrily, taking a firmer

115

grip on his sword and wishing he had brought his shield, too. 'You could have let him go.'

'To tell the burgesses that a knight is being murdered in the Church of All Hallows Barking?' demanded the swordsman coldly.

He pushed back his hood, and a mane of dark hair tumbled out. The swordsman was female. The others followed suit, and Geoffrey was nonplussed and very disconcerted to find himself facing four young women, all tall and strong – one was even taller than him – and approaching with determination and bloodlust etched clear on their faces. Other than a clear desire to kill, they were attractive, with dark eyes and olive skin. It seemed Emma and Sybilla had been speaking literally when they referred to the 'children', because the four warriors were clearly Sybilla's daughters.

'People say we are witches,' said the spokeswoman as they advanced. 'They claim we dabble in the dark arts, and that is why we are so formidable in battle. My name is Haweis, and I am the second born. Mabel is the eldest, and was named after my grandmother, God rest her murdered soul.'

Mabel, who was the tallest of the quartet, nodded. She was evidently the large, silent type, more than happy to let her more eloquent younger sister do the talking. Geoffrey looked her up and down and decided she was probably the most dangerous, because she seemed the most comfortable with her weapons. Meanwhile, Haweis continued to speak.

'These are my younger sisters: Cecily and Amise. Our mother wanted sons, and had us trained in the knightly arts when she produced only daughters.'

'But you carry her tokens?' asked Geoffrey, bewildered. He had never heard of such a thing.

'It makes us look more convincing,' said Haweis, smiling at his confusion. 'Who has heard of knights who do not carry emblems of the lady they serve? Their absence would arouse suspicion. I suppose you found the one Amise lost last night, and that is what drew you to our mother?'

Geoffrey thought of himself as a liberal-minded sort of man, and his years of travelling and reading meant that he was surprised by very little. But he had never encountered girls trained in swordplay, and he found the prospect of fighting them disturbing. He had always taken pains to spare women when he had been engaged in battle, and was reluctant to come to blows with them now.

'I have never fought women before,' he said, wondering what would happen if he put up his sword and walked away. He realized they would kill him, so the sword stayed where it was.

'I am more proud of my girls than I would be of any boy,' said Sybilla, beaming fondly at the warlike quartet that ranged in front of her in a protective wall. 'They are stronger, more intelligent and far more ruthless than men.'

'They should have joined the Crusade, then,' replied Geoffrey. 'That venture attracted folk with those particular talents.'

'We did,' said Haweis. 'But it was too tame for us, so we left during the siege of Antioch. There were better things to do than sit in the mud and starve like peasants.'

Geoffrey gaped. 'You went on Crusade? But how did you—'

'How did we fool people over our sex? That was easy. When you are tall and strong like us, few ask impertinent questions. We kept ourselves to ourselves. There were other women on the Crusade, so I do not know why you find our presence so remarkable.'

'Probably because the others did not go pretending to be knights,' said Geoffrey, aware that all four were coming closer as they talked.

'You are wasting time,' said Sybilla impatiently. 'Kill him. And do it properly this time.'

Six

G eoffrey was surprised by the speed and ferocity of the attack that followed. Without warning, the four women launched themselves at him simultaneously, drowning out his protests that he would sooner fight away from the holy confines of a church. He parried Haweis's first blow, which was so hard it made his fingers numb. While she prepared herself for a second, big Mabel moved in, swinging a mace with incredible skill. Geoffrey ducked behind a pillar, and she struck it with such force that splinters of stone flew off in all directions. Sybilla screamed at her daughters to hurry, while Geoffrey weaved around the piers, aiming to stay out of their way for as long as possible.

The two younger daughters edged behind him. One darted forward with her sword and, while Geoffrey's attention was taken, Mabel struck a monumental blow that would have killed him outright had it not been for the protection afforded by his armour. As it was he staggered, and Haweis used the opportunity to dive at him with her dagger. He felt the blade glance off his mail and decided he had had enough of chivalrously declining to attack. They would kill him if he continued to fight defensively, and he was certainly not ready to sacrifice his life for good manners.

Ignoring the pain in his left shoulder, he went on the offensive, assaulting Mabel and Haweis with a series of hacking blows. They retreated fast and in alarm, while the younger pair tried to slip in a sortie from behind. One succeeded in striking his helmet with her sword, but Geoffrey whipped out his dagger and hurled it at her. She dropped with a scream and her sister's attack faltered. The older women were not so easily distracted, and ignored her sobs and their mother's wails of horror.

'Enough,' shouted Geoffrey, as Mabel hefted her mace and Haweis grasped her sword in both hands. 'I will kill you if you fight me any longer. Give up and go home.'

Mabel hesitated, glancing at her injured sister and weighing up the situation. Sybilla screamed at her to attack, while Haweis was so angry she seemed beyond reason.

'Never!' she yelled furiously. 'You have murdered Amise, and will pay with your life.'

She dashed towards him with her sword raised high. Geoffrey waited until the last moment, then jigged to one side, so her hacking blow met thin air and she staggered off balance. He kicked out and knocked her from her feet, perfectly timed to stumble into Mabel, who was racing forward with her mace. Both women tumbled to the ground, so Geoffrey dropped his sword and swung around to grab Cecily. With one arm wrapped tightly around her neck, he snatched her dagger from its sheath and pressed it to her throat. She went stiff with fear.

'Enough!' he said a second time, aware of the aching throb in his arm from Mabel's mace. The two older sisters exchanged a glance, and then climbed slowly to their feet.

'Let her go,' ordered Sybilla. There was a tremble in her voice, and Geoffrey supposed she had only ever seen her daughters in the position of slaughtering their opponents, not losing to them. She looked down at the girl who lay in her arms, blood dripping from a jagged wound on her face. 'You have already killed one of my daughters. Do not deprive me of another.'

'She will recover,' said Geoffrey. Amise's cut bled furiously, and the resulting facial scar might well deter future suitors, but she would live if the injury was properly tended. He addressed Mabel and Haweis. 'Put up your weapons. Now.'

Cecily gave a whimper of fear that did more to convince them than any words. They obeyed, although Haweis left the strap of her sword untied, so she would be able to draw it

119

if Geoffrey lowered his defences. She glowered at him, her eyes dark with hatred and rage.

'You will not get away with this,' she whispered. 'I will repay you for what you have done.'

'You attacked me,' Geoffrey pointed out. 'So you must accept the consequences. But the monk you stabbed has escaped and is probably telling everyone he meets that there are female knights in his church. You should leave before people come to see whether it is true. Your family already has a reputation for sorcery, and the discovery of women dressed as men will only make matters worse.'

Mabel and Haweis gazed at the door in alarm. It was open, and a trail of blood marked where the wounded priest had crawled away. Mabel was no fool, and neither was Sybilla, although Geoffrey thought Haweis lacked proper judgement. Mother and eldest daughter exchanged a glance and Sybilla nodded agreement. Geoffrey pushed Cecily away from him, a little harder than was necessary, and watched as they hauled the injured Amise to her feet, concealing her bleeding face with her cloak. With her mother on one side, and the beefy Mabel on the other, they aimed for the door.

'I will not forget this,' snarled Haweis, and Geoffrey was sure she was not referring to his generosity in letting them escape when he could have slain the lot of them.

'Go,' he said tiredly, in no mood for bandying words with a woman who was beyond reason. He had met zealots on the Crusade, and knew from experience there was no point in arguing with them.

'I will see you dead,' she hissed. 'No one wounds a Bellême and lives to tell the tale.'

'Hurry,' said Geoffrey, wanting them gone so he could see whether Mabel had done serious harm to his shoulder. 'You do not want to be here when the monk brings the city guards.'

'Why not?' she demanded. 'You are the one who spilled blood. We were just defending ourselves. There are five of us to pit our word against yours.'

'The priest will know who stabbed him,' Geoffrey pointed

out. 'And the citizens of London will consider female knights an aberration. Go, before they hang you.'

She knew he was right, despite her determination to quarrel, and followed her mother and sisters out of the church, scowling furiously. Big Mabel paused when she reached the churchyard gate, and Geoffrey thought she was about to yell some insult or threat, but she took her dagger and touched it to her forehead, as a mark that she had yielded with honour and acknowledged his victory. Haweis shoved her hard, furious at the gesture, but Mabel was far too large to be jostled, and merely sheathed her weapon to concentrate on carrying Amise to safety.

Geoffrey was not far behind, no more happy to be discovered in a place where blood lay in pools on the floor than were the Bellême women. Folk did not take kindly to knights practising their killing skills in holy places, especially when it was Norman warriors befouling Saxon sanctuaries. When he reached the gate, a shadow dived at him. Haweis had hidden behind a yew tree and taken the opportunity to attack, thrusting her dagger towards Geoffrey's stomach. He had been anticipating such a move, and her weapon hissed through empty air as he jumped away. Her face was dark with fury.

'I will kill you sooner or later, Geoffrey Mappestone, and you will wish it was today, so you do not live the rest of your short, miserable life in fear.' The fierce expression in her eyes left Geoffrey in no doubt that she meant every word.

'Go home, woman,' he snapped. 'And do not forget you are not the only one with a sharp sword. I will not be so forgiving a second time.'

She glowered at him before following her sisters, aiming for some hideaway in the north of the city. Geoffrey glanced around to see whether Emma was lurking nearby, waiting to attack him when he thought the danger was over, but the place was deserted. He wondered what had happened to the injured monk, and walked around the side of the church to look for him. It would be a pity to let a man bleed to death, just for the want of a little medical attention. He found him huddled against a buttress in a feeble attempt to hide.

121

'Have they gone?' the monk asked in a hoarse whisper, his face white with shock.

Geoffrey nodded and knelt next to him, noting the wound was not serious, although it had terrified the poor man out of his wits. He rummaged in his pouch for one of the strips of clean linen he kept for such eventualities, and bandaged the bleeding arm. The Benedictine smiled gratefully.

'I am sorry I did nothing to help. I had no weapon, and would not know how to use it if I did . . .'

Geoffrey helped him to his feet. 'The wound may fester, so you should summon a surgeon or a wise woman to tend it.'

'And what about you?' asked the monk softly. 'Did they harm you?'

'No,' replied Geoffrey, not entirely truthfully; his shoulder ached viciously. However, he was determined Mabel should never know, no matter how serious the injury. He had his pride, after all.

The monk regarded him intently. 'You do not need to pretend with me. Come to my house. I have a tonic that will help both of us. Taken with wine it eases the most griping of pains.'

It sounded good to Geoffrey, and together they limped through the graveyard to the man's small home. It was a simple affair, comprising a single ground-floor room. A fire smouldered in the hearth, and over it bubbled a pot of stew. The monk barred the door, then fetched his potion, pouring a small amount into two cups and adding a generous measure of wine. He swirled it around and drained his goblet in a single swallow. Geoffrey followed suit, wincing as the stuff burned its way down to his stomach. It made his eyes water and he coughed.

'You will notice the difference in a few moments,' said the monk, smiling at his reaction. 'My name is Brother Edred, priest of All Hallows Barking by the Tower. It is a famous church, and has stood on this site for four hundred years. But I am sure its sacred walls have never before been sullied by the likes of what happened today.'

'You are probably right,' said Geoffrey, aware of a warm, tingling sensation spreading through his stomach. He started

122

to feel slightly light-headed. It was not unpleasant, although he suspected it would impair his ability to fight the likes of Mabel and Haweis if they came after him again that day.

'Sybilla has been here before,' Edred went on, sitting near the hearth and holding unsteady hands towards the flames. 'But I did not know her soldiers were women, nor that they would bare their weapons in my church. I hope they do not return – not them or Abbess Emma of Alménches.'

Geoffrey flexed his arm tentatively, relieved to discover the numbness was wearing off. Mabel had not broken bones after all. 'Where is Alménches?' he asked.

'In Normandy, I suppose,' replied Edred, in the tone of voice that suggested that if Alménches was in Normandy, then it might as well be in Hell. He was a Saxon, after all. 'They say she rarely visits her abbey, and spends most of her time plotting to further the interests of her family. They also say she prefers to speak to the Devil than to God.'

'That is said of most Bellêmes,' said Geoffrey, who had learned long ago to take gossip with a hefty dose of salt. 'Emma may be unpopular because her brother is the Earl of Shrewsbury.'

'No,' said Edred firmly. 'Rumours like this nearly always have some basis in truth. I have caught her myself, stealing holy water and poking around that part of the churchyard where we bury felons. Graves have been disturbed.' He pursed his lips and looked meaningfully at Geoffrey.

'You think she did it?' Geoffrey was sceptical, sure the Abbess of Alménches had better things to do than to scrabble about in graveyards after rotting corpses.

'She did it,' replied Edred with absolute conviction. 'I caught her with muddy hands after one such desecration, although I pretended not to notice. It is never wise to tackle such folk directly, lest they call on their familiars to put an end to you with claws and fangs. But you know why she wants the bones of men who have been buried in unhallowed ground, do you not?'

'No,' said Geoffrey truthfully.

'She intends to kill the King with witchcraft,' said Edred in a whisper. 'I have tried to warn him – he employs me

123

when his regular clerks need an additional scribe – but he will not listen.'

Geoffrey was not surprised. Even a powerful Norman abbess could not dispense with a strong king like Henry – whether she was in possession of dead men's body parts or not.

'I am sure there is nothing to worry about,' he said, pleasantly relaxed. He wondered whether Edred would lend him his bed for a while, because he felt like sleeping.

'Then you are wrong,' said Edred firmly. 'She means to murder the King. Will you tell him?'

'He would not believe me.'

'He might. You seem like an honest fellow – the kind of man a king would want in his service.'

'Yes,' agreed Geoffrey drowsily. 'That is the problem.'

The following day, Geoffrey wrote to his sister, informing her that the King anticipated an uprising along the Welsh borders, and warning that royal help might not arrive as quickly as she might expect. He did not trust Henry, and thought he might abandon Goodrich regardless of the arrangement he had made. But Joan was strong and resourceful, and Geoffrey hoped she would be able to prepare for the impending onslaught if given sufficient warning.

When he had finished, he sat in the window and gazed out at the seething mass of faces that hurried along Eastceape. Roger had dragged Helbye and Ulfrith to view the public lavatory again, declaring that they needed to recall every detail, because he intended to build a similar one when he returned to his home in Durham. Durand had declined the invitation, preferring to shop for trinkets in the market before they left for Winchester that afternoon, so Geoffrey had been left alone to write his letter and to ponder the events that had occurred since his arrival in England.

First, he considered Hugh. Geoffrey thought that if the young man had carried messages between various members of the Bellême family – and possibly notes from Matilda to the King – he could not have been as stupid as folk suggested. Had he been killed because he had learned the secret of Greek Fire, and certain members of the clan wanted to ensure he did not tell anyone else? Or had he been murdered by the King's agents, because Henry wanted to show the Bellêmes what happened to those who attempted to parley with him when he was determined to crush them? There was also the strange fact that the parchment containing the message had been rammed into Hugh's mouth, but Geoffrey was certain he had heard him yell before he was thrown to his death.

Then Geoffrey thought about Oswin, stabbed in his bed after his household had been rendered helpless with a soporific. Because Matilda had employed a similar method to gain access to Geoffrey, he could not help but suspect her of the crime. However, she had told him that she had been waiting impatiently for Roger to succumb, which indicated she had not been elsewhere stabbing landlords. He wondered if poisoned ale was something favoured by the Bellême family in general, rather than Matilda in particular, and if one of her siblings had killed Oswin. Emma was alleged to be a witch, and probably had access to such potions, while the fiery Sybilla and her daughters seemed willing to kill for any reason. Geoffrey was certain Bellême himself would not have been so subtle. He would have marched into the Crusader's Head with his sword and slaughtered the entire household, not just the slumbering taverner.

Next Geoffrey considered Petronus, shot then strangled. Was the ambush in the woods to prevent him from delivering his messages to Bishop Maurice? Maurice later claimed to have received all he expected, so perhaps Petronus had carried missives for someone else, too. Petronus hailed from Shrewsbury Abbey, and Bellême was the Earl of Shrewsbury. Geoffrey thought it reasonable to assume that Petronus had business with someone other than Maurice, someone in the service of Bellême. But who? The gawky Philip, who half-listened to conversations and then reported them, garbled, to his aunts? Or perhaps the sardonic Beaumais, who openly confessed to being a vassal of Bellême, but who still haunted Henry's Court?

And what of the meeting between Emma and Sybilla in All Hallows Barking? Were the sisters simply trying to devise ways of keeping their estates while their brothers suffered the full consequences of Henry's wrath? Matilda had claimed as much, but Emma and Sybilla did not trust her judgement, and thought she would allow herself to be beguiled by Geoffrey, who would then betray them all. He supposed he should not be surprised: in a country where the name Bellême was spoken with such fear and hatred, the family would be used to looking for treachery around every corner.

And what about Edred's claim that Emma had been raiding his churchyard for body parts to use against the King? Could that be true? Geoffrey supposed that if she was as powerful a witch as everyone seemed to believe, then it was possible she might try. He considered sending a letter to Henry, to warn him, but was afraid that it might be construed as a threat rather than friendly advice. He decided to leave the matter well alone. It was not his concern, and there was no reason why Henry should believe him when he had already chosen to ignore Edred.

He sighed and stretched, stiff from his encounter with Sybilla's daughters the previous day. The sun poured through the window, and there was an unmistakable feel of spring in the air. The day was mild, and he could detect the scent of early flowers above the foetid stink of the street below. It was far too pleasant a morning to stay in, so he decided to go for a walk, to see for himself the splendid new Cathedral of St Paul. His dog wagged its tail eagerly when he stood, more than willing to go for a stroll when the sun was shining and there were new smells to investigate.

He set out along Eastceape, where he met Durand coming the other way, a length of red ribbon fluttering in his hand. Geoffrey sincerely hoped he did not intend to use it to keep his hair out of his eyes. The squire fell into step with him, chatting about the lovely baubles that had been for sale in the market, while Geoffrey wished he would discuss something more manly than jewelled hair combs and nice brooches for cloaks.

They neared a fish market, where Durand began to complain about the smell, and Geoffrey saw two men carrying a long box. It was not a large box, nor did it look heavy, but the sight of it jarred a memory at the back of his mind.

The men who had accompanied Emma on her visit to All Hallows Barking had carried a long, thin box. But that was not all. He had seen a similar chest spirited away from the Crusader's Head on the night of Hugh's murder. Were these boxes one and the same, or was there a carpenter somewhere who produced many such items?

Geoffrey studied the men. One was a hawk-faced fellow who was clearly a knight. The other was heavily cloaked, as though he wanted to disguise himself. He was tall, but thin, and seemed to find carrying the box more of an effort than his stronger companion. Geoffrey did not recognize either, and they paid him no particular attention, so he decided the incident was probably irrelevant and dismissed it from his mind.

He and Durand crossed the polluted Walbrook stream, then walked along Westceape with the dog at their heels. It was not long before they saw the great cathedral towering over the surrounding rooftops, even though it was far from completed. When they drew closer, the sound of masons and carpenters at work drowned out the rattle of carts and the yells of traders. Hammers pounded and rang on wood and stone, saws scraped, and pulleys and winches creaked. Apprentices ran everywhere, fetching and carrying materials for their masters, mixing mortar, counting nails, measuring ropes and cutting wood for the mass of scaffolding that swathed the emerging building. Geoffrey stood for a few moments and regarded it in awe.

The nave was all but finished, and was a pile of Romanesque arches that soared into the sky. There was to be a mighty tower over the central crossing, and that part of the church was being strengthened accordingly to take the weight. He walked slowly, admiring the carvings around the heads of the doors and over the windows. He recognized one or two faces on some of the statues: Bishop Maurice had been used for the Angel Gabriel, while a likeness of King Henry had been plastered on St Michael. After a few moments, Durand became bored, and wandered away to sit on a pile of stones and watch the masons.

'What do you think?' came a voice from behind Geoffrey.

127

It was Bishop Maurice, standing with his arms around two giggling wenches. The bishop's face was flushed, and it appeared he had just enjoyed an invigorating session with them. He gave them a fatherly hug and dismissed them, first planting a wet kiss on their cheeks. They took the coins he offered and fled down the aisle, where their tinkling laughter echoed back through the stones.

'Are you asking what I think of the cathedral or your choice of company?' asked Geoffrey, thinking one was magnificent, while the other was unremarkable.

'Those ladies visit me for the benefit of my health,' said Maurice smugly.

'I remember you mentioning your malady,' said Geoffrey, supposing he had better take a polite interest, although he would have preferred talking about the cathedral. 'How often are you obliged to avail yourself of their services?'

'These two only oblige me once a day,' replied Maurice. '*After* Prime, of course. It would not do to ease my agonies before the sacred mass. Other kindly ladies help if I am overcome during the afternoons or evenings. As I told you at Westminster, my physician tells me women are the only cure. My goodness!' he breathed suddenly. 'Who is *she*?'

Geoffrey followed the bishop's gaze and saw him looking at Durand, wrapped in his cloak and with his fair hair tumbling to his shoulders. His back was towards them, so Maurice could not see his face.

'That is my squire,' Geoffrey replied shortly. 'His name is Durand.'

'No, *her*,' said Maurice in a whisper, eyes only for the golden-headed apparition. 'She who is interested in the work of my masons, and who perches on my stones like an angel.'

'He is interested in the masons, right enough,' said Geoffrey caustically. 'But not for what they are doing to your building.'

'I must have her,' said Maurice, spellbound. Durand stood and minced towards the masons. The bishop's eyes almost fell from his head. 'How often do you meet a woman interested in the art of craftsmen, and with whom you

128

can have a proper discussion after you have finished your medicine?'

'Not often, I suppose,' admitted Geoffrey, who liked an intelligent woman himself when he could get one. He thought about Matilda, and wished she was not a relative of Bellême. 'But Durand will disappoint you, My Lord Bishop. He prefers to talk about ribbons and bracelets than architecture.'

'But you do not,' said Maurice, turning to smile at him. He gestured expansively. 'What do you think of my cathedral?'

'Superb,' replied Geoffrey sincerely. 'It will be one of the wonders of the world.'

Maurice beamed. 'I like to think so. It will be the largest in the land – bigger than Durham.'

'So I see,' said Geoffrey admiringly.

'She has gone!' exclaimed Maurice, looking to where Durand had been standing just a few moments before. He gazed around in disappointment. 'Where did she go? My angel!'

'Flew up to Heaven, I imagine,' muttered Geoffrey, guessing Durand had seen nothing he liked among the masons, so had gone to inspect the carpenters instead.

'If you know her, you must put in a word for me,' said Maurice earnestly. 'I am fully booked for the next two days, but can find her a spot on Friday. She will not regret coming, I can promise you that. What did you say her name was?'

'Durand. I will give him your message, but do not blame me if he takes you up on your offer.'

Maurice laughed. 'You are teasing me! I like a man with a sense of humour, and they are difficult to find these days with political battles roiling about our ears. I shall be glad when Henry bans the Bellêmes from our country, because I think it will be a better place when they have gone.'

'Better for England,' said Geoffrey, wondering whether the bishop was being entirely truthful with him. He had not forgotten Wulfric's claim that Maurice had been among those who had gathered at the Crusader's Head to discuss Greek Fire, the resurrection of Mabel de Bellême and the fall of King Henry. 'But I feel for Normandy.'

'I attended that monk's requiem earlier today,' said Maurice, walking outside to show Geoffrey plans for his central tower. 'Petronus. You said you were there when he was shot.'

'Did he carry messages for anyone else, do you think? Other than to you from Abbot Ralph?'

'I expect so,' said Maurice carelessly. 'Shrewsbury is a long way away, and if you are going to make a lengthy journey, you will want to be of as much use as possible. You would carry other messages, if there were folk ready to pay, would you not? It is practical economics.'

'Do you think he carried messages from Bellême's supporters in Shrewsbury?'

'Yes, I would think so. It would not be illegal. Bellême is to be charged with various offences on Easter Saturday, but at the moment he is a free man and can do what he likes. In fact, I would be surprised if Petronus had *not* carried messages for members of Bellême's following.'

But Petronus had not confessed to doing so, Geoffrey thought, wondering whether that was significant. 'Perhaps that was why he was killed,' he suggested. 'To see what news he had.'

Maurice nodded. 'These are dangerous times, and there are rumours that the Bellêmes have devised a terrible weapon, which will destroy their enemies in a wall of fire. The King, obviously, is keen to get his hands on the details, so he will know how to counter it. Petronus may well have been killed to see if his documents mentioned this weapon.'

'But if he carried that sort of information, then surely he would have travelled less conspicuously? Or, if he insisted on being open, then he would have travelled with a substantial guard to protect him?'

'You would think so. But since he is dead, we shall never know why he did what he did. Have you ever been to Arundel? It is another of Bellême's fortresses.'

'No,' said Geoffrey, startled by the abrupt question. 'Nor his castles at Shrewsbury and Bridgnorth, neither.'

'Pity. I would have appreciated your comments on its military architecture, since you are a man who has an eye for a fine building.'

'There are rumours that Mabel de Bellême, the Earl's

mother, is still alive,' said Geoffrey, wanting to see what the prelate would make of that story, and thinking that he might as well gossip if Maurice was predisposed to talk.

'There are not,' said Maurice. 'There are rumours that *she has risen from the dead* and come to help her beleaguered children. That is not the same thing at all.'

'Do you believe it?' asked Geoffrey warily, thinking Maurice was a strange churchman if he put faith in the efficacy of the black arts.

'The Bellêmes are a powerful family, deeply steeped in a tradition of evil, and it is possible they have discovered some way to cheat death and bring Mabel back again.'

For some reason, the day suddenly seemed chillier to Geoffrey. A cloud drifted in front of the sun, and caused a shadow to fall across the church. Geoffrey glanced at Maurice, and saw he was thinking much the same thing: that even mentioning the allegedly long-dead witch seemed to blight their day. Geoffrey repressed a shudder, while Maurice started to walk towards his cathedral. He glanced around him nervously and lowered his voice.

'You see? Even discussing that fiend causes the sun to hide his head. I am going inside my holy church, where the likes of Mabel cannot follow. Will you come? I will say a mass for you, and then I had better find myself a woman. Discussing the Bellêmes has affected the balance of my humours.'

Geoffrey followed him, thinking that if he were to inveigle himself into the service of Bellême to please the King, then he needed all the masses he could get, even if they were spoken by venal prelates like Bishop Maurice.

Geoffrey spent so long at the cathedral that it was too late to leave for Winchester, so he and his companions were obliged to delay their journey until the following day. To while away the evening, Roger diced with Helbye and Ulfrith, while Geoffrey read a scroll Maurice had lent him about the use of pulleys in constructing large buildings, listening to the tap of rain against the window shutters. Durand had washed his hair, and huddled close to the fire, running his fingers through his locks to dry them. He had put some sort of scent in the water,

131

and its sweet aroma filled the room, masking the earthier odours of burning wood and wet cloaks. Roger grumbled that the perfume put him in the mood for a woman, and Geoffrey was reminded of Bishop Maurice and his medical complaint.

It was not long before there was a knock on their door, and a dripping messenger arrived with a scrap of parchment. It was from Edred at All Hallows Barking, who urged Geoffrey to visit him as soon as possible, but to approach with caution. Geoffrey was bemused and inclined not to go, since he thought the summons might be a ruse by the Bellême daughters to lure him out alone. He supposed it might also be Matilda, who would want to know whether he had delivered her message to the King.

But it was difficult to read Maurice's scroll in the unsteady light of a single candle, and Geoffrey was bored with watching Roger's brazen attempts to cheat Helbye and Ulfrith. After a year in Roger's service, Ulfrith had come to realize that Roger's consistent good luck was suspicious, but the lad was too simple to identify exactly how he was being fleeced of his meagre wages. Geoffrey was more than ready to go out and test his wits against the Bellême women.

'Wait until the end of this game and I will come with you,' offered Roger, who was on the verge of bankrupting the guileless Ulfrith for the third time that evening.

'No,' said Geoffrey, thinking he would be less noticeable on his own, and better able to sneak up on the church and see what was happening. 'Stay here.'

'Then I will come,' offered Helbye, standing slowly and unable to suppress a wince. He had been quiet most of that day, and Geoffrey suspected that the sudden change in weather from sunny to wet had made his old bones ache. Geoffrey declined to drag him away from the fire, and gestured for him to sit again.

'You cannot go alone,' said Ulfrith. 'Stay here and help me win my wages back from Sir Roger.'

'Take Durand,' suggested Roger. 'He can fetch me if there is trouble.' The disgusted tone of his voice indicated that he did not imagine Durand would be of any help by himself.

The squire looked up in horror. 'But it is past eight o'clock and pitch dark. The city will be full of rogues and vagabonds. Besides, it is raining and I have only just finished drying my hair.'

The others regarded him uncertainly, wondering whether he was making a joke. It was inconceivable to a man of arms that drizzle might prevent him from straying out of doors, and in a country like England, where it rained often, such an attitude would see them inside for months. Durand stared back defiantly, and Geoffrey thought he saw the glitter of self-pitying tears in the man's eyes. He threw him his cloak without a word, and opened the door to walk down the hallway into the street, standing in the shadows to scan the deserted road for signs of an ambush. His dog sat next to him and sniffed the air eagerly. It was an unfriendly beast, and if anyone had been lurking nearby it would have growled. Geoffrey glanced down at it, and it wagged its feathery tail, so he felt sure no one was waiting for him there, at least.

With Durand grumbling behind him, he set off down Eastceape, along the same thoroughfare that had thronged with people the previous morning. Now it was dark and empty, with the only illumination coming from the houses of rich folk whose glassed windows allowed the light to flood out. Geoffrey saw shadows flitting here and there, and sensed that London was just as much the domain of robbers and criminals during the hours of darkness as was Southwark.

It did not take long to reach All Hallows when there were no carts or processions of monastics to dodge around. When Geoffrey saw its dark mass against the skyline, he slowed and approached cautiously. His dog kept close, although whether it was because it detected menace in the air or because it sensed Geoffrey's unease the knight could not say. Durand kept closer still, and Geoffrey had to push him away twice, because all he could hear was the squire's ragged, terrified breathing.

There seemed to be nothing untoward, so he dipped down the lane that ran parallel to the church, as he had done the previous day, and doubled back to enter through the rear door. He saw Edred's little house with its windows barred and shuttered for the night, and eased towards the vestry door, where he spotted a shadow. He gestured for Durand to stay where he was and advanced alone. He glimpsed a long garment, and could hear soft intakes of breath: whoever it was was shivering. He moved forward until he reached the porch. The shadow was Edred.

'What do you want?' Geoffrey whispered softly, keeping well hidden as he spoke.

Edred almost leapt out of his skin. 'God forgive you, Sir Geoffrey!' he muttered, recognizing the knight. 'It is not kind to sneak up on elderly monks and frighten them into their graves.'

'What do you want?' Geoffrey asked again. The churchyard was very quiet, and only the patter of rain on leaves made any sound.

'I wanted you to see this for yourself,' Edred replied, still shaken. 'Come.'

'Come where?' asked Geoffrey uneasily. He had not taken such care in his walk from the tavern only to be led into an ambush at the church.

'Into my vestry,' said Edred. 'Emma is here, performing some unspeakable act of evil under the mistaken impression that she is alone.'

'Then how do you know about it?'

'I have served this church for twenty years and always rise to recite the divine offices, despite the fact that I always do so alone. When I came to say compline, she was here. So, I sent for you.'

'Is she waiting for Sybilla?'

'The Bellême women *have* been using poor All Hallows for their assignations during the day,' said Edred. 'But they do not come at night – well, until now. Come and see.'

Geoffrey allowed himself to be let into the vestry, where he was instructed to peer around the same door he had hidden behind the day before. This time, the church was so dark it was almost impossible to see anything, and the edges of the nave were in complete blackness. A single candle burned within, and Geoffrey could make out the dark features and grey mane of Emma, standing in front of the altar. Geoffrey's dog started to nose its way forward, but it stopped dead in its tracks and released a low, frightened whine. Its tail dropped between its legs and it cowered, as if someone were threatening to kick it. It stood that way for a moment, then fled. Edred gave Geoffrey the kind of look that indicated the dog's reaction was extremely meaningful.

Geoffrey felt himself jostled, and saw Durand had disobeyed his orders and had followed, wanting to see why he had been dragged out on such a miserable night. He regarded Emma with pursed lips.

'What is *she* doing here at this time of night?' he whispered indignantly.

'That is Emma of—' began Edred.

'I know who she is,' interrupted Durand importantly. 'I met her once when she visited my abbey. She is Emma, Abbess of Alménches, a woman who is said to find praying in churches distasteful, which is an odd thing for a nun to admit.'

'Keep your voice down,' warned Geoffrey. 'I do not want her to think we are spying.'

'But we *are* spying,' Durand pointed out sulkily. He turned to Edred. 'How did she get in? Do you leave your church unlocked? I know some chapels leave doors open on wet nights, for beggars.'

'Beggars have a place in my home, if they need one,' said Edred. 'But I do not leave my church open after dark. King William Rufus turned a blind eye to the black arts, and they flourished in his reign. King Henry has not yet managed to stamp them out and I do not want All Hallows sullied by that sort of activity.'

'Then how did she get in?' pressed Durand. 'Through the vestry door?'

'I noticed yesterday that one of the window shutters was broken, then pushed closed to hide the damage. I think she did it when she was last here.'

'She did,' said Geoffrey. He recalled Emma going to a window and hearing the splintering of wood. She had been preparing ahead.

'I told you she has been in the graveyard, digging in the

135

section where we bury felons,' said Edred unsteadily. 'Do you believe me now?'

'We can conclude she is not here for any innocent purpose, or she would have come during the day,' mused Geoffrey. 'A church open all night is of no use to her, because she might be disturbed by beggars coming to sleep, but one always locked would make for a very private place during the hours of darkness. She probably does not know you say your offices through the night.'

'There is no reason she should. Some of my parishioners are aware of my habits, but most do not care. I do not scream my devotions from the rooftops; they are between me and God.'

'Then what is she doing?' asked Durand, turning to look at Emma again. 'Why would she want to visit a locked church in the dark and damage its windows to do so?'

'That is why I called you here. She is going to do something terrible, and I want credible witnesses.'

'We could just stop her,' suggested Durand.

'I do not want her to know we are here,' said Edred fearfully. 'Her demon nieces took a sword to me once, and I do not want them to do so again. I want you to see what will certainly be a wicked act, and then I want you to tell the King, so he can ensure it never happens again.'

Geoffrey and Durand fixed their attention on the shadowy figure near the altar, with Geoffrey thinking it would be an odd tale to take to Henry – that he and his squire had spied on Bellême's sister and watched her defile a church without making any attempt to stop her. Henry would want to know why they had allowed her to proceed.

Emma remained still and quiet, staring at the pewter cross with an unreadable expression, her thick hair tumbling around her shoulders in a silvery sheet. Then there was a scraping sound, followed by a thud, and someone else joined her. Emma and her new companion did not seem to think they needed to keep their voices low in the deserted building, so it was easy to eavesdrop on their discussion.

'You are late,' Emma said accusingly. 'I have been waiting

136

for more than an hour, and you know how these places make my skin crawl.'

The other person did not reply, and Geoffrey eased forward in an attempt to see his or her face. It was covered by a hood, and he could not even tell whether it was male or female. The figure was taller than Emma, but Sybilla was taller than her older sister, and he thought Matilda was, too, while all four of Sybilla's daughters would be larger than their aunt. It might even be Bellême or one of his brothers. Or a retainer. Geoffrey cursed under his breath when he realized that unless the figure removed the hood they might never know.

The hooded figure made a gesture to indicate that Emma was to begin. The abbess stepped up to the altar and laid several bowls on top of it. Geoffrey heard Edred begin a prayer in a frightened whisper, and knew it would be hard for a good priest to watch his church defiled and not be able to prevent it. He wondered whether he should step forward and announce his presence after all. Geoffrey was not a deeply religious man, but he was uncomfortable watching sacred places sullied, and it was obvious Emma was about to do something deeply unpleasant.

'Move the candle,' Emma snapped at her companion. 'I cannot see.'

There were four small bowls on the altar now, and she set about pouring some of their contents into another, larger, one. The church was soon filled with a foul smell, like rotten eggs. Sulphur, Geoffrey thought. And he knew perfectly well what sulphur was used for: Greek Fire. He wondered whether Emma intended to manufacture some on the altar in front of his very eyes. If she did, then his duty was clear. He would allow her to finish, then step forward and lay claim to her bowls and potions, and the secret ingredient of Greek Fire would be revealed at last.

After a few moments of pouring and mixing, Emma turned to her companion. 'Do you have it?'

The figure passed her something, and Geoffrey wished she was using a brighter candle.

'In the name of my mother,' cried Emma, in a loud voice that had her companion glancing around uneasily, 'whose murdered soul wanders the earth. I do this for you.'

Geoffrey heard a whimper behind him, and thought it was his dog, but it was Durand; the dog had long since gone. Edred crossed himself furiously, and sprinkled holy water over the three of them.

'Do not call her too loud,' advised Emma's companion in an unsteady whisper. 'She may come, and I do not want to see her yet. Not until . . . well, you know.'

Geoffrey wished the figure would elaborate. Until what? What were they waiting for? Had Emma really devised a way of bringing the murdered Mabel from her grave? Emma tossed whatever her companion had brought into her bowl with a flamboyant gesture. There was a bright flash and a puff of reddish smoke, like something summoned from Hell.

The sudden noise and noxious smell was apparently as unexpected to Emma and her companion as it was to Geoffrey, Durand and Edred. Her companion shrank backwards, throwing up his hands to protect his face, while Edred raised the volume of his prayers, forcing Geoffrey to nudge him, lest he gave them away. Durand was so frightened he was close to tears.

'That was not supposed to happen,' said Emma, apologetically in the silence that followed. 'I must have added too much olive oil.' She seemed puzzled by her mistake.

Olive oil, mused Geoffrey. Could that be the secret ingredient of Greek Fire? It did not sound very likely, but the Crusaders' best alchemists had worked on the problem for three years, and had not been able to produce any. It would be ironic if the thing that made the devastating substance stick to its victims and burn so fiercely was something as ordinary as olive oil. It was a staple food in the Holy Land, although it was rare and expensive in England. He wondered how much of it would be needed, and whether Emma had sufficient stockpiles to make the kind of quantities necessary to defeat Henry.

'And now this,' said Emma, waving something theatrically. It was long and wizened, and Geoffrey thought it was a slug at first, but Edred crossed himself and muttered that it looked like the finger of a hanged man he knew had been stolen from

138

the churchyard a few days before. Geoffrey grimaced, sure the Greek Fire concocted by the Arabs had not contained body parts, and even more certain that this particular addition was Emma's personal fancy, rather than something essential. The potion cracked and sizzled, and it sounded as though the finger was being devoured.

'What is that?' asked the companion, pointing to a phial that was set aside at the far end of the altar, and had not yet been used. Geoffrey strained to hear his voice, but he spoke in the kind of hoarse whisper many people reserved for churches, so it was impossible to identify.

'A complex mixture of human blood, toad juice, charcoal and raisins,' replied Emma superiorly. 'It is imperative the balance is right, or the potion will not work. It goes in last – now, in fact.'

Everyone watched while she added a dash, and Geoffrey thought that anything containing raisins was a foul substance indeed. He detested the sweet, dried fruits, and decided that *they* could well be the secret ingredient that made Greek Fire so vile. They were brown and sticky, and the right colour. Another foul smell pervaded the church, and the bowl looked full to overflowing.

'You have made too much,' whispered Emma's companion accusingly. 'We only want a little, and you have made enough for an army.'

'I have my own needs,' replied Emma enigmatically. 'Go and check no one is outside, while I put this in a jar. I have been here too long already, waiting for you to bring me the oil, and I want to be gone. Matilda will wonder what I have been doing, and I do not want her to know.'

'Why not?' asked the companion, watching as she poured the solution into a pottery flask. Transferring a viscous solution from a wide-rimmed bowl to a narrow-necked jug was not easy, and some of it dripped on the altar.

'Because this is best kept between you and me,' replied Emma impatiently, spilling more in her haste to be done. 'It is never wise to tell too many people of your plans, because it is a natural condition of humans that they betray one another.'

'I will not betray you, Emmy.'

139

The abbess smiled. 'That is because you have not yet discovered your price. Everyone has his price, be it gold and silver, the life of a loved one, or the outcome of a war.'

'You are overly cynical,' said her companion, although Geoffrey thought she was probably right, especially where the Bellêmes were concerned. 'But why did this need to be done in a church? We could have hired a room in a tavern instead. It is cold in here, and I feel I am being watched.'

'You do?' asked Emma, looking around in alarm. 'Are you sure you closed the window properly after you climbed in?'

'Yes,' said the companion impatiently. 'I do not mean watched by people. I mean watched by beings who do not approve of holy places used for this kind of thing. They may do us some harm.'

'Do not be ridiculous,' said Emma dismissively. 'I have been doing "this kind of thing", as you so prosaically put it, for years, and nothing untoward has ever happened to me.'

'It probably explains why you do not like to be in churches, though. You sense you are not welcome. But tell me why we could not make this mixture in a tavern?'

'It is necessary to recite incantations, and they are more powerful when spoken in holy places,' replied Emma, upending the bowl and pouring the last of the potion into the flask. 'You cannot just hurl the ingredients together, or anyone could do it. Besides, the dark forces *like* to be summoned in churches. Now, go and ensure the coast is clear. I do not want anyone to see us leave.'

The figure departed obediently, and Geoffrey quickly closed the vestry door and slipped the bar across it. After a few moments, they saw the latch rise and the door shake, as Emma's companion gave it a good rattle to ensure it was secured. By the time Geoffrey decided enough time had elapsed to open it again, the companion had gone and Emma was walking briskly down the aisle with the pottery flask hidden in a basket.

'Will you follow her?' asked Edred, his face pinched and white with anxiety. 'To see where she goes, and to whom she gives this vile concoction?'

'There is no point,' said Geoffrey. 'She is going to her

140

lodgings, and we will learn nothing other than where they are. It would have been more useful to follow her companion.'

'It was probably a woman,' said Durand, sounding very certain. He had recovered from his terror now that the church was empty, and was back to his usual opinionated self. 'The Bellême women are large and tall. It was a sister or a niece.'

'Or one of their retainers,' said Edred. 'There is a courtier called Beaumais who is deeply involved in their affairs, and there is William Pantulf. They also have a steward called Josbert who is loyal to the point of lunacy. Then Bishop Maurice of London has been hankering after Emma, so it could have been him. A cloak like that would have hidden his corpulence, and the height was about right.'

'It could have been King Henry himself,' speculated Durand. 'He wants the secret of Greek Fire, and this may be the only way he can get it. The rumours that Bellême has it are rife, and it will not be good for his troops to think that the Earl has a weapon that will cook them inside their armour.'

Geoffrey walked to the altar, where Emma had left her candle burning next to the spilled potion. He was disturbed to see that the black sludge smoked slightly, where it had seared through the hard, ancient wood. He poked it with his dagger. It looked like Greek Fire, and the smell was similar, but the consistency was wrong. Emma needed to do more experiments before she perfected her mixture.

'It is too runny,' he said to Durand and Edred. 'It will probably burn like Greek Fire, but how will she use it? This watery substance cannot be propelled in balls using war machines.'

'It can be poured, though,' Durand pointed out. 'They could tip bowls of it over the walls of Arundel Castle on to the King's troops below.'

'Not easily,' said Geoffrey. 'How would you set it alight? It would not be easy to handle once it started burning, and would be just as likely to harm the defenders as the attackers.'

'Bellême would not care about that,' declared Durand knowledgeably.

141

He tried to take the candle from Geoffrey, to inspect the dark stain, but succeeded in knocking it from the knight's hand. When the flame touched the potion it immediately flared into a merry blaze. The stink of burning sulphur filled the air and produced a thick, choking smoke. Edred muttered a prayer, then emptied a bottle of holy water on to it, evidently anticipating that the sacred fluid would do battle with the demonic flames and douse them. The fire hissed, then burned more brightly. Geoffrey ran outside and gathered cold, wet earth in his helmet, which he dumped on the altar. After a few moments, smoke started to issue through the soil as the flames continued to smoulder.

'We shall have to carry it outside,' said Geoffrey, removing the cross and shoving it into Edred's hands. He took one side of what was basically a simple wooden table, and indicated that Durand was to take the other. Between them, they heaved it outside, and placed it in the churchyard, where it could do no harm. It continued to hiss and burn, even in the rain.

'It is demonic,' said Edred, appalled. 'It ignores holy water, and burns even when smothered in earth. Emma was right: her evil incantations have summoned up spirits that defy all natural laws.'

Geoffrey rubbed the soil away, and saw the substance had scalded a deep groove in the altar, but was beginning to flicker out. The wood surrounding it was wet, and difficult to ignite. It had done its worst and would burn itself out with little further damage if left to its own devices.

'It was careless of Emma to leave a candle so close,' declared Durand indignantly. 'What if we had not been here? It would have burned down to the stub and ignited that substance. Then this poor church would have gone up in flames.'

'Yes,' agreed Geoffrey soberly. 'And a fire would destroy all traces of her experiments. It was no accident she left the candle burning, Edred. She expects All Hallows Barking to be a mass of cinders and ashes tomorrow.'

Seven

It took three days to travel the short distance between London and England's capital city at Winchester. The spring was a particularly wet one, following what was said to have been a mild winter, and almost continual rain had turned the roads to mud. Riding along them was like wading through a river of slippery sludge, and Roger complained of the damage it might do to the horses.

Geoffrey was silent most of the way, thinking about what he had learned and witnessed and wishing his companions had gone to Normandy, where they could take refuge with the Duke. Durand would have gone in an instant, since he was far more interested in his own safety than in helping his master, but there were times when Geoffrey could not find it in his heart to condemn the man's cowardice, and the journey to Winchester was one of them. Geoffrey was touched by the others' loyalty, though, despite his concerns for their lives.

He considered the task ahead of him as he rode and came up with a plan he thought might work, but it relied on Roger being outside the castle where he could take messages to the King. He had decided that the King's prediction about what would happen when Bellême was confronted with the charges was accurate: Bellême would not stand by meekly while the King confiscated his estates – Arundel in the south, and Tickhill, Bridgnorth and Shrewsbury in the north. He would fight to keep them.

Because Arundel was closest to Winchester, and Bellême would not want to risk a two-hundred-mile trek north unless absolutely necessary, Geoffrey thought Henry was right in assuming that the Earl would fight from there first. It occurred to Geoffrey to gamble on that fact, and secure himself inside before Bellême arrived. But Bellême was unlikely to greet a past enemy in his stronghold with open arms, and Geoffrey decided it would be better to follow the King's recommendation and attend the Easter Court at Winchester, where he would meet Bellême 'by accident'.

He considered how he might persuade the Earl to hire him. Several ideas came to mind, but were discarded as impractical. He thought about seducing Matilda and having himself invited as her lover, but Emma and Sybilla were already aware that might happen, and it seemed a good way to get himself killed. Then he considered making some rebellious remark to the King, so he would be obliged to flee for his safety – and where better than with another of Henry's persecuted? But Henry had too many loyal men around him, and Geoffrey had a feeling he might be hacked to pieces before he could leave the building, let alone approach Bellême with his dilemma.

He tried to concentrate, and not to become distracted by the many questions that plagued him. Did the Bellêmes have the secret of Greek Fire, or did Emma still have some way to go before she perfected it? Had she actually been making the substance in All Hallows, or did her addition of dead fingers and raisins indicate she planned to do something else with her potion? Geoffrey was sure the Arabs did not include such ingredients or recite satanic spells, so it was possible the strange business at All Hallows had nothing to do with making a weapon. But what, then? It was obviously something sinister, or she would not have felt obliged to do it in a deserted church.

Or was she simply trying to keep her discoveries from the Earl? It was clear there was strife within the House of Montgomery-Bellême: the brothers were ranged against the sisters, and the sisters were every bit as greedy and acquisitive as their male kinsfolk. It would not surprise Geoffrey to learn that Emma was working for herself, and not for the clan as a whole.

However, the sisters were also divided, because Emma, Sybilla and the four daughters disapproved of Matilda and distrusted her judgement. He wondered whether they knew Hugh had been carrying her messages to the King, to negotiate a secret pact. Matilda had told Geoffrey she was acting for all three sisters, but was that true, or was she simply seeing to her own interests?

And what was young Philip's role? Was he what he appeared – the bumbling, illegitimate son of Philip the Grammarian, who Bellême casually dispatched to Henry's Court as security for his good behaviour? Since Bellême had no intention of behaving, Henry would be within his rights to execute Philip. If that happened, would Bellême care, or would he be incensed over the loss of a good spy?

And then there was Hugh. What had he been doing the night he was murdered and who had killed him? Henry, because he did not want to receive messages from the Bellême sisters? Matilda, so she could later claim she had sent the King offers of support as a way to gaining his sympathy? And what about the 'reply' in Hugh's mouth? Was it really from Henry, or was it written by someone else – perhaps one of Matilda's siblings – to prevent negotiations taking place? Henry claimed he had not heard from the sisters, but Geoffrey knew better than to believe anything *he* said.

Geoffrey sighed and flexed his shoulders, thinking next about Beaumais's warning that the King would try to kill him. Was that true? Or did the slippery courtier have his own reasons for spreading the seeds of distrust? There had been two incidents on the road to Winchester, but both attacks had been beaten off with ease, which led Geoffrey to assume they had not been instigated by Henry or Bellême, because both would have hired more competent agents.

'We have ridden far enough today,' said Roger. 'We should find a tavern.'

Geoffrey nodded through the drizzle to where a settlement nestled among the trees some distance ahead. 'That is Winchester. We will be there within the hour.'

'Very well,' said Roger reluctantly. He wiped rain from his eyes and attempted to engage his friend in conversation. 'Bellême is due to appear before the King's Court tomorrow, you say?'

145

Geoffrey nodded. 'That is why we should be in Winchester tonight, to get the feel of the place.'

'Have you got a plan?' asked Roger. 'You said you would by the time we reached Winchester, in case we are obliged to act immediately. And do not say the plan is to visit Bellême while the rest of us are on our way to Normandy. We are staying with you.'

'All I can think of is to go to Bellême and claim the King tried to kill me – it may even be true, given what happened in the woods near Westminster – and hopefully Beaumais will support what I say. He did warn me it might happen.'

'You have a wound to prove it,' said Roger, nodding at Geoffrey's shoulder, still bruised from where Mabel had struck it with her mace. It looked worse than it felt, and Geoffrey supposed it might make a suitably impressive injury to show Bellême. Of course, he would have to hope Mabel was not on hand to point out that it was her handiwork.

'I will say I have nothing to lose by joining him, and will go with him when he leaves for Arundel.'

Roger was not happy. 'But what if he wins this dispute with the King? You may find yourself bound to his service forever. Tancred will be furious.'

'Tancred is the least of my worries.' Bellême was the kind of man to kill petitioners, so simply marching up to him and offering allegiance was risky to say the least.

Roger's blunt face creased into a worried frown. 'Perhaps you should let me pretend I am you. I am not impeded by a stiff shoulder, and . . .'

'He *knows* me, Roger. But we should discuss the rest of my plan. Do you remember the system we devised in Jerusalem for sending messages at night? We used lamps to speak to each other, by moving them up and down.'

'Of course. You want me to look for waving lamps at Arundel?'

Geoffrey nodded. 'I will pass you two pieces of information from the battlements or a tower: first, which of the gates is the weakest in terms of its structure, and second, which is the weakest in regard to its defence.'

'How?'

'Arundel will have a main entrance. We shall call that number one. The one to its west will be two, and so on until we reach the beginning again. So, if I make two flashes, followed by three . . .'

'It means the gate immediately to the west of the main entrance is the weakest in structure, but the one to the west of it is the least well defended,' said Durand, who had been listening and was keen to show he had grasped the essence of the discussion.

'I am glad you understand,' said Geoffrey. 'If anything happens to me, you must do the flashing.'

Durand stared at him. 'But that would mean I am inside with you.'

'Yes,' agreed Geoffrey, surprised that he should think he would not be. Durand was his squire, and it was his duty to be at Geoffrey's side.

'But I do not want to meet Bellême,' whispered Durand, appalled. 'It is common knowledge that he is in league with the Devil, and, as a man of God—'

'You are not a man of God,' interrupted Geoffrey. 'You lost that honour by tampering with a butcher's son, and you are now supposed to devote yourself to becoming a warrior.'

'Tampering with a peasant does not sound overly serious to me,' said Roger. 'I always thought abbeys turned a blind eye to that sort of thing.'

'It was more than that,' said Geoffrey shortly, unwilling to reveal the grisly details of Durand's misdemeanour to Roger, who would certainly not understand. 'You must come with me, Durand. Bellême will be suspicious if I appear without a squire. But none of this may be necessary; Bellême might not flee to Arundel at all.'

'He will,' said Roger grimly. 'His other option is to hand all his estates to Henry and leave England like a beaten dog. Of course he will fight.'

'I am not going with you,' said Durand, white-faced with fear. 'You ask me to step into the lion's den, and I will not do it.'

'Yes,' said Geoffrey firmly, 'you will.'

*　　*　　*

The Conqueror had visited Winchester soon after his invasion of England, because it was the Saxon capital and the place where the treasury was held. He had seen no reason to change this, so the city had been allowed to remain England's administrative and financial centre. Henry also kept his treasure at Winchester. To make sure it was all there, and properly bulked up by taxes and fines, an army of scribes and monks worked for him, labouring as long as daylight would allow, and sometimes using the unsteady light of candles.

Winchester was different from London. It was less vibrant and colourful, but more wealthy and grand. The houses were larger, and the ones in the centre were built of stone, rather than timber. The fact that large numbers of courtiers gathered there frequently meant there were plenty of merchants ready to sell them what they wanted – fine cloth from France, spices grown around the shores of the Mediterranean Sea, exquisite jewellery from Italy and Spain, and good wines from Normandy.

'This is where we part,' said Geoffrey to Roger, as they neared the gates. 'We cannot be seen together from now on.'

Roger clasped his outstretched hand. 'I do not like this, Geoff, lad.'

'I know,' said Geoffrey. 'Will you take my dog? The last time he met Bellême there was a near-exchange of bites, and I do not want the Earl to kill me because it cannot control its roving teeth.'

'It is a good judge of character. Bellême deserves to be ravaged by wild beasts; he is one himself.'

'It is possible that the Earl has forgotten the biting incident,' suggested Durand timorously, loath to part with an ally, even the dog. 'And we need all the reinforcements we can get.'

'He *will* remember,' said Geoffrey, who suspected Bellême never forgot any kind of insult or injury, and the nip the dog had managed to plant had been a vicious one.

They parted, with Geoffrey and a sullen Durand heading for the centre, and Roger leading Ulfrith and Helbye to find a tavern – doubtless a seedy one – at the city's edge. Geoffrey

148

rode slowly, looking around with interest, and would dearly have loved to visit the merchant whose sign mentioned he sold books as well as pens, parchment and other clerkly supplies. But there was no point in going to Bellême carrying anything of value; the Earl would take anything that could be exchanged for gold.

It was already late afternoon, so Geoffrey found a small, quiet inn near the great Benedictine abbey. He had intended to stay in the monastery itself, thinking it would be safer than a tavern, but the city was heaving with people who were to take part in the King's Easter Court, and he realized there were unlikely to be vacancies. He paid for a chamber and sent Durand to buy food. He was bone weary, his shoulder throbbed and he wondered listlessly whether he would have the energy to play his part in the charade the following day. He lay down and waited for Durand to return.

When he awoke the sun had set and the street below was thick with shadows. Durand was still out. Geoffrey felt a pang of anxiety, knowing his squire would not deliberately linger in the streets of a strange town after the curfew had been sounded; it was not safe, and Durand would prefer to be inside with the door locked. Geoffrey left the bedchamber and walked to the main part of the tavern, where tables and benches were provided for those who wished to slake their thirst with jugs of ale. Several people were enjoying the hospitality of the landlord, mainly scribes and clerics, but Durand was not among them. Puzzled and not very pleased, Geoffrey saw he would have to go and find him.

He was still in full armour, so he fetched his sword, made sure there was a long stabbing dagger in his belt, and left the tavern. He had no idea where Durand might be, but hoped he found him fairly quickly, because he did not want to spend the entire night hunting for the man. He drew his cloak more closely about him, partly because it was cold, but mostly so it hid his distinctive surcoat. Crusaders were rare in England, and he did not want to draw too much attention to himself.

The streets were empty, and it seemed the curfew in the King's richest city was vigorously enforced. Monks and scribes had retired to their abbey or quarters, and Geoffrey

149

had the feeling Winchester, like London, became a different place at night. There was not a merchant to be seen, and those few folk who braved fines or imprisonment to go about their business after dark moved furtively, with their faces concealed by hoods or loose Phrygian caps with pointed tips.

A slithering sound behind him made him duck into an alley, but it was only a beggar with no legs, whose wheeled trolley made a hissing noise in the muck of the street. Then he saw other shadows and tensed. These were not prostitutes, robbers or other children of the night, but liveried soldiers carrying drawn swords. They walked briskly and turned a corner. Moments later, another man appeared, wearing a thick winter cloak and with his own weapon at the ready. Geoffrey saw flashes of red on his garments, similar to those on the soldiers' uniforms, and supposed he was their captain. He was tall and broad, and walked confidently, as though he was used to having his orders obeyed. A nobleman, Geoffrey assumed.

Just as he drew level with Geoffrey's alley, the mournful call of the night watch echoed along the street. Geoffrey heard the man swear, then was almost knocked over when he decided to hide in the same place. The stranger was even more startled to discover he was not the only one skulking in the shadows, but nodded agreeably when the knight raised his finger to his lips to indicate they should both be silent. Neither wanted to waste time explaining his business – no matter how legitimate – to the King's guards, who tended to turn such encounters into lengthy, ponderous occasions that involved exchanges of coins.

The night watch marched past, and Geoffrey saw that several held wriggling captives who were destined for a night in prison. The guard at the front carried a lantern, and threw its light into doorways and along lanes to search for curfew-breakers as he went. Geoffrey eased farther back into the shadows, and thought that those who had been caught must have been singularly stupid, given the noise the guards were making. When the watchmen had passed, and the street was silent once more, the stranger addressed Geoffrey in Norman-French.

'Why are you hiding in dark alleys at this hour?'

'Looking for my squire,' replied Geoffrey, thinking he could ask the same question himself. But he did not want to start an argument that might see the guards return and arrest them both, so he decided to overlook the man's peremptory behaviour.

'Probably looking for another master he thinks will treat him better,' said the man bitterly, as if this was something that happened to him regularly. 'None of them can be trusted. Name?'

'His or mine?' asked Geoffrey, trying to control his temper at the man's abrupt manner.

'Yours, of course,' said the stranger haughtily. 'I do not waste my time on servants. You are a knight and, although you have made an attempt to conceal it, a *Jerosolimitanus*, too. I saw your surcoat when the lantern went past. My brother was a Crusader, although he did not live to enjoy his glory.' He fingered the material of Geoffrey's tabard covetously. 'It was a pity. He had promised to give me his holy armour when he returned.'

Geoffrey peered at the man in the gloom, and could just make out dark hair and coal-black eyes. The stranger was not Bellême, whom Geoffrey would have recognized, but he was certainly a relative. Geoffrey supposed he was a brother – either Roger, Count of Marche or Arnulf, Earl of Pembroke. He considered his options. He could either lie about his name and escape to his tavern while he could, or he could tell the truth and insinuate himself into the Bellême household a little sooner than he had anticipated. He decided to take a chance.

'My name is Geoffrey Mappestone, and I came to Winchester to lend my support to the Earl of Shrewsbury against the King.'

The man regarded him in astonishment. 'Why would you do that? You must have heard that my brother's fortunes are waning, and that he is soon to lose all his possessions?'

'Your brother?' asked Geoffrey, pretending to be surprised.

'I am Arnulf, Earl of Pembroke. I also stand to lose my property to the King tomorrow.'

'Then you have my sympathy. Henry is a tyrant, who seized

the throne that rightfully belongs to the Duke of Normandy. I was in the Duke's service before I went on the Crusade, and any man who challenges Henry is a friend of mine.'

'My House needs friends,' said Arnulf keenly. 'We will not have justice tomorrow. Will you stand with us against him? Lend your sword to our cause?'

'Willingly,' said Geoffrey. But it was all far too easy, and he did not think any of the Bellême clan would accept allies quite so readily, no matter how desperate they were. Arnulf, like his brother, would – should – regard any offer of help delivered in a dark alleyway with the suspicion it deserved. 'But what makes you think you can trust me?'

'Experience,' said Arnulf with an engaging grin. 'I pride myself on being able to differentiate between good men and bad ones. Come.'

He led the way out of the alley and walked along the now-deserted street, far too fast and incautiously for Geoffrey's liking. With serious misgivings, but not sure what else to do now he had committed himself, Geoffrey followed. They turned a corner and walked straight into the night watch, who had stopped for an illicit ale at someone's house. The soldiers gave cries of excitement when they saw Geoffrey and Arnulf, and drew their swords.

'Put up your weapons,' Geoffrey said sharply, not breaking his stride. 'We are on the King's business. Stand aside.'

He was almost as astonished as Arnulf when the ruse worked, and the soldiers allowed them to pass. He shoved his way through them, spurred boots ringing as he walked.

'The *King's* business?' asked Arnulf. He sounded amused.

'Do you think they would have let us pass if I said we were with Bellême?'

'Of course,' said Arnulf, surprised. 'Even in these terrible times no one wants to earn my brother's disapproval. They would have stepped aside just as readily had you invoked the name of Bellême.'

He led the way to the widest, grandest street in the city, and headed for its largest and most luxurious tavern. He pushed open the door and walked inside, indicating Geoffrey was to follow. The interior was brightly lit and full of people.

Most wore the livery that people had learned to fear – that of the House of Montgomery-Bellême, which was black with flashes of red. It was said that the colours represented evil and blood. Geoffrey saw terrified pot boys moving around the tables, supplying the Earl's retinue with ale and food, and saw a white-faced taverner standing near the fire and wringing his hands in despair. And at the centre of the tavern was Bellême himself, looking just as Geoffrey remembered him from their encounter two years before.

Robert de Bellême, Earl of Shrewsbury and lord of vast estates in Normandy, was a large man with jet black hair and the same coal-dark eyes as his brother and sisters. He wore full armour, and the size of his retinue indicated he did not mean to go before the King as a sorry penitent the following day, but intended to put up a show of might. Geoffrey wondered what he would do if fighting erupted between Bellême and the King. Which side should he fight for? Then he sensed it might not matter, because just seeing Bellême in the flesh reminded him of how much hatred the Earl had mustered for him the last time they had met: he might not live to see the King's Court the following day. He gripped his sword, determined that if he was to die, he would take some of the Bellême clan with him.

Bellême was laughing rapaciously, while the landlord looked as if he was about to cry. Geoffrey soon saw why. The Earl had removed the man's shoes and was waving a hot poker around his feet while two soldiers held his arms to prevent him from running away. It was the kind of thing Bellême liked to do for entertainment, and why he had earned his reputation for cruelty.

'Brother,' said Arnulf, striding towards him. Bellême was not pleased to be distracted from his fun, although the landlord whispered a prayer of relief. 'I have found someone who intends to speak in your defence tomorrow.'

Geoffrey had offered to do no such thing, but it was too late to correct Arnulf, and he took a deep breath before staring into the malevolent eyes of the most hated and feared man in the civilized world.

153

'Geoffrey Mappestone,' breathed Bellême, as if he could not believe his eyes. 'I thought you skulked in the Holy Land, away from King Henry and his usurping ways.'

'You know him,' said Arnulf in satisfaction. 'I thought as much when he offered us his support. I am not often wrong in my judgements.'

'And what do you judge from him?' asked Bellême disdainfully. Geoffrey sensed that he and Arnulf disliked each other, and it was not just the sisters who were at loggerheads.

Arnulf shrugged. 'We cannot be overly fussy about who we recruit. Your temper has lost us too many friends, so we are obliged to take them where we can. He will do, as far as I am concerned.'

'Like Bishop Giffard?' asked Bellême coolly. 'You trusted him, and look what happened.'

'That was not my fault,' said Arnulf. 'You were the one who told him about Greek Fire, not me. It is *your* fault the King knows about our weapon.'

'You told me he was sympathetic to our cause,' snarled Bellême. 'And instead I learn he is fanatically religious and believes Henry to be the rightful King of England. He was no use to us at all and, worse, he immediately informed Henry that we are working towards making Greek Fire.'

'It does us no harm to be feared by Henry,' said Arnulf, unrepentant, while Geoffrey thought his powers of observation were not as acute as he believed if he imagined the unsmiling, hair-shirted Bishop of Winchester was anything other than a deeply religious man. 'It will make it more difficult for him to gather troops against us.'

Bellême sneered, evidently thinking Henry had troops enough already. Arnulf became defensive.

'Then ask Geoffrey. He went on the Crusade and will have seen Greek Fire used in battle.' He addressed Geoffrey directly. 'Would *you* willingly fight an enemy who possessed Greek Fire?'

It was a question loaded with pitfalls, although Geoffrey did not think Arnulf had intended it to be so. Bellême understood its implications, though, and waited for Geoffrey's reply, like a snake watching a mouse. Geoffrey hesitated. He could say he would not engage in a frontal assault where Greek Fire was likely to be thrown at him, but that would tell Bellême he was a coward. However, to deny that Greek Fire was a terrifying weapon would make him a fool.

'I have fought enemies who have used it,' he replied carefully.

'You have seen it in action?' asked Bellême curiously. 'Our brother, Philip the Grammarian, *said* he had, but I think his accounts of what it can do are either exaggerated or in error.'

Geoffrey was not surprised Bellême was sceptical of Philip's claims. Philip had never been close enough to any fighting to know what Greek Fire could do, let alone to understand how it was deployed. If he had secured the secret, then he had not done so based on personal experience. Geoffrey began to feel hopeful that the House of Montgomery-Bellême did not comprehend the true nature of the substance, and would therefore not be able to use it to its full devastating advantage.

'Special machines are needed to launch it,' he said. 'Ones that have been adapted to deal with the fact that it can ignite spontaneously. It is very dangerous without the right equipment, and just as likely to kill the user as the victim.'

He hoped his warnings might put them off. He did not want to see Greek Fire used against the King's troops – or any troops – if it could be avoided. It was one thing for Bellême to have a vat of Greek Fire at his disposal, but another altogether to put it into action against his enemies without destroying half his own men in the process.

'You should not have brought Giffard to our meetings,' said Bellême, turning on Arnulf and abruptly changing the subject. Several courtiers jumped uneasily. 'We have lost the element of surprise. I cannot imagine why you thought he might rally to our side, when he is a dour man who has never swerved in his allegiance to the King.'

'Allegiances come and go,' said Arnulf carelessly. 'As well you know.' He gestured with his hand in a way that indicated

155

he thought the tavern was less full of supporters than it should have been.

Bellême ignored the criticism, and turned his reptilian eyes on Geoffrey again. He stared for a long time before speaking, while Geoffrey pretended to be unconcerned by the penetrating scrutiny. 'I thought you were in Antioch,' he said eventually.

'I came back,' said Geoffrey, meeting his gaze. He sensed that to look away would indicate weakness, and he did not want Bellême to think him easily intimidated. It had been a long time since he had felt himself to be in such dire danger.

'For me? I am touched,' said Bellême. He put his hand on his heart and adopted a simpering expression that made some of his retainers laugh sycophantically. He looked around suddenly and his face assumed a wary expression. 'Where is that dog of yours? You did not bring it, did you? I will kill it if you have!' He drew his sword and began to look under the tables.

'I came for my sister's sake,' said Geoffrey. 'Henry will not help her fight off the raids from her Welsh neighbours.'

He was pleased with himself, thinking that if anyone told Bellême that Geoffrey had visited the King at Westminster Palace, he would now have a plausible reason for being there: to try to persuade Henry to support Joan. Geoffrey could claim that he had decided to change his allegiance when Henry had refused. It was the way things worked in the modern world, where loyalty was bought and sold like any other commodity, and Bellême should not find Geoffrey's story remarkable.

'Prince Iorwerth has been active around the Marches on my behalf,' agreed Bellême with satisfaction. 'At least *he* is a loyal ally.'

'I am tired of Henry and his bullying ways,' Geoffrey pressed on. 'The Duke of Normandy would make a better king.'

'Will he indeed?' asked Bellême. Geoffrey saw he was still looking for the dog. When he did not find it, he kicked a man who was sitting near him and indicated he was to vacate his stool. When the courtier backed away with obsequious bows, Bellême put his feet on it, unwilling to leave his ankles exposed to stealthy canine fangs.

'You once offered me a post in your command,' said Geoffrey, grateful that he had had the foresight to leave the dog with Roger. It was not a greatly loved pet, but he did not want it skewered by Bellême, nevertheless. Meanwhile, the landlord had begun to weep, silently and desperately, as if he knew the absence of an animal to slaughter meant he might take its place.

'You think I should employ you now?' asked Bellême, leaning back in his chair.

Geoffrey shrugged with a nonchalance he did not feel. 'I cannot return to Tancred while Joan is in danger.'

'And it is Henry's lack of support for her that has turned you against him?' Bellême glanced back at the landlord, and Geoffrey saw he was losing interest in the discussion and wanted to get back to his torture. He wondered whether he would be next in line for fried feet, when the landlord was dead.

'That and the fact that he also killed my dog,' said Geoffrey with sudden inspiration.

For some reason, Bellême accepted the brazen lie, although he was reluctant to believe what was close to the truth. He nodded for Geoffrey to sit at his table.

'He killed your dog,' mused Bellême, thrusting the poker into the fire. The landlord's weeping grew a little louder. 'And you have decided to make him pay. Tell me, how did he slay it?'

Geoffrey was tempted to invent something truly wild to satiate the Earl's ghoulish curiosity, such as claiming Henry had done it with his teeth or suffocated it by sitting on its head, but the terrified whimpering of the landlord reminded him that he was dealing with a brutal man who was not noted for his sense of humour.

'He had it shot,' he replied instead.

'Pity,' said Bellême with genuine regret. 'It was fierce and ungovernable, and would have made good breeding stock for my bitches. I have never seen such an animal before.'

Neither had Geoffrey, although he was not proud of it. The dog was not a paragon of loyalty, like other men's animals, and graced Geoffrey with its presence only as long as it was fed regularly and not prevented too often from terrorizing sheep and geese. People were either afraid of it or they admired its aggression and viciousness.

'Wine,' said Geoffrey to the landlord. The man stood there blinking stupidly. 'Move!' shouted Geoffrey. He watched the man scurry away and hoped he was not foolish enough to bring the jug back himself. He doubted he could deliver him from Bellême a second time.

Bellême smiled coldly, knowing exactly what Geoffrey had done. 'He was entertaining me before you interrupted us, and now you have sent him on an errand of your own. I doubt he will want to come back now.'

'I apologize,' said Geoffrey, watching Arnulf and the rest of Bellême's audience drift away now the landlord had been reprieved and the sport was over. They were soon alone. 'I thought he was on hand to see to his guests.'

'I hear you have met my kinswomen,' said Bellême conversationally. He leaned forward suddenly and gave Geoffrey a thump on the shoulder that almost dislodged him from his seat. Fortunately, it was not the one Mabel had tried to mangle, and Bellême looked disappointed when all that happened was that Geoffrey spilled the wine a pot boy had just brought. Geoffrey supposed the daughters had exaggerated the 'defeat' they had inflicted on him. He grimaced as the wine slopped on the floor, then drained what was left. He needed fortification if he was going to spend the evening with Bellême.

'Your sisters are not as hospitable as you are,' he said. 'They tried to kill me: twice. And once was in London's much admired public lavatory, if you can believe it.'

Bellême laughed mirthlessly. 'They think you did away with Hugh.'

'Then they are wrong. Whoever murdered him was inside the Crusader's Head, and I have never crossed its threshold.'

Bellême was thoughtful. 'I saw Hugh's body myself and the place where he died. You are right: his assailant would

158

have had to be inside the tavern to kill him. Perhaps you can be of use to me after all.'

'How?' asked Geoffrey warily.

Bellême gave another of his glittering smiles. 'By discovering the traitor who killed him. I know you uncovered your father's murderer two years ago, so now you can put your skills to work for me.'

'That will entail a journey to Southwark,' said Geoffrey, wondering how he would explain to the King that he had been accepted into Bellême's service – but unfortunately not at Arundel.

'No,' said Bellême. 'I do not intend to let you out of my sight now you are here. You are a dangerous enemy and I want you where I can see you. You do not need to travel to Southwark. My family have already interrogated the taverner and his patrons, so you can speak to them and piece together the information they have obtained collectively.'

'But they may not have asked the right questions,' objected Geoffrey, thinking that Bellême's task was likely to prove impossible.

'There is no point in returning to Southwark,' insisted Bellême. 'Oswin the taverner is dead, stabbed in his sleep. His loyal pot boy fled during the funeral and has not been seen since. And the other servants and patrons know nothing – or are too frightened to say if they do. You will have to make do with what we have.' He lowered his voice conspiratorially, so only Geoffrey could hear. 'You see, I believe the person who murdered Hugh is a member of my own household – perhaps one of my own family. I want to know which.'

'I will do my best,' said Geoffrey, wondering why it was his misfortune to be set unreasonable quests by rich and powerful men.

'You will,' agreed Bellême. 'Because I intend to hang whoever killed Hugh with my own hands. If you do not discover who murdered him within a week, I shall hang you instead.'

The King's Easter Court was held the day before Easter Sunday at the great hall at Winchester and was an important occasion. The King processed in his finery, flaunting his wealth, while the soldiers, who marched on his either side to protect him from the watching crowds, provided a solid reminder that he was strong as well as rich. The Royal Treasury, which Geoffrey was disappointed to learn was no more than a sturdy and heavily guarded hut, had been raided for sceptres, orbs, crowns and other symbols of authority, presumably to show any watching Saxons that their Norman overlords had the country well and truly under their control.

There was a lot of cheering and blasting of horns as the King rode triumphantly around the city, and there was an additional air of excitement because it was the last day of the gloomy season of Lent: the following morning would see the lifting of dietary restrictions for monks and laymen alike. There was also a good deal of optimism regarding the fate of Bellême. People he had terrorized now stepped forward to witness his downfall, confident in the knowledge that the King was about to expel him once and for all.

Geoffrey did not feel comfortable riding in Bellême's retinue. Folk turned out of their houses to watch them pass, and none seemed friendly. Some gathered handfuls of dung to toss in their direction, although none were actually aimed at Bellême himself. People were not stupid, and did not want to be run through for spoiling the Earl's fine robes with a dash of manure. Geoffrey was fairly well protected from the onslaught, because he was in the middle of the soldiers who followed in Bellême's wake. He suspected he was actually under guard, although no one had attempted to relieve him of his weapons.

The hall at Winchester was similar to Westminster's, although not so large. It had been cleared of tables and benches, so people could cram inside to watch the proceedings, and Geoffrey was not surprised that a large crowd had gathered to watch the Earl of Shrewsbury and his family get their just deserts. He looked for Durand among them, but the squire had evidently decided the whole adventure was far too dangerous, and had escaped while he could. Geoffrey cursed Tancred for lumbering him with such a cowardly retainer.

Bellême shouldered his way through the assembled masses to stand near the front, and his arrival completed his family's number. Standing on either side were his two brothers, making for a physically impressive trio in their ermine-fringed cloaks and the black and red of their House. They were unmistakably kin: Bellême and Arnulf had black, flowing locks that they had allowed to grow fashionably long, while Roger, Count of Marche, had short hair that stood to attention on the top of his head.

Roger was the thinnest and Arnulf was the shortest, although he was still head and shoulders above most courtiers. Arnulf possessed neither the austere surliness of Roger nor the sheer unadulterated menace that exuded from Bellême. He smiled more often, and affected a careless attitude, as though he could do little about the events that carried him along to his destiny and was prepared to make the best of what happened. On the surface, he was the most pleasant of the three, although Geoffrey had learned – unlike Arnulf himself – that it took more than one meeting to determine a man's character.

Behind them were their sisters. It was customary for women of their age – even the youngest was well into her forties – to conceal their hair with veils, wimples or mantles, but all three sisters allowed theirs to tumble in sheets down their backs, displaying glossy locks for all to see. Emma's was more grey than black, but it was still an impressive shock nonetheless. She sported a brown habit to indicate she was an abbess, although it was the only concession she made to her vocation. Her fingers were encrusted with jewels, and the gold cross she wore around her neck was one of the largest Geoffrey had ever seen. Next to her was Sybilla, who immediately spotted Geoffrey. She nudged Emma, and both glowered at him. He was the first to look away. Behind them were four tall knights, all hooded with their faces in shadow, although a bandage could be seen gleaming palely on one.

Standing slightly apart was Matilda. Her dark eyes did not possess the malevolence of the others, and her face was more ready to break into a smile that bespoke humour rather than spite. She was not smiling now, though. She looked nervous. Geoffrey glanced at Emma, and wondered whether she had some potion concealed in her clothes that she intended to

161

use on the King, as the monk Edred had believed. He shuddered at the thought. If that happened, then the next most powerful man in the court would seize control. And that was Bellême.

Horns sounded brassily and a stir of anticipation rippled through the crowd. The King had arrived. He walked through the centre of the hall with his courtiers and nobles streaming behind him, while a pair of burly squires – neither of which was young Philip – pushed people out of his way. Philip was near the end of the procession, and Geoffrey did not miss the long stare that passed between him and his aunts. Matilda, though, was the only one who smiled. He grinned back, and the knight sensed genuine affection between them.

There were others in the King's retinue whom Geoffrey knew, too. Near the front was Bishop Maurice of London in his ecclesiastical splendour, while Edred was one of an army of scribes who carried parchment and pens, evidently brought from London to assist with the drafting of the many writs, charters and documents that would result from this important occasion. Bishop Giffard was there, lean and thin and with his hair shirt visible under his religious habit. Geoffrey felt a presence at his side and turned to see Beaumais, the man who had openly professed loyalty to Bellême when Geoffrey had met him at Westminster. The courtier smiled, and inclined his greasy head in greeting.

'I see you took my advice. The King intends to kill you, so you have come to Bellême, where you will be safe.'

Geoffrey was sure his safety had not improved, but said nothing. The King marched to the far end of the hall and climbed the steps to a raised dais, where a massive throne had been placed. He sat and allowed his squires to scurry around him, making him comfortable by plumping up cushions and pouring him wine. Meanwhile, Beaumais scanned the people who stood in a silent semicircle around Henry's throne. He sucked in his breath, and shook his head vigorously. Geoffrey saw several others in the Bellême retinue do the same.

'William Pantulf has defected,' Beaumais hissed, pointing at a nobleman who stood behind the King. 'He vowed to serve Bellême, but he has broken his oath. This is a bitter blow.

162

The Welsh listen to him, and he may encourage princes like Iorwerth to abandon us and follow Henry instead.'

'Why do we need the Welsh?' asked Geoffrey. 'If Bellême is exiled, nothing they can do will help.'

Beaumais glanced at him. 'If there is another war, we will lose without the Welsh. Pantulf has struck a foul blow against us with his disloyalty.'

'War?' asked Geoffrey uneasily. He had not anticipated a war; just a siege in Arundel Castle.

Beaumais nodded. 'You did not expect us to go quietly, did you? But the King speaks. Listen.'

In order to heighten anticipation, and possibly to show Bellême that he did not respect him, Henry dealt with several minor cases before he indicated that the Earl of Shrewsbury was to step forward. By this time, Bellême was livid. He shoved his brothers aside and stood in front of the King, where he made the most perfunctory obeisance. It did not pass unnoticed, and Henry gave a thin-lipped smile.

'Robert de Bellême, Earl of Shrewsbury,' he announced in a ringing voice. Everyone in the hall was absolutely silent, determined not to miss a single word or nuance that was uttered. 'You are here to answer to us, Henry of England, on a number of charges – forty-five in total. You have collected taxes you had no right to take. You have continued to fortify your castle at Bridgnorth, even though you did not seek our permission to do so. Your brothers, Arnulf, Earl of Pembroke and Roger, Count of Marche, are similarly charged.'

Arnulf and Roger went to stand next to their brother, and Geoffrey could see Bellême struggling to control his rage at the humiliation. Henry sensed his vassal's discomfort, and did all he could to heighten it. It was obvious that he did not have the slightest intention of allowing Bellême to keep his English estates, and equally apparent that Bellême still entertained some remote, albeit futile, hope that some arrangement might yet be reached – if he managed to hold his temper.

'And your sisters can come forward, too,' ordered Henry coldly. 'Emma, Abbess of Alménches, Sybilla fitzHaimo and Matilda de Mortain.'

'We have done nothing,' objected Emma indignantly, remaining where she was. 'Our brothers rebelled, but *we* did not.'

'We stand with our brother,' said Sybilla between gritted teeth, pushing past the abbess to go to Bellême's side. 'Any action against him is an assault against us all.'

'Are you *my* loyal subject, then?' asked Henry archly of Emma. 'Will you renounce all ties to the House of Montgomery-Bellême and swear allegiance to me? No? I thought not. Stand with your brothers, madam, and hear what I have to say. You, too, Matilda de Mortain.'

Fuming, Emma shoved her way forward, although she declined to stand near Bellême, who glowered at her angrily. He was clearly furious that she should attempt to dissociate herself from him so publicly. Sybilla gazed defiantly at the King, and Geoffrey could tell from her fierce expression that she was more devoted to Bellême than the others. Matilda, meanwhile, stood with her head bowed. Geoffrey wondered whether she was trying to indicate submission, and make Henry aware that she was willing to negotiate if only he would hear her out.

'Read the charges in full,' ordered Henry, leaning back and clearly enjoying himself. He was not alone, and there were unpleasant smiles all over the hall from nobles and poor folk alike, as the hated Earl was made to listen when Bishop Maurice stepped forward and began to list all manner of offences, most of them blatantly contrived. The King had set his spies on Bellême, and every minor error he had made over the last year was dutifully recorded. If anyone other than Bellême had been accused, Geoffrey would have thought the King was being unreasonable, petty and unfair.

Bellême's followers began to mutter rebelliously at the injustice, although Bellême merely clenched and unclenched his fists as Maurice droned on, while King Henry's eyes never left his vassal's face. When Maurice reached the thirtieth charge Geoffrey noticed that something peculiar was happening to Emma. She began to sway, and then she dropped to the floor in what appeared to be a swoon. Maurice hesitated for a moment, but then continued with his monologue. Emma, meanwhile, began to shudder and convulse. Then she started to mutter.

Geoffrey spoke several languages, but he did not recognize the one Emma began to intone, and, judging by the vicious sound of many of the words, it was not one any Christian man should be familiar with. It sounded like the language of witches, and he involuntarily took a step backward. Others did the same, unnerved by the peculiar sounds that were emanating from the writhing abbess.

'She is speaking the Devil's tongue,' Beaumais whispered to Geoffrey, sounding more matter-of-fact than the knight felt the situation warranted. 'I expect she is summoning her mother.'

'Her mother is dead,' said Geoffrey.

'That is irrelevant,' said Beaumais. 'Abbess Emma believes Mabel will be a powerful lady once her severed head is reunited with her body. Until then, she often answers Emma's calls for assistance.'

Geoffrey glanced at Emma's siblings. Bellême watched his sister with a face wholly devoid of expression, and Geoffrey did not know whether he was pleased or angry that his long-dead mother was about to be invited to King Henry's Easter Court. Roger's mean mouth was hanging open, as if in disbelief. Arnulf backed away, half-fascinated and half-horrified, and crossed himself quickly. Geoffrey could not decide whether it was a Christian man's fear for his soul, or whether he was distancing himself from whatever happened in case it did not succeed.

Sybilla's face was also blank, but her eyes were hard and cold, and, again, Geoffrey could not tell whether she condoned her older sister's performance. Matilda closed her eyes and made no secret of the fact that she wished she was elsewhere. The four 'knights' gathered around their aunt, and Geoffrey saw all carried daggers and suspected they would kill anyone who tried to prevent Emma from doing whatever it was she had in mind.

The next thing that happened was the release of a foul smell accompanied by smoke, both coming from under Emma's habit. Then there was an odd popping sound, and a woman near Bishop Giffard started to scream. Geoffrey tore his eyes away from Emma to the King, and saw an expression of abject horror on the monarch's face. But he was not looking at the swooning abbess.

Geoffrey followed his gaze to a cloaked figure who stood in the shadows at one side of the hall holding a small bow with an arrow nocked into it. The arrow was pointing at Henry.

Eight

G eoffrey eased his way through the crowd towards the archer. Henry had ducked behind someone, and the archer was obliged to move to bring him into his sights again. Geoffrey glanced at the dais and saw Henry was using Philip as his human shield, which may have been what had stilled the archer's hand. It was all very well being paid by the Bellêmes to shoot the King, but no man would risk killing one of their kinsmen while he did it. Philip, meanwhile, was blissfully unaware he was saving the King from certain death. He, like everyone else, was watching Emma go through her moaning, smoking contortions, and no one seemed aware of the King's mortal danger.

Geoffrey reached the archer and jostled him, so the arrow sped harmlessly towards the roof, where it embedded itself in the painted ceiling. The archer regarded him furiously, obviously not understanding why someone from the Bellême household should interfere with him. He nocked another quarrel and took aim a second time. Then there was a thump and he dropped to the floor, an arrow protruding from his own chest. Geoffrey gazed around wildly and saw the King's soldiers had been well trained and, like Henry himself, recognized a diversion when they saw one. The hostile archer had exposed himself when he had stood to shoot, and one of them had picked him off.

Geoffrey saw the fallen bowman was dead. He kicked the weapon under a stack of benches, looking around to see if Emma had hired a second killer to take over if the first one failed. But she had apparently been confident that her plan would work, and no one else whisked a weapon from his cloak to commit regicide. Geoffrey glanced at the King and met his eyes. Henry nodded slightly, and gave the slightest of smiles. Geoffrey hoped it was an acknowledgement of the fact that he had spoiled the man's aim, and not that he thought Geoffrey had had a hand in the attempted murder. But Henry's archers were lowering their weapons on his orders, and Geoffrey comforted himself with the fact that he would hardly tell them to do that if he thought a threat still existed.

He eased away from the archer, knowing it would not be wise to be discovered next to a corpse when the fuss surrounding Emma had died down, especially since that corpse was probably one of the Bellêmes' most faithful retainers. He glanced around guiltily, but no one seemed to have noticed that he had moved. Indeed, Beaumais was still talking to him, and the courtier was not even aware that Geoffrey had been gone. He started to relax, and hoped Bellême's attention had also been focussed on his sister's odd antics. He saw it had: Bellême was looking just as bemused as everyone else.

'What is wrong with her?' the Earl demanded. His earlier unreadability was replaced by irritation, and Geoffrey had the impression he had not known what Emma intended to do. 'Has she been at her portions again? I told you to make sure she did not have any this morning, Sybilla.'

'She said she wanted to be alone, to pray for our family,' objected Sybilla, chagrined by the rebuke from the brother she adored. 'She must have taken something then.'

Bellême sighed in exasperation. 'You know perfectly well that she does not pray, and I *told* you not to leave her alone today. We have problems enough without folk accusing us of witchcraft.'

'She is no witch,' protested Sybilla unconvincingly, while Matilda rolled her eyes at the ceiling. Geoffrey tried to prevent himself from smiling, and could not imagine who Sybilla thought she could fool, when her sister lay on the floor with smoke and foul smells issuing from her clothing as she screeched words that were clearly magical incantations.

168

He did not think he had ever seen a more brazen display of the dark arts.

'Then what does she think she is doing?' demanded Roger, eyeing Emma in disgust. 'She cannot summon our mother, if that is what she is trying to do. Old Mabel will not come *here* in broad daylight, with a hall full of people to laugh at her poor decapitated corpse.'

Geoffrey did not think many people would be laughing if Mabel de Bellême appeared *sans* head and started to make her way through them. He was unable to suppress a shudder. It seemed the only reason Roger thought Mabel would not appear was because it was the wrong place and time. Geoffrey was not a superstitious man, but the rumours about the Bellêmes and their diabolical talents made him uneasy nonetheless.

'I thought Emma would behave here,' protested Sybilla, not liking the fact that she was being blamed for his sister's dramatics.

Bellême shook his head in disbelief. 'Why would you think that? Now douse her with a bucket of water, before she sets us all alight.'

'There is no need for that,' said Emma, abruptly scrambling to her feet. The crowd around her backed away in alarm, as though they expected her to explode, turn green or spray them with some vile substance. 'I am quite recovered.'

Indeed, she was so recovered that Geoffrey saw the whole attack had been carefully choreographed. She was completely back to normal, with the exception of a few tendrils of smoke curling from under her habit. Geoffrey looked on the floor and saw broken glass, and assumed she had mixed two volatile compounds to produce the fog and stench.

'Have you quite finished, madam?' demanded Henry archly. Geoffrey saw he was angry, but, since her attack had failed and the archer had been dispatched permanently, he had apparently decided to ignore the attempt on his life in the interests of completing the Bellêmes' humiliation. He was about to pronounce sentence on them, and Emma would soon be gone from his realm anyway.

'Yes, thank you,' she replied, smoothing down her hair and

169

straightening her clothes. 'I suffer from a falling sickness. It is something that afflicts us holy women from time to time.'

Her eyes flicked in the direction of her archer, but since he lay dead under a bench, she could not see him. She realized her attempt to kill the King had failed, and her eyes glittered with frustrated anger.

'A falling sickness?' asked Henry caustically. 'That must be inconvenient.'

'Sometimes,' she replied. 'But I am used to it. Now, you were saying, My Lord Bishop?'

Maurice cleared his throat and resumed reading, while Bellême and his siblings turned towards the King again. Geoffrey saw the exchange of angry glances that passed between Emma and Sybilla, while the four 'knights' shifted uneasily. Matilda's expression was blank, although Geoffrey was under the impression that she had not been included in the plot, and neither had Bellême. And Arnulf and Roger? Geoffrey had no idea.

Maurice hastily finished his arraignment and began rolling up the parchment. Emma's fit had upset him. Had he also been aware of the plan, and was disappointed that it had failed? Or did he dislike demonic languages assailing his ears? He backed away, relieved to have discharged his duties and more than happy to let the King take over. Henry regarded his assembled vassals in silence.

'Well?' he asked eventually, addressing the entire clan, although it was Bellême he looked at the hardest. 'What do you say?'

'These are grave charges, sire,' replied Bellême icily. 'I must beg your leave to consult with my family, and decide how best to answer them. I would not wish to speak in haste and tell Your Majesty something that later transpired to be incorrect.'

'Very well,' said Henry, the voice of reason. 'You can have until the end of this afternoon. Bring the next case, Pantulf!'

A shambling man stepped forward, and began to tell Henry in a high-pitched voice that his neighbour stole the water he needed for his mill, but no one listened to his piteous

170

entreaties. Instead, all eyes were on the Bellêmes as they left the hall, apparently intending to return to their fine lodgings and discuss the accusations. Geoffrey followed – he had no choice, given that he was back in the middle of Bellême's soldiers. Beaumais walked with him, still agog at the spectacle Emma had provided.

'I have heard that God afflicts holy folk with conditions like that,' he gushed. 'It must be a confounded nuisance, and will inevitably occur at the most awkward of moments.'

'I do not think it had anything to do with her holiness,' remarked Geoffrey, astonished that Beaumais should think Emma's display was even remotely connected with Christianity.

Beaumais waved a hand to indicate he thought Geoffrey was wrong. 'Still, Bellême cannot blame her for getting in his way when she cannot help herself.'

Geoffrey regarded him askance. 'Getting in his way?'

Beaumais looked shifty, as though he realized he had said something he should not have done. He prevaricated. 'But you heard how ridiculous these charges are! The King commits most of them himself, and it is an outrage that he persecutes his nobles for following his example.'

'You have not answered my question. What did Bellême intend to do?'

Beaumais sighed. 'He was going to wait until the last charge was read, then kill Henry with his sword. But Emma's fit meant the guards were more alert, and he saw he would not have succeeded.'

Geoffrey concurred; the guards were certainly alert after they had shot the archer.

'Bellême will not be pleased with Emma,' Beaumais added, stating the obvious.

Geoffrey thought the Bellêmes would be more successful if they co-ordinated their attempts at regicide, and realized Henry had had a luckier escape than he knew.

It was a tense walk through the city to the tavern, with people jeering or simply standing silent and accusing. Geoffrey did not recall when he had ever felt quite so uncomfortable, and that included after the sack of Antioch when the citizens had screamed bitter curses at the looting Crusaders. The cavalcade reached the inn without mishap, and filed through the door, where retainers and family alike jostled to stand as far away from the enraged Earl as possible.

Bellême drew his sword and paced furiously, hacking at tables to vent his frustration. His reputation was such that everyone knew he might divert his frenzy from furniture to a person, to allow the sight of flowing blood to soothe him. His gaze settled on a cat sunning itself on a windowsill, but the animal became aware it was the subject of hostile attention and fled before he could harm it. He thrust his sword through the window instead, shattering the shutter and smashing a pot on the other side.

'Foolish women!' he howled. 'You have ruined me! I had a plan and you foiled it.'

'We did what we thought was right,' said Emma primly, looking very much the abbess. 'I cannot imagine why my archer failed me. He does not usually miss what he aims at.'

'I think he was pushed in all the excitement,' said Matilda, and her eyes lingered briefly on Geoffrey. His stomach lurched. Had she seen him jog the archer's arm? Or was there nothing significant in the way she had caught his eye? If she knew the truth, he doubted he would live long once she told her brother.

'I do not care,' snarled Bellême. 'What are we supposed to do now? I could go back to the King and claim I am innocent of these outrageous charges, but he will find me guilty regardless. Then he will demand our estates – from every last one of us – and the House of Montgomery-Bellême will be banished from this land forever. Do you have any idea how much these estates are worth?'

'A little,' said Emma insolently.

'Then why did you not leave matters to me, as I ordered?' Bellême was all but screaming, and spit sprayed from his mouth. 'There are only two roads open to us now: we can go back to Henry and allow him to strip us of our property. Or we can ride to Arundel, which I took the precaution of preparing for a siege. Neither appeals. I would sooner have had Henry dead and word sent to the Duke of Normandy to come and take the English throne.'

'Brother,' began Sybilla gently, taking a step towards Bellême and attempting to lay a hand on his arm. 'Calm yourself. And, in any case, the Duke would not make a very good king.'

'Stupid, ignorant women!' screeched Bellême, rounding on Emma again. 'I would not have allowed *him* to rule! I would have recommended a regent: me. You have lost me more than you can possibly know with your pathetic attempt to "help" today.'

'Saddle the horses,' said Arnulf to his squire, making a decision in the silence that followed. 'I will not stay here to be treated like a common criminal by Henry. I shall go to Arundel.'

'And what about Philip?' asked Matilda, hands on hips. 'He is Henry's hostage, and if we race away to Arundel, Henry will kill him.'

'Poor Philip,' sneered Roger unpleasantly. 'Let us all forfeit our chance of saving something from this mess so we can prevent *his* miserable neck from being stretched.'

'It is not his fault we have come to this,' argued Matilda. 'He should not have to pay the price.'

'Life is unfair,' remarked Arnulf, pushing past her and making for the door. He paused and looked back at the silent retainers. 'Well? Will you stay, so Henry will not kill Philip? Or will you ride south with me?'

There was an immediate bustle of activity, as folk ran from the chamber to make ready for what promised to be a hard and fast journey. All were relieved to be away from the Earl, who was still spitting his fury and reducing the tavern's fine furniture to firewood. Matilda stood with her head bowed, although the expression on her face was more calculating than distressed. After a moment, Geoffrey saw her waylay a servant and whisper something in his ear. He nodded and hurried away.

Geoffrey headed for the stables to prepare his horse, which Bellême had arranged to be fetched the previous night on the grounds that he thought Geoffrey might desert him if allowed

173

to collect it himself. The knight had barely reached the door when there was a terrific screech of rage from one of the chambers on the tavern's upper floor. Sensing trouble, he turned back.

'Thief!' The next thing Geoffrey knew was that Durand was tumbling down the stairs, followed by a very angry Emma. 'He was in my chamber, after my holy relics.'

Bellême started towards the squire with murderous intent, evidently thinking that a thief would make a perfectly suitable substitute for tables, cats and benches. He raised his sword.

'No!' squealed Durand in terror, on his knees with his hands clasped as he appealed to Bellême. 'I was not stealing. I am here to meet my master, Geoffrey Mappestone. We became separated yesterday, and I have been looking for him ever since.'

Bellême swung away from Durand and came towards Geoffrey, his eyes flat and blank, and his face lit with a savage light that Geoffrey thought was a long way from being human. He had seen a good deal of bloodlust on the Crusade, but none of it was as terrifying as Bellême's. He drew his own sword and braced himself, hoping Bellême's soldiers did not join the fight and make it an uneven one too quickly. Rescue came from an unexpected quarter.

'It is all right,' said Arnulf, striding forward and pressing his brother's arm to make him lower his weapon. 'The wretch is telling the truth. Geoffrey *was* looking for his squire last night when he met me. Doubtless he told the fool to meet him here, and he became confused about where to wait. Foolish oaf!' He eyed Durand disparagingly.

'Is this true?' asked Bellême, advancing to the point where the knight could see that his eyes were abnormally bloodshot. His temper was only just under control.

Geoffrey nodded. 'Tancred has charged me to make him into a knight, although I think the task is beyond my abilities.'

Bellême regarded the cowering Durand in astonishment, taking in his unmanly posture and flowing hair. Durand started to cry and real tears ran down his face. He was the most miserable, cowardly specimen Geoffrey had ever

174

encountered, and he was heartily embarrassed to admit an acquaintance with him. He made up his mind to send him back to Tancred at the earliest opportunity.

'A knight?' asked Bellême in disbelief. 'Him?'

'Do you have any advice?' asked Geoffrey unhappily. 'I need all the help I can get.'

Bellême's face creased into a cold smile. 'My advice would be to skewer him and tell Tancred he died in battle. Take him out of my sight. If I see him again, I shall do you the favour of killing him.'

The journey to Arundel was one of the least pleasant Geoffrey had ever undertaken. Not only was the weather foul, with gusting sheets of rain in their faces the whole way, and their horses skidding in the long, snaking quagmire that represented one of England's busiest highways, but Bellême had a temper to match. He refused to stop for anyone, and Geoffrey saw several peasants disappear under his hoofs as he rode. It seemed the more he thought about his sister's misguided attempts to kill the King, the more angry he became, so his rage festered and threatened to consume him completely.

Durand wept inconsolably, and Geoffrey soon grew tired of the snide comments from Bellême's knights for his owning such a feeble squire. He began to wish Bellême had killed the man after all. He tried every tactic he knew to stop Durand's weeping – threats, kindness, anger, sympathy – but nothing worked. He eventually discovered what Durand had been doing among Emma's relics. The previous night, the squire had gone to the abbey instead of fetching food as Geoffrey had ordered, and more time passed than he intended. Loath to break the curfew, he spent the night there. The next day he learned Geoffrey had secured himself a place in Bellême's retinue, and decided to wait for him at the inn. When he heard Bellême return in such a fury, he had fled upstairs in terror, where he had been caught trying to climb into the chest Emma said she used for storing her relics.

'You tried to get inside a reliquary?' asked Geoffrey, aghast. 'I thought you respected holy things.'

175

'I do, but it was the only open chest in the room, and I was frightened. The other one was locked.'

'The other one?' asked Geoffrey, most of his mind still on the fact that Durand might have put himself in serious danger by tampering with objects that were sacred. Only a fool risked the wrath of Heaven by dealing disrespectfully with items that had once belonged to saints.

'The long, thin box. But it was too small for me, and it was locked anyway, so I had to opt for the other one.'

'Long, thin box?' echoed Geoffrey, his thoughts whirling. Was this the same chest he had seen being ferried around London on three separate occasions: once outside the Crusader's Head after Hugh's murder, once at All Hallows when Emma met Sybilla, and once near St Paul's when Geoffrey had been going to visit the cathedral? How many of these long, thin boxes were there, and what did they contain? Could it be a weapon that would allow Greek Fire to be propelled at an enemy? If that were the case, then Emma was further along with her experiments than he had thought.

'Yes, long and thin,' snapped Durand, shattered nerves making him testy. 'Locked.'

'Were there any gaps that allowed you to see inside?'

'I was too frightened to look,' said Durand, dabbing his tear-reddened eyes with a piece of embroidered silk. 'But it smelled nasty, like rotting clothes. I was terrified to the point of fainting!'

'Keep your voice down!' snapped Geoffrey, aware that Beaumais and several guards were finding Durand's unmanly confessions very amusing. He supposed they had not seen many weeping squires, since it was unlikely Bellême would tolerate them for long.

'I did not know the other chest contained holy things,' said Durand hoarsely. 'I just wanted to hide until the shouting and noise was over. I do not like arguments that involve breaking windows and smashing tables with swords. Unfortunately, Abbess Emma's reliquary was not empty, and there was no room for me inside it, anyway.'

'I imagine not,' said Geoffrey. 'She is hardly likely to tote an empty box on her travels. What was in it? Bones?'

He thought about Old Mabel and what Emma intended to do with her.

'A couple of skulls,' replied Durand with a tearful shudder. 'Both recently dead, with hair and flesh still attached. One looked familiar. And a large pot of something black and smelly.'

'Greek Fire?' asked Geoffrey with quickening interest. 'The stuff she made in All Hallows Church?' He spoke in a low voice, so that Beaumais and the others would not hear.

'Similar,' said Durand, patting daintily at his nose with the silk. 'But thicker and stickier. She must have boiled it down to concentrate it.'

'Or perhaps it was not the same substance,' mused Geoffrey. 'I told you what she spilled in All Hallows was too runny. Perhaps what you saw was not what she made, but the real thing.'

'It was not burning,' said Durand helpfully.

Geoffrey regarded him askance. 'You only ignite it when you are ready to use it.'

'Then perhaps the bowl I saw is the sum of her supplies,' suggested Durand hopefully. 'We have been regaled with rumours that she has cisterns of it, but perhaps she is limited to what Philip the Grammarian sent her from the Holy Land – a sample.'

'I was under the impression that he sent her the formula, but perhaps you are right, and he sent her a pot of it instead. That would be good news for Henry. The Crusaders had samples, too, but no amount of analysing and experimenting helped us to reproduce it. It contains a secret compound that I believe is only available in the East.'

Durand sniffed and drew a piece of scented linen from his scrip in which to blow his nose. Geoffrey saw Beaumais nudge Arnulf and point at him.

'Do you know why Emma has those two skulls?' asked Durand, dabbing his nose like a lady of some breeding. Geoffrey heard Arnulf snigger.

'Edred said she had been digging in his graveyard for the corpses of felons. You say the heads you saw were

177

recently dead, so it seems likely they are the fruits of her grave-robbing.'

'You have not answered my question,' said Durand pettishly. 'I asked if you knew *why* she has these skulls, and you have only told me where they came from.'

'Very well,' said Geoffrey, fighting down his irritation with the man. 'Tell me, since you obviously think you have the answer.'

'I do have the answer,' said Durand with complete conviction. 'They are to be joined to the headless body of Mabel de Bellême, Emma's murdered mother!'

Geoffrey regarded him uncertainly. 'That is an unpleasant conclusion to have reached.'

'Nevertheless, it is true. Old Mabel's killers took her head and it was never recovered. Everyone knows that. So, until the real one appears, Emma is obliged to use ones stolen from graveyards.'

Geoffrey started to laugh. 'You have a lurid imagination . . .'

'It is true! Emma wants the original head back, so she can reunite it with the body and use Old Mabel to get the Bellêmes what they want in this world. Their powers will increase a hundredfold once she succeeds. Until then, she is obliged to use different heads.' Durand sounded completely convinced, and Geoffrey began to reconsider the possibility, despite his initial scepticism.

'So, her chest is not a reliquary at all,' he mused. 'It is a repository for a pair of spare heads and a pot of Greek Fire.'

He glanced behind him, to where a bouncing cart only just managed to keep pace with them. It was piled high with items the Bellêmes considered essential – including both the long, thin box and the 'reliquary' – and Geoffrey was faced with the sudden, nasty realization that the rest of Mabel de Bellême might be closer than he had thought. Durand said that the long box stank of rotting clothes, which was exactly how a pile of ancient bones in their grave clothes might smell.

Durand's assumptions seemed wild and improbable, but Geoffrey had an uncomfortable feeling that he had just answered one question that had been nagging at him for several days. He recalled Emma telling Sybilla at All Hallows that their mother was waiting 'outside', and Geoffrey had seen the abbess escorting the long, thin box towards the church before she had entered. He had questioned Sybilla about it, but she had been enigmatically vague. He saw that Emma had been speaking literally after all, and Old Mabel had indeed been nearby.

And Old Mabel had been at the Crusader's Head, too, he thought, present for the demonstration of Greek Fire. He himself had seen her spirited away after Hugh had been murdered. Then, later, she had been carried past St Paul's Cathedral by two cloaked men. Mabel, it seemed, spent a lot of time travelling hither and thither. He grimaced, thinking it was distasteful to take ancestors from their graves and haul them around the civilized world in the hope that they might walk again.

Meanwhile, Durand cast a fearful glance to where Bellême rode at the head of the cavalcade. 'Do you think we will escape this horrible adventure alive?'

Geoffrey smiled encouragingly. 'We shall do our best.'

But his best was evidently not good enough, because Durand began to weep afresh at the notion that he might accidentally encounter Bellême and be run through for exercise. Geoffrey knew this was not out of the question, but suggested Bellême might not be so antagonistic if Durand acted in a more manly way. Durand sobbed that he did not know how, dabbing his nose with his scented linen and shaking his golden curls in agitation.

In the end, Geoffrey banished him to ride with the women, hoping to shame him into stopping his tears. Durand wrung his hands in gratitude, and Geoffrey watched him take a place behind Matilda, who regarded him with as much disgusted disdain as had Arnulf and Beaumais. Emma, who rode significantly close to the cart, simply scowled, so Durand dropped farther back, as unwilling to ride near Bellême's sisters as he was to ride near Bellême himself.

The ride was exhausting, and every step jarred Geoffrey's sore shoulder so he longed to stop. The distance between Winchester and Arundel was about forty-five miles, and

179

Bellême claimed he had once made the journey in three hours, but that day he was forced to ride more slowly or risk half his court travelling on foot after their mounts had either dropped dead beneath them or turned lame.

They had left Winchester at about noon, and no one except Geoffrey seemed to find their escape suspiciously easy. They followed an ancient track across the South Downs through the village of Exton and over Old Winchester Hill, then on to Linchdown, through Cocking and Bignor, and finally following the path of the River Arun to Arundel itself, arrived just after the sun had set.

Arundel, 5 March 1102

Bellême flung the reins of his horse to a groom, and then strode across Arundel's wide bailey towards a wooden hall-house. Geoffrey dismounted and looked around, handing his gloves to Durand, who was bedraggled and unhappy. Geoffrey saw Mabel, the largest of Sybilla's four daughters, regarding his squire in disbelief, as if she could not imagine how a man could be so pathetic. Geoffrey ignored her, and began to assess his surroundings with the eye of a professional soldier.

The stronghold was cleverly designed and the site well chosen, standing on a rocky spur that overlooked the river. In the centre was a motte, perhaps seventy feet high, topped by a substantial central tower, which was full of chambers, galleries and battlements for soldiers and archers to keep watch over the surrounding countryside. It was well guarded, and Geoffrey wondered how he would reach it with a lamp to pass his messages to Roger and Helbye.

On either side of the motte were raised baileys, which were surrounded by ramparts and a wooden palisade topped with spikes. The palisade boasted several shooting platforms, and Geoffrey saw it would be difficult for an invading army to come close without exposing itself to a hail of missiles. He saw immediately why King Henry had assumed the confrontation between his troops and Bellême's at Arundel would take the form of a siege: a frontal attack would be suicide.

The baileys contained a number of buildings. The outer court had enclosures for animals and sheds for their fodder; the inner one was protected by an additional wall, and was dominated by the hall. This comprised a vaulted undercroft for storage, a large chamber on the first floor for communal meals and sleeping quarters, and some tiny rooms on a top floor for the Earl and his siblings.

Geoffrey gave the reins of his horse to Durand and ordered him to make sure it was fed and cleaned before he retired for the night. Durand sniffed wetly, then, before Geoffrey fully understood what he was doing, the squire leapt on to it and thundered out of the gate into the darkness beyond. Durand had fled for his life.

Geoffrey gaped in astonishment. He had not known his squire possessed the courage to mount so bold an escape from under Bellême's nose. Bellême whirled around at the clatter of hoofs, but waved away offers by those willing to hunt Durand down. He was not worth the effort, and Bellême had more important matters to attend to. He gave Geoffrey a sharp glance, as though he thought the knight might have engineered the incident himself, and then turned away. Geoffrey wondered how long the squire would last on a spirited warhorse before he was thrown and killed. Or worse, as far as Geoffrey was concerned, whether he would damage the beast by riding it recklessly in the dark.

Two men came to welcome Bellême to his stronghold. One was plump and smiling, with a tonsure barely visible in a mass of curly brown hair. He wore the robes of a Benedictine, and Geoffrey wondered whether all members of that order were fat, since he had not seen a slim one for some time. The monk was obviously a person of rank, because Bellême greeted him politely.

The second man was a grim-faced knight with beetling eyebrows and a hawk-like nose. He was lean and tall, with deep-set eyes, and everything about him bespoke dourness. Although he wore the livery of Bellême's house, his uniform contained less red and more black than anyone else's. His hair was shorn to an uncompromising shortness

181

at the back and sides, and his gloves and cloak were cut in the military fashion – functional and with no regard to current popular style.

'The fat fellow is Ralph d'Escures, Abbot of Sées,' said Beaumais, seeing Geoffrey's interest and coming to talk to him. 'Sées is the mother house of Shrewsbury Abbey, so when Ralph is in England, he is obliged to pay homage to Bellême.'

'Abbot Ralph,' mused Geoffrey thoughtfully. 'He *was* in Shrewsbury recently, because a monk called Petronus tried to deliver messages from him to Bishop Maurice just a week ago.'

Beaumais nodded. 'Petronus was murdered near Westminster. I went with Maurice to inspect the corpse and to help remove the messages from the man's person.'

'Did you?' asked Geoffrey. He had wondered whether Petronus had carried missives other than the routine ones sent by Ralph to Maurice. Beaumais was a slippery sort of fellow, and Geoffrey wondered what his 'help' had entailed. 'Did Petronus have any messages for you?'

'Why would Abbot Ralph send anything to me?' asked Beaumais in surprise, although that was not what Geoffrey had asked: his query had been a more general one, concerning whether Petronus had carried *anything* for him. He was not sure whether Beaumais's misinterpretation had been deliberate, so decided to lie.

'Petronus told me his pouch was full of missives for different people, not just ones for Maurice.'

'Really?' Beaumais's voice was flat. 'He should not have done. He was told to maintain secrecy.'

'Is that why he was killed?' asked Geoffrey, wondering whether Beaumais was aware that he had just admitted to knowing more about Petronus's business than he should have done.

'We do not know who killed him,' said Beaumais. He sounded angry. 'But we have our suspicions, and the King is at the top of the list.'

'Why?'

'Because Petronus carried important information,' replied

Beaumais shortly. 'I had hoped to see an issue resolved when he arrived, and his death interfered with my plans.'

'The issue had nothing to do with Greek Fire, did it?' asked Geoffrey, careless that his conversation was becoming an interrogation. Beaumais did not seem to mind. He appeared to be the kind of man who enjoyed talking about his own affairs, even when he should have kept some of them to himself.

'It most certainly was not,' said Beaumais with some feeling. 'I do not want to become embroiled in *that*, thank you very much. It was about another matter entirely.'

'One less important,' stated Geoffrey, deliberately dismissive. It was an obvious ploy – making it sound as though Beaumais was involved in something irrelevant in the hope that his ego would balk. Beaumais would have to be a fool to fall for such a tactic, so Geoffrey was startled when he did.

'My business is *very* important,' Beaumais argued indignantly. 'More than any foreign weapon.'

'What can be more important than a way to defeat the King?'

'The King will not be brought low by weapons alone. Emma has other plans.' He beamed fondly at the abbess who, despite looking travel-weary and dishevelled, smiled back, before busying herself with her boxes.

'What plans?' pressed Geoffrey. 'A potion?'

He thought about Emma and her activities in All Hallows Barking. Was it Beaumais who had brought her the olive oil? The figure had been the right height and build. Or did Emma's plans involve the contents of the reliquary and the long box, so the potion containing olive oil, sulphur, fingers and raisins was designed to restore flesh and muscles to long-dead bones and had nothing to do with warfare?

'It will involve potions,' acknowledged Beaumais, gratified to show off his superior knowledge. 'And other items.'

'Items carried in that narrow chest?' asked Geoffrey, nodding to where Emma was supervising its unloading. The attention she lavished on it indicated that she considered it either valuable or fragile. The other Bellêmes watched wordlessly as it was carried inside with a care that verged on reverence.

Beaumais beamed at him. 'You have it! But do not talk

too loudly, my friend. The Bellêmes are sensitive about it, and you would be wise not to cross them. Their mother would disapprove, too.'

'Mabel's bones are in it,' said Geoffrey, to test whether his assumptions were right. 'And her head is in the other chest – the "reliquary".'

'No,' said Beaumais, already forgetting he was not supposed to talk about the matter on pain of upsetting Old Mabel. 'We do not have her own head yet, but it is only a matter of time before we do. And then the fortunes of the House will turn. Do you know the man who is with Abbot Ralph?'

'No,' replied Geoffrey, although he had seen him before. He had been one of the two men who had carried the long box near St Paul's. His companion had been cloaked and hooded to prevent himself from being recognized, but the knight had not bothered to hide his face.

'That is Josbert of Brèval. He is Bellême's most trusted servant, and he has been working hard to prepare Arundel for the siege that is about to follow. Will the King come, do you think?'

'Oh, yes,' said Geoffrey. 'He will come.'

Bellême and his siblings headed for the hall, along with Abbot Ralph, Josbert, Beaumais and a number of others, so Geoffrey followed for want of anything else to do. The building was surprisingly pleasant, with sumptuous wall hangings and fresh reeds scattered on the floor. While Bellême paced furiously, none of his fury exhausted by the ride, his company waited nervously to see what he would do next. Geoffrey found a spot near the back of the hall and sat on the floor, feeling exhaustion wash over him.

Food was brought, and Bellême was persuaded by Sybilla to sit and eat. As bread and meat restored the family's strength, conversation broke out. It comprised mostly bitter sniping between Emma and Bellême, with the others taking sides. Sybilla agreed with everything Bellême said, no matter how ill-informed or outrageous, and Geoffrey thought it a pity he should inspire such blind loyalty.

Abbot Ralph did his best to keep the peace, but his efforts

were mostly ignored, while Josbert sat next to Bellême and scowled at anyone who spoke. Geoffrey hoped the King would break the siege quickly, because being locked in a confined space with such people promised to be no fun at all. He also hoped the King would strike sooner than in a week, since he was sure boredom would lead Bellême to carry out his threat to hang Geoffrey, regardless of whether or not he had managed to identify Hugh's killer.

It was not long before he lost interest in the angry, strife-filled chatter of the Bellêmes, and closed his eyes. He did not feel particularly safe in the hall, but it was dark and not a good time to wander outside in the wet looking for a better place to sleep. He removed his cloak and used it as a pillow. It was not the first time he had slept sitting up, and he was sure it would not be the last.

He was asleep almost instantly, and when he awoke the hall was dim and shadowy. People lay everywhere, huddled in blankets and cloaks, and the fire had been banked. At the far end of the hall men still spoke in soft voices, and Geoffrey saw Bellême sitting with Josbert, poring over documents and planning their strategy. He was about to sleep again when he became aware of someone inching towards him. He eased himself up, and when the attack came, he was ready for it. He knocked the dagger from his assailant's hand before it did more than snake towards him. It clattered to the floor with a ringing sound that had many sleepers grumbling and turning restlessly. Carrying a torch, Bellême strode down the hall to see what was happening.

'Oh, it is you,' he said when he saw Geoffrey twisting the arm of the would-be knifeman and forcing him to his knees. 'I might have known.'

'Who is he?' asked Josbert, who had followed Bellême and was regarding Geoffrey with suspicion.

'He is the man who will uncover the traitor who murdered Hugh. Then we shall hang him.'

This was not quite the agreement Geoffrey thought they had made.

'No,' said Josbert shortly, before Geoffrey could voice his objection. 'I do not care what you have hired him to do. Get

185

rid of him. More castles have fallen through treachery than through battle, and I want no strangers here. Kill him now, or send him away tomorrow with the other expendables.'

Bellême turned to him in astonishment. 'Do you dare to give me orders?'

'If you want your siege to be successful, then I do,' replied Josbert tartly, unruffled by Bellême's ire. Geoffrey warmed to him a little. 'I can leave now, if you would rather appoint someone else.'

'You will stay,' snarled Bellême. 'And so will Geoffrey. I want to know who murdered Hugh and I do not trust anyone else to uncover the truth. You are right: there *is* treachery in my retinue, and I want an outsider to expose it for me.'

'Why?' demanded Josbert, with what Geoffrey considered to be rash abandon. 'An insider – like me – understands the factions in your following. This man does not.'

'You will be far too busy to bother with the murder of my nephew, while my brothers and sisters have their own plans afoot, some of which would see me sacrificed in order to see them reprieved.'

'I do not think they—' began Josbert.

'Then you are a fool,' snapped Bellême. 'Everyone is out for himself. Am I right, Geoffrey?'

'I should think so,' agreed Geoffrey cautiously. Of all the Bellêmes, Sybilla and her daughters were the only ones who had shown loyalty to any other family members, and they were seriously deranged.

'Emma strives to make our mother whole again,' Bellême went on. 'That is a good thing, but she imagines Mother will side with her against *me*, her favourite child. Foolish woman! Sybilla is so loyal she is a menace, and I dislike her perverted daughters pretending to be men. Matilda flaunts her prettiness in the hope that gullible men will help her. Roger wants to inherit my lands in England, while Arnulf . . . well, who knows what Arnulf plans? I distrust a smiling face.'

'Matilda does not flaunt herself,' said Josbert gallantly.

'She allowed that pawing Bishop Maurice to avail himself of her charms,' Bellême pointed out acidly. Geoffrey knew that was true, because he had been disappointed in her.

186

'Only to help you,' said Josbert tartly. 'Maurice has visited Arundel and *I* was afraid he would remember it well enough to give the King details about its defences, so she bedded him and quizzed him about what he recalled. She says he knows little that can harm us and is satisfied that the King will not learn from Maurice how long we can survive a siege. She did well.'

Clever Matilda, thought Geoffrey, recalling that Maurice was puzzled to have been asked questions about a castle when he had wanted to chat about the sexual experience they had shared. She had questioned a potential enemy with care and at depth, and the man had not realized what she was doing.

'We shall see,' said Bellême ungraciously. He wagged a finger at Josbert. 'But I want Geoffrey to hunt out this traitor, so do not kill him until his time is up.' He glanced meaningfully at the knifeman Geoffrey still held, obviously thinking he was under Josbert's orders.

Josbert regarded Geoffrey venomously. 'I shall be watching you,' he said, before striding back to his parchments at the far end of the hall.

'You and everyone else,' muttered Geoffrey, thinking that so many people were going to watch his every move he was probably the safest person in the castle. He released the knifeman, deciding to let Bellême deal with him.

'Amise,' said Bellême disdainfully, dragging the hood away from the would-be killer's face to reveal Sybilla's youngest daughter. She had removed the bandage she had worn earlier to reveal a long swelling cut that ran the length of one cheek.

'He was sleeping like a baby,' she spat furiously. 'While I am scarred for life.'

'Then you should choose your enemies more carefully,' said Bellême in a menacing whisper. 'And you will make one of me if you kill him. But you do not have long to wait. If he cannot find my traitor, you shall have the honour of hanging him yourself. But you will leave him alone until then.'

'Look!' cried Amise, pointing to her face. Her voice was loud, and people sat up, disturbed from sleep. Confused voices began to echo through the hall. 'How will I ever marry? Who will take me?'

'Anyone I decide to give you,' replied Bellême harshly. 'Lands and estates are what matter, not looks. You will marry well, because it is in my interests that you do so. And it is your own fault you are so horribly disfigured, anyway.' Geoffrey winced, thinking that he might have expressed himself a little more gently. 'You elected to fight like a man, so you must accept being injured like one.'

'I shall never forgive him,' spat Amise. 'Never.'

'Good,' said Bellême, pleased. 'Revenge is a good thing to cultivate.'

Amise glowered at him before stalking away. Bellême watched her go with a chuckle, evidently amused by the thought of a maimed girl seeking vengeance in the middle of the night. Geoffrey saw he was going to be in for a very long week.

The following morning was fine, and Geoffrey woke when the servants came to light the fire and set up tables for breakfast. He watched them struggle with temperamental trestles and load them with bread, fruit, salted fish and oatmeal. Wisely, everyone waited for Bellême to take what he wanted first, and then there was a concerted rush. Geoffrey saw a number of people stuff bread into their clothing, and knew they were planning ahead, anticipating a time when it would be scarce, and they would be reduced to catching rats and eating victuals they would not pass to a beggar in normal life.

As soon as breakfast was cleared away, Josbert issued orders. Some people were instructed to collect their belongings and leave, while others were told to stay. Soon, a stream of folk headed for the gates, carrying all they could. Some were minor nobles who had thrown in their lot with Bellême and who were now forced to fend for themselves, but most were villagers who had fled to the castle for safety. Josbert checked each person who left, and any scrap of food or livestock was confiscated. Geoffrey felt sorry for the peasants who wept because a cow or a sheep was all they owned, but Josbert cared nothing for that.

188

By the end of the morning, he had animals penned in both baileys, and every storeroom was filled. Pantries and butteries were full to overflowing with grain, salted meat and fish, and sacks of dried peas and beans, while a second well was being dug in the inner bailey, lest the one in the outer court should become contaminated or run dry. Arrows had been commandeered by the cartload, and Geoffrey saw Josbert expected the siege to last for months.

Other people arrived, trying to gain access, but most were turned away. One was not, and Geoffrey saw Matilda hurry forward to embrace Philip, the hostage who had been at Henry's Court. No one else seemed very interested, and although Emma also came to greet him, she did not display the warm affection of her younger sister. Geoffrey lounged behind a water barrel, so he could overhear what was being said between aunts and nephew.

'Did you receive my message?' asked Matilda, holding Philip at arm's length and looking him up and down to ensure he was unscathed.

Philip nodded eagerly. 'And it is as well that you warned me you all planned to flee, or Henry would have hanged me for certain. He has never liked me, and would relish an opportunity to make sure there was one less Bellême in the world.'

'He would not,' said Emma scornfully. 'You mean nothing to him, and he would not bloody his hands over you. Now, had *I* been the hostage, things would have been different . . .'

'I managed to escape,' Philip said proudly, ignoring her. 'On my own. I thought Bishop Maurice might help me, but he was more interested in sleeping with a new serving wench.' He glanced defiantly at Emma. 'I really did think Henry might kill me, after what you did yesterday.'

'He would have been within his rights,' said Matilda, casting an admonishing glare at her sister. Emma raised her eyes heavenward, to indicate she thought they were both overreacting. 'News came this morning that we are declared outlaws for vanishing without answering the charges laid against us. But I am glad you escaped. How did you do it?'

'I climbed out of a window and dropped on to a compost heap. The guards heard me fall and fired arrows, but I managed to jump into the river and float away.'

'Did you bring what I asked?' demanded Emma. 'A lock of Henry's hair and one of his fingers?'

'No,' said Philip apologetically, although Geoffrey considered Emma's request an unreasonable one. Philip might have managed to snag hair while the monarch slept, but a finger was an entirely different proposition. 'I tried, but he never sleeps alone and would have noticed me removing a finger. I have some toenail clippings, though.'

'They will have to do, I suppose,' said Emma, sighing to indicate her disappointment. 'And what have you discovered about the map?'

'I do not think Henry has it. There is a chest where he keeps things he does not want his clerks to see, and it is not there. You say it should have come into his hands a week ago, but it has not.'

Geoffrey frowned. The archer who had ambushed them near Westminster had allegedly muttered 'map' as he died. Durand had assumed he had been trying to say Mappestone, and had interpreted it as evidence that the attack was directed against Geoffrey. But what if he had indeed been saying 'map', and referred to the one Emma had hoped Philip would take from the King? That would imply Petronus had indeed been carrying missives other than those from Ralph to Maurice. He had known he was in danger, and had hoped two knights would be enough to protect him. He had been wrong. When the attack failed, both archers had been shot for incompetence, and someone else had hunted down the injured Petronus and strangled him. So, who had taken the map Petronus had carried?

The probability that the archer Geoffrey had caught had been shot by someone in the King's hunting party, combined with the fact that Emma expected the map to be in the King's possession, indicated that the ambush had originated with Henry. Furthermore, the fact that the ambush had occurred a week earlier fitted well with what Emma and Philip were talking about. The mess was beginning to make sense to

Geoffrey. It explained why Henry or his men had killed the archer, and even why the King had insisted on riding immediately to Westminster, abandoning his morning hunt: he had wanted his agents to complete their business without interference from Geoffrey.

But what map could be so important that it called for a monk to be murdered? A map telling Emma where she might find the secret ingredient to Greek Fire? Beaumais had all but admitted to Geoffrey that he was the recipient of some of Petronus's messages, so it was possible the map was his. He had gone with Bishop Maurice to see whether he could find it on Petronus's body, but was too late: the map had gone. Bemused, Geoffrey turned his attention back to the discussion.

'Will my grandmother be angry?' Philip asked Emma in a voice that was fearful.

'No,' said Matilda, before Emma could answer. 'Old Mabel knows you did your best. Go to the kitchens and eat. We will talk more later. I am proud of you.'

When he had gone, the sisters regarded each other soberly.

'What does this mean?' asked Emma. 'That the King has committed the thing to memory and destroyed the only copy in existence? If that is the case, we shall never have it, and our mother will be doomed to wander the earth headless forever.'

So, that was it, thought Geoffrey. It was nothing to do with Greek Fire, but with the location of Old Mabel's head. He could only assume that the knights who had killed her and stolen her skull had made a chart saying where they had buried it. If the Bellême clan really did believe that uniting head with body would give them supernatural powers, then it was not surprising they were prepared to go to such lengths to have it. But Geoffrey was surprised Henry was willing to enter the quest for it, too.

'She will not,' said Matilda sharply. 'You may frighten the others with tales of corpse-raising, but you do not convince me. Corpses do not rise from their graves because they want their heads back.'

'Her bones come together almost every night,' said Emma

in a voice that was strangely distant. It made the hairs on the back of Geoffrey's neck stand on end. 'They rattle and heave, and her tortured soul screams out that she must be whole. She has promised us great rewards if we succeed – rewards that will see Henry writhe with envy.'

'Well, I have never heard her,' said Matilda doubtfully.

'You do not have the Gift,' said Emma dismissively. 'She calls to me all the time. If we do not discover her head soon, she will become so angry that who knows what she might do? You know what she was like when she did not have her own way.'

'But you said you had another head that would suffice – you arranged for Hugh's to be severed, on the grounds that he was a Bellême and mother might be appeased by it.'

Geoffrey was disgusted, but recalled what Durand had said when he had discovered the two heads in Emma's 'reliquary'. He claimed one had been familiar, and he had been right.

'Well, she is not appeased, and she still wants her own. Let us hope this siege does not last long, or she may decide to look for it herself. Just imagine what *that* would do for our reputations.'

'It would make little difference,' said Matilda dryly. 'We are already feared, and a walking headless corpse will not surprise most people. Will it, Geoffrey?'

Geoffrey remained stock still, hoping he had misheard, but Matilda walked to his barrel and pulled him out.

Emma pulled a disagreeable face to indicate she did not approve of eavesdroppers. 'Do you have any idea where it might be?' she demanded of him. 'Have you heard the King mention maps, or know whether he has dispatched his best agents to unusual places with spades?'

'No,' replied Geoffrey. 'Are you sure he knows you are looking for your mother's head?'

'He knows,' said Emma with conviction. 'And he will try to stop us from getting it.'

'I can see why,' admitted Geoffrey. 'Yet another Bellême ranging herself against him – especially one like Old Mabel – will not be an attractive proposition.'

'We do not want her to fight for us,' said Matilda with a

hard look at her sister. 'Some of us just want her poor body whole in its grave, to see her soul at peace.'

'And the rest of us think that uniting head and body will increase the Bellême power beyond anything that the world has seen before,' snapped Emma. She gave a rather nasty smile. 'But I doubt *you* will be here to see it, Geoffrey. You will hang in a few days.'

Nine

G eoffrey had two tasks to complete in Arundel Castle: bring about its fall for Henry and discover who had murdered Hugh. Since he considered the latter more pressing, and did not trust Bellême not to shorten his allotted time out of sheer malevolence, he decided to make a start on questioning anyone who might have been involved in the death. He began at the bottom, with servants and grooms, but the Bellêmes were cautious about what they revealed to their retainers, and none knew anything of relevance. He saw he would have to move higher up the chain, to the siblings themselves.

This was easier said than done, because by the end of the first day, everyone was more interested in the arrival of a smattering of the King's troops, who established a camp some distance away. Bellême led a sortie against them, but the skirmish ended in stalemate, and Bellême cantered back having killed a dozen of Henry's soldiers and lost twelve of his own.

On the morning of the second day, there was a shout of alarm, and Geoffrey ran with others to see a massive contingent of King's men approach. They pitched their tents and soon had the castle surrounded. Work began immediately on counter-fortifications, and long before sunset the air rang with the sound of hammering and sawing. Henry had not simply gathered his forces and descended on Arundel: he had come prepared. He had timber and metal, and evidently intended to construct siege engines in full view of the castle's occupants, letting their fearful imaginations work in his favour. Geoffrey admired his strategy. It was something he would have done himself, wearing down his opponents'

194

minds, so they would be more willing to surrender without a fight.

'He did not wait long,' remarked Arnulf, watching their preparations uneasily. 'I suspect our flight to Arundel did not surprise him at all. He anticipated what we would do.'

'Rubbish!' asserted Bellême scornfully. 'He did not expect us to take a stand against his injustice.'

'Of course he did,' argued the surly Roger. 'He *wanted* us to run away. As soon as we left Winchester he declared us outlaws: we have played directly into his hands.'

'I agree,' said Arnulf.

'Well, I do not,' retorted Bellême angrily. 'Did you hear he issued another summons to me this morning, ordering me back to Winchester? He had no idea I would come here.' He saw Geoffrey listening, and his face broke into a scowl. 'Why do you skulk here when you are supposed to be learning who murdered my nephew?'

'People refuse to talk to me,' said Geoffrey with a shrug. 'I told you it would be difficult to solve the crime so far from where it was committed.'

'Everyone will answer any questions you put,' said Bellême in a loud voice, glaring around at his assembled clan. 'Anyone who is uncooperative will answer to me.'

'Well, I shall not be quizzed,' said Josbert sullenly. 'I have nothing to say to the likes of him.'

'Then I shall assume you have something to hide,' declared Bellême, glowering at his assembled household. 'So, you will all – *all* – answer anything he asks. Is that clear?'

There were rebellious mumblings, and Geoffrey thought Bellême had done him a grave disservice. By giving him authority, Bellême had ensured they would be on their guard and less likely to reveal something inadvertently in the course of a conversation. He had also ensured no one would volunteer information, while the likes of Josbert and Roger would reply just enough to claim they were following Bellême's orders, but refuse to divulge anything useful.

When Bellême stalked away to sit in the hall and gaze broodingly into a goblet of wine, Roger and Josbert turned their backs on Geoffrey. He decided to talk to them later, because he would learn nothing from them while they still smarted over Bellême's sharp orders. He approached Arnulf instead, who was by far the most amiable of the three.

'I am sorry,' said Bellême's youngest brother, backing away with his hands raised. 'I need to check my horse. I will talk to you another time – if I am not busy.'

Geoffrey interpreted Arnulf's response as a more polite version of the message given by Roger and Josbert. He left the battlements and wandered to the inner bailey, where he spotted Matilda sitting on the wall that surrounded the well.

'You took a risk at that tavern in Winchester,' she said, indicating that he should perch next to her. 'My brother is unpredictable, and might just as easily run you through as accept you into his service. I credited you with more sense than trying to secure an allegiance with him.'

'I am supposed to discover who killed Hugh,' said Geoffrey, cutting to the chase. 'Any ideas?'

'Emma and Sybilla believe *you* did it. They applaud Robert for obliging you to discover the identity of the murderer on pain of death, because they think you have no way out of your predicament.'

'And you? I doubt you would have come to my bedchamber for favours if you thought me a killer.'

'Perhaps.' Her black eyes glinted with humour. 'But perhaps not. I wasted my time with you that night. You did not intervene with the King on my behalf, and now I am locked in a castle surrounded by hostile troops, even though I have done nothing wrong.'

'Henry would not have listened to me anyway,' said Geoffrey. 'His mind was already made up, and you can see his point: your House has taken part in three invasions to put the Duke of Normandy on his throne, and he will never have peace as long as you are in England.'

She raised her eyebrows and started to laugh. 'You are a bold man! You tell me King Henry is *right* to place me and my family in this position? No wonder no one here trusts you!'

'I did not say I agreed with him,' said Geoffrey, realizing that honesty was probably not a good policy at Arundel, and that he would be wise to dissemble if he did not want to be

196

hanged as a traitor before his week was up. 'I was just putting his side of the argument.'

'Then I strongly advise you not to.' She was still laughing at him. 'Robert is imaginative when it comes to killing, and I doubt he will be merciful if he thinks you side with Henry.'

'Tell me what you know about Hugh,' said Geoffrey, thinking he had better change the subject before he incriminated himself further. 'People claim he was a halfwit. Is it true?'

'Yes,' said Matilda. 'Or he would not have allowed himself to be caught and killed. My brothers think he used a slowness of speech to hide a clever mind, but they are mistaken.'

'But you trusted him,' said Geoffrey. 'He carried your messages to the King.'

'I would rather you did not mention that around here,' said Matilda, although she did not seem overly concerned. 'Robert suspects that my sisters and I tried to negotiate with Henry, but he does not have definite evidence, and I do not want you to give it to him.'

Geoffrey scratched his head, wondering whether he was in danger from her, too. If she really did not want Bellême to know what she had done, then the only way to ensure he never did would be to kill the one person in the castle who had details. Or was she merely trying to make him nervous because it was something all Bellêmes did so well? Geoffrey had never before encountered so many people he found impossible to understand. He narrowed his eyes as a thought occurred to him.

'When you came to my room that night, did you expect me to have the map revealing the whereabouts of your mother's head? I recall you referring to Old Mabel's "property".'

'Emma does. She thinks you killed Hugh because he had seen the chart, and you wanted to ensure he never told anyone what was on it.'

'And it would have had to be a map – a picture – because Hugh could not read,' surmised Geoffrey. He recalled Oswin the landlord saying as much. 'A letter with words would be meaningless to him.'

'To all of us, except Emma and Sybilla,' said Matilda. 'Emma was taught to read when she entered the Church,

197

and Sybilla learned so she could be of use to Robert.' She sounded disgusted that such effort should be expended for the sole purpose of pleasing a brother.

'But you were not interested in a map.' Geoffrey watched her intently. 'You were more concerned about the reply from Henry, although at the time you pretended it was the other way around.'

She smiled wryly. 'I admit that keeping my estates was more pressing than trying to ascertain the whereabouts of a skull that was probably tossed into a river years ago. But Emma and the others are obsessed by it.'

'Because they think it will save them from their current predicament by supernatural means? It is not an unusual reaction: some people pray, others put skull to rotting corpse. I suppose this is what Wulfric meant when he said he had overheard Old Mabel referred to as the "head" of the family.'

'Do not be facetious or I shall answer no more questions,' said Matilda sharply. Geoffrey surmised that she did not know whether Emma and her siblings were right to be fanatical in their search for the thing, and wanted the option of taking their side if they transpired to be right. 'But, on the occasion you mention, I was indeed more keen to know whether the King had responded to my suggestion. I am still uncertain whether to believe the reply you say you read.'

'I did not lie.'

'That is not what I meant. What I am saying is that I do not know whether it came from Henry, or whether someone else wrote on his behalf. And now Hugh is dead, I doubt I ever shall. He may have delivered my message to Henry, as I asked, but he may have shown it to someone else and delivered their response instead. He was not especially trustworthy, as it happens.'

'So, who do you think killed him?'

'A number of people, for all kinds of reasons. And do not forget that Oswin, the landlord of the Crusader's Head, was also killed to prevent him from talking.'

'To prevent him from talking about the meetings your family held in his tavern with Old Mabel in attendance? Or to stop him telling anyone about the fact that your family has Greek Fire?'

'Or about the fact that I may not have been the only one trying to reach Henry to suggest a truce. Or perhaps Hugh's death has nothing to do with my family's troubles, and he died for reasons none of us have yet considered.'

'Like what?'

'Hugh had an unnatural fondness for Philip, his cousin. It is not unusual for young men to form such attachments, but my brothers disapproved. Why do you think they attacked King William Rufus so many times? It was because he, too, had a penchant for men.'

'Are they sufficiently averse to homosexuality to kill Hugh for it?'

'You know my brother. He will kill if his wine is too warm or he does not like the colour of a man's tunic. And, although Roger and Arnulf are gentle saints by comparison, they also have foul tempers. Meanwhile, my sisters did not like Hugh's slow speech and transparent attempts at cunning – although he sometimes acted as their go-between, too.'

'Like Bellême, you seem to think the murderer is one of your own kin,' observed Geoffrey.

'They are the most likely culprits,' she agreed carelessly. 'But then there is Beaumais, who is everywhere and the friend of all. Meanwhile, Josbert was also in London that night. And another suspect might be William Pantulf, who was our ally until yesterday and is now in the pay of the King. Have I helped you at all?'

'No,' said Geoffrey gloomily.

Matilda walked away leaving Geoffrey to wonder how he was ever supposed to solve the murder so far from where it had happened, with so many possible culprits, and when it was in no one's interests to see him uncover the truth. Matilda was more helpful than most, and did not give the impression she wanted to run him through every time they met, but even she had lied to him. The story she had told him the night she had entered his bedchamber differed in several ways to the one she told now.

First, she had given the impression that Hugh had been

in her pay; now she confessed that she had not trusted him. Second, she had pretended to be more interested in the information pertaining to her mother's "property" than the message purporting to be from Henry; now he knew it was actually the other way around. And third, she had originally been convinced that Hugh's death was connected to *her* errand; now she disclaimed responsibility. Geoffrey filed the information away to consider later. He did not think she had killed Hugh, or she would not have tried to hunt down the message later, but there were many questions he wanted answered about her curious relationship with her nephew.

He walked through the inner bailey, looking for someone else to interrogate. He saw Emma and Sybilla together, so decided to tackle them next. Bellême was not far away, and Geoffrey thought the fierce sisters might be more prepared to speak to him when their brother was within hearing distance. As he walked in their direction, four women intercepted him. They were Sybilla's daughters, but in place of their mail, they wore dresses that accentuated the tall, graceful lines of their figures – except Mabel, who looked better in armour.

'I did not kill Hugh,' he said, pushing past them to reach Emma and Sybilla. Amise looked as though she wanted to renew the argument about who was responsible for scarring her face, but Geoffrey did not have the time or the inclination for that. 'So, who else might have done it?'

'You are becoming desperate,' jeered Haweis, the prettiest daughter, eyeing him with dislike. 'And your week is not even up yet.' She exchanged a triumphant glance with her sisters. Amise seemed delighted at the prospect of Geoffrey's failure, although Cecily and Mabel did not join in their gloating. Cecily seemed distracted, and kept glancing over Geoffrey's shoulder as though looking for someone; Mabel remained grim-faced, and Geoffrey thought she was more like her dour uncle Roger than her flamboyant mother.

'Well?' he asked, turning his back on them and speaking loudly to Emma and Sybilla, so Bellême would hear what he was doing. 'What do you know about Hugh's death?'

'I saw his body,' said Emma spitefully. 'Did you know that

the eyes of a murdered man hold a picture of his killer? I saw your face in his eyes.'

'When did you see his body?' asked Geoffrey, supposing he should not be surprised that she, of all the Bellêmes, should be party to such grisly information. 'The night he died?'

'*I* was not there,' replied Sybilla. 'I was across the river in London, with some of my daughters.'

'I did not mean you,' said Geoffrey brusquely. 'I was talking to Emma.'

'I saw him within an hour of his death,' said Emma, glancing at her brother out of the corner of her eye and noting he was listening. 'It was not a pretty sight, although Arnulf had been kind enough to cover him with a cloak and remove the rope from his poor dead neck.'

'I will do the same for you, Geoffrey,' offered Haweis with an unpleasant smile.

'And I will prove *you* are the guilty man,' added Amise. In the light of day her wound looked worse than ever. It was swollen and raw, and had been badly sewn, so that when the infection drained Geoffrey thought it would heal badly and give her a lopsided look. 'You will not escape justice.'

'I am not talking to you,' said Geoffrey irritably. 'Did your mother never tell you it is rude to break into the conversations of your elders with childish remarks? Now, go away.' He saw Bellême grinning, while even Emma's thin lips softened into a semblance of a smile. It seemed few people told the female warriors what to do. He turned back to the older women. 'Did Hugh ever bring messages for you? Or deliver them?'

'Occasionally,' admitted Sybilla, aware that her brother was watching and anxious to be helpful. 'We were expecting one from him the night he died.'

'The map detailing the location of your mother's head,' said Geoffrey.

Emma's eyes widened in astonishment. 'How do you know about that? It is a secret that has never gone beyond the family, despite the fact that we have been hunting for the last twenty-five years.'

'Matilda told you!' declared Sybilla angrily. She turned to Emma. 'You see? She cannot be trusted with her penchant

201

for pretty men and chatter over a pillow. She had no right to tell him this.'

'She told me nothing,' said Geoffrey. 'If she had, I would have known about it when we met in All Hallows Church, and I would not have asked some of the questions I did.'

'Then who?' demanded the fiery Haweis, drawing a dagger. 'I will slit his gossiping throat.'

'I reasoned it out for myself,' replied Geoffrey tartly. 'The evidence is there; it just needed to be reviewed logically. Did someone murder Hugh so he would never deliver this map to you?'

'You mean the King?' asked Emma bluntly. 'He is the one with the most to lose if I bring my mother into the Bellême battle lines.'

'Perhaps,' said Geoffrey. 'He probably knows about your quest – which suggests to me that your family's business is not as private as you think.'

'No,' said Bellême, coming to join them. 'The King did not kill Hugh. I told you before: Hugh was murdered by someone here, in this castle.'

'Nonsense, brother,' said Emma sharply. 'You have become obsessed with the notion of a traitor, and it is irrational. We are all on the same side.'

'We are not,' said Bellême, equally sharply. 'There are as many sides as there are Bellêmes. Any one of us would betray another in an instant if he thought it would improve his lot. If you believe otherwise, you are deluding yourself.'

'*I* would not,' cried Sybilla in dismay. 'I am loyal to you, Robert, and so are my daughters.'

'I know,' said Bellême, although he did not sound pleased and gazed disparagingly at the foursome. Mabel seemed especially uncomfortable in her feminine finery, and Geoffrey noticed that she had declined to don the soft leather shoes that went with the embroidered kirtle, and still wore chain mail boots. It made for an odd combination.

'There is a difference between murder and a disloyal plan to save our own estates,' snapped Emma. Geoffrey saw her bite her lip, and supposed she had not intended to let that particular piece of information slip.

202

'What plan?' asked Bellême silkily.

'Matilda tried to negotiate us a separate agreement with the King,' elaborated Sybilla, smiling fawningly at her brother, and seeming oblivious that by betraying Matilda she had just proved his point that the siblings would sell each other for personal advantage. 'I did not think it was a good idea, but she insisted, and Emma agreed.'

Geoffrey saw Emma wince, and supposed the cat was well and truly out of the bag now. Bellême, however, did not seem surprised by the news. It was even possible he had intercepted the message, and had sent the reply purporting to be from Henry himself. Did that mean he had also killed Hugh? Geoffrey hoped not, aware that that particular solution would not reprieve him from hanging.

'It is not what you think,' hedged Emma. 'Matilda and I reasoned that if the King allowed us to keep our estates, then we could use them to help you when you next invade England. We have not plotted against you.'

Bellême regarded her dispassionately. 'Betrayal of me is a far more grave offence than the murder of a nephew. And I am vexed about the latter, so you can imagine how I would feel about the former.'

'You should not tar us all with the same brush, Robert,' said Sybilla desperately. 'Some of us would sooner die than betray you.' She glared at Emma. 'It was their idea, not mine.'

While Bellême and his sisters bickered, Geoffrey watched Cecily. Her attention was a long way away, and her eyes were fixed on a point just above Geoffrey's left shoulder. He glanced behind him, and saw she was paying close attention to the comings and goings at the hall. Suddenly, her expression changed from hopeful eagerness to blushing confusion. Geoffrey looked behind him a second time, and was somewhat bemused to see Beaumais. The sardonic courtier saw the assembly and gave a jaunty wave in their general direction, oiled hair glinting in the sun. Cecily gave a delighted grin; she was not the only one, and Emma also inclined her head with a meaningful smile.

How many Bellême women did Beaumais have under his spell? Geoffrey mused. Emma he could understand, because they were of an age and Beaumais had already spoken of her with some affection. But Cecily seemed an odd choice, although she was comely enough if a man had a penchant for fighting women. Geoffrey allowed himself the satisfaction of a smile. If Beaumais intended to keep two Bellême women happy simultaneously, then he would have his work cut out for him. Neither were the kind to share, and he thought Beaumais was playing with fire, taking on a self-confessed witch and a female knight at the same time.

Meanwhile, Bellême was addressing Geoffrey, forcing him to pull his attention away from the gaudy courtier's dangerous liaisons. 'It seems you have made some headway with your enquiry. Perhaps you will evade my noose after all.'

'But then, perhaps not,' hissed Amise, so Geoffrey knew she would do all she could to see him fail.

When so many people were crammed into a small space, it was difficult to find a safe and quiet spot, but Geoffrey succeeded eventually. The stables had been raised next to the hall-house, but not right against it, so there was a narrow strip of space between the two buildings that was concealed from the casual passer-by. The far end was blocked by rubble, so the tunnel could only be accessed from one direction. Geoffrey stole straw from the stable and made himself a bed there, preferring the chill of the open air to the sticky humidity of indoors.

The next morning, his third day at Arundel, he resumed his investigation, knowing he would need every available hour either to question witnesses or to analyse the information he had gathered – although he suspected he would not be overwhelmed with that, given the family's taciturn and unfriendly nature. The first person he met was Arnulf, who was humming to himself. It seemed a good omen, so Geoffrey approached him with a friendly smile.

'My brother's inquisitor,' said Arnulf, his expression instantly wary. 'I appreciate you are in a difficult position, Geoffrey, but I do not want to be interrogated by you.'

'Just one question. How soon after Hugh's death did you arrive at the Crusader's Head?'

'That is easy.' Arnulf sounded relieved, as though he had

204

anticipated that Geoffrey would ask something more difficult. 'I was there when it happened.'

'You were?' asked Geoffrey in surprise. 'I did not see you.'

'But I saw *you*. I decided it would be better to maintain a low profile, so Josbert and I hovered near the back of the crowd.'

'Then I did see you. I spotted several figures with expensive cloaks towards the rear of the onlookers, but could not see their faces. Was it you who ran forward – twice – to get a better view?'

'That was Josbert. The first time he was acting on my orders, because I wanted to be sure it was Hugh who had been killed. The second was of his own volition. We all like to see a corpse, and I suppose he could not restrain himself.'

Geoffrey suffered from no such compulsion, and he supposed it was just another incidence of the Bellême family's macabre penchant for death and suffering. He imagined such nobles would attract like-minded men, and Josbert was certainly the type who might prefer the sight of a body to an attractive woman or a pleasing building.

'It was not you who made off with the box containing your mother's bones, was it?' he asked, recalling the curious comings and goings at the back of the crowd while Hugh was being cut down.

'It was not!' replied Arnulf in some distaste. He moved closer to Geoffrey, so he would not be overheard. 'Sybilla, Emmy and Robert are hopeful that our cause will gain power if we bring our mother back to life, but I do not believe in such things, and neither does Roger. We are soldiers, and we know that once you are dead, you stay dead. Our Abbess of Alménches may be the most powerful witch in the civilized world, but she will not succeed in this.'

'Is she?' asked Geoffrey. 'The most powerful witch in the civilized world?'

'She thinks so, but I have never seen her do anything that cannot be explained rationally. She has an extensive knowledge of herbs and potions, and this allows her to pretend she has supernatural skills, but I think it is all

205

trickery. She should have left our mother in peace, where she was buried. If Old Mabel's bones really do cry out at night, it is because they do not want to be ferried around in boxes when they should lie in the cool earth.'

He gave Geoffrey a quick smile, then headed for the hall, where breakfast was being served. Geoffrey was not hungry, and did not want to join the jostling, grabbing crowd for scraps, so instead intercepted Roger, who was striding away from the hall.

'No,' said Roger, lips tightening into their habitual mean line as he moved away. 'I do not want to talk to you.'

'So, *you* are the one with something to hide,' Geoffrey called after him. 'You are the only one who has declined to talk.'

Roger stopped dead in his tracks and came back, as Geoffrey knew he would. He also anticipated that it would be with a dagger in his hand, and raised his own to indicate that Roger was not the only one ready to use steel. Roger sighed furiously, and thrust his knife back into his belt. He folded his arms and stared straight ahead, and Geoffrey supposed he was waiting for the interrogation to begin.

'Were you present in the Crusader's Head when Hugh was killed?'

Roger shook his head.

'Arnulf was,' said Geoffrey, hoping to loosen the man's tongue.

'Well, I was not,' snapped Roger. 'Next question.'

'Where were you, then?'

'That is none of your affair.'

'Then I shall assume you *were* in the Crusader's Head.'

Roger was outraged. 'You cannot! I have not admitted it.'

'Few murderers confess to their crimes, but that does not make them innocent.'

Roger swallowed. 'You cannot think I am the killer,' he said, glancing around him uneasily. 'How could I be? I was busy trying to bribe those guards on the London Bridge to let me and the others cross later that night, but they would not hear me out. I was there for the best part of an hour, until it was almost dark.'

206

Geoffrey recalled how the guards had refused him, too, because the King had had one of them maimed for breaking his rules. He rubbed his chin thoughtfully. If Roger had arrived back at the Crusader's Head after dusk, then he probably had not murdered Hugh, because Hugh was already dead by the time darkness fell. Geoffrey also recalled the guard saying that 'better men' than him had demanded to cross that night and had been refused. He supposed the better man may well have been Roger in his finery. So, he was reasonably certain Roger was telling the truth about trying to bribe his way across the bridge, but the question still remained as to whether he was telling the truth about the timing. He could have killed Hugh, *then* gone to argue at the bridge.

'Why were you so keen to cross the river that night?' he asked. 'Why not wait until morning?'

'Why do you think?' snapped Roger. 'I wanted to spend the night in good lodgings, not in the filth of Southwark.'

'Then why not meet in London in the first place? Why travel to Southwark at all? And why not meet openly? Family gatherings are not illegal.'

'Ours would have been construed as such,' said Roger resentfully. 'If Henry had learned we planned to discuss our strategy over the impending Easter Court, he would have seen it as treason – and he would have been right, technically speaking. Southwark is a safer place for that kind of thing. Besides, not all the family intended to return to their city lodgings that night; some had other plans.'

'What plans?' asked Geoffrey. 'Who did not want to return?'

'You will have to ask them,' said Roger stiffly. 'I do not betray my kin. However, I can tell you that Arnulf has a liking for Southwark's Winchester Geese, and Matilda was going to decide what she did after she had received some message or other from Hugh. Of course, his death changed all that.'

'But *you* wanted to return to the city?' asked Geoffrey, trying not to smile at Roger's idea of not yielding his family's secrets.

'I did, and was prepared to pay a princely sum for the privilege. But, as it transpired, we were busy all night at the Crusader's Head, discussing Hugh. My gold would have been wasted, because none of us travelled to London until the next day.'

'Perhaps you were not at the tavern when Hugh was murdered,' said Geoffrey. 'But you were there later, because I saw you myself.' He gestured to Roger's distinctive hair, cut short on top so it stood up, like a brush. Geoffrey had seen the hair and he had observed the glitter of silver thread in a handsome cloak. He did not know what to think about Roger's story, but knew he had not told the complete truth. Roger scowled at him and stormed away, furious that his word was questioned by a mere knight, no matter how justified.

The new information took Geoffrey no nearer the truth. It told him that virtually the entire Bellême clan was in the area when Hugh had died, although Roger claimed to be off bribing guards and Sybilla said she had not attended the meeting at all. It also told him that the family had lingered after the death and that any of them could have murdered the landlord, Oswin. He saw Beaumais, and wondered what he had to say for himself.

'Do you have any theories about who killed Hugh?' he asked, thinking that the man had ideas about everything else, so would surely have an opinion to offer about something as significant as a murder.

'It was not Emma,' he said quickly. 'Folk often blame her for mishaps, because she dabbles in witchcraft. But *she* did not kill him.'

'She was not one of my main suspects,' lied Geoffrey. 'What about Cecily?'

Beaumais seemed surprised by his choice of suspects, but considered the question carefully. 'I would imagine Cecily is more of a dagger woman. I do not know how she would fare with hangings.'

'She seems fond of you.'

Beaumais looked at him warily. 'Is she?'

'You must have noticed the way she looks at you.'

'I have not, actually. I have enough to manage with Emma, thank you very much. One Bellême is plenty for anyone, as you have doubtless discovered with Matilda.'

'I have not—' began Geoffrey, startled.

Beaumais cut across his reply. 'Now, *she* would be worth the risk. But Cecily? No! She is a child, and I prefer women. However, a dalliance with Cecily would not be wise for you, either.'

'Why not?'

'There is no point in attracting a young woman when your untimely death will break her heart. If you must have a younger woman to balance what Matilda offers you, then try Mabel. She is more practical about these things.'

'I shall bear it in mind,' said Geoffrey, thinking he would have to be desperate to take on Mabel. He changed the subject. 'Were you at the Crusader's Head the night Hugh was murdered?'

'I was in the tavern's stables for a while,' replied Beaumais vaguely. 'Discussing something with Emma.'

'In the stables?' asked Geoffrey curiously, thinking it would be an uncomfortable place for a frolic. The inn itself had been sordid, and he imagined the stables would have been worse.

'It was Emma's idea, if you must know. She likes dark places. But you must not misunderstand her. Her heart is in the right place, even if her head occasionally leads her astray.'

'Her mother seems to have a similar problem,' remarked Geoffrey. 'Head and body wandering the Earth in different directions.'

'Hush!' exclaimed Beaumais in alarm. 'It is not wise to make comments about Old Mabel. She may hear and exact revenge. I am lucky to have Emma to protect me, or I might be in serious danger.'

'Why? What have *you* done to offend the long-dead Mabel?'

Beaumais glanced around him surreptitiously. 'I failed to secure that map – the document that says where her head might be found. I understood that Petronus was bringing it, but by the time I saw him, it had been stolen.'

'By whom?' Geoffrey was under the impression that Emma and Matilda had expected Hugh to deliver that particular item

209

to them the night he was murdered. Was there more than one of them?

'By the men who murdered Petronus, I imagine – Henry's agents.'

'I see,' said Geoffrey, wishing Beaumais had told him this when they had discussed the matter earlier. He did not understand the slippery courtier at all, keeping secrets one day and revealing them without a second thought the next. 'How did Petronus come to have this map?'

'From Abbot Ralph,' said Beaumais. 'Ralph is bound to Bellême because Shrewsbury Abbey is on Bellême land. Ralph discovered the map and sent it with Petronus to be delivered to me. But I failed to secure it, and Emma says her mother was very angry.'

'Lord!' muttered Geoffrey.

'Bellême thinks *he* was Mabel's favourite, but it is Emma. Poor Emma, besieged on every side.'

'So are we all,' Geoffrey pointed out, indicating the King's troops outside. 'But why "poor Emma" especially?'

'Sybilla is supposed to be her best ally, but *she* makes it clear her first duty is to Bellême. However, I think Sybilla is only loyal to him because she believes he will win this war with Henry and she wants him to reward her later. Of course, Bellême is not the kind of man to give rewards.'

'No,' agreed Geoffrey. 'However, while he may forget to repay loyalty, he will not forget treachery. Emma should be careful. If Henry wins this siege, and the family is exiled, they will all have to live together in Normandy. Sybilla's loyalty to Bellême is probably prudent.'

'I can see that,' said Beaumais worriedly, as if it had not occurred to him before. 'I should tell Emma, before it is too late. You are right. We do not want an enemy like *him* snapping at our heels.'

'*Our* heels?' queried Geoffrey, amused.

But Beaumais had already gone, hurrying to seek out the woman who seemed to have secured his friendship. Geoffrey did not trust Beaumais. He had encountered such men before, and knew them to be sly and difficult to catch out. On the surface, Beaumais was a brainless gossip, but he also had access to sensitive information, and Geoffrey could not decide whether he was merely a slack-tongued courtier who thrived on intrigue, or a cunning manipulator who knew exactly what he was doing.

Geoffrey glanced at the sky and saw a flock of birds fluttering across it. He wished he could join them, away from the warring, treacherous House of Montgomery-Bellême. As he looked up, he saw Bellême, Roger, Arnulf and Josbert on the watchtower roof. Usually, the roof was thick with lookouts, but these had been ousted to stations on the floors below. Geoffrey looked away, not wanting to know what the Bellême brothers were doing, since he was sure it was either unpleasant or sinister.

He glanced at an outbuilding that had been commandeered by the Bellême women for their personal use. Sybilla and Emma were sitting outside, while the four daughters had taken up stations to prevent anyone else from going too close to them. Geoffrey decided not to wander in that direction, unwilling to see the bones of Old Mabel gather together and go for a walk across the inner bailey. Meanwhile, Beaumais had been intercepted by Abbot Ralph, and they muttered in low voices near the stables. Cecily watched them intently, and Geoffrey changed direction again, wondering if there was anywhere in the castle he could walk without encountering his suspects.

He went to his hiding place behind the stables and thought about what he had learned, but could see no connections that made sense. Most confusing was the map, which Matilda had expected Hugh to bring to her, and which Beaumais had expected from Petronus a day later. Geoffrey could only assume that Emma was being cautious, and had sent more than one agent to secure it. Since she obviously believed that finding the head was the key to Bellême victory, then it made sense that she would have more than one plan in play to lay hands on it. Unfortunately for her, neither had worked.

After a while, Geoffrey decided to see whether Philip knew anything that might be relevant, although speaking to such a lowly member of the clan bespoke desperation. As he walked across the bailey, he saw nothing had changed: Bellême,

Josbert, Roger and Arnulf were still on the watchtower, the women still clustered around their outbuilding, and Beaumais and Ralph stood near some bales of hay, so Geoffrey could only see their heads.

Suddenly, there was a loud bang, followed by a lot of screaming. Smoke swirled around the women's building, but the origin of the sound was difficult to pinpoint. It might have come from anywhere, because the close proximity of the buildings made for confusing acoustics. Geoffrey glanced up at the tower and saw four figures framed against the sky: the brothers and Josbert were straining forward to see what had happened. Beaumais and Ralph were still by the hay, but made no attempt to move towards the commotion.

When Geoffrey arrived, a ring of people stood around someone lying on the ground. There was a sharp stink of sulphur, with something deeply unpleasant that immediately reminded him of the Crusade. It was singeing flesh. The screams that had immediately followed the explosion had petered out, and the only sound was the whisper of horrified voices. Geoffrey saw that the clothes and hair of whoever lay on the ground were smoking furiously.

Mabel, taller than the others, spotted him at the back of the onlookers and elbowed her way through them to grab his arm. He was inclined to resist her powerful tugs, but he did not want to create a scene, and allowed himself to be propelled towards the casualty. It was Cecily. A thick, black, sticky substance adhered to her chest and neck, and low yellow flames flickered across her clothes. There was an acrid stench of burning that had more than one person turning away in revulsion. Smoke seethed this way and that, blown by the breeze.

'You are familiar with the ravages of Greek Fire,' said Mabel, her voice hoarse with emotion. 'We are not, because we left the Crusade at Antioch. Help her.'

'Greek Fire?' cried Josbert, breathless from what must have been a very rapid dash from the tower. 'Douse the flames immediately, before she sets the entire castle alight.'

Before Geoffrey could stop him, he had seized a bucket of water – a number of these were scattered around, ready for use if King Henry deployed fire arrows – and hurled it over Cecily. There was a hiss, and a lot more smoke, but when the steam had blown away flames still licked across her body. There were sharp intakes of breath from those unfamiliar with Greek Fire and its idiosyncrasies. Josbert watched in dismay when he saw he had done nothing to help. Emma elbowed him out of the way and scraped handfuls of dirt to throw on the flames, but that did no good either.

'Water and sand are useless against Greek Fire,' snapped Mabel impatiently. 'We all know that. Let Geoffrey help. He knows what he is doing.'

Geoffrey knelt next to the prostrate figure, and used a stick to scrape some of the hot tar from Cecily's skin, although he knew he was doing too little and too late: she was already dead. He felt the great veins in her neck, but there was no life beat. He pushed on her chest, because he had learned from Arab physicians that this sometimes made the heart beat again, but he hoped it would not. The Greek Fire had seared its way to the bone in places, and if she lived it would be a short and agonized existence.

'I am sorry,' he said gently to Sybilla, who watched with a face that was a fixed mask of horror.

'It hit her chest,' Geoffrey explained to Bellême a short while later. The hall had been cleared of servants, and the Earl paced back and forth as he fired his questions at the one man in the castle who had seen Greek Fire in action. 'She probably died more or less immediately, when the stuff burned her throat.'

Beaumais and Ralph were there, too, occasionally adding a remark. Emma stood with the sullen Josbert, while to one side, alone and impassive, was Big Mabel. Matilda and the other two daughters were with Sybilla in a private chamber, trying to soothe her grief. Roger and Arnulf sat on either side of the hearth, speaking to each other in low voices and exchanging their views on the devastating weapon that was being created on their behalf. Arnulf seemed a good deal more enthusiastic about it than Roger, who kept informing his younger brother that it was unsoldierly.

213

'And this is how it works?' asked Bellême. 'It kills its victims instantly?'

'Not always,' said Geoffrey, reluctant to recall the horrors that Greek Fire had wrought on the Crusader army. 'If it had hit a limb, rather than her torso, then she might have survived.'

'And this is the weapon we will use on Henry?' whispered Abbot Ralph, so low that he could barely be heard. The portly monastic's face was white, and Geoffrey knew from the sour smell around him that he had been sick.

'It is what he plans to use on me,' retorted Bellême, although this was news to Geoffrey. 'He *has* used it on me! How else do you think my niece died?'

'You think Henry's troops propelled it across our ramparts?' asked Josbert. 'I thought it was fired from within. I thought *she* was experimenting again.' He pointed an accusing finger at Emma.

'Well, I was not,' replied Emma shortly. 'I was preparing a potion we might try on King Henry at some point, containing the toenail clippings Philip secured for me. Tell him, Mabel.'

'Yes,' said Mabel flatly, so Geoffrey did not know what to believe. Was she lying to support her aunt, because the female Bellêmes needed to stick together against the males? But did she resent doing so, because Emma's tampering had brought about the horrible death of a beloved sister? Or was Mabel merely shocked at her first sight of genuinely dirty warfare? He recalled the salute she had given him after their skirmish in All Hallows Church, and imagined she had principles when it came to fighting, like Geoffrey himself. A weapon like Greek Fire flew in the face of all of them.

'But you do not deny that you have been meddling?' demanded Josbert archly.

Emma bristled indignantly. 'Of course I have! I am some way from perfecting the substance, and if I do not "meddle" then it will not be ready when we need it. Tell him, Robert.'

'I have ordered her to continue her experiments,' said Bellême, still pacing. 'We do not know when we shall need it, so the sooner it is ready the better.'

Geoffrey leaned against a wooden post and considered the evidence. The watery substance that Emma had spilled in All Hallows was not the same stuff that had killed Cecily, which was thicker and identical to that used by the Arabs. So, was Cecily killed with some of the real Greek Fire Durand had seen in Emma's chest, which was probably a sample sent by Philip the Grammarian, or had Emma's experiments paid off and she had finally succeeded in making her mixture properly sticky? And if she had perfected the formula, did that mean she had moved on to the next problem: how to deploy it?

Or was Cecily killed by the Bellême brothers and Josbert, who had been on the roof of the tower with all archers conveniently banned so no one could see what they were doing? If Emma had made Greek Fire, then Geoffrey was certain Bellême would want to practise with it. Or was it something to do with Beaumais and Ralph, who alone did not rush to the scene of the accident to see what had happened? Was that why Ralph had vomited, because he had been appalled at what the substance had done to his victim?

Or was Bellême right: Henry had the secret of Greek Fire, and was preparing to end the siege earlier than anyone had anticipated? Geoffrey had examined the watchtower, the place where Emma had been working and the spot where Beaumais and Ralph had stood, but there was nothing to indicate that a missile had been projected from any of them. He concluded that the Greek Fire may well have come from outside. He sincerely hoped Bellême would not charge him with solving Cecily's murder, as well as Hugh's.

'He is the only one here, other than Emma, who knows about Greek Fire,' said Josbert, indicating Geoffrey with a finger that shook with outrage. 'He must have killed Cecily.'

'He did not,' said Bellême. 'I was watching him when she died. He had nothing to do with it.'

'What makes you think he did not delay the explosion until he was safely away?' demanded Emma. 'I have read about such devices in foreign texts, where wicks soaked in oil are used to light candles at predicted times. Why not the igniting of Greek Fire?'

215

'Is this true?' asked Arnulf of Geoffrey, sounding very interested. He gazed around at his siblings. 'It could be important, and would add a new dimension to this weapon. We need all the advantages we can get if we are to defeat Henry, and a delayed igniting of Greek Fire could be a godsend.'

'That would make it even more hideous than it is already,' said Roger with a black scowl. 'I like to look a man in the eye when I slay him, and I disapprove of killing when I am not there to see it.'

'That *is* a disadvantage,' conceded Bellême ruefully. 'I, too, like to see the faces of the men I slaughter. But we cannot be too choosy in our current predicament. Tell us, Geoffrey. Can Greek Fire be ignited from a safe distance using some sort of timing device?'

'I do not know,' replied Geoffrey honestly.

'He would say that,' snapped Josbert. 'He is hardly likely to admit to such knowledge when it will see him hang for the murder of a Bellême.'

'He did not do it,' said Mabel quietly. She spoke so seldom that everyone turned to look at her. 'Emma has been experimenting with Greek Fire, and my mother, sisters and I have been helping. Look at my hands.'

She held a couple of meaty paws in front of her. They were covered in small marks. Some were burns, and others were dark stains from some sort of tar or pitch.

'So?' demanded Roger testily, sounding as though he thought she was wasting his time. 'What of it, woman? You should wear gloves if you are concerned over your lily-white skin.' His tone was sneering, knowing such a consideration would not be an issue for the mannish Mabel.

'My point is that anyone who has used Greek Fire will be marked,' said Mabel. She regarded Roger with hard, cold eyes. 'Or his gloves will, if he is unmanly enough to be concerned about the silken quality of his skin. Geoffrey's hands are unscathed, and he does not own gloves.'

'How do you know they are unscathed?' snarled Roger, not liking Mabel's tone.

Mabel snatched Geoffrey's hands and hauled them under

Roger's nose. The knight was almost pulled from his feet, and was reminded that she was a very powerful woman. 'And I know he has no gloves because I saw his squire ride off with them.'

Bellême clapped slowly and mockingly. 'Well done, Mabel. But you are forgetting something: *I* have already ascertained Geoffrey's innocence, because I told you I watched him in the inner bailey most of the morning. I would have noticed him lighting oily wicks or ferrying bowls of Greek Fire around. We did not need your deductions.'

Mabel regarded him steadily. 'But you did not convince us. Josbert did not accept your testimony, and neither did Roger. It is what happens in a family where lies and subterfuge are considered virtues, and honesty and truth are regarded as weaknesses.'

Geoffrey winced, thinking she should have remained silent, but Bellême merely looked at the rest of his family. 'So, Geoffrey is cleared of any involvement in Cecily's death, and Mabel is too honourable to have murdered her sister.' He treated her to a glance that was contemptuous. 'I am innocent, too, obviously. What about the rest of you?'

He gazed around challengingly, and Geoffrey saw several people thrust their hands into sleeves or under cloaks. Geoffrey was amused at the 'obviously' added to the end of Bellême's statement, and thought he was just as much a suspect in the death of Cecily as anyone else, especially since he made no move to expose his own hands for general scrutiny. Emma removed her gloves and Geoffrey saw skin that was marked, like Mabel's.

'Here,' she snapped. 'But I have been working on the weapon I hope will save our House from an embarrassing rout, so of course *I* am marked. But I was not doing it when Cecily was attacked.'

'I will not show my hands like a naughty child,' growled Roger, striding towards the door.

'Nor I,' said Arnulf, following him. Wordlessly, Josbert did the same, while Beaumais made no effort to remove his gloves, either. Abbot Ralph flapped unblemished white fingers at anyone who happened to be looking, although no one took much notice and he seized the opportunity to slip away, too. Emma also took her leave, although whether it was because she had other matters to attend to, or because the conversation was uncomfortable, Geoffrey could not tell. Beaumais scurried after her.

'So,' said Bellême, when the door had closed and only he, Geoffrey and Mabel remained. 'We are left with a second mystery: who killed Cecily? Emma, because she is an incompetent witch and made a mistake in her formula? Matilda, who hates Sybilla for telling me about her plot to deal with King Henry behind my back? Arnulf or Roger, because they feel Sybilla's daughters give her too many voices in the castle? Beaumais, because Cecily had an eye for him?'

'Or Josbert, because he disapproves of women warriors?' asked Mabel.

'It will be the same traitor who killed Hugh,' said Bellême with certainty. 'He continues to work against me. You must double your efforts to uncover him, Geoffrey. Your time is running out.'

Geoffrey's heart sank. As far as he was concerned, there was no evidence that the death of Cecily had anything to do with the murder of Hugh, and two separate enquiries would almost certainly mean he would not solve either in the allotted time.

'No,' said Mabel. 'I will do it.'

Bellême was amused. 'Why do you think you will succeed?'

'Because it is important to me,' replied Mabel simply.

Ten

That evening, no one would talk about anything other than what had happened to Cecily, and Geoffrey found it hard to bring any discussion around to Hugh. In the end, he gave up, and climbed to the battlements of the gatehouse, to look out across the slowly darkening countryside. Josbert followed, ever suspicious of the unwelcome intruder, and watched intently as Geoffrey paced back and forth, so the knight did not know how he would ever manage to send his signal to Roger and Helbye.

There were a number of towers studded along the walls, but the largest was the gatehouse. It was built of Purlborough stone, and had been the first section of the fortress to be upgraded from wood to masonry. The wall to his right led to the massive motte and watchtower, while to the left was a smaller wooden tower placed to give maximum coverage to the archers defending Arundel's main entrance. The gatehouse was three storeys high, plus battlements, with large chambers at each level containing the portcullis mechanism, piles of arrows and hearths for heating any missiles that might be dropped on to the heads of attackers.

Geoffrey leaned on the battlements and gazed at the ground below. It was a long way down, and he recalled Philip telling his aunts about how he had escaped from Winchester by leaping out of a window. A compost heap had softened his fall, but there was no rotting vegetation around the walls at Arundel. Geoffrey did notice, however, that the gatehouse garderobe shaft emptied into a midden almost directly beneath him, and its recent increase in use meant that the waste was not being channelled away as intended by the castle builders.

It had gone from a trench to a heap, and it stank accordingly. Geoffrey moved away, repelled.

He stayed for a long time on the gatehouse roof and Josbert grew restless, as Geoffrey knew he would. Josbert would never admit defeat by leaving him alone, but still chafed at the time he was wasting by making his point. Had Josbert killed Cecily, and wanted to prevent Geoffrey from discovering any evidence to prove his guilt? Geoffrey thought it possible, but did not believe Josbert possessed the imagination to conduct experiments with Greek Fire on his own. He was a good soldier, following Bellême's orders carefully and reliably, but he was not a thinker.

Eventually, Josbert muttered something to one of his captains, who immediately came to stand close to Geoffrey, and left the gatehouse. A few moments later, when Geoffrey was considering leaving himself, Josbert returned with parchments and a lamp. Geoffrey watched in surprise as Josbert began to scan a document.

'You can read?' Literacy was not a skill Geoffrey would have attributed to a man like Josbert, and he wondered whether he had underestimated him in other ways, too.

Josbert turned away from him to indicate that he did not want to talk.

'Did you write this?' asked Geoffrey, reaching for a parchment written in a firm round hand scribed by someone comfortable with pens.

Josbert snatched it from him. 'Leave that alone. It is mine, and not for prying eyes.'

'I only wanted to know whether your talents extended to writing as well as reading,' said Geoffrey, the germ of an idea forming at the back of his mind. 'Or whether you use a scribe.'

'Abbot Ralph scribes for me,' replied Josbert stiffly. 'I do not trust anyone else. I *can* write, but I find it time-consuming and tedious. Now, you will excuse me, because some of us have work to do.'

Geoffrey went back to watching Henry's ever-growing army, trying to assess whether the King might have a weapon that could propel Greek Fire into Arundel's inner bailey.

220

He supposed that such a device would look something like a mangonel, with an A-frame and a throwing arm, and would be easy to spot. But he could see nothing suitable, and supposed that if Henry had fired the weapon, then he had quickly camouflaged the machine he had used. After a while, Geoffrey became aware that he was not the only one assessing Henry's troops: Mabel was similarly engaged, also trying to ascertain whether the King had killed Cecily.

'You think my sister was killed by someone inside Arundel,' she said, coming to stand next to him. It was a statement and not a question. 'You agree with Bellême.'

'I do not know,' said Geoffrey, watching as the fields beyond the castle began to twinkle with a hundred cooking fires. The smoke drifted towards them, tinged with the scent of roasting meat. He glanced at the door that led to the stairs, and saw Josbert still watched him intently.

'But you have your theories,' remarked Mabel. 'Will you share them with me?'

'How well do you know Beaumais?' he asked.

She regarded him silently for a moment. 'Well enough to know that he would not have the courage to kill in broad daylight with half the House of Montgomery-Bellême looking on.'

'But it was a *cowardly* attack,' Geoffrey pointed out. 'Hurling Greek Fire at a young woman is not the act of a hero. Or perhaps it was not aimed at Cecily, but Emma or your mother.'

'Possibly,' admitted Mabel. She regarded him with steady black eyes, and Geoffrey thought they might have been friends, had she not been the wrong sex and fighting for the wrong side. 'I want to solve this wicked deed, Geoffrey, so we will make an agreement. You will tell me anything you learn about Cecily's death, and I shall tell you something to help you now. *I* was at the Crusader's Head when Hugh died. I escaped with my grandmother's bones after the murder. I believe you saw me.'

Geoffrey recalled the two shadowy figures moving with their burden through the back of the crowd. One was large

221

– Mabel – while the other had been smaller. 'Who carried the other end of the box?'

'It is my decision to tell you about my role in the affair, but I cannot make that choice for my companion, too. My sisters were with my mother at the time – in London, not Southwark. Emma took only me that night, because she wanted me to carry the chest. My mother would never tell you this, because she does not want to help you – she still believes you are the killer.'

Geoffrey recalled Sybilla saying that she had been with 'some' of her daughters the night in question, and had not been near the Crusader's Head. Mabel's story indicated she had told the truth.

'But Emma was there. I suppose she was demonstrating her Greek Fire? I smelled it very strongly that night. It has a distinctive odour, and once you have smelt it in battle it is not easy to forget.'

Mabel nodded. 'That is why Emma called the meeting – to show off her progress with the weapon. It was a display aimed to impress not only my uncles, but my grandmother, too.'

Geoffrey regarded her askance. 'Do you think Old Mabel's bones appreciated the display?'

Mabel was unsmiling. 'I have no idea, although I am inclined to believe that mouldering skeletons tend not to appreciate very much. However, although I was there, I did not murder Hugh. He was a halfwit, and I do not kill those unworthy of my military skills.'

'Who else was there?' asked Geoffrey, suspecting that her fine principles would not interfere with her slaying her sister's killer if she ever discovered his – or her – identity.

'Roger and Arnulf were *near* the tavern at *around* the time of Hugh's death, but I do not know where they were the exact moment he was hanged. The same is true for Josbert and Matilda, who were also present. Bellême himself was *not* there – at least, I did not see him. Beaumais was in the stables for part of the time with Emma, but there is no way of telling whether he ventured into the tavern at some point. But I have at least narrowed your list of suspects down a little. You can discount my mother, Haweis, Cecily, Amise and me.'

'Thank you,' said Geoffrey, aware that she was quite capable of lying for reasons of her own. 'But how do you know I will keep my part of the bargain, now you have told me what you know?'

'Honour,' she said simply. 'There are still a few of us who possess some.'

She walked away, leaving Geoffrey staring after her thoughtfully. He stayed for a long time on the battlements, thinking about the events of the day. And Josbert watched him the entire time.

The following day, a Wednesday and Geoffrey's fourth at Arundel, was cloudy and cool, and the overcast morning and the death of Cecily cast a pall of gloom over the castle's inhabitants. Bellême was irascible and aggressive, and broke the jaw of a servant because the man spilled ale he claimed they could not afford to lose. As a consequence, the hall emptied quickly when the meal was over.

Geoffrey was among the first to leave and escaped to the outer bailey, where he saw the portly Abbot Ralph sitting on a water barrel and looking as miserable as Geoffrey felt. Geoffrey went to perch next to him, thinking that the fat churchman was one of the few he had not questioned since his arrival. He did not know why he had been tardy about it, and saw uncomfortably that time was slipping through his fingers more quickly than he realized.

'Do my unblemished hands prove my innocence of Cecily's death in your eyes, as they do in Mabel's?' Ralph asked as Geoffrey made himself comfortable.

'Yes,' said Geoffrey. 'I cannot imagine why you would want her dead.' He did not reveal that he could not say the same about Beaumais, who had been with Ralph at the time of the murder.

'You wonder why I did not rush to see what had happened when she screamed,' said the abbot, regarding Geoffrey with sombre eyes. 'It is because I hate bloodshed. It makes me faint, and I could tell by the tenor of the shrieks that something vile had occurred. Beaumais is the same, he says.'

Geoffrey recalled the acrid scent of vomit later, when they

had discussed Cecily's death in the hall, and supposed Ralph was telling the truth. He decided to reserve judgement about Beaumais, though.

'I did not kill Hugh, either,' added Ralph.

'I know. You were not in London at the time. Your messenger, Petronus, had travelled directly from Shrewsbury with missives from you, which he could not have done had you been elsewhere.'

Ralph smiled and Geoffrey thought his face a pleasant one. 'Not everyone can put two apparently disassociated facts together and draw a logical conclusion. You should have been a scholar.'

'I wish I had,' said Geoffrey ruefully. 'Then I would not be in this situation.'

'What dreadful crime *did* you commit to see you assigned to such a place? A *Jerosolimitanus* is not the kind of man my lord of Shrewsbury usually admits into his service.'

'Then you have not met many Crusaders,' said Geoffrey, who thought that the band of ruthless, greedy killers who had murdered and robbed their way across the civilized world to 'rescue' Jerusalem from the infidel represented exactly the kind of person Bellême would recruit.

'All *Jerosolimitani* have God's thanks,' said Ralph fervently. 'No matter what happens to you here, you can be certain of a place in Heaven when your time comes. It must be a comforting thought.'

'I hope God and His angels are a little more discerning than that,' said Geoffrey, thinking that if there was any justice, then very few Crusaders could expect to see the pearly gates. He was also not ready to find out, and intended to live longer than a few more days. He changed the subject. 'Beaumais says you sent a map with Petronus, which reveals the location of Old Mabel's head.'

'I know he thinks that,' said Ralph softly. 'But it is not true. I do not approve of witchcraft, and would never help Emma bring her mother back. Mabel is in Hell, and we do not want those sort of creatures prowling the Earth and interfering in human affairs.'

'Do you believe Emma will succeed?'

'Not if God is watching,' replied Ralph. 'But the map has nothing to do with me. You must remember, however, that Petronus travelled from Shrewsbury, which is under Bellême's control. *I* did not send this chart, but Petronus might have secured it from another loyal subject and carried it south.'

'Do you think he took it willingly, knowing what it was and what it could mean?'

'He was an intelligent man. He probably anticipated being promoted within the abbey for his pains.'

'But how could he have discovered it in Shrewsbury, of all places?' Geoffrey was unconvinced.

'Shrewsbury is the heart of Bellême's English domains. It is possible that the map was sent there because it was seen as the safest place for it. You may not like Bellême, but there are plenty of others who would do anything to please him and share his fortunes.'

'His fortunes do not look promising at the moment,' Geoffrey pointed out wryly. 'Petronus should have given the map to the King instead.'

'Perhaps he intended to, but now he is dead we shall never know.' Ralph regarded Geoffrey keenly. 'You should not be here. A man who thinks has no place in Bellême's household.'

'You do not seem to be his kind of man, either.'

'I am supposed to be in Shrewsbury on abbey business,' said Ralph ruefully. 'But Bellême summoned me to Winchester to help him answer the charges brought by the King – I have some training in the law, you see. But it was obvious there was no defence to those accusations, and the King was merely playing games with him. I tried to ride for Shrewsbury when we left the Court, but Bellême insisted I come here and I had no choice but to obey. I deplore my own cowardice, but I did not want to end up slaughtered, like that landlord.'

'You mean Oswin of the Crusader's Head?' asked Geoffrey.

'No, the landlord in Winchester. Bellême said he did not like the fact that the man was relieved to see him go. Therein lies a warning to us all.'

Geoffrey was disgusted, recalling the poor fellow Bellême

had terrorized the night before their flight to Arundel. Ralph seemed to share his repugnance, and they sat in silence for a while.

'I do not know why the Earl is so keen to discover Hugh's killer,' said Geoffrey eventually. 'He slaughters people because he feels like it, so why should he care about Hugh?'

'I have done business for Bellême in Southwark before,' said Ralph absently, so Geoffrey did not know whether he was working towards an answer or simply reminiscing. 'I knew Oswin, and he confided in me, although I tried to discourage him from doing so – the less said about what went on under that roof, the better. But he dictated a letter before he died, telling me what had transpired the night of Hugh's murder. He knew he would not live long, and wanted someone to know the truth.'

'The truth?' asked Geoffrey hopefully. 'What did he say?'

'I had already been summoned to Winchester, but the messenger intercepted me *en route*. Oswin said he was sure *you* were innocent of any part in Hugh's death. He also said there was a meeting of the Bellême clan that evening, to witness Emma's progress with her weapon, and listed those present in the inn or its outbuildings: Roger, Arnulf, Beaumais, Emma, Matilda, Mabel and Josbert. Bellême declined to enter the tavern, but Oswin saw him outside in the shadows.'

'Bellême was there?' asked Geoffrey. Mabel had told him he was not – or rather, that she had not seen him, which, Geoffrey realized, were not one and the same. Then he remembered that Bellême had told Geoffrey he had seen Hugh's body and the place where he had died, and had agreed that the young man's killer had to have been *inside* the Crusader's Head, not outside. Of course Bellême had been there – to witness the Greek Fire, if for no other reason.

Ralph nodded. 'That is why I fear you will never solve the case – or not in a way that will free you. Oswin said they all came and went on mysterious errands several times that day.'

'Did he believe these errands were private or family business?' asked Geoffrey despondently, thinking that as soon as he was getting somewhere with his elimination of suspects, someone like Ralph came along and muddied the waters all over again.

'He did not say.'

Geoffrey considered what had happened just before Hugh had died. The window had been open, and he would have heard a fight or an argument had a stranger entered Hugh's room. There was also Oswin's claim that Hugh had ordered wine for three before he had died, and no one bought wine for uninvited strangers. Therefore, Geoffrey was able to conclude that Hugh knew his killer or killers. What next? There had been a yell, and Hugh had been tipped out of the window to die of a broken neck. He had howled, but how had he shouted with a mouth full of parchment?

'Did Oswin's letter say anything else?' asked Geoffrey, a little desperately.

'Only that the family was in factions, and brothers spied on sisters because Bellême was afraid one was trying to make peace with King Henry. Nothing you do not already know.'

'Oswin was right,' said Geoffrey. 'The sisters *were* trying to negotiate. When they received no reply, Emma attempted that ill-fated business with the archer and her smoking potions at Winchester.'

'I doubt the sisters actually contacted the King,' said Ralph, after considering the matter for some time. 'Henry always uses considerable finesse in his dealings with difficult magnates, and he would have listened if any Bellême had appealed to him. He might not have agreed to their terms, but he would have heard what they had to say.'

Henry had said as much, too, Geoffrey recalled. Was it true? Was Hugh's death exactly as it appeared: Matilda had chosen him to be her messenger but the letter had gone undelivered and another person had written a reply, pretending to be from the King? Were the suspects for Hugh's murder just the male members of the family, because it was in their interests not to allow a treaty with the women, which would weaken their House?

But why kill Hugh, and not Matilda herself, to ensure she did not do it again? If Bellême did not care about dispatching a nephew, then he would not balk at slaying a sister. Or

227

would he? Perhaps the spectre of his mother, on the verge of returning from her grave, was enough to keep his murderous fingers from his rebellious siblings' throats.

Geoffrey rubbed his head tiredly. How could Bellême be the killer? He would not have charged Geoffrey to uncover the culprit, if he were the one responsible. But Geoffrey knew Bellême was a complex man, who might well enjoy seeing someone struggle to solve a murder for which he was responsible. It would afford him great amusement to watch how Geoffrey would proceed once he had the knowledge, especially during a siege, when there was nothing to do and the hours hung heavily.

'You will find your culprit is one of Hugh's uncles or aunts,' concluded Ralph soberly. 'But Bellême will never allow you to reveal which.'

'Especially if it is him,' said Geoffrey, feeling that his situation was more bleak than ever.

Another day passed, and Geoffrey was able to discover nothing more about Hugh. He questioned virtually everyone in the castle, even those who had not been in Southwark that night, but no one gave him more information. Haweis and Amise refused to talk to him at all, unless it was to remind him of how much time he had left to live, while Bellême himself said he was too busy to answer questions.

Roger was equally unhelpful, while Josbert admitted he was in the Crusader's Head when Hugh was killed, but said he would challenge Geoffrey to a duel if he spoke to him about the matter again. Geoffrey decided to accept the challenge soon, because it was a more noble end than hanging – and he might even win. Only Arnulf was prepared to talk. He confessed he had been in Southwark with both brothers, saying they all wanted to see for themselves the progress Emma had made with Greek Fire, and acknowledged that he had wandered off alone as the afternoon had progressed, but claimed he knew nothing about why Hugh was killed. The only thing he added that Geoffrey had not known was that Philip, the King's hostage, was there, too.

Geoffrey went to speak to Philip, who was as blunderingly clumsy around his uncle as he was with the King. Bellême

228

made it clear that he had little time for the man, although his aunts and female cousins seemed to tolerate him well enough. Matilda was especially fond of him, and always sprang to his defence when Bellême turned on him for some paltry or contrived reason.

'You were in Southwark the night Hugh died,' said Geoffrey, when he eventually cornered Philip alone. The squire looked ready to run away, so Geoffrey held his arm. 'What were you doing there?'

'I was invited,' squeaked Philip in alarm. 'Bellême said I might be useful.'

'Doing what?'

'Something for the family.' Philip jutted out his chin defiantly. Tears glittered in his eyes, and Geoffrey felt sorry for him. He had lived so long in Henry's court that the family no longer trusted him, and his own bumbling inefficiency made matters worse. Poor Philip belonged nowhere, but was desperate to be accepted.

'What?' pressed Geoffrey. 'Delivering messages? Keeping watch? Fetching and carrying?'

'Carrying,' said Philip in a whisper. 'No one else was brave enough to do it, but I was.'

'Carrying what?' asked Geoffrey, trying to understand what the lad was saying. 'Were you spiriting Greek Fire away from the tavern after Hugh was killed?' He thought about what he had seen with his own eyes. 'No, not Greek Fire. I do not think Emma owns much of that, and she would probably prefer to carry it herself. You took care of something many believe to be truly dangerous.'

Some of Philip's confidence returned, and he held his head a little higher. 'Something dangerous and irreplaceable. Emma trusted *me*.'

'Your grandmother's bones,' said Geoffrey in satisfaction. 'I saw two people moving them on several occasions, but I certainly recall them on the night of Hugh's death. I saw you.' And Mabel had been the other, he thought. Philip had probably been helping Josbert the time Geoffrey had seen them near St Paul's Cathedral, and perhaps at All Hallows Barking, too.

'I will not tell you the identity of my companion,' said Philip, in the kind of voice that indicated he might, if sufficiently bullied. 'Leave me alone. I do not want to die next to you at the end of a rope.'

'Did you deliver messages to the King for your aunts?' asked Geoffrey.

'I offered, since I was in a position to get near His Majesty, but they said it was too dangerous. They trusted Hugh more.'

'Why was that?' asked Geoffrey. 'I have been told he was short of wits.'

'That was why everyone liked him,' said Philip, a little bitterly. 'When you are obviously stupid, people give you more freedom. It is only us intelligent men who find our movements restricted.'

'I see,' said Geoffrey. He wondered whether the lad might be jesting, but his expression was quite serious, and he supposed Philip really did see himself as some kind of intellectual. However, Geoffrey was sure he did not have the wits to kill Hugh and get away with it, so he joined Ralph and Sybilla on Geoffrey's list of eliminated suspects. He released the agitated young man and looked for someone else to question. He saw Beaumais, and sauntered towards him.

Geoffrey felt he still did not have Beaumais's measure, no matter how much time he spent with him. The siege seemed to suit Beaumais, because he was lively and invigorated. He watched people disintegrate in the claustrophobic situation with apparent relish, and seemed to gather strength from their decline. He was always well groomed, with his hair slicked into its immaculate bob, although Geoffrey noticed that others had already become careless over appearances, something he considered as an early sign of a deteriorating morale. He studied Beaumais's locks, intrigued by their shininess.

'Olive oil,' explained Beaumais, primping with some pride. 'It is a marvellous substance, and makes the hair glisten in a manner that ladies find very attractive.'

'Really?' asked Geoffrey uncertainly. 'Do you not find it makes you smell of cooking?'

'I have become used to its odour, and Emma tells me it is seductive.'

'Does she know you have been raiding her supplies?' asked Geoffrey. She would not be pleased when she learned that one of her ingredients for Greek Fire was being squandered in such a fashion.

'I do not use hers,' said Beaumais haughtily. 'I have my own.'

Geoffrey stared at him, remembering the meeting of Emma and someone in a cloak in All Hallows Church, when olive oil had been supplied. So, he thought, her companion must have been Beaumais after all. Beaumais provided Emma with oil, but kept a little back for his personal use. He happened to glance at the man's hands while his attention was caught by a sudden fight between two chickens. They were marked with black streaks, and burned. Beaumais had, without question, tampered with Greek Fire.

On the sixth and last full day, while leaning over the gatehouse's battlements, Geoffrey saw two figures in the distance whom he recognized as Roger and Helbye. They cheered him enormously, although he still had not managed to send them his signal. He knew what he needed to say: the best place for a frontal assault was the gatehouse, because its ramparts were less steep than those leading to the other entrances, while the little postern door – the third along – was the least well defended. All he needed to do was to flash his lamp once, then three times, and he would have had the satisfaction of knowing he had passed damaging information about Bellême to the King. However, waving a lantern from the battlements was not easy, because all the towers were heavily guarded. Geoffrey had made several attempts and had been thwarted each time.

As he stared towards the besiegers' camp, he could hear carpenters sawing and hammering on the war machines that would eventually be used against Arundel. The noise went on day and night, and even in the darkness blacksmiths' furnaces glowed, indicating the King meant business. The racket alone was having an impact on the defenders. Bellême skulked with a face like thunder, and killed a servant for running up some stairs when he happened to be coming down them. Then he ordered the body flung at the besiegers, although Geoffrey was not sure what he hoped to achieve, other than making the tactical error of informing Henry that there were serious problems brewing within.

The same day Emma stood on the gatehouse roof with her hands over her ears and screamed, which resulted in a lot of jeering from the besiegers. They were gratified to know that even a few days of noise could unnerve the castle's occupants, and Josbert was not pleased that she proved their strategy was working in so spectacular a fashion. He dashed to the tower to drag her away himself. Meanwhile, Sybilla was distraught with grief for Cecily, and Matilda was irritable and uncommunicative. Amise tried three more times to catch Geoffrey unawares with her dagger, and he was obliged to threaten to scar her other cheek if she did not desist. Roger and Arnulf demonstrated that they could be just as brutal as their older brother in their treatment of the servants, and Geoffrey was not surprised the family had so few real friends and supporters.

Later, Geoffrey was lying in his spot behind the stables, trying to make sense of the mass of facts and details he had accumulated over the last six days, when he heard yelling. He joined the people running to the hall to see what had happened. Beaumais jogged next to him, having emerged from a barn. Moments later Matilda followed. The straw clinging to their clothes and hair, especially to Beaumais's sticky locks, suggested they had been engaging in more than a casual conversation.

Geoffrey stood on a plinth at the base of a pillar, so he could see over the heads of the people in front. A body lay on the floor, and there was a knife sticking out of it. Geoffrey saw it was Haweis, Sybilla's prettiest daughter. Sybilla knelt over her child, wailing, while Matilda, Mabel and Amise gazed at the body with eyes that bespoke abject shock. After Cecily's death, all three daughters had reverted to wearing their armour, although it had not saved Haweis: Geoffrey saw her attacker had slipped his blade into the vulnerable point underneath her arm. He waited to see what would happen,

232

and was alarmed, but not particularly surprised, when he heard his name spoken.

'Geoffrey did it,' declared Amise. 'He has hated us since we defeated him in that London church.'

'No,' said Mabel quietly. 'He would not have killed her unless she attacked him first.'

'Perhaps she did,' suggested Amise spitefully. 'None of us want him here – the killer of Hugh and the creature of King Henry.'

'He is not Henry's creature,' said Matilda bitterly. She gazed at him challengingly, virtually telling anyone watching that he might have done more for her if he was better able to secure the King's ear.

Bellême strode forward and bellowed Geoffrey's name in a voice that stilled every mutter and shuffle. He was angry, and no one wanted to catch his attention when his temper was up. Some folk, wiser than others, slipped out while they could, preferring to learn what had happened later than to be near the unpredictable Earl. With a sigh, Geoffrey jumped from his plinth and walked to the front of the hall. Bellême had his dagger drawn, and he pointed it at Haweis when he addressed the knight.

'Did you do this?'

'No,' said Geoffrey, thinking there was little else he could say. He did not think that telling the Earl he had been thinking behind the stables all afternoon would do him much good.

'Liar!' shrieked Amise. 'We left her alone for a moment, and it was the opportunity you have been waiting for. It is *your* dagger sticking out of her.'

'Mine is here,' said Geoffrey, pulling it from his belt.

'You stole one, then,' snarled Amise. 'Who is without his dagger?' She gazed around the gathered throng, although only a fool would have admitted that the murder weapon was his, stolen or not.

'I will kill you myself,' said Sybilla, snatching the knife from Bellême, wielding it in a way that suggested she had probably secured some knightly training herself. 'First you maim Amise, then you burn Cecily and now you stab Haweis.'

233

'He killed no one,' said Abbot Ralph, bravely interposing himself between the furious woman and Geoffrey. 'He has been with me all day, so he cannot be your culprit.'

'Are you sure?' asked Bellême in the kind of voice that indicated *he* was not.

Ralph nodded. 'He has been helping me with letters explaining why I have not returned to Shrewsbury. You must look elsewhere for your villain.'

Bellême took the weapon from Sybilla. 'I said your daughters were *not* to wear mail in my castle. You know I do not like it. It is perverted.'

'They need to defend themselves,' flashed Sybilla, angry with her brother for the first time since Geoffrey had known her. 'There are hostile troops all around us, and I do not want them exposed to stray arrows – or stray Greek Fire.' She glowered at Geoffrey again.

'Her armour did not save her from a dagger,' Bellême pointed out unpleasantly. 'What was she doing here anyway? The hall is used as a dormitory for the night watch at this time of day, and she should not have been here.'

'She was assisting me,' said Emma, softly. She stood in the shadows to one side and emerged to stand beside Sybilla.

'Really?' snarled Bellême. 'Doing what? Sending messages to the King, to tell him how to destroy my defences and take my castle?'

'Of course not!' cried Sybilla, appalled. 'You should know us better than that. My daughters have been gathering herbs for Emma to help *defend* us against Henry.'

'Witchcraft!' sneered Bellême in disgust. 'But never mind that. Who killed Haweis? Abbot Ralph says it was not Geoffrey, so you must invent another suspect.'

'I do not know,' said Amise in a low voice. 'But when I find out, I shall kill him myself.'

'Yes, yes,' said Bellême dismissively. 'You women are very interested in killing, but it has brought you nothing but pain. You should leave the slaughter to us men and concentrate on feminine virtues.'

'Such as what?' demanded Sybilla, unusually sharp with

her favourite brother. 'Making marriages with men who desert us? Haweis was to have wed your faithful servant Pantulf, and now look at her.'

At the sight of her dead daughter, she started to weep again. Mabel went to stand next to her, offering comfort in the form of a reassuring presence, while Matilda tried to quell the shuddering sobs with a hug. Emma stood with her hands in her sleeves, aloof from the squabble.

'I mean virtues like counting the family gold and ridding our homes of rodents,' said Bellême, who seemed to have as odd an idea of feminine virtues as his sister.

'I do not know who killed her,' said Mabel, regarding the body of her sister with quiet affection. 'The hall was deserted when we left her, because the night watch had not arrived. Anyone who saw us enter might be responsible.'

'We went upstairs to deliver the herbs to Emma,' said Amise, glowering at Geoffrey in a way that suggested she still regarded him as guilty, whether he had a priestly alibi or not. 'She was not there, so we left them and came back to the hall immediately. Haweis was only alone for a moment.'

'I was on the roof,' said Emma, looking hard and long at Beaumais and Matilda, so that Geoffrey suspected her attention had been glued to the barn when the murder had occurred. She had watched her sister enjoying the company of the man who professed to be her own lover. Geoffrey rubbed his eyes, and wondered why people insisted on creating such complex problems for themselves with their infidelities and betrayals. It was so much simpler to be loyal.

'Why did you leave Haweis here at all?' asked Bellême. 'Why not take her upstairs with you?'

'She twisted her ankle,' said Amise, casting a venomous glower at Bellême. 'We have been obliged to wear "maidenly" shoes that do not fit, and she fell over. She waited here because stairs hurt her.'

'It is true,' said Mabel. 'The shoes that went with the dresses were impractical for a castle under siege, so I continued to wear my mail boots. Haweis did not and took a tumble.'

'Josbert!' roared Bellême, suddenly bored with the whole

affair. 'Bury her in a place where she will not leak and poison our water, and let us be done with the matter.'

'I will do it,' said Emma with dignity. 'She was a good girl, and deserves more than to be tossed into a shallow hole. I shall ensure she has a decent burial.'

'As you please,' said Bellême, indicating he thought it of small importance. He turned to Josbert. 'But woman or not, she was a Bellême, and I want to know who killed her. Find out, then hang him.'

Josbert started to object that he was too busy, but Bellême was already striding out of the hall, scattering people before him like leaves in the wind. He either did not hear or did not care what Josbert thought of the commission, and the castellan gazed down at the dead Haweis with a face as black as thunder, as though it was her fault that he had been given such an unreasonable task. Then his eyes lit on Sybilla, and his expression softened.

'You should lie down,' he said, gruffly kind. 'I will bring you some wine.'

'She does not need wine,' snapped Amise. 'She needs justice – to see a murderer hang.'

'Tell me who is the culprit, then,' suggested Josbert. 'You must have some idea. And do not tell me it was Geoffrey when the priest has exonerated him.'

'We do not know,' sobbed Sybilla. 'This is what happens when you trust people outside the family. It was Beaumais's idea to break the siege by witchcraft and now look what has happened!'

'*I* did not kill Haweis,' said Beaumais, startled. 'I have been with Matilda . . . discussing goats . . .'

Matilda nodded agreement, not looking at Emma, while Geoffrey tried to hide his amusement at the bizarre choice of subjects. Beaumais had said the first thing that came into his mind. Emma glared angrily at her sister, but still managed to smile at Beaumais. Geoffrey wondered whether she was prepared to blame Matilda. He knew people could be blind where love was concerned.

'Beaumais is right to place his faith in witchcraft,' said Emma softly. 'There are only two things that can save us

236

now: Greek Fire and our mother coming to the battle lines. But neither will happen if we stand around chattering. Come, my sisters, and let us continue this vital work.'

'God help us!' muttered Matilda to Geoffrey as she prepared to follow Emma to the upper chamber they used for sleeping and plotting. 'Arundel is dangerous even for Bellêmes now. It is not just you who needs to watch out for daggers in his back.'

'Emma knows exactly what Beaumais was just doing,' warned Geoffrey, glancing to where Emma paused at the bottom of the spiral staircase to wait for her sister. 'You should be careful.'

'I am always careful,' said Matilda with her enigmatic smile.

'Do *you* know why Haweis was killed?' asked Geoffrey. 'Was it because she was helping Emma, and someone disapproves so strongly of witchcraft that he will do anything to thwart her?'

'Or perhaps Haweis was trying to smuggle messages to Henry without the rest of us knowing.'

'You tried as much using Hugh.'

'But I was trying to save *all* us women, not just myself.' Matilda's expression was unreadable. 'However, I have sent no messages since we arrived here.'

Emma gave an impatient sigh, so Matilda abandoned Geoffrey to follow her sister upstairs.

'You saved my life,' said Geoffrey to Ralph when the others had gone. 'Sybilla would have attacked me if you had not stepped forward. And you took a risk, because I have not seen you at all today.'

'But I saw you,' said Ralph. 'I know you are innocent, and God will overlook my lie under the circumstances. But stay away from this business, my friend. The family is beginning to fall apart in great jagged pieces, and they will slash anyone who comes too close.'

As the sun set at the end of Geoffrey's last evening, Amise came to gloat. He was on the roof of the gatehouse, watching the sun sink in a blaze of orange and red, and wracking his

237

brains for a solution to Hugh's murder. There were plenty of guards nearby, but a stiff breeze blew and they were trying to keep to the leeward side for warmth. For a short while, Geoffrey was alone, but he knew it would not last and that by the time he had grabbed a torch to send his message the opportunity would have passed. It was still too light to signal, anyway, and there was no point in forfeiting his final few hours to contact Roger at a time when the big knight was unlikely to be looking. Even as the thought went through his mind, more guards came on duty and his solitude was over.

It had been a pretty day, with only the merest wisps of cloud visible. The sun caught in the nearby River Arun, turning it into a scarlet snake that wound through the fields surrounding the castle and away to the woods in the distance. It lit the King's banners, and for a while the incessant hammering stopped as workmen went to eat their evening meal. It would start again as soon as they finished, but for the moment it was peaceful. Geoffrey breathed deeply, savouring the scent of new-sown crops and wood smoke from the camp fires, and wondered why he never appreciated beauty until he thought he was about to see it for the last time.

'Enjoy it,' came Amise's voice at his elbow. 'It will be the last sunset you will see. My uncle plans to hang you at dawn tomorrow, because he knows you are no closer to finding Hugh's killer now than you were at the beginning of the week.'

'Oh,' said Geoffrey, turning to face her. 'I thought he might have forgotten about it.'

She sneered. 'I have reminded him of his promise every day – to give me the honour of killing you. I think I shall hang you here, because it is the tower closest to the King. He will see what happens to men who anger the House of Montgomery-Bellême.'

'Go away, Amise,' said Geoffrey. 'If this is to be my last night, then you are not the person I choose to spend it with.'

'I shall stay if I please.' He started to leave, but she blocked his way. 'This time tomorrow you will be hanging from the battlements.'

'Show me,' said Geoffrey.

She regarded him uncertainly. 'What?'

'Show me,' repeated Geoffrey. 'I want to see the place you have chosen. I might not like it.'

She eyed him uneasily. 'You want me to show you the place where I will kill you?'

Geoffrey nodded, thinking she was remarkably slow in the wits. 'In an hour.'

'Why then? Why not now?'

'Because I do not want to see it now. It is my final evening, and I intend to do what I like.'

He pushed past her and ran down the spiral steps, glad to be away from her irritating presence; he had seldom met anyone who harboured such grudges. But he was pleased with himself, because Amise had given him an idea, and all he had to do was wait until it was dark. He went to his hiding place near the stables, wriggled into a comfortable position and closed his eyes, trying yet again to solve the riddle of Hugh's death before his time ran out. His mind wandered, and he found himself contemplating the various romances that had blossomed since the drawbridge had been raised and frightened people had found solace where they could.

First, and most obviously, there was Beaumais and Emma, although Emma was more keen than Beaumais, who was inclined to rove. Matilda also grew lonely very quickly, and she had twice offered Geoffrey a repeat of their performance at the inn in Southwark. He was tempted, but there were few places they could be guaranteed privacy, and he did not want to be run through on the pretext that he had defiled Bellême's sister. Beaumais obliged her when he thought Emma was otherwise occupied, and a sturdy captain called Foucon stepped forward manfully when Beaumais thought she was not.

Not to be outdone by her frolicking sisters, Sybilla had recruited a paramour, too. She selected Josbert, although Geoffrey could not imagine why, other than the fact that there was not much choice once Beaumais and Foucon had been taken. Bellême's soldiers were an unkempt, unruly horde to whom no self-respecting lady would give a second glance and, unless Sybilla attempted incest and wooed a brother, there was only the portly Abbot Ralph left.

Geoffrey dragged his thoughts back to Hugh, and was about to review what he had learned yet again, when he heard voices in the stables. Bellême had recently declared these off limits, on the grounds that someone might kill a horse for meat. He claimed he might need all his steeds for engaging Henry in battle, although few believed him; they all knew he wanted them well-fed in case he felt like escaping.

Geoffrey was intrigued by the low voices emanating from a forbidden place, and cocked his head in an attempt to hear what was being said. However, although he could make out words, he could not recognize voices, because they were whispering.

'Robert is beginning to think that I am the traitor,' one was saying.

'He cannot act without proof,' said the second.

'Do not speak drivel!' snapped the first. 'My brother does not need proof before he acts! He is not a monk or a lawyer! Did the King need "proof" when he invented those charges against us?'

'No, but—'

'Then do not blather about matters you know nothing about. You are worse than your father. No wonder he died so soon on the Crusade.'

The second voice was Philip's, Geoffrey surmised. And the other must be either Roger or Arnulf, given that he referred to Bellême as his brother. But which? Geoffrey stood, intending to watch them when they left. It would be useful to know who believed he might be accused of treachery, because it could imply a guilty conscience. Geoffrey moved stealthily in the dusk, but stopped abruptly when he saw he was not the only one listening to the discussion. Someone in a dark cloak was standing outside the stable door, straining forward in an attempt to hear. Geoffrey could see nothing of his face, but found his attention caught by a long pale hair that adhered to the back of his cloak.

Then everything happened very quickly. Philip and his uncle emerged from the stables and the man in the cloak darted to one side. Geoffrey could not tell whether he had hidden or had moved to confront them. Geoffrey heard a dagger whipped from a sheath, so he pressed back into the shadows, not wanting to become involved. The sound of a body hitting the ground was followed by running footsteps. When they had receded, he eased from his hiding place and peered around the corner. Someone was lying on the floor, and he thought he glimpsed someone disappear around the far end of the stables. Geoffrey slipped away, hoping he had not been seen. He did not think that being found near a corpse would do his cause any good, and he decided that someone else could raise the alarm.

Geoffrey was concerned that the glorious day might mean a later dusk than usual, and that Roger might not be watching for a signal on the grounds that it was still too light. So, once the knight had ascended the tower with Amise at his heels, he knew he would have to prolong their discussion, to make sure the light had faded sufficiently. It was not something he wanted to do, given the probable topic of conversation, but he could think of no other way and did not think she would agree to another delay. It was not pleasant listening to her describe what she planned to do to him, although it came as no surprise to learn that she intended to make the experience last as long as possible.

'I have tested my plan with Roger since we last met,' she said, pleased with herself. 'He was more than happy to spend an hour helping me prepare.'

'I am sure he was,' said Geoffrey, thinking that organizing a hanging would probably be exactly the dour Roger's idea of a good time.

'We are all looking forward to tomorrow,' she went on. 'My mother and Emma. My uncles Robert, Arnulf and Roger. Beaumais, Josbert and Philip, although Philip is a pathetic specimen and says violence distresses him.' She issued a snort of disgust. 'Did you know the King wanted to make him into a knight – to succeed where others failed? The task is almost as impossible as converting your womanly squire into a soldier.'

Geoffrey agreed.

'Matilda says your death is a waste of a good man,' Amise went on. 'She says there are too few of you here, but I think she refers to your abilities in the bedchamber rather than your integrity. Mabel agrees with her, although *she* knows nothing about bedding men. She is more likely to bed a woman.'

'Mabel is the only decent one among you,' said Geoffrey, hoping to annoy her into blathering a little longer. It was almost dark enough to send his first signal.

'She is becoming addled,' said Amise shortly. 'But I am not here to discuss the wits of my sister. I came to show you how you will die.' She leaned down to point out a specific piece of masonry, to which she intended to secure one end of the rope.

'I cannot see,' said Geoffrey. It was dark enough now for Roger to be watching, and if he was not, then Henry would have to find his own weaknesses to probe. 'We need a lamp.'

'*I* can see,' she said accusingly.

'Well, I cannot,' he said, pretending to squint. 'Fetch a lamp or I shall leave.'

She sighed and snapped her fingers at the guards, who regarded each other uneasily and declined to obey until she took several steps towards them. Captain Foucon – Matilda's soldier-lover – shook his head in disapproval, but did what she asked, thrusting the lamp into her hands and making it clear he was watching her very carefully. He was wise enough to know that unguarded flames and a wooden roof in a besieged castle were not happy bedfellows.

The gatehouse's battlements comprised upright sections that were taller than a man's head, which afforded an archer protection while he fired at invaders, and knee-high spaces – gaps – between them through which he could shoot. Insofar as the signal was concerned, Geoffrey's task was to make Amise walk across one of the gaps once, leave a short interval of time, and then cross three times in quick succession. If he could make her repeat the operation, then he could be certain that Roger had received the correct message.

'Now,' he said, shielding the lamp with his body, so the light would not be seen by anyone watching from Henry's camp. 'Tell me again.'

He moved back to expose the lamp and, obligingly, she

242

carried it across the gap. That was the first part of his signal completed. She pointed to the stone, and he went to join her. He took the lamp from her, ready to start the second part.

'This one would be better,' he said, crossing the gap to inspect another stone. One. He immediately trotted back and looked at the one she had selected. Two. 'No, I think you are right. Although . . .' He made his way back again, still holding the lamp. Three. It was done.

'You are wrong,' she said angrily, grabbing at the lamp and starting to walk back to her own stone. Geoffrey held on to it, not wanting a fourth blaze to occur too soon and confuse Roger.

'Look,' he said, pointing at nothing. She bent her head and studied the parapet for some time before shaking her head in irritation, snatching the lamp and marching back across the gap again. It had been long enough, and Geoffrey was now on his second set of signals. She had just made the first flash.

'Here!' she said, pointing with a jabbing finger.

Geoffrey retrieved the lamp, readying himself for the next three. 'You are wrong. This one is better.' He crossed again. One. But Foucon was becoming suspicious and Geoffrey knew he did not have much time before the soldier stopped him. 'Let me see.' He crossed again. Two.

'Hey!' shouted Foucon in anger when he realized Geoffrey's peculiar behaviour had a very distinct pattern. 'He is signalling to the King! Grab him.'

Geoffrey dodged him and darted across the gap to make his final flash, just as Foucon powered into him hard enough to drive the breath from his body. The lamp flew from his fingers, and spilled oil immediately set the top of the tower alight. Soldiers rushed to stamp it out, and it was all over in a moment. Geoffrey had succeeded in sending two complete signals, and all he could hope now was that Roger would remember what they meant and pass the correct information to the King. His sister would be protected from Welsh raids, and Geoffrey could die safe in the knowledge that he had done all he could to ensure her protection.

Foucon was furious that a signal had been made on his watch, and Geoffrey thought that he might hurl him over the battlements there and then. But Foucon knew better than to deprive Bellême of his morning sport, and settled for shoving Geoffrey roughly down the spiral stairs, across the bailey and into the wooden hall. He gathered several soldiers to help him *en route*, and Geoffrey wondered what the man expected him to do in a castle surrounded by battalions of mercenaries.

He did not care that he had been discovered, because he was enormously satisfied at having used Amise to betray the castle and outwitted his captors at the same time. Meanwhile, Amise trailed at his side screaming all manner of threats and insults. Geoffrey knew he could incense her further by ignoring her, which he did with pleasure. Since he was due to be hanged the following day he felt he had nothing to lose by incautious and offensive behaviour now.

By the time they reached the hall, Foucon had Geoffrey surrounded by at least a dozen guards, and they made a lot of noise as they entered. Bellême was trimming his fingernails with a dagger, slouched in a chair on the dais. He did not look pleased when Foucon bundled Geoffrey in front of him and jabbered his accusations. He sighed, and fixed the captain with a glower that silenced him as immediately and effectively as if a bucket of water had been thrown at him.

'Well?' Bellême asked Geoffrey. 'Have you used my torches and my niece to signal to Henry?'

'Ask Amise,' said Geoffrey. 'She was the one who waved the lamp all over the place, not me.' He was pleased to see Amise blanch when her uncle's beady gaze settled on her.

'No!' she cried. 'I was showing him the place where I intend to tie my rope tomorrow. There were no messages.'

'Foucon says there were,' said Bellême.

'Foucon is a fool,' she replied angrily. 'I was just showing Geoffrey—'

'The ropes. Yes, I heard the first time.' Bellême scowled at the captain. 'You have allowed your imagination to run wild. Why would he signal to Henry, when Henry is no more his friend than I am? What would he tell him anyway? "I will die tomorrow so make sure you are awake early"?'

'He was signalling,' persisted Foucon stubbornly. 'He made sure the lamp moved back and forth in a regular pattern. And then he almost set the tower alight when I tried to stop him.'

'Now, that *is* serious,' said Bellême, uncoiling himself from the chair. 'A fire would finish us for certain. But there is not much harm Geoffrey can do tonight. Stay with him until tomorrow, when we will be free of his threat. Send these men back to their posts.'

Geoffrey was not surprised to learn that Bellême had already assumed he had failed in his quest to identify Hugh's killer, although he thought he might have at least asked. Abbot Ralph had been right: it did not matter whether he solved the mystery, because Bellême was going to hang him regardless.

'You want *me* to look after him?' asked Foucon, regarding Geoffrey uneasily. 'On my own?'

'You heard,' snapped Bellême. 'God knows, you gambol in the barn with Matilda readily enough, and she is far more dangerous than poor Geoffrey Mappestone. Take his sword, if he is too much for you. Have you seen Philip? I sent for the lazy boy an hour ago.'

'Not since this morning,' said Foucon. He glanced nervously at Geoffrey. 'I do not—'

'Philip wants me to trust him, yet he cannot obey my simplest commands,' said Bellême angrily. 'Send someone to hunt him out, or I shall hang *him* tomorrow, too.' He glowered at the hapless Foucon. 'Why are you still here?'

'I thought—'

'Are my orders not clear?' snarled Bellême. 'Do not let Geoffrey out of your sight until dawn – not that there is anywhere for him to run. He should have dashed out of the gate when we first arrived, like his cowardly squire.'

Geoffrey sincerely wished he had.

245

Eleven

A while later, a yell of outrage pierced the air. It was Roger, and he had found the body of the man stabbed earlier that evening. Emma and Sybilla wanted Geoffrey hanged even before the corpse's identity was announced, but Bellême pointed out that he had been with Foucon since dusk, and could hardly have murdered someone with a captain trailing in his wake. Geoffrey was not sure whether Bellême genuinely believed the murder had occurred after he had been put under guard, or whether he already knew the killer was someone else – perhaps someone with his blessing.

Matilda released a howl of anguish when torches were brought and it was discovered that the dead man was Philip. She gathered him in her arms, and Foucon laid a rough hand on her shoulder as a gesture of sympathy. It did nothing to quell her shuddering sobs, and was hastily removed when Bellême indicated with a flick of his head that he was to resume his duties guarding the prisoner. Reluctantly, Foucon returned to Geoffrey, although he clearly longed to be with his woman. Matilda did not notice whether he was there or not, and it took all three brothers to prise her away from Philip.

While the Bellêmes secreted themselves in an upper chamber to discuss the latest murder, Geoffrey borrowed pens and parchment and wrote letters to Joan and Tancred. When he had finished, he stared into the fire, thinking about Hugh, while Foucon watched him. Geoffrey thought it remarkable how impending death sharpened his mind, because he found he was able to see facts far more clearly than before, although they still did not yield the answer he needed.

246

He gave his letters to Ralph, who promised to see them delivered when the siege was over, made a scanty and inadequate confession, and wandered into the inner bailey with Foucon at his heels. Dawn was not far off, because the stars were beginning to fade, and he realized that the night had gone more quickly than he had anticipated, time trickling away like grains of sand through an hourglass.

Arundel's baileys were busy, even at that hour, because the hall was so crowded and noisy with snoring that few slept well. Boredom was a major problem during a siege, and Geoffrey thought Josbert remiss not to have devised activities that took people's minds off the fact that nearby was a hostile army waiting for their blood.

He took a deep breath and gazed at the star-blasted sky, then closed his eyes and listened to the sounds of the night – a child whimpering in a dream, a cat screeching, the clatter of pots from the kitchen by scullions already working, and the low mumble of conversations around the yard as guards and others whiled away the hours of darkness.

Matilda was one of those awake and wandering aimlessly. She gestured that she wanted to talk, but Geoffrey preferred to be alone. Matilda, however, was determined to have her way. She followed him, breaking into a run when the knight walked faster in an attempt to elude her. Foucon did likewise, so that the three of them made for an odd procession in the dark.

'Where are you going?' she demanded breathlessly, snatching Geoffrey's arm to make him stop and ignoring the fact that Foucon was pleased to see her. Her eyes were puffy from crying, but she seemed to have regained control of herself.

'To remove my armour,' said Geoffrey, moved to pity by the signs of her grief and resigned to being polite. 'Since I am to die this morning I have little to fear from daggers. It will be pleasant to spend some time without it.'

'I am sorry things worked out like this. I believed you would solve the riddle and save yourself.'

'Not when no one would talk to me,' said Geoffrey shortly. 'Doubtless your brother knew that when he set me the task, and this is just another example of his idea of fun.'

'You may be right.'

247

She followed him back into the hall, where they found an unoccupied corner and she helped him with the many buckles and clasps that held the mail in place. When it was off, Geoffrey felt light and free, standing in no more than shirt and leggings, almost as though he was naked. Foucon had relieved him of his sword, but had left his dagger, which he tucked into his belt.

'I wish I could have helped you,' said Matilda, watching him fold his surcoat and stuff it under a bench. Abandoning that particular item was a wrench for Geoffrey, because he had worn it since joining the Crusade, and it had seen him through many dangers. 'But I know nothing of any use.'

'I eliminated you from my enquiry earlier in the week,' he said, smiling. 'I do not think you murdered the man you hoped would arrange a meeting with Henry. You had too much to lose from Hugh's death. However, I did catch you out in some lies.'

'I am sure you did,' she replied, smiling wanly. 'Lying is what us Bellêmes are good at, after all, and I confess I gave you different versions of my tale when we met in Southwark and here in Arundel. But you are right: I did not kill Hugh, because I *did* want him to carry messages declaring my desire for a truce. My sisters still believe you killed him, you know. They are quite certain.'

'In that case, we can eliminate them, too,' said Geoffrey. 'They would not continue to believe me to be the culprit, if they had killed Hugh themselves – at least, not to each other. Besides, I know from Mabel that Sybilla was not in Southwark that night, but in London with her other three daughters. Meanwhile, Emma was far too engrossed with Greek Fire and your mother's body. She would not have had time to kill Hugh.'

Matilda nodded. 'She *was* busy that night. My brother is not easily convinced of anything, and she had those two very important projects she wanted him to support. She thought of nothing else.'

'So, we have made progress already. The remaining suspects are Bellême, Arnulf, Josbert and Beaumais – but not Philip, who had escaped from the King to wander in

Southwark the night Hugh died, because I think he and Hugh were killed by the same man.'

Tears welled into her eyes and she looked away. 'Philip could never kill by stealth, no matter how hard he tried to be like the rest of us. But what about Roger? Why is he not on your list? He would not hesitate to kill his own mother if he thought it would benefit him.'

'His mother is already dead,' said Geoffrey wryly. 'But he might have another opportunity to strike at her if Emma's plans come to fruition.'

'Then let us hope they do not,' said Matilda, dabbing her eyes with her sleeve. 'Robert and Sybilla are desperate for Emma to succeed and bring Old Mabel back, but I do not see how she will help us. She was a dangerous lady with her plots and love of poisons. They will not be able to control her, and it is not wise to introduce yet another divisive factor into our family. Roger and Arnulf agree – Roger because he remembers Mabel too well, and Arnulf because he says he does not want to see her without her real head.'

'Perhaps Old Mabel is the killer of Hugh,' suggested Geoffrey facetiously. 'There is something I had not considered before.'

'No,' said Matilda, after a moment of serious thought. 'I saw her that night, and she was no more than bones in a box. Emma had not succeeded in raising her then, and she has not been successful since, despite her claims that the skeleton calls for her to get on with it.' She sighed, and returned to a subject that was more important to her. 'Poor Philip. He was harmless, despite his inflated opinion of his intellect. I planned to take him home with me when all this was over, where he would be safe.'

'You loved him,' said Geoffrey, curious that someone like Philip had secured the affections of a sharp and clever woman like Matilda.

'He was the son of my favourite brother, and I loved him for his sake. Philip the Grammarian and I were close as children.' She took a deep breath, and he saw the topic was painful for her. 'But you still have not explained why Roger is no longer a suspect for Hugh's murder.'

'As I said, whoever killed Hugh also killed Philip. And I know Roger did not kill Philip, because Amise said he was with her on the gatehouse roof at the time. She did not know about Philip's death when she gave Roger the alibi, so I am inclined to believe her. Also, if Roger had been the murderer, he would probably not have been the one to discover the body.'

'But you are still left with Arnulf, Beaumais, Josbert and Robert,' said Matilda. 'Can you not narrow it down further?'

'Why? Do you think your brother will be satisfied if I present him with a shortlist?'

'No,' she said, taking him seriously. 'Especially if he is on it.'

'Him and Arnulf,' said Geoffrey thoughtfully, supposing it must have been Arnulf who had met Philip in the stables. It could not have been Roger, because he had been with Amise. Did this mean Arnulf was the killer? Geoffrey realized it did not, because he had no way of knowing whether Philip was stabbed by Arnulf or the person listening to their secret conversation.

'Speak of the devil and he will appear,' said Matilda softly. 'Here is Arnulf now and Josbert with him. I cannot imagine what Sybilla sees in Josbert. I would sooner couple with a goat.'

Arnulf grinned in a friendly fashion when he approached Geoffrey, a stark contrast to the unsmiling presence behind him, although both regarded Geoffrey's abandoned armour curiously.

'What are you doing?' demanded Arnulf. 'Do you not want to wear it when you die?'

'Would you want soldiers squabbling over *your* corpse to claim it? It is better to leave it here.'

'Can I have your surcoat, then?' asked Arnulf eagerly. 'I have always wanted one of those. My brother Philip promised me his when he came back from the Crusade, but he died at Antioch and that was that. He did not bother to send it to me.'

'Very little was returned to us after his noble death,' said

Matilda bitterly. 'I, too, would have liked something of his to remember him by.'

'Greek Fire,' said Geoffrey. 'He sent the formula for Greek Fire, and probably a pot of it, too, so that Emma could see what it could do. The Bellêmes did not do too badly from his demise.'

In fact, he thought they had done a good deal better from Philip's death than they would have done had he lived, because Geoffrey doubted whether he would have shared his secret weapon with them. He had not been a sharing sort of man, as Geoffrey had discovered when caches of food had been discovered in the remains of his tent after his murder. He thought it a shame that such a miserable specimen should claim a special place in Matilda's heart, but supposed he should not be surprised, given the alternatives presented by her other siblings.

'The surcoat,' prompted Arnulf, not to be side-tracked. 'May I have it?'

'If you like,' said Geoffrey reluctantly. He supposed he would sooner Arnulf had it than Bellême or Josbert. At least Arnulf had been civil to him, unlike most of the castle's inhabitants.

Arnulf grinned in delight and pulled the garment over his head. 'I knew you were a good man. I sensed it the first time we met in Winchester, and I am seldom wrong in my judgements.'

Geoffrey saw Matilda and Josbert exchange the kind of glance that indicated they were less impressed with his evaluating abilities, but they said nothing. He watched Arnulf struggle into his tunic. It was disconcerting to see such a familiar item on someone else, and he did not like it at all. When Arnulf asked for his belt, too, to hold it in place, Geoffrey refused and Foucon fetched him a length of rope instead. Arnulf tied it several times before he was satisfied, tearing off his gloves in his impatience as he did so. Josbert watched with rank disdain, as if he could not imagine why Arnulf would want such an unsavoury object. To take his mind off the fact that a Bellême would now wear the much-loved garment, Geoffrey thought about Hugh.

251

'On the night of Hugh's death, why were you in Southwark?' he asked Josbert.

The castellan scowled. 'I have told you before: it is none of your affair.'

'You were on the King's business. Bellême said there was a traitor in his house, and he was right.'

Josbert sneered. 'Do not accuse *me* of Hugh's death to save your own skin. Bellême knows I was in Southwark that night, and he knows it was not for the King and it was not to kill Hugh.' The fierce expression on his face told Geoffrey he would get no more from him.

'I have changed my mind,' said Geoffrey abruptly to Arnulf. 'If you want my surcoat, then you must buy it. Give me ten silver pennies.'

Arnulf started to laugh. 'But you will be dead in a few hours and there is nowhere to spend your money. Do not be ridiculous, man!'

'Then give it back,' said Geoffrey uncompromisingly.

Arnulf backed away, hands in the air. 'Very well. I have no wish to deny a dying man's request. Give him what he wants, Josbert.'

'Me?' asked Josbert, startled. 'I do not want the filthy object. If you want it, *you* pay him.'

'I cannot reach my pouch with this on,' said Arnulf. 'And I do not want to take it off and put it on like a woman trying on kirtles. Give him the silver, Josbert. You can have it back at dawn.'

Geoffrey had seen that Arnulf's pouch would be difficult to reach: the surcoat was tight, because Geoffrey had less bulk around his middle, and he knew Josbert – who controlled the fortress's purse strings – would be asked to pay. In order to do that, he would have to open his own pouch. When he did so, muttering resentfully as he counted out the coins, Geoffrey made a grab for them and several pieces of parchment fluttered to the ground. He reached them before Josbert and started to read, while Josbert regarded his odd behaviour with open-mouthed astonishment.

'The knowledge contained there is nothing to do with you. It is a list of supplies and how long they will last at the current rate of consumption. You, of all people, should not be worried about starvation.'

'True,' said Geoffrey, handing the parchments back to him.

Josbert slapped the coins into his hand. 'There. Enjoy them while you can, because no miracle is going to save you now.'

He stalked away and Arnulf went with him, swaggering in his new surcoat. Geoffrey was sorry to see it go, and watched wistfully. Matilda turned her black eyes on him, amused.

'Why did you want so much money? Will you swallow a coin in the hope that the rope will not break your neck if there is silver lodged inside it?'

Geoffrey regarded her askance. 'Will it work?'

'I would not think so. It is something Emma said she read once. But why did you demand silver?'

'To discover the identity of Hugh's killer,' said Geoffrey. 'I know who it is at last.'

'Dawn is here,' said Foucon nastily, not liking the way he was ignored by Matilda because Geoffrey was there. He gestured to the window, where the first light paled the eastern sky. 'It does not matter what you have reasoned, because Bellême will not believe you now anyway. He will assume you are making a last-ditch attempt to save your life, and will not take any accusations you make seriously.'

'That is true,' said Matilda in an unsteady voice. 'He will not. Not now.'

Geoffrey did not want to be rounded up like a common criminal and dragged to the gatehouse for his execution, so he saved Bellême the trouble and went there of his own volition. Matilda stood at his side while he gazed over the slowly lightening fields. Henry's campfires, which had burned out during the night, were being rekindled, so men could cook bread on hot stones and perhaps warm a little salted beef to eat. Smoke drifted across the fields like wispy clouds.

'Tell me who killed Hugh and Philip,' she said. She glared at Foucon when he attempted to come closer, so he backed off and went to lean on a turret, out of earshot. 'Perhaps I can persuade my brother to listen, if you have a convincing argument.'

'That is the problem,' said Geoffrey, leaning over the parapet and shivering as the wind cut through his shirt. 'It does not matter *who* killed them. What is important is *why*. And I do not know why.'

'Then *who* will have to do,' said Matilda encouragingly. 'That is what he charged you to discover, after all. He cannot claim it is not enough and kill you anyway.' They exchanged a glance that told each other they knew perfectly well Bellême might do just that. 'So, who was it?'

'Arnulf.'

'Arnulf?' she asked in astonishment. 'But why?'

Geoffrey grimaced. 'That is the point I have just made. I do not know why, only that he is the culprit. Bellême will ask the same question, and he will also be extremely unsatisfied when I say I do not know. Without proof of *why* Arnulf saw fit to murder his kinsmen, my information amounts to nothing more than an accusation based on circumstantial evidence.'

She took a breath. 'All right. Tell me *how* you know Arnulf is the villain.'

'I learned three things when I sold my surcoat. First, the noose around Hugh's neck was distinctive. I watched Arnulf tie an identical knot with the cord Foucon gave him to put around the tunic.'

'Arnulf has always made odd knots,' admitted Matilda thoughtfully. 'Even when we were children. But it was foolish of him to tie a tell-tale bow on a murder victim.'

'Very,' agreed Geoffrey. 'But he was probably rushed and did not think about it. However, Emma told me she saw Hugh's body within an hour of his death, and she also mentioned that *Arnulf* had removed the rope from Hugh and covered him with a cloak. I thought nothing of it at the time, but I now see that Arnulf knew the knot might betray him, so he took it away under the guise of showing respect to his nephew's body. The second thing I learned was that Arnulf's hands are scarred.'

'He removed his gloves to try on the surcoat,' said Matilda,

254

nodding. 'You are right: his hands were marked, indicating he has had dealings with Greek Fire.'

'But not as much as Beaumais. I still do not know which of them – if either – killed Cecily.'

'What else? You said you learned three things from selling your tabard.'

'The last concerns Josbert. When I snatched at his silver, I did not want the coins. I wanted to see the writing on the documents in his pouch. I have had my suspicions about him for a while – there is more in his refusal to speak to me than mere surliness, and I think he is simply nervous that he might inadvertently let something incriminating slip if he answers my questions.'

'Josbert is a loyal vassal,' said Matilda thoughtfully. 'He might well use those tactics to ensure he did not accidentally betray Robert. He is solid and reliable, but does not have the wits of a Bellême – or a Mappestone. So, what did you learn from the parchment, other than that the siege will not last more than six months, because we are consuming more food than he had predicted?'

'Josbert can write, but his style is unsteady and childish, because he does not use it often – Ralph helps him here with his neat round hand. However, the writing listing the castle's victuals was identical to that of whoever scribed the message that was stuffed into Hugh's mouth.'

'*Josbert* wrote the reply from the King?' asked Matilda with huge eyes. 'The one that was supposed to make me think Henry wanted nothing to do with me and my proposals?'

'Henry said he had not received messages from you, and I suspect he was telling the truth: your missive, sent with Hugh, was not delivered. Then, probably to deter you from dispatching another, Josbert issued you with a reply of his own, purporting to be from Henry.'

'But why would Josbert – or any of my kin – thwart my negotiations for a peaceful settlement?'

Geoffrey shrugged. 'He might resent the fact that you could have been pardoned and kept your property while Bellême did not. He might believe your negotiations would weaken Bellême's position, and underline the family's factions and weaknesses. Perhaps he secretly loves you and thinks that if he is expelled to Normandy, then he wants you to go too.'

She laughed, then became serious. 'But surely he must see that if some of us keep lands in England, they can be used as a foothold for others in the future? What benefits one will benefit the rest.'

'Henry knows that, which is why I imagine he would be unlikely to grant your request anyway. But Josbert certainly destroyed your hopes.'

'It is a pity it did not occur to you to inspect his handwriting sooner, or to examine Arnulf's knots. You might have been able to save your life.'

'Or shortened it. How long do you think Arnulf and Josbert would have allowed me to live after I made my accusations? I *should* have guessed their identities sooner, though, because of something the landlord of the Crusader's Head said to me.'

'Go on,' invited Matilda.

'Oswin claimed Hugh ordered wine for *three* people before he died – it was why he reasoned Hugh had not killed himself, because suicides do not order drinks for themselves and two friends first. The two people with Hugh when he died were the killer and his accomplice. Arnulf and Josbert.'

'And you know Josbert was Arnulf's "accomplice" because . . . ?'

'Because he wrote the letter that was rammed in Hugh's mouth,' said Geoffrey impatiently. 'Arnulf does not read, so I doubt *he* knew what was on the parchment. Josbert probably told him it was a gag to prevent Hugh from making any noise. Arnulf was rushed, and agreed without thinking. Josbert put his own plan into action that night, using the corpse Arnulf had so conveniently provided. I saw him inspect Hugh's body myself: twice. Arnulf said the first time was on his orders; the second time was of his own volition. Arnulf assumed a love of the sight of corpses was what drove him, but Josbert had just realized it was an excellent opportunity to make sure his parchment was still in place. He probably killed Oswin, too – not only for throwing away his painstakingly written letter, but to prevent him from telling anyone that he and Arnulf had been with Hugh before he died.'

'But he was too late,' mused Matilda. 'Oswin had already talked to you. Josbert bolted the stable door, but the horse was no longer in it.'

The horse had bolted twice, thought Geoffrey, because Oswin had dictated his letter to Abbot Ralph, too, telling a kindly mentor all that had happened, because the landlord had sensed Hugh's death was a catalyst that would turn the Bellêmes against him.

'And poor Philip,' said Matilda softly. 'You said Arnulf also murdered Philip.'

'Yes,' said Geoffrey, thinking of the discussion he had overheard near the stables. It was obvious what had happened. Arnulf and his nephew had made some pact to benefit each other, and Arnulf had decided Philip was too much of a liability inside a castle under siege, where tempers were frayed and unsettled. He had executed him to ensure he said nothing incriminating, probably hoping that Geoffrey, who was soon to die, would provide a convenient scapegoat.

There was a commotion in the bailey below as Bellême emerged from the hall rubbing sleep from his eyes and servants ran to tend to his early morning needs. Arnulf and Roger were with him, and Geoffrey felt a pang of regret when he saw his surcoat adorning a murderer. He wished someone else had asked for it, because he felt he would rather even Bellême took possession of it than the smiling killer.

Matilda turned to Geoffrey. 'It is light. You do not have long left.'

'Bellême was right all along,' said Geoffrey, making no move to end the conversation. 'There *is* a traitor in his house. The traitor represents a danger to you, too, and you should trust no one.'

'I never have,' said Matilda. She sighed. 'I wish there was something I could do to prevent this, Geoffrey. I dislike hangings. They always seem so unsporting.'

'I dislike them, too,' came a quiet voice from behind. It was Mabel, who had ignored her uncle's orders and wore full knightly regalia. She had polished and cleaned it, so she looked resplendent. She gave Geoffrey a shy half-salute, and he realized she wore it to honour him. 'You say Arnulf killed Hugh? That is no surprise. He smiles too much.'

'Josbert does not, though,' said Matilda. 'He never smiles at all.'

'Better that than false friendliness,' said Mabel. 'Did Arnulf kill my sisters, too?'

'I am not sure,' replied Geoffrey, although the burn marks on Arnulf's hands suggested he had had access to the incendiary device at some point. 'I do not know *why* Arnulf killed Hugh, so it is hard to say why he might also have murdered your sisters. Their killer might have been Josbert.' He thought hard, trying to remember whether the castellan also had damaged hands, but his mind was blank.

'Beaumais has burned hands,' suggested Mabel.

'And he is the kind of man to change sides to suit his own needs,' added Matilda. 'He frolicked with me in the barn, even though he has promised himself to Emma. I knew it would not take much for him to break his allegiance.'

'Is that why you did it?' asked Mabel. 'I did not understand why you chose a weak, vacillating fellow like him, when there are stronger men available. You wanted to test his loyalty to Emma?'

'Loyalty in the bed and in battle are not comparable,' said Geoffrey, thinking it was unfair to accuse Beaumais of being a traitor simply because he was unable to resist Matilda's charms.

'You are a man,' said Matilda scornfully. 'You would say that. But the reality is – and every woman knows it – that a man who cannot be trusted in the bedchamber cannot be trusted anywhere.'

A cockerel crowed, long and loud, saving Geoffrey the need to respond, and Mabel glanced over the parapet to the ground below. 'You intend to jump. That is why you dispensed with your armour.'

'I see,' said Matilda, nodding slowly. 'You did not do it to enjoy an hour unencumbered with metal, but to make yourself lighter, so you do not land with such a crash.'

'It is a long way down,' said Mabel doubtfully.

'The ground offers a better fate than the one Amise has in mind for me.' Geoffrey inhaled deeply, relishing the sweet scent of clean air tinged with wood smoke, and wondered whether he would be able to make his leap before Matilda and Mabel could stop him. That they had so easily guessed his plan did not bode well for its success. Mabel was a large, strong woman, and it would be difficult to break away from her once she had grabbed him.

'You must aim for the soft ground near the garderobe shaft,' said Matilda, uncharacteristically delicate when she referred to the ordure that had accumulated in a squelching heap. 'That is how Philip escaped from Winchester – he jumped into a compost heap. Is that what gave you the idea?'

'Yes,' admitted Geoffrey, who had determined upon this after abandoning a more risky plan that involved taking Bellême hostage and demanding safe passage on pain of slitting the man's throat.

'Do not forget that Arundel's walls are higher than the ones at Winchester,' added Mabel helpfully. 'We are three storeys. And a pile of shit is not as pleasant as landing in a heap of rotting vegetation.'

'I will bear it in mind,' said Geoffrey. He looked from one to the other and smiled when he understood they were not going to prevent his escape.

'What is the plan?' asked Matilda. 'Jump into the mud, then claim sanctuary in the church?'

'That would involve running uphill,' said Mabel, assessing the landscape with a professional eye. 'Head towards the river, where the land slopes down. Then do what Philip did: leap into the water and allow the current to tow you to safety.'

'Aim *left* of the garderobe shaft,' instructed Matilda, leaning over the parapet to inspect the ground. 'The right side slopes too acutely and you may fall on to harder ground.'

'Unfortunately, that is where Foucon is standing,' said Geoffrey, who had reviewed all his options very carefully when he had been with Amise the night before. He knew exactly which gap he needed to drop through for the best chance of survival. 'I shall have to make do with the other.'

259

'No,' said Mabel, reaching for her sword. 'I will clear it for you.'

'I would not become involved, if I were you,' warned Geoffrey, touched that she was prepared to risk her life to help him, but not wanting her to hang in his place – which would surely happen when Bellême found out what she had done. 'Your mother will not want to lose another daughter so soon.'

'He is right, Mabel,' said Matilda. 'This is not an occasion for steel, but for cunning.'

'We need a diversion,' said Mabel, nodding. 'It will not take much to distract Foucon, Matilda: he is besotted with you. Meanwhile, his soldiers are looking very shabby today. They need smartening up.'

'Look!' said Matilda urgently, pointing towards the bailey. 'Robert is on his way already. Wait for my signal, and make a good jump, Geoffrey.'

'God's speed,' added Mabel, touching him lightly and briefly on the shoulder. She drifted away, scanning the countryside as though her sole purpose was a survey of the castle's defences. Matilda went in the opposite direction, aiming for Foucon.

'That ridiculous man thinks Arnulf is the killer,' Geoffrey heard her announce, accompanying her words with a tinkling giggle to indicate she thought his conclusion ludicrous. Foucon laughed, too, although his tone was more wary than amused. Matilda flounced past, rubbing her arms. 'It is very cold in the wind, Foucon. Come this way and let me tell you more of what he said.'

Foucon was torn. He was under orders to guard Geoffrey, but would far rather talk to Matilda and put himself back in her good graces. He glanced down to where Bellême had started to climb the spiral stairs, and evidently decided that Geoffrey was unlikely to escape with Bellême blocking his only way out. He scowled at the knight to warn him to behave, then followed Matilda. Meanwhile, Mabel had completed her circuit of the tower and was approaching from the other direction.

'Look at this,' she shouted furiously to the remaining

guards. 'You are filthy, slovenly vermin who are not fit to stand in my presence.'

'Why?' demanded one of the guards, offended. 'What have we done?'

'Someone has used the turret as a urinal. Come here, all of you. I want you to see this for yourselves before I report the matter to Josbert.'

The soldiers followed, half amused by her outrage at something they did all the time, and half afraid that Josbert might agree with her and punish them. Geoffrey moved nonchalantly in the direction of the gap above the garderobe shaft, while Matilda leaned over the parapet and treated the delighted Foucon to an expanse of bare bosom. But Foucon was no fool, and did not like the fact that Geoffrey was moving out of his line of vision. Suddenly, Matilda started to shout.

'One of the siege engines is on the move! Sound the alarm! Do not just stand there! Move!'

Within moments, the top of the tower was in chaos, as guards darted here and there, jostling each other for space to see whether she was right. They were worried, because the completion of a war machine meant the castle would soon be in for some sustained battering, as missiles assailed it night and day. Their lives would become more miserable than ever. Geoffrey heard Bellême's voice on the stairs, demanding to know what the racket was about. He did not have much time.

He walked to the gap, now free of soldiers, and looked at the ground below. It was so far down that he saw the folly of his plan. Even if he managed to hit the muck and not the ground, he was likely to pummel into it so hard he would die anyway. But Bellême was already on the roof, joining the soldiers who clamoured that they could see a siege engine moving. Geoffrey had two choices: he could allow Bellême to hang him, or he could take his chances with the midden. He sat, aware that Mabel was watching him covertly. Then he swung his legs over the gap and forced himself to drop.

He felt himself airborne, dropping straight down with a

261

stomach-clenching suddenness, while the foetid brown sludge of the midden rushed up to meet him.

Geoffrey hit the ground with a tremendous crash that drove the breath from his body and made filth fly in all directions. He immediately felt himself sinking, and foulness seeped into his mouth and eyes. For a moment, he could only lie still, and there was a distant sense that he had broken his spine. Then he found his legs still worked, and his arms, and he was fighting to escape the clinging muck. It was more difficult than he had anticipated, because the trench was deeper than he had thought. Choking and gagging on the vileness, he began to flail wildly, aiming to reach solid ground or something that would allow him to claw his way free.

He managed to seize a handful of grass, but his fingers were oily, and he could not grip it hard enough to help himself. With horror, he felt himself sink deeper. With a desperation borne of panic, he made a monumental effort to hurl himself to one side. With a sucking plop, the midden released its prize, and he was able to crawl away, where he lay on his side gasping for air.

But his respite was not to last. A soldier on the battlements above had edged past Matilda and happened to look down at the ground below. He saw exactly what had happened, and started to raise the alarm. Geoffrey heaved himself on to his hands and knees, then grabbed at the walls to pull himself upright. His legs felt as though they were made of rubber, and the sprint across the open land to the river suddenly seemed a very dubious proposition. He was not sure he could make it.

More shouts echoed from above, and he saw that if he did not run soon, his great leap would have been in vain. In moments, archers would grab their bows and release volleys of arrows, and few could miss at such a short distance. He thrust himself away from the wall and started to run. His wet clothes weighed him down, and he felt as though he was running through honey. Each unsteady, staggering step seemed to take an eternity, and the river did not seem to be coming any closer at all.

A heavy stone thumped into the ground at his side, showing

that the guards were not waiting until the archers arrived, but were trying to hit him themselves. A second stone followed the first, so close that he felt the wind of it passing close to his head. The ground was uneven, and to his horror, he lost his balance, tumbling into the grass and losing vital moments. He dragged himself upright and plodded on, aware of heavy missiles thudding all around him. He tried to move faster, but the ground was pitted with molehills and burrows, and he was afraid that if he fell again it would be the last thing he did. Then an arrow hissed into the ground near his heels.

Just when he thought he could run no farther, the land dipped and the river was in front of him. He skidded down the bank, then rolled head over heels until he hit the water with a splash. He plunged downwards, surrounded by foam and bubbles that turned quickly from white to brown to black as he sank. Then he hit the bottom, and felt his feet slide into soft mud. He struggled furiously, knowing that if he became entangled in the river's bottom, then his wild bid for freedom would be at an end.

Just when he thought the river might win, he felt himself come free, and kicked towards the light above. The current tugged at him, and he allowed himself to drift, knowing that the farther away from the castle he was when he surfaced, the less likely he was to be hit by Bellême's marksmen.

He broke through the surface, and drew a great gasping breath into his burning lungs. A hissing sound to his left made him look back at the castle, where archers all along the wall nocked arrows to their bows. Another came a hand's breadth from his shoulder, so he turned and swam as hard as he could, aiming for the middle of the river where the current was strongest, and would take him away faster. But he was a sitting duck, and saw the only way to escape was to duck again.

He took a deep breath, and dived, aiming to one side in the hope that the archers would be less able to predict where he might be. Out of the corner of his eye he saw trails of bubbles where more arrows zapped into the water where he had been, and saw he would have been hit for certain if he had not jigged away from his original course.

When he felt as though his lungs would burst, he surfaced

263

again. Within moments, arrows pattered around him, and he realized how deeply determined Bellême was that he should not escape. He drew another breath into his protesting lungs, and dived again. This time, he could not go so deeply or swim so far before he was obliged to come up. The hail of missiles was unrelenting, and he knew it was only a matter of time before one hit him.

He was bracing himself for another dive, when the shooting stopped as abruptly as it had begun. Bewildered, Geoffrey glanced back, and saw the archers looking in the opposite direction. Then there was a low whistling roar, like a thunderbolt, followed by a crack, and Geoffrey saw a cloud of dust rising from one of the walls. Arundel Castle was under attack! A great shriek split the air, and a second missile was launched. This one hit the wooden watchtower, but did little damage. There was a smashing sound, and a great black stain began to dribble down it. It was Greek Fire, but it had not ignited. Geoffrey thought Bellême would be relieved, because it could have had the entire structure in flames. Part of his mind noted that it had come from outside the castle, which meant that Bellême had not been the only one working to produce the substance.

But it was no time to speculate or to watch the confused milling of guards on the battlements as the realization dawned that the King might also possess a deadly weapon. Geoffrey swam as hard as his exhausted muscles would allow to the opposite bank, and clambered out. An arrow thudded nearby as one determined bowman continued to follow Bellême's orders. As soon as he was free of the clinging mud and slippery roots that formed the riverbank, Geoffrey ran until he was certain he was out of range. Only then, chest heaving and legs shaking from exhaustion, did he turn to look at the castle.

He heard another low roar, and saw a stone smash into the palisade near the gatehouse, but although shattered wood flew in all directions, it made little impact on the stone. The siege machine was too far away to do real harm, and its aim was flawed: it was being used before it was properly assembled or calibrated. Meanwhile, Bellême's guards fled in all directions, because although the missiles were unlikely to breach walls, the flying splinters they created could kill or maim onlookers. One person remained unmoving and unflinching, however, and Geoffrey could see by its size that it was Bellême. He held a bow, and Geoffrey realized it had not been an archer who had continued to fire after the others had stopped, but the Earl himself.

'Hey!'

The voice so close made Geoffrey spin around, anticipating more trouble when Henry's soldiers assumed he was one of Bellême's men making an escape before he starved. His flagging spirits received a boost when he saw Roger trotting across the uneven ground to meet him. The dog was at his heels, and released a delighted bark when it saw Geoffrey. It scampered towards him in a rare display of affection, then threatened to trip him over by winding itself around his legs, attracted to the powerful smells that clung about him from his brush with the midden.

Geoffrey staggered towards Roger, wanting to put as much distance between him and Bellême as he could, lest the Earl employ some of the witchcraft for which his family was famous, and make his arrows fly farther than they should. He refused to answer any questions until they were safely concealed behind a large tree.

'We had your message,' said Roger, removing his cloak and throwing it around Geoffrey's shoulders. Geoffrey gathered it around him gratefully. 'You said the gatehouse represents our best hope of attack, but the postern gate is the least well defended.'

'Yes,' said Geoffrey, wondering why Roger was scowling at him. 'Our system worked.'

'So, why are you here, then?' demanded Roger huffily. 'Did you not trust me to get it right?'

'No,' said Geoffrey tiredly. 'I mean, yes.'

'Then why did you dive off the battlements to deliver the message to Henry in person?' asked Roger icily. 'It was a foolish thing to do and quite unnecessary. You would have been better to stay where you were. This siege will not last for long now we have your information.'

265

'And neither would I,' said Geoffrey, explaining what would have happened if he had not made his bid for freedom. 'But I have done what I was ordered to. I am leaving for Dover tonight.'

'Henry wants to see you first,' said Roger. 'It was him who ordered the war machines fired to improve your chances of escape, so remember to thank him.'

Geoffrey was glad Henry had deployed his mangonel, because no one could now accuse Matilda of causing a diversion to allow him to escape. He suspected that she had not seen it move as she had claimed, but no one in Arundel would be able to prove that. Indeed, she was probably enjoying adulation as an observant lookout.

'And what about the Greek Fire?' asked Geoffrey. 'I saw it hit the watchtower. Did Henry give the order for that to be used, too?'

'Greek Fire!' snorted Roger in disgust. 'What Henry has is nothing like Greek Fire! It is too wet, and he cannot get it to stay alight. You saw what happened when they gave it a trial run: it trickled down the wall and did nothing more inconvenient than leave a nasty stain.'

'You mean Henry does not have the secret?' asked Geoffrey, knowing that Roger regarded his questions as stupid, but suddenly overwhelmed with weariness.

'He does not have real Greek Fire,' reiterated Roger. 'His stuff is entirely too sloppy. He cannot make it go where he aims. And he cannot make it burn.' Roger made a list on his fingers, somehow reaching five points, when Geoffrey had counted only three.

'Like Emma's. Hers is too wet, too.'

'If hers is the same as his, then neither of them has the secret.'

Geoffrey followed Roger through a well-organized camp to where a bigger and gaudier tent than the others was located upwind from the stench always associated with any kind of military station. A royal standard fluttered in the breeze, and Geoffrey noticed there was even a tent for the King's horses, should the weather turn bad and they needed shelter.

'Geoffrey,' said Henry, coming to greet him with a smile. He started to touch the knight's shoulder, but became aware of the unpleasant smell that clung to his clothes and let his hand drop to his side. 'I did not expect to see you so soon. I imagined you would remain with Bellême and surrender when we broke the siege. Escape was a dangerous thing to attempt.'

'Not as dangerous as staying would have been,' said Geoffrey.

Henry gestured that he was to sit on a bench inside the tent, while he reclined in a large chair opposite. After a moment, he rose and moved it away, wrinkling his nose fastidiously. He expressed polite interest when Geoffrey gave a brief account of his experiences, but the knight had the impression that he only wanted information pertinent to the siege. Geoffrey did not mention his partial solution to the murder of Hugh, nor that the answer had only come to him moments before he was due to hang. Roger and Helbye would be a much more appreciative audience than the King.

'Well, I am glad you are still with us, even if a tactical error was made in trying to save your life,' said Henry, interrupting before he had finished.

'Revealing to Bellême that you have Greek Fire?'

Henry grimaced. 'Revealing to him that I do *not* have Greek Fire. I gave the order for the mangonel to fire a couple of rocks, but your sergeant interfered. Saying he was a Crusader who understood Greek Fire, he wound the engine we have been using to practise, and launched a pot before I could stop him. You probably saw what happened: the vessel smashed and it dribbled down the wall but did not ignite as it was supposed to have done.'

'It needs refinement,' agreed Geoffrey. 'The Crusaders never did learn the secret – the element that makes it difficult to douse. Nor did we work out how to propel it where it is meant to go.'

'Has Bellême?' asked Henry eagerly.

'I do not know. My squire saw a pot of a substance I assume was real Greek Fire among Emma's belongings, but her supply is limited – and becoming more so. Her own attempts at reproducing it are no more successful than

267

yours.' Geoffrey knew he would have noticed if she had possessed vats of the stuff. It was difficult to conceal much in a castle under siege, but especially barrels of a smelly and dangerous substance. 'And she does not have enough to defeat a large army.'

'Elaborate,' ordered Henry.

Geoffrey struggled against his overwhelming tiredness to give an answer that made sense. 'Emma's Greek Fire, like yours, is too thin. Hers burns better – she added olive oil and raisins, and that may be why.' He did not mention that she had also included a dead felon's finger or that she chanted incantations to the Devil while she did so. 'But it is still not perfect.'

'But how did she lay her hands on a sample of the genuine substance?' demanded Henry. 'As soon as Bishop Giffard told me what Bellême was doing I sent my best agents to the Holy Land to procure some, but they have not been successful.'

'How long have you known about Emma's experiments?'

'Bellême tried to recruit Giffard to his ranks last autumn, and we discovered then what Emma was trying to do. But you have not answered me: how did Bellême acquire real Greek Fire?'

'Philip the Grammarian found some on the Crusade. He must have sent the formula and a sample to Emma, so she could use her talents to create more. However, I believe one ingredient is found only in the East, which is why she has not met with total success.' He rubbed his chin thoughtfully, recalling the day when Philip the Grammarian had been killed.

'What?' asked Henry, watching him. 'You have just thought of something new. I can tell.'

'Philip died during a raid at Antioch. But he did not die fighting the Turks, no matter what his kinsmen claim. I saw him running away myself. Later, when I oversaw his burial, I noticed he had been stabbed in the back.'

'Really?' Henry was torn between annoyance and being intrigued. 'You did not mention this when I asked you about him at Westminster Palace.'

'I have only just remembered,' Geoffrey lied, wishing he was not so tired and his wits were sharper, especially around a man like Henry. 'But the wound was from a straight blade, not a curved one, indicating he was not killed by Turks, but by another Crusader. He was not popular, and I assumed someone had taken advantage of the confusion in the raid to dispatch him. I was right, but I did not understand the killer's motive at the time. I assumed it was because he had been hoarding food when the rest of us were starving. I was wrong: he was murdered for Greek Fire.'

'But the secret ended up with Emma. Why would another Crusader give her the Greek Fire when he could have kept it for himself?'

'Her nieces took it to her,' said Geoffrey, watching Henry's eyebrows rise. 'They told me they stayed with the Crusade until Antioch – where Philip was killed. They claimed they went home because they were bored, but I suspect they returned because they wanted to take the Greek Fire to Emma. Philip probably planned to sell it to one of the Crusader leaders at Jerusalem. Just imagine the prestige that would have come from being the man responsible for providing the means to bring the Holy City into Christian hands.'

'I wonder whether Young Philip knows about this. Still, I doubt he is man enough to do anything about avenging the death of his father.'

'He plotted,' said Geoffrey, recalling the discussion near the stables with Arnulf that had resulted in his murder. 'But not successfully. He is dead.' He rubbed his head, wanting the interview with the King to be over, so he could change his clothes and sluice the foulness from his hair with clean water. He edged closer to Henry, in the hope that the King would find the stench so distasteful he would bring the audience to an early conclusion.

'Is he?' asked Henry a little sadly, standing and rummaging in a chest to produce a large pomander that he pressed over his nose and mouth. His next words were muffled. 'That is a pity. He was not a bad boy, although he had an inflated sense of his own intelligence. Who killed him?'

'Arnulf, probably.'

'It is best we keep the information about the Grammarian and his discovery to ourselves,' said Henry, moving towards the door, where there was a breeze. 'I do not want rumours spread that Emma the Witch has real Greek Fire, as well as the ability to raise long-dead ancestors from their graves.'

'She will not succeed in that. They are still missing her head.'

'It was stolen after her murder twenty-five years ago,' said Henry. 'And do not look at me in that accusing manner, Geoffrey. I was a child when Mabel de Bellême met her well-deserved end. The loss of her skull had nothing to do with me.'

'Do you know what happened to it?' asked Geoffrey, sure Henry was right, but unable to shake off the feeling that the King knew more than he was prepared to admit.

'I do not think anyone knows,' said Henry, his face all but invisible under his pomander. 'But that has not prevented tales of its reappearance, and maps that identify its alleged whereabouts.'

'Maps,' said Geoffrey, knowing he should probably keep quiet, but too weary to think clearly. 'That was why that monk – Petronus – was murdered. Archers were hired to ensure he did not deliver his messages. They bungled their attack, and were killed in their turn. But one of them whispered "map" as he died.'

'So your squire said,' said Henry, his voice still muffled as he looked out at his camp. 'The attack had nothing to do with me, although I cannot vouch for my courtiers. They all know the damage that might be done if Mabel's head is reunited with her body.'

'The priest of All Hallows Barking caught Emma robbing graves,' said Geoffrey, wondering whether Henry was genuinely interested in something outside the tent or whether the King just could not look him in the eye. 'He was afraid that she was using stolen body parts to make some kind of attempt on your life. She had two heads in her reliquary, one of which was Hugh's.'

'Did she, by God!' exclaimed Henry in distaste. 'The Bellêmes are an odd family, Geoffrey. Young Philip even

270

claimed some toenail clippings from me, although I cannot imagine why.'

'For Emma's potions,' said Geoffrey. 'You were lucky: she had actually instructed him to acquire hair and a finger.'

'Potions? She has been trying to sicken me with charms?' Geoffrey nodded, and the King was thoughtful. 'Then I am grateful I exchanged my clippings for some of Philip's own. Perhaps her spell worked, and that is why he met his untimely end. She has been a busy lady: manufacturing Greek Fire, concocting charms to kill her monarch, raising her mother from the grave.'

'She has had plenty of help: Sybilla and her daughters, Beaumais.' He did not mention Matilda.

'So, Edred was wrong,' mused Henry, now standing outside the tent and speaking to Geoffrey over his shoulder. He raised his hand when the knight started to follow, to indicate he was to remain where he was. 'Emma did not rob graves to harm me, but to excavate some unfortunate's head for her mother. She is a clever woman, who knows truth always takes second place to what people believe. I have no faith in magic, Geoffrey, but my subjects do, and they might well turn to Bellême out of fear that Old Mabel will haunt them if they do not.'

Geoffrey knew he was right. Wars had been won and lost on account of what people believed. Faith had certainly been important in ensuring the fall of Jerusalem, and he had seen with his own eyes that superstition and religious fanaticism were powerful weapons. When the King disappeared from his line of sight, he seized the opportunity to escape. Roger was waiting for him, and he headed towards his friend, grateful that the interview was over and he was free to leave. He was not pleased when Henry followed, the pomander still pressed hard against his face.

'My armourer will equip you with what you have lost,' he said. 'Although I am afraid he will have no Crusaders' surcoat. I expect you want to return to Tancred now you have discharged your duties?'

'Today,' said Geoffrey, trying not to shiver in the biting wind lest the King mistook it for fear. He wondered whether

Durand was at the siege camp, and whether his horse had been well cared for.

'How about later?' the King suggested pleasantly. 'I have another task for you. I know you will not refuse, because this time it will benefit your sister directly. Bellême's mercenaries are causing chaos along the Welsh border, and I want you to ride north to see what can be done.'

'But I—'

'Do not argue,' snapped Henry. 'I need all the men and resources available to me, because crushing Bellême is the greatest challenge I have yet faced. You will go to the Marches with William Pantulf, and together you will ensure the Welsh do not rise and add their strength to Bellême's. The security of a nation is at stake here, Geoffrey. You cannot refuse me.'

'You cannot, lad,' muttered Roger. 'All this is true. The Welsh under Prince Iorwerth *are* massing, and Bellême's troops *are* all over the borders causing mayhem. We were born here: we cannot let our birthplace be ravaged by the likes of Bellême's mercenaries. Henry needs us both.'

'Thank you, Roger,' said the King dryly. 'I am pleased I have your support.'

'You do,' said Roger, unabashed by what was obviously a reprimand. 'And I am more than happy to enter your service and see this tyrant driven from your shores. But then I am leaving. I have other business to attend to, besides saving England.'

'Do you indeed?' said Henry, amused, despite his irritation at the big knight's presumption. 'Then why, pray, are you prepared to fight for me?'

'Several reasons,' said Roger baldly, ignoring Geoffrey's warning glance to say no more. 'First, I do not like Bellême. Second, one of his sisters gave me wine that made me sleep through an invasion of my bedchamber, and no woman does that to a son of the Bishop of Durham.' He drew himself up to his full, considerable height, while Geoffrey closed his eyes, thinking it was unwise to remind the King that he was the offspring of another of Henry's enemies.

'And third?' asked Henry warily.

272

'And third, I have not had an opportunity to loot anything since the fall of Jerusalem, and my treasure is running low. I would like to strip a few of Bellême's strongholds.'

'Very well,' said Henry, hiding a smile. 'You have my permission to loot anything of Bellême's, but you will not touch a penny of mine. I shall also require a percentage of anything you take. Let us call it a Loot Tax.'

'But that is not fair,' objected Roger, horrified. 'We were allowed to keep everything in the Holy Land.'

'But this is England,' said Henry softly. 'And we have laws in England. They do not call me the Lion of Justice for nothing.'

'They do not call him Henry the Clerk for nothing, either,' grumbled Roger imprudently as they left. 'He wants to tax everything, even looting. It is not right, Geoff, lad.'

Twelve

G eoffrey missed his armour and sword and, although the
mail given to him by Henry was adequate, it was not
of the same quality as that which he had been forced to
abandon. The surcoat Henry had provided he vowed never
to wear, because it was one emblazoned with Henry's own
colours, and implied that Geoffrey was one of his knights.

The only familiar thing Geoffrey still owned was his horse.
It and his squire were in Henry's camp, where Durand was
entirely unrepentant for running away, claiming he would be
hanging in Geoffrey's place if he had not taken his fate into
his own hands. Geoffrey thought he was probably right, and
could not find it in his heart to condemn the man, although
he disapproved of the fact that he had lied about it to
Roger, telling him that Geoffrey had ordered him to save
the horse.

Practising with his new armour and weapons was easier
than Geoffrey would have liked, because skirmishes along
the Marches were frequent and bitter. The Welsh knew better
than to take on Henry's forces in open battle, but that did
not stop them from swooping down from their mountain
strongholds to raid English settlements and farms, steal
cattle, kill villagers and burn houses and barns. He heard
the fighting was not so bad where Joan lived, and hoped she
was managing to fend off the raids. He considered deserting
Henry to help her, but knew he could do more good in the
north, where royal troops were more likely to break the back
of the simmering Welsh revolt.

The summer was long and hot, and reminded Geoffrey of
the Holy Land, with the sun beating down relentlessly and

274

the ground baked dry and hard under his feet. As the weeks passed, he wondered whether it would ever end, or whether he was doomed to spend the rest of his life hunting phantom raiders in the rugged mountains of North Wales.

'You cannot rest until this is over,' Roger said one sultry night, after they had spent a fruitless day trying to dislodge a pack of bandits from a village near the Welsh border. 'You will never be safe in England until Bellême is expelled.'

'But I do not live in England, so whether he is here is irrelevant to me. I shall be glad to see him gone for Joan's sake, but all we are doing now is sending him as angry as a swarm of bees to Normandy – where he will vent his fury on other innocent people.'

'We could kill him,' suggested Roger helpfully. 'That would solve the problem.'

'He would be succeeded by one of his brothers,' Geoffrey pointed out, absently ruffling his dog's fur. 'And they are no better. Roger is surly, aggressive and held in check only because he is afraid of Bellême. And Arnulf murders his nephews for reasons I do not understand.'

It was late, and the sounds of the summer night wafted around them as they spoke – the occasional pop from the dying fire over which they had cooked their supper, the distant bleat of sheep and the whine of an insect. The air was sweet with the scent of ripening crops, and the harvest would soon be ready for gathering. Geoffrey hoped Bellême's rebellion would be stamped out before then, because folk would starve if they could not gather the grain that would see them through winter.

'Pantulf will join us tomorrow,' said Roger drowsily. 'He has been trying to negotiate with the Welsh again, and vows he will bring Prince Iorwerth with him when he comes.'

'I know,' said Geoffrey, who was concerned about Pantulf's role in the campaign. Pantulf had changed his allegiance from Bellême to Henry at the Easter Court, and Geoffrey was never happy with men who were inconstant. He did not like the fact that the King had put Pantulf in charge of breaking down Bellême's Welsh alliances, and feared he might change sides again.

'Once we have Iorwerth's support, Bellême's revolt will crumble,' said Roger, trying to find a comfortable position on the hard ground.

'I know that, too,' said Geoffrey, wondering whether Roger thought him an idiot, unacquainted with the politics of the war he fought.

'Without Iorwerth causing mayhem along the Marches, Bellême will be left with only Arundel and his three northern castles,' Roger rambled on. 'Henry will be able to concentrate his forces on those, instead of wasting men hunting phantom Welsh raiders around here. You will be with Tancred before Christmas. Sooner, even.'

'I hope so,' said Geoffrey, not sure Bellême would be so easy to defeat, even with the loss of Iorwerth. He was a desperate, cornered man and, in Geoffrey's experience, such men tended to be more dangerous adversaries. 'I just hope he does not stoop to using Greek Fire or his risen mother.'

But Roger was already dozing, leaving Geoffrey to take the first watch. He stood and went to check that the guards were alert and in their places, then wandered through the camp to ensure all was as it should be. Helbye was asleep, rolled into his cloak and his face lined with fatigue. Durand was next to him, twitching and jumping like a dog that dreamed of chasing rabbits. Ulfrith was near Roger, flat on his back and snoring like an overweight merchant.

Satisfied, Geoffrey went to sit near the fire again. He estimated it was probably nearing midnight when his dog pricked up its ears and gave a low whine. Geoffrey was immediately alert and, within moments, he heard the distant drum of horses' hoofs. Anticipating an attack, he ordered the guards to wake the others and drew his sword, listening to the advance of the riders with his head cocked to one side. They came closer, and he signalled for his soldiers to take cover, archers along the roof of an abandoned hut and soldiers concealed among the trees of a small copse. The hoofs slowed when they approached the camp. Geoffrey stepped out and raised his hand.

'Geoffrey,' said the leading rider as he dismounted. Geoffrey dismissed his men from their alert. The horseman was Pantulf, who looked as though he had just stepped from an audience with the King, rather than a long and hard ride over rough country. 'Bishop Maurice said you would be here. He also said you have declined reinforcements.' There was disapproval in his voice.

'More men will not make a difference here,' replied Geoffrey, sheathing his sword. He leaned down to grab the dog by the scruff of its neck. It did not like Pantulf, and had already bitten him twice. 'We will only fall over each other when we try to track the enemy into the hills.'

'He is right,' said a slight, black-haired man who rode behind Pantulf. He leapt from his pony with the agility of a monkey. 'More men here would be worse than a waste.'

Geoffrey studied him in the firelight. His eyes were dark, and his colouring reminded the knight uncomfortably of Bellême, although he knew it was common enough in the Celtic countries. The newcomer clicked his fingers at the dog, which trotted towards him, wagging its tail. Geoffrey was impressed. It was not a friendly beast, and he admired anyone it did not immediately try to savage.

'This is Prince Iorwerth,' said Pantulf, gesturing towards him with a careless flick of his hand. His voice was smug. 'I told you he would come.'

'Welcome, Iorwerth ap Bleddyn,' said Geoffrey politely, using the Welsh language he had learned as a boy. 'Our fire is low, but we can stoke it up and offer you bread and meat, if you are hungry.'

Iorwerth gave a delighted grin and answered in kind. 'I have never heard a Norman speak our tongue before, but Pantulf tells me you are an unusual man. He also says you have made an enemy of the Earl of Shrewsbury. That was not wise: Bellême is a powerful man.'

'Not for long,' said Geoffrey. 'In England, at least. King Henry is determined to see him exiled, and he usually gets what he wants.'

Iorwerth jerked his head at Pantulf, confident that the aloof nobleman could not understand a word he said. 'Master Traitor there says Henry will grant me dominion over most of Wales if I abandon Bellême. Is that true?'

277

'I can show you Henry's letter authorizing Pantulf to make the offer,' said Geoffrey. 'As long as you do not make too many raids on to English soil when this is over, Henry will probably leave you to rule as you see fit.'

'Then that is what I shall do,' said Iorwerth, pleased. 'It was expedient for me to remain loyal to Bellême while he was strong on the Marches, but it is time I developed new alliances. I do not trust Pantulf, but I believe a man who addresses me in the language of kings.'

'What are you two gibbering about?' demanded Pantulf. He glared at them, not liking the way the Welsh prince had immediately imparted what were clearly confidences to a comparative stranger.

'No one "gibbers" in Welsh,' said Iorwerth in thickly accented Norman-French. 'For your information I have just informed Sir Geoffrey that I *shall* rally to the King's cause. I shall order my troops to stop fighting Henry and turn their attention to Bellême instead.'

He patted the dog, vaulted into his saddle and cantered away with his men, leaving Geoffrey and Pantulf rather startled at his abrupt leave-taking. Geoffrey coughed from the dust the cavalcade had stirred up, while Pantulf tried to brush it from his fine clothes. When the clatter of hoofs had died away, Geoffrey offered Pantulf a seat on a conveniently placed stone, while he knelt to coax the campfire's embers into life, and Roger went to oversee the standing down of the troops.

'Do you believe him?' asked Pantulf, staring into the flickering flames.

'Yes.' Geoffrey smiled. 'You have just ended this vicious campaign, Pantulf. Bellême cannot fight Iorwerth as well as Henry, and I predict he will be gone from England by autumn.'

Pantulf was pleased with himself. 'Our days of bloody skirmishing are almost at an end, and we shall ride for Bridgnorth at dawn. The King is already on his way there with his army.'

'Henry has left Arundel?' asked Geoffrey, surprised he should give up after three months of siege. The supplies

278

list Geoffrey had snatched from Josbert before his escape suggested they would not last much beyond the end of summer, and the royal war machines would be ready to do serious damage to the castle defences long before then. One hard push would see Arundel fall.

'Arundel has surrendered,' said Pantulf. 'I heard the news a few days ago. The King became bored of sitting outside, doing nothing, so he took a few soldiers to the Bellême stronghold of Tickhill, instead. The moment Tickhill saw that the King himself had come, it gave up.'

'And I suppose word was immediately sent to Arundel?' asked Geoffrey, who knew how such tactics worked. 'Tickhill's loss would be a bitter blow to Arundel's defenders, and they would lose heart.'

'They lost heart *instantly*,' said Pantulf in satisfaction. 'Arundel yielded to Henry the same day.'

'And Bellême?' asked Geoffrey hopefully. 'Is he captured?'

'Most of the family escaped during the confusion, but Bellême was not among them: he had left earlier and has been fortifying his northern castles. So, some of the clan are at Shrewsbury and some are at Bridgnorth, but all are ready to fight.'

Geoffrey started to wonder how it was possible for Bellême to slip away when the King had had Arundel surrounded, but then recalled that Henry was a clever man, and supposed Bellême's escape was part of some plan. There would be pockets of resistance from the Earl's supporters for as long as he possessed powerful fortresses like Shrewsbury and Bridgnorth, and Geoffrey suspected that Henry would want those smashed as decisively as Arundel and Tickhill, to ensure the rebellion was well and truly extinguished.

'We have orders to travel to Bridgnorth as soon as possible,' said Pantulf. 'We leave at first light.'

'No,' said Geoffrey firmly. 'Henry asked me to help you secure Iorwerth, and I have done that. It is time for me to leave this troubled land.'

Pantulf gave a tight smile. 'You have no choice. You and I are in a similar position: we were loyal to Bellême and were persuaded to accept a new master. Henry trusts neither of us completely, and we would be wise to do as he asks until he does. Your estates lie on the Marches, and you would not like him to give them to someone else.'

'I do not care,' said Geoffrey, not bothering to point out that he had never been loyal to Bellême. 'But my sister would be furious, and I am more afraid of her than I am of Henry. Very well, we shall go to Bridgnorth. Do you know where it is?'

'In Shropshire. I know this part of the country well, which is why Henry will give me Stafford Castle when the Earl is finally defeated.'

'Is that why you abandoned Bellême?' asked Geoffrey, startled. 'For Stafford Castle?'

'Yes,' said Pantulf with a predatory grin. 'The King approached me with his offer the day before Bellême came before his Easter Court, and it seemed too good an opportunity to pass up. Besides, Henry will oust Bellême from England if it is the last thing he does. Bellême's day is almost over, and only a fool follows a falling star.'

Geoffrey poked the fire with a stick, and was grateful his own ambitions were more modest. The shifting, unsteady alliances and friendships at court were unfathomable and unpredictable, and he could think of little he would like less than being one of Henry's castellans. He saw the first tendrils of light begin to brighten the eastern sky and stirred himself. There was plenty to do if they were to break camp at dawn and ride to meet the King in Shropshire.

Bridgnorth, August 1102

Bridgnorth had once been no more than a tiny hamlet atop a rocky cliff that plummeted down to the River Severn. Then Bellême had raised a fortress there. When he saw the splendid location, Geoffrey understood exactly why Bellême had chosen it: the castle would be difficult to invade from any direction; war engines would be unable to reach it; and any forces attempting to scale its cliffs would face a volley of arrows and anything else the defenders cared to hurl at them. Geoffrey saw they were in for another siege, because only an insane commander would pit his troops in open warfare against the defenders of Bridgnorth.

280

He and Pantulf spent three days scouting the land around the castle, and eventually agreed on a site that was suitable for use as headquarters. They erected a tent large enough to hold a sizeable table and drew plans of the castle's oval bailey, earthworks, motte and wooden keep. Then they devised strategies for an attack, should the occasion arise. Pantulf's illustrations were better drawn and more attractive to look at, but Geoffrey's were more accurate.

The King arrived within the week, accompanied by blasting trumpets and braying horses, which Geoffrey knew were to ensure that the castle's inhabitants knew they were now surrounded by an experienced and determined force: the troops that had brought the mighty Arundel to its knees. He hoped Bridgnorth would see the futility of resistance and surrender soon, because he did not want to kick his heels at another prolonged siege when he could be riding to Antioch.

The King was not the only familiar face to arrive. Bishop Maurice was there, too. The fat prelate arrived in a covered cart, which Geoffrey assumed contained scribes and writing tables so his affairs could be attended to while he was away on campaign. He was startled and rather amused to learn it contained several women and his personal physician. Maurice clambered inelegantly from his wagon as young women dropped into the grass all around him, causing a great stir among the watching soldiers. Geoffrey hoped Maurice was willing to share, or there would be fighting for certain: pretty girls could not wander freely around a camp full of bored men and expect to emerge untouched.

'Oh, no!' groaned Durand, who stood at Geoffrey's side to watch the new arrivals. 'Not Maurice! Every time we meet he tries to seduce me, and I am not interested in fat old men.'

He slunk away, while Geoffrey folded his arms and laughed. The squire's flight had not gone unnoticed, however, and the bishop approached Geoffrey, his eyes glittering with lust.

'It is her!' he breathed. 'The lady with the locks of an angel.'

'I will order him to cut them,' said Geoffrey irritably.

'I must have her!' pressed Maurice eagerly. 'She eluded me once in London and again when I visited the siege camp at Arundel, but I shall not allow her to slip through my fingers a third time.'

'You met him at Arundel?'

'When you were still inside the castle, and she was free to take another lover.' Maurice heaved a regretful sigh. 'But she would not have me, and your friend Roger said she was not for sale. But I *will* have her, no matter what it takes. Pass her a message: I pay well. I will even add something for you, if you allow me to entertain her for an hour tonight. Tell her to come after compline.'

'We shall see,' said Geoffrey, thinking that extra money might come in useful for the return journey to Tancred, but aware that Durand preferred his men younger and slimmer than the portly Maurice.

'You should go to the King's quarters,' said Maurice, rubbing his hands in delight when he saw Geoffrey might be prepared to be generous. 'There is someone there you know.'

Maurice would say no more and, with some trepidation, Geoffrey approached the handsome tent with the royal standard that he had last seen at Arundel. Servants scurried here and there, fastening the ropes that held it up and carrying the King's possessions inside. Henry was in deep conversation with Bishop Giffard, and their earnest, sober faces suggested they were discussing something important: finance. He backed away, not wanting to know whom Henry next planned to tax to pay for his war against Bellême. He came up hard against someone and turned to apologize, but his words stuck in his throat.

'I did not believe Abbot Ralph when he said you had escaped,' said Beaumais, as startled to see Geoffrey as Geoffrey was to see him. 'I thought you had been hit by the archers.'

'As you see,' said Geoffrey, indicating he was whole and healthy. 'How is Abbot Ralph? Bellême did not . . . ?'

'Even he knows better than to harm a man of God. He made Ralph give up your letters, though, then read all manner of sinister meanings in the fact that you are fond of your sister and that you apologized for not returning sooner to Tancred. Emma and Amise even entertained the notion that you killed their kinsmen on *Tancred's* orders! But your letters were sent to their intended recipients after Arundel surrendered.' He smiled spitefully.

'God's teeth!' muttered Geoffrey, supposing he had better send others as soon as possible. His sister would not be pleased if she grieved for him, only to find he was alive, and neither would Tancred. 'Where is Ralph now?'

'Shrewsbury,' said Beaumais. 'But Bellême will want him at his beck and call again soon. Men of integrity are few and far between now that *I* am no longer in his service.'

'You have changed your allegiance.' Geoffrey was not particularly surprised that a man like Beaumais would abandon Bellême when he saw him as a lost cause. 'Why?'

'I served him for as long as I could. But then the King pointed out that he will soon be defeated and his followers exiled. I do not want to be exiled, so I reconsidered my position.'

'No,' said Geoffrey, regarding him intently and knowing he was not telling the truth. 'You have always been the King's man. You played a dangerous game with Bellême!'

'I do not know what you are talking about,' said Beaumais stiffly. 'I have never made a secret of my loyalty to Bellême.'

'To Bellême, no,' said Geoffrey. 'But you have done well to conceal your allegiance to Henry, whom you have served since we met at Westminster Palace in March, if not before.'

'You are wrong,' said Beaumais coldly. 'I—'

'While we were there, you said Henry might kill me. It was a lie: Henry would not kill me, because I am too useful to him alive.' Geoffrey spoke bitterly, because he disliked being a pawn in games played by men like the King. 'You told that story to ensure I would go to Arundel with Bellême.'

'It was not my idea and I did not want you there. I was afraid you might betray me with some of your pointed questions, but Henry insisted. He wanted more than one agent inside Arundel, and he decided on you. I was to recruit you if I needed help.'

'But not the other way around.' Geoffrey recalled Bishop Giffard mentioning there would be other spies in Arundel, and should have guessed one was the man who had spent time in Henry's Court.

'Right,' agreed Beaumais. 'I was more important, so *you* were to help *me*. My task was to spread unease and dissent, so the garrison would be more ready to surrender than one that was united. You helped me there, by telling Matilda that Arnulf killed Hugh and that Josbert prevented her from negotiating with the King.'

He smiled, but Geoffrey did not think it was a pleasant expression. The knight realized he should have suspected why Beaumais was always ready to chatter and gossip: he was spreading lies and suspicion. He also recalled that Beaumais had thrived on the claustrophobic conditions of the siege, while others had cracked. The misery and frustration were part of his plan.

'Are your activities why Arundel surrendered so quickly after Tickhill?' Geoffrey supposed that if Beaumais had so damaged morale in a week, he had probably brought folk close to collective suicide after three months.

'They helped, and the siblings are more like bitter enemies than allies now. Henry also wanted me to send him messages about the state of Arundel's defences, but Bellême had it too well guarded.'

'I managed,' said Geoffrey, gratified to see the man look surprised. 'So, Henry gave himself two chances with his secret spies.'

'Three,' corrected Bellême. 'There was one other, apparently. But I was the most important.'

'I suppose he thought my very obvious presence would distract from yours.' Geoffrey was not pleased that he had been the tethered goat to help the slippery Beaumais.

'And it worked well. While you were there I was able to do what I liked. It became far more difficult after you left.' He sighed and stretched. Geoffrey detected a strange odour, and noticed the man's hair still glistened with large quantities of olive oil.

'Has Emma succeeded in making good Greek Fire yet? Or in raising her mother from the dead?'

'Her Greek Fire is better than Henry's. It burns well, because of the unique adjustments she has made to the basic ingredients. The only thing she cannot do is propel it towards the enemy.'

'But it was you who provided her with olive oil,' said Geoffrey.

'Are you insane?' demanded Beaumais indignantly. 'I had changed sides by then. I am hardly likely to provide my enemy with the raw materials to defeat my new master, am I?'

'But you met her at All Hallows Barking, where she added olive oil to her Greek Fire for the first time,' said Geoffrey, not mentioning that she had added raisins and severed fingers, too.

'I most certainly did not,' said Beaumais shortly. 'I told you before: I have my own supplies of olive oil. It is imported from Sicily, and is far too expensive to waste on Emma's experiments. I imagine it was Arnulf who met her at the church.'

Geoffrey thought for a moment. 'I see. But although he may have provided her with the oil, he was actually thwarting her by giving her ingredients that were tainted or of poor quality.'

Beaumais grinned at him. 'You understand the Bellêmes better than I thought. That is exactly what he did. I had a good look at his oil, and I certainly would not use *that* on my hair! He did not want Emma to become too powerful you see. He is greedy and self-serving, and feels as much threatened by his own family as he does by enemies like the King.'

'Who can blame him?' muttered Geoffrey. 'But I should have guessed Arnulf was the person with Emma in All Hallows, because he called her "Emmy", and I have heard no one other than him refer to her like that. I was blinded by the fact that I thought it was you.'

You probably saw me "assisting" Emma in Arundel, but,

285

like Arnulf, I was deliberately more hindrance than help –
although I acted out of loyalty to Henry, not to further my
own interests.'

Geoffrey was not so sure about that, but he said nothing.

'Was it you who extinguished the fire she set in All
Hallows, then?' Beaumais asked. 'Yes, it must have been,
or how would you have seen her and Arnulf working there?
She was furious about that, since she was sure her device
would work and destroy any evidence she might have left.'

'Her device,' mused Geoffrey. 'A candle set to burn down
and ignite a dangerous substance at a later time. She confessed
to knowing about that sort of thing when Cecily died. Now we
learn she did more than just know about them: she actually
used them.'

'She is a formidable lady, and that is why I did all I could
to hinder her experiments with Greek Fire.' He showed
Geoffrey hands that still bore scars. 'At great personal risk,
I might add.'

'However,' said Geoffrey, still thinking, 'while you deny
involvement in the plan to make Greek Fire, you were
certainly involved in the one to unite Old Mabel with her
head. You expected Petronus to deliver information regarding
its whereabouts before Easter, and I am sure you would have
passed that knowledge directly to Emma, had it arrived.'

'But before Easter, I still believed that Old Mabel's resurrection would win the war against Henry. Now I know
that even if Emma does succeed, Old Mabel will make no
difference to the Bellême fortunes for two reasons: first, I
doubt anyone will be able to control her, and second, I do
not think she will be able to do much anyway – not without
a head, and Emma still does not have one that fits.'

'The one she stole from All Hallows was no good? What
about the one she took from Hugh?'

'They were too big, and Mabel will not want an overly
large head on her body when she comes back to life. Well,
who would?' Beaumais shuddered, then walked away to
pay homage to the King, leaving Geoffrey staring after him
thoughtfully.

*   *   *

Geoffrey was heartily sick of the whole business, and did not want to remain in Bridgnorth with men like Pantulf and Beaumais, who changed sides any time they thought it was personally expedient. Their actions went against everything he believed in, and he found their company distasteful. He determined to stay as far away from them as possible, although it was not always easy, because they believed they had something in common and often sought him out.

'It is easy to serve Henry,' said Pantulf lazily one day, when he came to sit with Geoffrey to eat his midday meal of bread and salted beef. 'Especially when he promises me a prize like Stafford Castle.'

'And *I* shall be Sheriff of Shropshire,' said Beaumais gleefully. 'What about you, Geoffrey? What did Henry promise you if you came to his side?'

'A new surcoat,' said Geoffrey shortly.

He wondered how Henry could begin to trust men like them, and knew that if Bellême won any kind of victory, they would slip back to him in an instant. He was about to leave on the pretext of mounting a patrol, when Bishop Maurice joined the little gathering, and began to pester the knight yet again about securing the services of 'Angel Locks', making it difficult for Geoffrey to escape.

'Let me show you the siege plans,' said Pantulf suddenly to Beaumais. 'You, too, Maurice. Come.'

Geoffrey could hardly believe his ears. 'I do not think that is a good idea,' he said, thinking he had not worked so hard drawing maps and drafting strategies simply so Pantulf could show them to the first traitor who happened to pass. 'The fewer people who see them, the better.'

'They may have suggestions,' said Pantulf. 'Maurice has been to Shrewsbury, while Beaumais knows Bellême well, and is better able to predict how he might react in certain situations.'

'Our plans will be no good if they slip into the wrong hands,' warned Geoffrey, not caring whether he offended Beaumais or Maurice. If the King wanted to trust someone like Beaumais with strategic secrets, then that was his affair, but he did not think Pantulf should do it. And there was no need to confide in the Bishop of London at all, given that the prelate's presence was more closely related to the efficient administration of Henry's tax system than to warfare.

Pantulf waved a dismissive hand at Geoffrey's objections and led the way to the tent where the large table stood, still covered in diagrams. He brushed most aside with a sweep of his hand and took others from a locked chest. Eagerly – too eagerly Geoffrey felt – Beaumais and Maurice leaned forward to study them. Maurice reached across the table to point at something, and knocked over a goblet of wine, so that dark red liquid shot out across Geoffrey's plans, making the ink run.

'Careful!' he snapped, mopping up the spillage with his sleeve. He examined the map critically and decided that, luckily for Maurice, the stain did not obliterate any of the important details. The mess was ugly, but it was a working battle plan, and its prettiness was irrelevant.

'Sorry,' said Maurice with a sheepish grin. He glanced at Pantulf. 'Now, where did you say you will station the main troops in this particular attack?'

Pantulf began to reply in great detail and, disgusted with the whole affair, Geoffrey left them to it, and spent the rest of the afternoon gambling with Roger and Helbye in a blatant flouting of the rules Henry had set to maintain discipline in his camp. That afternoon, restless and unsettled among folk of whom he was deeply suspicious, he took his horse out for some exercise. His dog loped at his side, enjoying the opportunity to stretch its legs.

The countryside around Bridgnorth was gently rolling, some of it dedicated to crops, but most left for grazing the many sheep that were farmed in the area. There were large tracts of woodland, too, not the dense wild forests like the ones farther south or in Wales, but areas of mixed oaks, beeches and elms, dappled with pleasant glades. Geoffrey aimed for a track he had followed before, knowing it was relatively free of roots and other obstacles that might trip a warhorse.

After about an hour he became aware of voices, carried towards him on a soft summer breeze. He knew none of Henry's men would be so far outside the camp – soldiers needed permits to forage in the woods, and none had been granted that day. He supposed it was possible that a noble had had the same idea as him, and wanted to exercise his steed, but most seemed lethargic and lazy, and tended to let their squires manage the care of their mounts.

Hoping the discussion was nothing more threatening than a couple of poachers, Geoffrey eased his horse forward. He had no particular plan in mind, other than to ensure that the voices did not belong to someone who should be inside the castle, and which would mean that Henry needed to tighten the blockade. He dismounted, looped his reins over a tree stump and advanced on foot. His dog kept pace, straining forward as if it were hunting. Eventually, he came close enough to see the owners of the voices, and eased behind a tree when he identified one as Bishop Maurice. The prelate faced a second man and was passing him documents.

Geoffrey frowned when he noticed one scroll was stained with wine. What was the prelate doing out in the woods with the King's siege plans? He eased around his tree to try to see the identity of the second man, then felt his jaw drop in shock when the fellow turned slightly and he had a clear view of his face. It was Robert de Bellême.

Geoffrey stood stock still with his mind racing. Had Bellême slipped out of Bridgnorth using some secret passageway known only to him? Geoffrey had come across such devices in the past – there was one in his own home in Goodrich – and Bellême was just the kind of man to install such a feature. But Geoffrey had been told that Bellême was in Shrewsbury, so why was he at Bridgnorth?

The meeting of prelate and Earl certainly explained why Maurice had been so keen to learn about the besiegers' plans. He was not only passing the maps to Bellême, but was elaborating on them by repeating the details Pantulf had been so willing to provide. As Geoffrey listened, he heard Bellême quizzing Maurice on specifics, and the bishop answering without hesitation. He cursed himself for not seeing sooner that Maurice was not to be trusted. Wulfric, the pot boy at the Crusader's Head, had told him months before that the prelate was among those who attended clandestine meetings in Southwark. Geoffrey realized that Maurice must have been the King's enemy for a very long time.

He edged closer, wanting to hear exactly what Maurice said. It was too late to prevent the information from changing hands, so the most useful thing Geoffrey could do now was to learn the extent of the damage the bishop's betrayal had caused. He certainly had no intention of challenging them. The Earl had a formidable reputation as a warrior, and was dressed in full armour. Geoffrey was clad only in boiled-leather leggings and a chain-mail tunic, and was not willing to squander his life fighting an enemy so much better equipped.

But he had not taken his dog into account. It had met Bellême on a previous occasion, when it had been kicked, and it was not an animal to forget such an insult. It began to growl. Geoffrey pushed it with his foot, willing it to be quiet. It promptly barked. Bellême moved like lightning, striding towards the tree and pushing away the branches before Geoffrey could do more than turn and look at the path that would allow him to escape. With a triumphant cry, Bellême hauled him from his hiding place and threw him to the litter of leaves that comprised the forest floor.

Geoffrey scrambled to his feet and made an insulting bow, thinking he was doomed anyway, so he might as well enjoy himself by aggravating the Earl before he was run through.

'Good evening, My Lord,' he said pleasantly. 'I did not expect to see you again.'

'Well, I expected to see you,' snapped Bellême, in the kind of voice that indicated he did not regard it as a pleasure. Geoffrey's dog snarled from behind the safety of its tree. 'I see you still possess that miserable beast. You told me the King had killed it.'

Geoffrey wished he had. 'I was mistaken.'

'You lied to me,' said Bellême, more curious than angry. 'I did not know you lied. You have misled me on previous occasions, but you have never told me an outright untruth.'

'There is a first time for everything. Did Matilda tell you I discovered Hugh's killer? It was Arnulf, but I did not think you would believe me.'

'She mentioned it, but she and Arnulf have always despised each other and she has many reasons for wanting him discredited. Perhaps it is just as well you escaped, because I would have believed you when you identified Arnulf as my traitor, and I would have killed him. And I would have been wrong to do so, because you have just shown me that you are a liar.'

'You would have kept your word and let me live?'

'Of course not. But I knew you would rise to the challenge of completing a task in a set period of time, and there was no one better suited to investigate Hugh's murder. I was quite serious when I said I wanted to know the identity of the traitor, and I was furious when you escaped without giving me a proper report first. I could not trust Matilda's version of your reasoning. But it is all irrelevant now. I have learned that *all* my siblings are traitors in their own way. There is not one who would sacrifice himself to save me, and even Sybilla now wishes she had nailed her loyalty to another mast.'

'We should not stay here, My Lord,' said Maurice, looking around nervously. 'Geoffrey will have guards with him, and I do not want to be caught here with you.'

'He is alone,' said Bellême, his cold black eyes boring into Geoffrey's as though he wanted to read his mind. 'Or his friends would have made themselves known by now. We shall dispatch him and continue our discussion uninterrupted.'

'But it is time we were going,' argued Maurice. 'We do not have the leisure for this kind of thing.'

'I would not betray the King if I were you,' said Geoffrey to Maurice. 'He is not a fool, and will find you out sooner or later. Your vocation will not save you, either.'

'Bishop Maurice believes in me,' said Bellême smoothly, cutting off the prelate's reply. 'I will win this campaign, Geoffrey. Even as we speak there are men gathering to ride to my aid – mercenaries from Normandy and Crusader knights who know how to fight. The King will not defeat me.'

'You must not linger,' said Maurice to Bellême urgently. 'Ride back to Shrewsbury, before one of the patrols finds you and your campaign ends in capture.'

'*Back* to Shrewsbury?' mused Geoffrey. 'So, you did not escape from Bridgnorth?'

Bellême glowered at him. 'How could I? You have it sealed up like some ancient relic. I cannot even get word to my followers through my secret doors. But it does not matter. Bridgnorth will hold Henry's attention while I strengthen my position at Shrewsbury. It was always my intention to defeat him there, anyway.'

'Do not tell him all this!' squeaked Maurice in alarm. 'He will pass your plans to the King.'

'He will be dead,' said Bellême, drawing his sword. 'Fetch the horses, Maurice. We shall be done with Sir Geoffrey in a few moments, then we shall ride – you to the King before he notices you have gone, and me to victory at Shrewsbury.'

Maurice opened his mouth to object, but Bellême lunged at Geoffrey, so he hurried away, unwilling to witness a slaughter. While the dog barked furiously, Geoffrey drew his sword and met Bellême's advance with a stroke of his own. He followed it with a hefty kick aimed at Bellême's knee.

The Earl howled in pain, and came at Geoffrey with a series of sweeping blows that were so powerful they made whistling sounds through the air. One hit the trunk of a tree and splinters flew in all directions. Geoffrey dodged away, lighter of foot and more agile than the heavier man in his full armour. He ran all around a thick oak tree and managed to stab at the Earl's back. Bellême gave a scream of outrage and turned faster than Geoffrey had thought possible. He hurled a dagger, and only good luck saved Geoffrey from being skewered. While he ducked, Bellême struck with his sword, and more of the tree flew apart.

'You will blunt the blade,' taunted Geoffrey, circling him. 'Did no one teach you never to cut down trees with your sword?'

He skipped to one side as the Earl came at him yet again, his eyes red-rimmed and longing for blood. Geoffrey teased him about his speed, hoping to encourage wild attacks that would tire him. Geoffrey's shorter reach would not allow him a good strike, and his only chance was to wear the bigger knight down. But Bellême was an experienced warrior, too, and knew exactly what Geoffrey was trying to do. He controlled his rage, and came after Geoffrey in shorter, faster spurts to keep him on his guard, forcing him to use valuable energy of his own to leap away from attacks that never came.

They lunged, weaved and swiped, but neither sword met its target, and Geoffrey soon felt sweat coursing down his back. Bellême's face was red and shiny, and Geoffrey imagined he must be half cooked inside his armour. He redoubled his efforts, trying to force the Earl to move as much as possible in the hope that sweat would drip into his eyes and blind him for a vital moment, or make his sword slippery in his hand.

The sun began to set, making it difficult to see. Geoffrey's arms and legs started to ache, and he wondered how long they had been fighting, wielding their heavy weapons. Bellême was tiring, too, and made mistakes. Once he allowed Geoffrey to come too close and was rewarded with a stinging slash to the elbow that made him swear viciously. But then he found some demonic strength, and came after Geoffrey so fast that the smaller knight tripped as he staggered backwards. Geoffrey saw Bellême's face lit with a savage smile, and rolled away just in time to prevent himself from being pinned to the ground through his middle. Bellême stabbed again, and Geoffrey felt the blade slice through the leather of his leggings and rake down his calf. He struggled away, trying to regain his feet before Bellême moved in for the kill.

But Bellême would not give Geoffrey the time to stand, and kept him rolling with savage stabs. Geoffrey twisted violently, then abandoned his sword to grab Bellême around the knees. Both toppled to the ground, with Bellême scratching and punching like a tavern brawler. He struck Geoffrey hard on the side of the head with the handle of his dagger, and Geoffrey felt himself begin to black out. He fought desperately against the encroaching darkness, knowing that if he swooned he would never wake.

'I always knew you would die by my hand,' Bellême whispered. He abandoned his dagger and his fingers began to tighten around Geoffrey's throat. 'I knew I only had to be patient.'

Just when his world was beginning to turn silver around the

edges, Geoffrey jerked one knee upwards as hard as he could, full into Bellême's groin. The Earl's grip eased immediately, and tears of agony rolled down his cheeks. Geoffrey pulled away and tried to stand, searching for his sword among the litter of last year's leaves, so he could kill the man and bring an end to his reign of terror. But Bellême was not a man to let pain slow him down. He, too, scrambled to his feet and began another of his hacking attacks. This time Geoffrey had no weapon to counter the blows, and his injured leg slowed him. He jerked away and limped to a tree, where the two of them ducked and weaved around it for an age, while Geoffrey felt himself become weaker and slower.

'Someone is coming,' came Maurice's urgent whisper through the trees. Geoffrey heard the rumble of hoofs, and knew Maurice was telling the truth. 'They must be Henry's men. Run, while you still can, My Lord Earl. If you are caught, they will kill you for certain.'

Bellême hesitated, and Geoffrey dived at him while his attention wavered. But Geoffrey's strength had ebbed, and he did no more than make the Earl stagger. Bellême, meanwhile, had gained new energy from learning he was on the verge of capture. He kicked out, knocking Geoffrey from his feet. Geoffrey tried to move away, but his limbs were slow to obey him. He was aware of his dog barking again, and saw it dart forward to sink its hard yellow teeth into Bellême's leg. The Earl bellowed in fury, and kicked out fiercely, but the dog hung on. Cursing foully, the Earl raised his sword and aimed it at Geoffrey, who only just managed to roll away in time. He sensed he would not be able to do so again.

'Hold him still,' Bellême ordered the bishop, still trying to dislodge the dog. 'He is a danger to us both alive. We must kill him, or we are undone.'

'I cannot,' said Maurice, his eyes wide. 'My vocation forbids the spilling of blood.'

'You have brought about the spilling of blood by passing me your plans,' Bellême pointed out, swiping at the dog and missing. He winced as its fangs sank deeper.

'That is different,' said Maurice. He glanced behind him,

panic-stricken. 'The horsemen are here. Stay if you will, but *I* will wait no longer.'

His words finally penetrated Bellême's brain. With a sudden surge of strength, the Earl kicked away the dog, vaulted into his saddle and wheeled his horse around, aiming to trample Geoffrey under its hoofs. Geoffrey predicted what he intended to do and jerked away. Bellême hurled a dagger as a parting shot, trying one last time to kill the man who had been such a thorn in his side. It hissed harmlessly into the ground, but Geoffrey decided to lie still anyway. The Earl would not see his dagger had missed in the gathering dusk, and it seemed prudent to play dead until he had gone.

'You have killed him, now go!' urged Maurice desperately, while the dog yapped furiously around the horse's feet. 'I cannot be found here with you.'

Bellême turned his horse and was gone, while Geoffrey struggled to his feet, aware that if any horsemen were coming, they would not be on his side. He had given no orders for patrols in that part of the woods, and suspected they would be Bellême's men.

'There,' said Maurice, glancing wildly around him. 'I have driven him away, and you had the sense to feign death. But we should not stay here, because he does not like men who tell him lies.'

'Lies about what?' asked Geoffrey, flexing his cut leg.

'There are no soldiers coming,' said Maurice. 'Come! Quickly!'

'Why are you . . . ?' began Geoffrey, but Maurice shook his head.

'Will your horse bear my weight as well as yours? We must be away as fast as possible.'

'Both of us would kill it,' said Geoffrey, hearing the weary slur in his words. 'You are not exactly feather-light.' He gathered his scattered weapons, feeling the ground tip and sway as he leaned down; even exhausted and dazed he followed his knightly instincts and refused to ride without them.

'Better it than us,' said Maurice, clambering into Geoffrey's saddle. He offered his hand and Geoffrey took it warily. 'Hurry!'

Geoffrey climbed slowly behind Maurice. The poor beast snickered angrily at the weight, but Geoffrey urged it into a canter, hoping it would be able to see in the failing light, and would not stumble and dump them both on the ground to die at Bellême's mercy.

'Tell me, bishop,' he said as they went. 'Whose side are you really on?'

'The side of right,' said Maurice. 'And that is all you need to know. Now hurry.'

Thirteen

Maurice refused to answer Geoffrey's questions until they were well away from the woods and could see the King's campfires in the distance. Then he closed his eyes and heaved a sigh of relief. Geoffrey slid to the ground to spare his horse, leading it across fields and scrub, and feeling his strength return. He took several deep breaths, and leaned down to inspect the wound in his leg. It was just a scratch, and needed no more than a rinse with clean water to see it heal.

The daylight soon faded, and night was full on them as they made their way home. The moon was obscured by clouds, and in the distance Geoffrey could hear thunder. A flicker of lightning told him that a summer storm was brewing somewhere to the north, and the air smelled metallic. His dog whimpered. He leaned down and patted its head, grateful for its intervention in the fight.

'Now,' he said to the portly bishop. 'You had better tell me what you were doing. King Henry will not be pleased when he learns you have been meeting his enemy in secret.'

'Fool!' snapped Maurice. 'Do you think I went there of my own accord? Put my head in the lion's mouth for fun? There is nothing Bellême can offer that would make me take that sort of risk.'

Geoffrey squinted up at him. 'You were on the King's business?'

'Of course,' said Maurice, aggrieved. 'It was *his* idea that one of his most trusted ministers should pretend to cross to Bellême and feed him information that will bring about his downfall. *And* he decided that a prelate would make a better traitor than one of his nobles. I have been the King's agent for months now – since Christmas, in fact.'

'You attended Bellême's clandestine meetings in the Crusader's Head,' said Geoffrey, recalling what the landlord and his pot boy had told him.

'Yes,' said Maurice huffily. 'And I would not visit a place like *that* unless the King ordered me to do so. I was so unnerved by the whole venture that I was obliged to partake of some of the Winchester Geese immediately afterwards, to soothe my ragged nerves.'

Geoffrey recalled the taverner telling him that, too. 'Being a double agent cannot be easy.'

'I am not a *double* agent,' snapped Maurice angrily. 'That implies I am a traitor to both sides, and I am not. I am loyal to the King, which is why I am prepared to risk my life for him.'

'You are the reason the King knew about Bellême's Greek Fire,' mused Geoffrey. 'And about the plan to unite Old Mabel with her missing head, so she could join their battle ranks.'

'Me and Bishop Giffard both.' Maurice sighed and ran a hand over his perspiring pate. 'But I deplore this sort of activity. I am not built for the excitement spying brings. My heart is pounding, and if I do not have a woman soon I shall expire.'

'What did Henry tell you to do today? Why does he want Bellême to have our plans?'

But Maurice was more interested in the state of his health than in satisfying the knight's curiosity. 'I feel quite sick, you know. I have never been so frightened in my life, especially when you appeared and I could see him thinking that I had led you there. You almost had us both killed, and the King's plan thwarted at the same time. I *should* have let Bellême finish you off.'

'Well, I am grateful you did not.'

'Your fight looked set to continue for hours, so I decided my only option was to draw it to a close myself,' said Maurice resentfully. 'I could hardly leave while you still battled, or he would have assumed I had summoned him there to have him murdered. And, worse, he would have dismissed the information I gave him. You put me in a quandary.'

'I apologize.'

'I set my horse loose, so he would hear its hoofs and think soldiers were coming. I do not *think* he will return to see whether a patrol really came, so he probably still believes I am his man.' Maurice was anxious. 'You should not have followed me.'

'I did not,' said Geoffrey. 'But if you hold secret meetings in the future, you would be wise to whisper, not bawl loud enough to be heard on the opposite side of a forest.'

'I tried to make him speak more softly, but he said there was no one around. That man is too confident for his own good.'

'So, the King *ordered* you to give our battle plans to Bellême?' said Geoffrey, wanting to be sure he had not misunderstood.

'Yes,' said Maurice. 'He thinks I understand maps, because he made me draw one of Arundel.'

'You asked me if I had been there when we met at St Paul's Cathedral,' recalled Geoffrey. 'You had been told to make a map, and wanted to speak to anyone who might give you further information.'

'Exactly,' said Maurice. 'Matilda de Mortain asked the same of me when I bedded her once. She questioned me relentlessly about what I remembered of the place. I played the bumbling fool, because it seemed a good idea at the time. Then Beaumais found out about my dalliance, so I was obliged to tell the King myself, before he did it for me.'

'You asked whether Beaumais had gossiped about it to me,' recalled Geoffrey. 'At Westminster.'

'I do not trust Beaumais. He is spiteful and sly. When I eventually plucked up the courage to tell Henry about Matilda, I anticipated that he would be angry, but I think it gave him the idea that plans of all the castles in his kingdom might be useful. I worked for weeks on Arundel, trying to recall every passage and chamber.'

'Speaking of charts, my squire heard the dying archer at Westminster say "map". Do you know anything about who killed him and Petronus? I know the map he referred to had nothing to do with sketching castles, although I suspect the King was involved.'

'My servants would need to be paid a lot more than *I* could afford to induce them to murder a man of God on my orders. I do not know who killed poor Petronus.'

'And the two archers?'

'That was Beaumais. He was proving his loyalty to Henry, and killed them for their incompetence when they failed to secure the map from Petronus. He was part of the King's hunting party that day, and it was his arrow that killed the man you had caught. Then he slipped away to finish the other one. Henry knew what he was doing, but did not stop him.'

'Beaumais slips from side to side like a serpent. How do you know he did not strangle Petronus?'

'Because I was with him,' said Maurice with a heavy sigh. 'I thought he might try to snatch the map for Bellême. But he merely executed the archers for failing to carry out the King's instructions. You probably heard us arguing about it later, in Westminster Palace. I do not recall ever being so angry. I disapprove of wanton slaughter.'

'So what happened to this map?' asked Geoffrey, who had a vivid recollection of the furious, low-voiced altercation that had taken place between the two men that day. 'It was not on Petronus's body, and it seems the archers did not take it, or they would still be alive.'

'No one seems to know,' said Maurice. 'Beaumais thought you took it, but I know that was not possible: you did not have the opportunity, because you ran straight into Henry and he escorted you to Westminster. Your friend Roger did not have it, because his belongings were thoroughly searched that afternoon by the King's agents. We have no idea what happened to the thing.'

'Perhaps Beaumais was lying about its existence,' suggested Geoffrey, concealing his astonishment that anyone should be able to search Roger without being caught. Roger was very protective of his possessions. 'To make himself seem more important in the eyes of the King.'

'It exists,' said Maurice with conviction. 'Petronus saw it himself. But, if you know what is good for you, you will put it from your mind. You will not want to know what it contains, believe me.'

'It reveals the whereabouts of Old Mabel's head.'

'How do you know that?' demanded Maurice, startled. 'Did someone tell you? Beaumais?'

'I reasoned it out for myself. Emma is toting her mother's bones all over the country in the hope of restoring them to life, and it is common knowledge that Old Mabel was decapitated. It is not a huge leap in logic to assume a resurrection is unlikely when the body is in two separate locations.'

Maurice shuddered. 'I hope a resurrection does not occur at all. I do not want to do battle with the likes of Old Mabel; I am not sure my religious skills are up to it. Still, the map seems to have disappeared, and the Bellêmes are not in a position to go hunting for heads anyway. Their day is almost over, and soon it will not matter whether Old Mabel makes an appearance or not. Beaumais thinks it is unlikely now – it is why he changed his allegiance.'

'The King should not trust him,' said Geoffrey distastefully.

'I quite agree,' said Maurice fervently. He shuddered. 'I cannot tell you how vile it was passing Bellême those plans. I shall never do anything like that again. My poor heart would not allow it.' He did indeed look shaken. His face was pale and his hands were unsteady on the reins.

'You can regain your strength with a woman,' Geoffrey suggested helpfully.

'Yours?' asked Maurice eagerly. 'Only a paragon like Angel Locks will be able to restore the balance of my humours tonight, after what I have been through.'

'You mean Durand?' asked Geoffrey. 'I can ask him, if you like.'

'I do not know why you persist with this charade,' said Maurice irritably. 'I am a man who is intimately acquainted with women, and I know a lady when I see one. Angel Locks is one of the most glorious creatures I have ever had the

301

pleasure to admire, and I cannot imagine why you always abuse her good name. You do not deserve her.'

'No,' agreed Geoffrey. 'I do not.'

Geoffrey and Maurice travelled the rest of the way to Henry's camp in silence, as the knight wondered what Henry thought he would gain by leaking sensitive information to Bellême, and Maurice was lost in a lecherous reverie about Durand. Geoffrey assumed the King intended to develop new plans of his own, although he felt they would not be as good. Geoffrey had worked hard, taking careful measurements and performing calculations that took into account the lie of the land and the number of men needed to storm the castle. Henry had not, and Geoffrey knew an ill-prepared attempt to take a fortress like Bridgnorth by force would fail.

'Do not worry,' said Maurice, as they approached the first outpost and soldiers stepped forward to demand their names and the nature of their business. 'The King knows what he is doing. Come with me to see him now. He will put your mind at rest.'

Geoffrey demurred, preferring to return to his own campfire, but Maurice claimed the knight owed Henry an explanation as to why he had almost thwarted his carefully contrived plot. Reluctantly, he followed the bishop to the royal enclosure, and listened while Maurice told the King what had happened in the woods that evening. Geoffrey suppressed a smile when the prelate allocated himself a role that was rather more active in the fight than the reality, but said nothing to contradict him. Maurice *had* saved his life with his ruse, and Geoffrey owed the man his gratitude.

Henry appeared to be satisfied with the way matters had ended, although he was not pleased that Geoffrey had almost foiled what he insisted was a clever ploy. Geoffrey rubbed the bridge of his nose, and hoped that the campaign against Bellême would soon be over. He was weary with nobles and their deceptions.

'Bellême is at Shrewsbury,' he said. 'Not Bridgnorth, as we thought. We should leave a small force here and march on Shrewsbury immediately. That is where he intends to make his final stand, and we should prevent him from becoming too firmly entrenched—'

'Not yet,' interrupted Henry. 'There are things that must happen first.'

'Such as what?' demanded Geoffrey, forgetting he was speaking to a monarch. 'Bridgnorth will surrender as soon as Shrewsbury falls: there would be no point in holding out, and the man you most want to defeat – Bellême – is at Shrewsbury. Why wait here?'

'My spies inform me that Bellême and Roger are at Shrewsbury,' argued Henry. 'But Arnulf is *here*, and I want him just as much as I do Bellême. He murdered young Philip, and I do not approve of the strong slaying the weak.'

'He killed Hugh, too,' said Geoffrey, aware that tiredness was making him incautious. The King had not been very interested in what Bellême had ordered Geoffrey to do during his week at Arundel, and Geoffrey had not mentioned that he had uncovered the identity of a murderer.

'How do you know?' asked Henry, startled. 'I thought I was the only one with the answer to that.'

Geoffrey was wary. '*You* knew Arnulf was the culprit? How? Is *he* working for you, too?'

'He is not,' replied Henry shortly. 'I have standards, and the treacherous Arnulf falls well below them. I sent my own agents to discover what had happened in the Crusader's Head that night – and not a moment too soon, because the landlord was murdered soon after they spoke to him. Arnulf was covering his tracks, but he had left it too late. My agents had already acquired all the information needed to solve the mystery.'

Geoffrey outlined what Bellême had asked him to do. 'So, when did *you* find out?' he asked.

'At my Easter Court. Had I known that Bellême would charge you with a similar investigation, I would have told you the answer and saved you some trouble. But you cannot blame me for not anticipating that those would be the terms of your joining his household.'

'So, why *did* Arnulf kill Hugh? I never did understand his motive.'

'Because Hugh was working for me,' said Henry simply.

303

He smiled at Geoffrey's astonishment. 'I offered him a percentage of any lands I took from his family, and he was mine in an instant. I thought his pretence of dim wits would protect him, but while he fooled some Bellêmes with his dithering and vacant grins, not all were convinced. They are a clever family.'

'So how did Arnulf discover that he was your agent?'

'Through Philip. Philip was *not* my man, lest you think I would stoop to using such a weakling to perform tasks so vital to the security of my kingdom. He was Arnulf's spy, a fact I had known for some time. Hugh invited Arnulf and Philip to his chamber in the Crusader's Head the night the clan gathered to watch Emma demonstrate her Greek Fire. Rashly, he confronted them with their treachery himself, instead of allowing me to deal with the matter.'

'So, Arnulf killed him,' surmised Geoffrey. He realized he had been wrong about one conclusion he had shared with Matilda: the two 'friends' for whom he had ordered wine were not Arnulf and Josbert, but Arnulf and Philip. Still, it did not matter much, since Arnulf had done the actual killing and the companion was merely a witness. He continued. 'Arnulf probably decided Philip was too great a risk, and saw it was only a matter of time before he let something slip.'

Henry nodded. 'Philip did not react well under pressure, and I imagine the growing stress of being in a castle with his bellicose relatives would have turned him jittery. I would not have trusted him, and Arnulf must have felt the same way. Beaumais saw him do it.'

'Beaumais was the man in the cloak who watched them talking in the stables before Philip was killed,' said Geoffrey in understanding. 'I should have guessed. I saw a long pale hair adhering to the back of his cloak, and there was only one person in the castle to whom that could have belonged: his lover Emma. Could Beaumais not have saved Philip?'

'It was not worth the risk,' said Henry. 'Beaumais had a job to do for me, and that was more important than Philip's life. Sacrifices – like Philip and Hugh – are unavoidable in times of war.'

Geoffrey thought about what he had learned. 'So, Hugh was

your agent. Did he act for anyone else? Did he bring you messages from other members of his family who wanted to parley?'

Henry shook his head. 'Geoffrey, Geoffrey! I have already told you the answer to that. I asked him to discover whether any of them were interested, but he said they were not.'

Geoffrey smiled maliciously. 'Then your spy was not all he seemed, either. Matilda entrusted him with several begging notes for you. He carried one the day he died.'

Henry gaped. 'Hugh deceived *me*? But why?'

'Because of the reward you promised him, I imagine. Had you pardoned the sisters, then his percentage would have been smaller. It would have been in his interests to see them *all* exiled.'

A faint smile flickered across Henry's dark features. 'You see? He was not as weak-witted as everyone believed. He was able and willing to manipulate most situations to his own advantage. Bellême will be sorry to hear he lost an opportunity to secure such an ally.'

'So, who murdered the others? We know Arnulf killed Hugh, Philip and Oswin, and Beaumais killed the archers in the woods near Westminster. But what about Petronus, Cecily and Haweis?'

Henry shrugged. 'I was not locked up in Arundel Castle, and so cannot know the identity of the other traitor in Bellême's family.'

Geoffrey regarded him warily. 'The *other* traitor?'

'Yes,' said Henry softly. 'There is one more who prefers me to Bellême, but I am not sure who he is. I only know him from his very helpful letters. When the time is right, he will come to me and I shall reward him. It is all arranged: he will show me a sign that only he and I know.'

'Lord!' muttered Geoffrey, bewildered by the complexities of Henry's relationships with the House of Montgomery-Bellême. He wondered what Henry would do if his faithful traitor transpired to be the Earl himself.

'Is there anything else?' asked Henry, eyeing a waiting pile of parchments meaningfully.

'I assume you have other plans ready, should we have the opportunity to attack Bridgnorth?' asked Geoffrey, wanting to work on them himself and thus increase their chances of success.

'No,' said Henry calmly. 'This castle will not be taken by force. You told me so when I first arrived, and I have no reason to disbelieve you.'

'But you told me to draw up plans—'

'So details of our "attack" could be passed to Bellême,' said Henry, as if it were obvious. 'He thinks I am impatient to see an end to this campaign, thanks to Bishop Maurice. He believes I will fight to take Bridgnorth and Shrewsbury. But I am a patient man. I will bide my time and Bridgnorth will soon be mine.'

'How?' demanded Geoffrey.

Henry smiled. 'You must wait and see, like everyone else.'

Geoffrey did not have to wait long. The royal troops had been camped around the feet of Bridgnorth Castle for less than three weeks when the gates opened and a small party rode out, holding their standards low to show the King their purpose was to parley, not to fight. There was an immediate commotion in the King's camp, as archers hurried to take up positions and scouting parties raced out to ensure no hostile army was advancing. Geoffrey saw his own patrols on their way, then went to the royal enclosure to see what was happening.

The first thing he noticed was that the three people in charge of the deputation were women, and the second was that they were accompanied by two knights. It was Emma, Matilda and Sybilla, ably guarded by Mabel and Amise. Geoffrey saw the puckered scar that marred Amise and was sorry that time had not rendered it less ugly. Mabel caught his eye and smiled – the first he had seen her give.

Beaumais was also there, but she did not acknowledge him. Sybilla gave the oily-headed courtier a glare that would have killed him on the spot if eyes were deadly weapons, and her expression was echoed by Amise. Emma was impassive. Beaumais did not seem at all discomfited by the fact that he was faced by people he had betrayed. He merely watched the scene unfolding in front of him with as much interest as any other onlooker. Geoffrey thought him incorrigible.

'You should not be here,' he said. 'Your presence may antagonize one of the women to do something violent, and it would be a pity to allow such an incident to interfere with a surrender.'

'I can protect myself,' said Beaumais, hair glinting in the sunlight. 'And you seem to be watching me, too, so I shall come to no harm.'

'That was not what I meant,' said Geoffrey, bemused by the man's brazen self-interest. 'I was thinking it would be a shame to lose a chance for peace because you want to spectate. I do not want my men to fight, if it can be avoided.'

Beaumais regarded him in astonishment. 'I thought knights liked bloodshed.'

Geoffrey saw there was no point in arguing. If Beaumais did not understand what he was trying to say in plain Norman-French, then there was no other way to tell him, short of forcing him away physically, and he did not want to make a scene.

'This is interesting,' said Beaumais, turning his attention to the activity in front of him. 'We shall soon have an end to this business. The King's spy will see to that.'

'Hugh?' asked Geoffrey. 'He died months ago. Or are you referring to yourself?'

'The other one,' said Beaumais. 'I told you about him before: the last of the King's brave agents, who risk their lives to bring about what he desires.'

'Is that how you see yourself?' asked Geoffrey, amused. 'Well, who is this paragon?'

'I cannot say,' replied Beaumais in the kind of voice that made Geoffrey certain he did not know. 'But he will play his part soon, and then we shall all be off to our new lives. I am to be Sheriff of Shropshire and I am anxious to make a start. Shrewsbury Castle will make fine headquarters.'

King Henry emerged from his tent to greet the Bellême sisters, having hastily donned some of his more regal attire. He wore a cloak fringed with ermine, despite the warmth of the day, and his tunic was sewn with gold thread. He also wore a crown. It was only a simple circlet of gold with one or two rubies at the front, but it was enough to turn him from a campaigning soldier into a monarch.

Meanwhile, the Bellême women had also been to some trouble over their appearance. Sybilla and Matilda were resplendent in floor-length supertunics and tight-sleeved kirtles, and their dark hair was decorously concealed under wimples held in place by jewelled diadems. Meanwhile, Emma had opted for the habit of a nun, and wore a plain brown tunic with a silver cross. Geoffrey supposed she was making the point that she was a high-ranking abbess and worthy of special treatment.

The three sisters dismounted, and Henry nodded to several squires that they should take the horses to water. Durand was one of them – he had taken to hovering around the King's tent because Bishop Maurice was usually preoccupied when he was near Henry and less likely to make advances. Durand, however, was reluctant to offer a Bellême his assistance. He hung back, but Henry glared at him, so he was obliged to move forward. Sybilla glanced at the golden-haired squire without much interest, then reached out suddenly and grabbed him by the front of his shirt.

'It is Geoffrey Mappestone's coward,' she said, regarding her catch like a cat with a mouse. Geoffrey had never seen a man look more terrified. 'Quaking and trembling like a grass in the wind.'

'My Lady,' Durand whispered, trying to free himself. He was not successful, and only made her tighten her grip. Emma also recognized him, and came to help her sister.

'I remember you,' said Sybilla nastily, while Durand looked as though he might be sick. 'You rode with us women when we travelled from Winchester to Arundel after the Easter Court. You were more interested in our baggage than you should have been, especially in our mother's box.'

'He was on the verge of climbing in with Hugh's head when I first met him,' said Emma harshly. 'Our brother should have run him through there and then.'

'I meant no harm,' bleated Durand. 'Please!'

308

Help came from an unexpected quarter. 'Leave him alone,' ordered Henry.

'Why?' asked Emma frostily. 'Is he your spy? You recruited Hugh, so perhaps you have a penchant for weak young men.'

'He has served me well enough,' said Henry, indicating that Sybilla was to release him.

She obliged reluctantly, and the squire fell to his knees, then scampered away. Geoffrey watched him go and pondered what Henry had meant. Surely Durand could not be his spy? He was far too concerned for his own safety to make an effective agent, and would be more of a liability than a help. He wondered whether Henry had protected Durand because he wanted another favour from Geoffrey and thought that the rescue of his squire might make him feel beholden. Henry, Geoffrey determined grimly, was going to be in for a disappointment, if that were the case.

When Durand had gone, Henry became gracious. He ordered food and wine, which was icily refused, so he flashed one of his best smiles and ordered servants to bring chairs from his tent and arrange them outside. Sybilla sat on the best one and allowed Henry's men to fuss around her with cushions, while Emma stood behind her, her face shadowed by her monastic veil. Matilda winked at Geoffrey as she took a seat next to Sybilla.

'It is time to discuss terms,' said Emma coolly.

'The terms of your surrender?' asked Henry innocently.

Emma's expression was hard. 'If you want to put it like that, then yes. But not in front of all these people.' She glanced significantly at the inside of the tent. 'In private, without an audience.'

'Very well,' said Henry. 'Only Bishop Maurice and Bishop Giffard shall be witnesses.'

'No,' said Emma. 'Just you.'

'I trust my bishops to be discreet,' said Henry, surprised. 'And so can you.'

Emma glowered at Maurice, evidently recalling past meetings in the Crusader's Head. Either that or she was among Maurice's conquests, and the black look meant something else entirely. 'Maurice and Giffard have betrayed us already. We shall talk to you alone or not at all. A bloodless capitulation is in all our interests, so you should hear what we have to say.'

Henry shrugged. 'If that is what you want, then so be it.'

'I do not think that is wise,' said Geoffrey as the King started to follow them inside. 'They are—'

'Do you think I cannot protect myself against women?' snapped Henry. 'In case you had not heard, ladies like me. It will be no trouble at all to woo this trio.'

Geoffrey had grave misgivings, but there was nothing he could do if the King was intent on being stubborn. He watched them disappear inside the royal tent and wondered if Henry would emerge alive, or whether they would strike him down and put their brother on the throne until the Duke of Normandy could come and claim his birthright.

He paced back and forth, and saw from their uneasy expressions that Maurice and Giffard were similarly anxious. Maurice was so concerned that he did not even notice Durand skulking around the edge of the crowd that waited to see what would happen. Pantulf and Beaumais lingered too, along with Roger and Helbye. Geoffrey trusted Pantulf not to make a hostile move, because he had proved himself by bringing Iorwerth to the King, but Beaumais was a wholly different proposition. Geoffrey watched him, resting his hand on the hilt of his dagger, and ready to spring at the first hint of danger.

Amise was furious that she had not been invited to the private meeting. She stalked around the tent with a scowl as black as thunder. Her scar gave her a vaguely demonic appearance, and Geoffrey saw Helbye catch her eye and promptly leave, muttering something about Bellême's 'devil army'. Although Geoffrey tried to stay away from her, it was not long before their paths crossed in the confined space of the royal enclosure.

'Traitor!' hissed Amise furiously. 'My uncle should not have given you a week to find Hugh's killer. He should have hanged you straight away.'

'Good day to you, too,' said Geoffrey, walking away.

She grabbed his arm. 'I hate you. But my feelings are irrelevant today. It is time we called a truce.'

Geoffrey regarded her with deep suspicion. If she thought she could make him lower his guard by offering the hand of friendship, she was sorely mistaken.

Mabel stepped forward. 'You must forgive my sister's manners, Geoffrey. It is not easy for either of us to be here, among enemies.'

'I imagine not,' said Geoffrey shortly, making a second attempt to leave. Mabel blocked his way, and he did not feel like engaging in a tussle to remove her. She was a powerful woman.

'We have things to tell you,' said Amise.

'I am sure you do, but they are not things I want to hear,' said Geoffrey coldly. 'Go away.'

Amise attempted to conceal her hostility with one of the falsest smiles he had ever seen. 'We now accept that you were right about Arnulf.'

'He admitted providing Emma with tainted olive oil for our Greek Fire, you see,' elaborated Mabel. 'She thinks that is why it has not worked properly, despite her fortifying it with demonic incantations and the fingers of corpses.'

'He betrayed his "Emmy",' said Amise, pronouncing the affectionate nickname with a sneer. 'He wanted her to fail so that he could work on the substance himself.'

Geoffrey recalled the marks he had seen on Arnulf's hands when he had donned the surcoat.

'We also know that Hugh never delivered Matilda's messages to the King,' said Mabel softly. 'And that Josbert planted a royal "reply" on Hugh's body.'

'Josbert said he was trying to *protect* Matilda,' Amise went on. 'He knew Bellême would kill her if he ever found out what she had done. But you made an erroneous assumption: you thought Josbert stuffed the parchment into Hugh's mouth *before* Arnulf pushed him from the window – as a gag.'

'No,' said Geoffrey, who had reconsidered his conclusions after his recent discussion with the King. 'Josbert was not in the chamber when Hugh was killed – I now know that was Arnulf and Philip. Josbert stuffed the parchment into Hugh's mouth *after* he was cut down, which was why Hugh was able to shout as he fell. I saw Josbert myself, although I did not realize at the time what he was doing. When Hugh was cut down, an onlooker from the rear of the crowd pushed forward – twice. That was Josbert – the first time to learn the corpse's identity, and the second time to plant his evidence.'

'We know,' said Mabel softly. 'Josbert told us everything before Arnulf knifed him.'

'Josbert is dead?' asked Geoffrey, startled. 'And Arnulf killed him? When?'

'During the confusion surrounding Arundel's surrender,' replied Amise. 'Josbert knew the King would hang the castellan who had held out against him for so long, so he made a final confession to us. When Arnulf heard he was spilling all his secrets, he was so angry that he stabbed him.'

'We both saw it happen,' said Mabel soberly. 'I think Josbert antagonized him deliberately, because he chose to die by a sword rather than a noose.'

'Henry would not have hanged Josbert,' said Geoffrey. Or would he? That the siege had lasted so long was largely because Josbert had prepared the castle. Mabel regarded him steadily, and Geoffrey saw she was sceptical of the King's mercy, too.

'Bellême was furious about Josbert's death,' said Amise. 'Arnulf knew he would not be safe in England, so he did the prudent thing and left for Normandy while he could – although he will lose all his English possessions now for certain.'

'He would have lost them anyway,' said Geoffrey. Amise glowered at him, and he edged away. He respected, even liked, Mabel, but Amise's close proximity was not pleasant, and he knew she was still waiting for an opportunity to kill him.

'It is almost over,' said Amise. 'But not quite. Tell us the truth: did you kill Cecily and Haweis?'

Geoffrey sighed, weary of her inability to see further than her own bigotry. 'Of course not! What is the matter with you? You are like your mother, so devoted to a single issue that you refuse to see the evidence that points you in other directions. It will be your downfall, as it will hers.'

'Who, then?' asked Mabel, silencing her sister's angry retort with a powerful – and probably painful – squeeze of the shoulder. 'I think you know.'

'Yes, I do.' Geoffrey spoke softly. 'It was the last of the King's spies. It was Emma.'

'Emma?' echoed Amise in disbelief. 'How did you reach such an outrageous conclusion?'

'Logic,' replied Geoffrey simply. 'Think about the facts. You said yourself that you were away from Haweis only for a moment. Therefore, whoever killed her must have been waiting in the hall. It was not Beaumais or Matilda, because they were frolicking in the stables at the time.'

'But Emma was on the roof,' said Mabel, confused. 'She told us she suspected Matilda and Beaumais were carrying on, and went to spy on them. That was why she was not in her chamber when we delivered the herbs she asked us to find.'

'Emma did know about Beaumais and Matilda, but she also knew that pretending to be the jilted lover would exonerate her from other accusations. She sent you for herbs, knowing that Haweis could not climb the stairs with her sprained ankle, and would be left alone. She hid in the hall and waited. And, if you recall, she kept her hands in her sleeves after Haweis was discovered. That was to mask the fact that they were covered in blood.'

Amise looked at Mabel in confusion. 'I saw her hands when we went upstairs to comfort mother. They *were* bloody, but she said it came from when she had tried to help Haweis.'

'Then she lied,' said Mabel flatly. '*I* found Haweis's body, and Emma went nowhere near it – to help or otherwise. If there was blood on her hands, then it came there *before* I raised the alarm, and that means . . .' She trailed off.

'I still do not believe you,' said Amise defiantly, addressing Geoffrey. 'You accuse Emma because you cannot think of anyone else. But she is grateful to us for helping her with our grandmother, who could not have been raised from the grave without our help.'

Geoffrey raised his eyebrows. 'Old Mabel is up and walking? Emma has succeeded?'

'You will have to wait and see,' said Amise spitefully. 'But not for long: I have asked her to visit you first.'

'I am sorry, Geoffrey,' said Mabel, glaring irritably at her sister to silence her. 'But I do not see *why* you believe Emma killed Haweis. I am not saying you are wrong, only that I do not understand.'

'Her motive is obvious. Haweis was the prettiest of you all, and Old Mabel had already rejected the heads of the felon and Hugh.'

Mabel gazed at him. 'Emma killed Haweis so she could use her head for Old Mabel?'

'She was probably desperate. She could not locate the original skull as long as she was locked inside Arundel, and her options were limited. Time was running out, and she needed Old Mabel ready as soon as possible. Remember who volunteered to see Haweis buried.'

'You are right,' said Mabel, her face drained of colour. 'Emma had wrapped Haweis in a sheet and would let no one see the body. The head lolled against my shoulder when I lifted it, and I thought it was odd at the time. Emma must have taken Haweis's head and substituted Hugh's or this felon's. So, we know why she killed Haweis, but what about Cecily?'

'Because of Beaumais,' said Geoffrey. 'Emma loved him, and did not like Cecily making moon-eyes at the man. She had access to Greek Fire, and she had already employed a device to cause a delayed explosion – when she attempted to incinerate All Hallows Barking. Perhaps Emma intended to use *Cecily's* head for Old Mabel, to kill two birds with one stone. But the Greek Fire spilled all over Cecily's neck, and would have made her head unusable.'

'Emma is not a traitor or a killer,' persisted Amise, although her expression was uneasy.

'Are you sure she can be trusted with your mother – and Matilda?' asked Geoffrey. 'Because you have just abandoned them with only the King for company.'

Amise dithered, but Mabel took Geoffrey's accusations

seriously. She walked briskly to the King's tent, while Geoffrey followed at a distance. If Emma did intend to kill her sisters, then it was an issue for her family to resolve, and he had no intention of becoming embroiled in another Bellême quarrel. But Mabel had nothing to worry about. As she approached, the flap of the tent opened and Henry emerged with all three sisters at his side. They were grim-faced, but alive. Mabel stopped mid-stride and gave Geoffrey a weary look, as though she felt he had misled her, while Amise merely sneered.

'We ate and drank nothing Henry offered,' Geoffrey heard Sybilla whisper to Mabel. 'As you recommended.'

'We will surrender this evening,' announced Sybilla in a tired voice to the crowd. 'We cannot win this confrontation, and the King says we can leave his kingdom without further persecution if we go tonight. We can each take a horse and a saddlebag. What we carry in that bag – jewels, clothes – is for us to decide, and he has promised not to interfere. Bishop Maurice will escort us to the coast.'

Maurice nodded enthusiastically, evidently more than happy to take several attractive ladies on a fairly long journey. Geoffrey wondered how many of them would be subject to his pawing advances before they reached the sea. He did not imagine they would take pity on his medical condition, and suspected the lecherous prelate would be in for a disappointing trip.

'I may owe you my life,' said Geoffrey to the happy bishop. 'But you owe me a horse. Mine is still winded from carrying you.'

Maurice laughed, then lowered his voice. 'You see? The plans I gave Bellême convinced him that he cannot win at Bridgnorth, and he has given the order for its surrender. That was what Henry intended all along, so your careful analysis of the castle did not go to waste. Do you still doubt the King's wisdom – or my loyalty to him?'

'No, but *he* might, if you interfere with the ladies entrusted to your care.'

'I will treat them as tenderly as any lover,' Maurice promised, rubbing his hands together. 'They will carry fond memories of their journey with me, I can promise you that.'

Suddenly, there was a sharp cry, and Geoffrey saw that the Bridgnorth deputation had already started back towards the castle. Sybilla was slumped in her saddle, and Mabel was trying to hold her upright. Then Sybilla dropped to the ground.

Fourteen

When Sybilla fell from her horse she was dragged some distance by the frightened animal before Mabel managed to control it. Geoffrey and several others, including Beaumais and Maurice, ran to see what had happened. The King, meanwhile, retired to his tent, declining to deal further with the feisty female Bellêmes.

When Geoffrey reached the women, he found Sybilla lying on the ground struggling to breathe. Her face was white and covered in a film of sweat. Emma stood silently to one side with a bewildered expression on her face, and Matilda moved away from her, as though she guessed Emma was responsible and wanted no part of it.

Mabel shot Geoffrey an agonized glance. 'She has been poisoned. Help her!'

'Ask Emma,' he said. 'There are many potions that can kill, and you will not save her unless you know which one she has swallowed.' And probably not even then, he thought.

Beaumais was indignant for his former lover. 'Oh, yes! Blame the witch! That is what everyone does when someone has a gripe in the stomach.'

'I am innocent,' whispered Emma, appalled. 'I would never harm my sister.'

'Henry did it, then,' said Amise accusingly.

'The King has no reason to hurt Sybilla,' said Maurice gently. 'He is not the kind of man to poison defeated enemies. Besides, she drank or ate nothing he offered. She only took what Emma had.'

'But I only gave her wine!' cried Emma. 'And I drank

some of it myself. So did Matilda, and we are well enough. I tell you I have done nothing!'

'But you killed Haweis,' said Amise furiously. 'So her head could adorn Old Mabel's bones.'

'I had no choice,' said Emma, white-faced and distraught. 'The future of our entire House is at stake, and desperate situations call for desperate measures. I am sorry about Haweis, but it was better she died quickly and painlessly by my hand, than slowly and painfully by starvation in Arundel. I did it for *all* of us, so that my mother could save us from Henry and defeat.'

'And Cecily?' asked Mabel, not bothering to point out that they had survived the siege without any intervention from her grandmother. 'Geoffrey says you killed her, too. Is he right?'

'That was because of me,' said Beaumais rather vainly, as he patted his oiled hair.

Emma closed her eyes in despair when Beaumais spoke, but snapped them open when she realized her troubles were only just beginning. Amise moved towards her with her dagger drawn. The abbess backed away, fumbling urgently in the pouch she carried at her side. Meanwhile, Geoffrey glanced at Matilda. She was a short distance away, watching the scene with detached interest. More solutions clicked into place as he went to stand next to her.

'I was wrong,' he said. 'Emma did not poison Sybilla, did she? Her shock at that accusation was real. So what happened, Matilda? Did you make sure she and you took the antidote to whatever you had added to the wine? You intend Sybilla to die, but Emma to be spared.'

'I intend Sybilla to die and Emma to be blamed,' corrected Matilda. 'It is always easy to blame the witch, as Beaumais says. Who else would know about poisons?'

'You should not let Sybilla die. She is your sister, and Emma is right: you have all lost this battle.'

'This battle is irrelevant. My actions today have nothing to do with Henry. It is about my brother, Philip the Grammarian. Sybilla killed him, four years ago.'

'But he died at Antioch,' said Geoffrey, bemused. 'And I can assure you she was not there.'

318

Matilda shook her head slowly. 'You do not have to wield a dagger in order to bring a man his death. A few weeks with our House has taught you that, surely?'

Geoffrey had already guessed that one of Sybilla's daughters had killed Philip the Grammarian, using the raid as a cover. He had also reasoned that they had left Antioch immediately, as soon as they had secured the formula for Greek Fire.

Matilda continued to speak in a whisper. 'Amise sent letters, informing Sybilla that she had done what was asked. Amise was the one who stabbed him – which should not surprise you, given your own interactions with the child – but the order came from Sybilla.'

'But why does Emma need to bear the blame?'

'Because her witchcraft almost destroyed us, and I do not approve. I know what she did to Haweis and Cecily – and I know what happened to Hugh's poor corpse. I do not want our mother raised from the dead, and I do not want us to use Greek Fire against our enemies. If we are to make a new life in Normandy, I do not want it said that we are *all* warlocks.'

'These are not good reasons,' said Geoffrey. 'They are—'

'Do not interfere, Geoffrey,' warned Matilda, her eyes flashing with a sudden fury. 'I did not help you escape Arundel so you could betray me. You would not have lived if Mabel and I had not helped you that day. Do not make me regret it.'

She turned when Amise gave a piercing cry and sprang at Emma with her knife. Emma issued a screech of her own, then the two women were rolling around on the ground, flailing and scratching. Geoffrey started towards them, aiming to put a stop to the sordid spectacle, but Matilda stopped him.

Emma had her hand in the pouch she carried at her side, and flung something in Amise's face. It was a small phial that broke and released something black and sticky. Amise screamed and put her hands to her eyes, allowing Emma to roll away. Geoffrey assumed the undignified fracas was over, and began to step forward again, intending to help Amise scrape the dark substance from her face before it did any harm. But Amise hurled her dagger in fury, screaming

319

all manner of hatred and threats as she began to claw at her cheeks.

It was pure bad luck for Emma that the knife embedded itself in her chest, because Amise could not see what she was doing. The Abbess's eyes bulged and she dropped to her knees. With the last of her strength, she drew something from her scrip and tossed it at her adversary. Flames erupted on Amise, blazing even more fiercely when they reached the pitchy substance. Geoffrey saw Emma's satisfaction as Beaumais and Maurice tried to smother the flames, and he recognized the distinctive smell of Greek Fire. He knelt next to Emma, although he could see she was beyond any earthly help.

'An undignified end,' she whispered. He was not sure whether she referred to herself or Amise.

'Greek Fire is terrible,' said Matilda, crouching next to them. 'I wish Philip had never found it.'

'It could have helped us win this war,' whispered Emma. 'I perfected it, you know, the day before Arundel fell. Arnulf's meddling in All Hallows confused me, but once he had confessed to what he had done I was able to make the appropriate adjustments and rectify the matter.'

Geoffrey recalled that Emma had been puzzled when her experiment had produced a dazzling flash and an explosion. Arnulf's interference had seriously impeded her progress.

'But now I know,' she continued weakly. 'The secret is to—'

'Do not tell us,' said Matilda quickly. 'It is better that it dies with you.'

Emma's bloodless lips parted in a ghastly smile. 'I used the last of Philip's sample on Amise, so you should be pleased that his murder is appropriately avenged. There is no more Greek Fire in Bellême hands, and the only other person who knows its formula is Sybilla: I told her last night. But you have ensured she will never tell, either.'

'I am glad,' said Matilda. 'I shall take our mother's bones and bury them in Normandy. And then perhaps our House can be free of all this evil.'

Geoffrey was not sure Henry would permit Old Mabel to

320

leave, and thought he might well have her buried somewhere no Bellême would ever find her. Old Mabel dead had proved every bit as dangerous as Old Mabel alive.

The light faded from Emma's eyes and she lay still. Geoffrey crossed himself, not so much for her as for himself. He thought it was not natural for a woman to take pride in her diabolical achievements as she breathed her last, when most folk were keen to absolve themselves of their sins. He glanced at Mabel, who leaned heavily on a pile of cloaks that covered Amise's still-smoking torso. He prised her hands away and removed the material to reveal a blackened head that looked barely human.

He laid a sympathetic hand on Mabel's shoulder, while Maurice stepped forward to mutter prayers. She lifted her sister's body as though it was a child's, and laid it gently across the back of her horse. Then she did the same for her mother. Emma was left where she was. When she had finished, Mabel reached out and laid one of her meaty paws on Geoffrey's shoulder.

'I doubt we will meet again, Geoffrey, but remember me well. Do not equate me with the murderers and schemers in the House of Montgomery-Bellême.'

'God's speed, Mabel,' said Geoffrey softly, thinking that the burly warrior was the only member of the entire clan he did not distrust. He hoped he would never encounter the family again, and made a silent vow never to set foot in their lands in Normandy, under any circumstances.

Beaumais crouched next to the woman who had been his lover. 'Oh, well,' he said ruefully. 'She would have had to go sooner or later anyway. I intend to be a bishop, and I can hardly do that with a witch as my mistress.'

'No, you should choose a Christian next time,' agreed Matilda. She turned to Geoffrey. 'It is over now. All the traitors are dead, and my dear Philip has been avenged. Look in the castle chapel after we leave; Mabel and I have put something there for you to remember us by.'

'It is not the formula for Greek Fire, is it?' he asked nervously. 'Or Old Mabel's headless corpse.'

She smiled wanly. 'It is something you will like – other

321

than a good woman. Perhaps you will come to see me if you ever visit Normandy? I enjoyed our tryst in Southwark all those months ago.'

'I might,' he said vaguely, not wanting to offend her with an outright refusal. She was an attractive lady, but there were plenty of others who were equally pretty and who did not come with dangerous siblings and a working knowledge of poisons.

'There is one other thing you should know,' she said, pausing with her foot in the stirrup. 'Sybilla passed a letter to your little squire when she pretended to manhandle him earlier today – you may recall me mentioning to you that she could write. It is on its way to my brother even as we speak.'

'Durand? Why would she give a message to Durand?'

'He is so terrified of us that he will do anything to avoid incurring our wrath. You had better hurry, Geoffrey. Who knows what the message contains?'

'I was wrong,' said Geoffrey, amused. 'Emma was not the King's last agent. You are.'

With a rush of understanding he saw that Emma would not have tried to have King Henry shot by hidden archers in the Easter Court if she had been a royal spy. That had been a genuine attempt at regicide, deriving from fear and desperation. Also, she would not have offered Bellême the secret of Greek Fire or tried to summon her dead mother. And she certainly would not have ordered young Philip to bring the King's toenails to add to potions she hoped would kill him.

Matilda flashed him a sudden grin that was full of mischievous pride. 'Yes and no. I sent Henry information – enough to secure his gratitude, but not enough to cause serious damage to my House. I could not predict who was going to win, you see, and thought it best to have a foot in both camps. Beaumais did not know I was a double agent – I made sure of that by careful quizzing during our sessions in the barn at Arundel – and I did not guess *your* true role. Henry is a clever man, keeping his spies unaware of each other.'

'So, the messages you sent with Hugh *did* reach royal

322

hands, and Henry's response was to order you to work against your family?'

'No. Henry was telling the truth when he said he had received no messages offering to parley. Hugh really did fail to deliver them, and Josbert really did find one and take matters into his own inefficient hands. I used young Philip to give Henry other information, although no one – not Philip and not Henry – knew that *I* was the sender.'

'How? Philip recognized you, surely?'

'He merely collected letters from pre-arranged places. Henry grew to trust his anonymous spy, but he did not know my identity until I revealed it to him today.'

'Why are you telling me?'

'I am in the mood for confession now this business is at an end, and you are someone I think will understand without judging me too harshly. So, we are even now. I helped you escape from Arundel, and you will not tell anyone I was Henry's spy. There is no point now, is there?'

Geoffrey supposed there was not, and watched as she rode to Bridgnorth Castle to pack the single saddlebag she was allowed to take when she quitted Henry's realm. He wondered what was in the message Sybilla had given to Durand, and had an awful feeling Sybilla had written out the revised formula for Greek Fire, which Emma had revealed to her the previous night.

It felt good to wear his own armour and surcoat again. Mabel had even made sure that Geoffrey's sword was included in the parcel that had been left in the care of Bridgnorth Castle's frightened chaplain. Since Geoffrey had not expected to see any of it again, discovering it awaiting his collection in the abandoned chapel had been a genuine pleasure. He returned the borrowed mail to Henry, and decided he could take on a hundred Bellêmes in the armour that was so comfortably familiar. He wondered how Mabel and Matilda had persuaded Arnulf to part with the surcoat – especially since Geoffrey still had the silver coins he had paid for it.

The first thing Geoffrey did after the royal forces had taken control of Bridgnorth was to look for Durand. But the squire was nowhere to be found, and his horse was missing. Helbye had seen him riding away as though the Devil was on his tail, but had assumed his terror was caused by the close proximity of Bellêmes. Maurice had also seen him leave, and waxed lyrical about his blond locks flying in the wind.

'I shall never have her again,' he said with a wistful sigh.

'Again?' asked Geoffrey warily.

Maurice handed him several silver pennies. 'That is what I promised you for persuading her to come to me. I am a man who keeps his word.'

'He came?' asked Geoffrey uncomfortably. 'Durand came to your tent?'

'Last night,' said Maurice with a fond smile. 'At around midnight.'

'It was dark, then,' said Geoffrey, wondering how Durand had managed to convince the rampant prelate that he had been of the fair sex, and how Maurice had not discovered the truth.

'Very,' agreed Maurice. 'She is a modest lady.'

'I do not want your money,' said Geoffrey, trying to pass it back. 'I am no brothel keeper.'

'Do not be so ready to refuse silver, Geoffrey,' said Maurice, pushing the coins back into his hand. 'These are turbulent times, and who knows when you might need it? But I must go. I have only Matilda and Mabel to escort to the coast, but I am sure we shall find something to while away the time. God bless, Geoffrey. And remember this advice: never say no to a woman or to coins. Follow that rule, and you will live to be a happy man.'

Geoffrey thought it very much depended on the women. He looked down at the coins and smiled. Durand would have some explaining to do when he caught him.

As soon as Henry was certain Bridgnorth was secure, he prepared to ride for Shrewsbury. He was also concerned that Durand might be about to pass a deadly secret to his enemy, but at the same time remained sceptical, claiming that Matilda would have mentioned the matter during their parley if it had been true. She was his spy, after all, and had

324

made herself known by passing him a piece of parchment with a sign drawn on it.

'It was the symbol we had agreed upon,' elaborated Henry, when Geoffrey looked blank. 'It was known only to me and to my agent.'

'How do you know she did not learn it from someone else?' asked Geoffrey. 'Like Emma?'

'Emma was not my spy,' said Henry, finding the notion amusing. 'It was definitely Matilda who sent me so many helpful messages. So, now you know why I wanted to linger at Bridgnorth when you were all for riding on Shrewsbury. I wanted to meet my anonymous helper.'

'Then why exile her? I thought you planned to reward her when she made herself known.'

'I *am* rewarding her,' said Henry. 'I am allowing her to leave with her life. I dislike traitors, of any kind, and I shall never pay them gold or land for their lack of honour.'

'I see,' said Geoffrey, wondering whether Beaumais and Pantulf knew about this particular policy. He could see Henry's point: a traitor was a traitor, and could never be trusted. It was right and just that Matilda should be exiled, and safer for Henry to have no Bellême in his kingdom. However, it also explained why Matilda had not bothered to mention the message Sybilla passed to Durand. It had allowed her a final act of revenge upon a man who had not fulfilled her expectations.

'Sybilla and another of her demonic daughters are dead, and so is Emma,' said Henry in satisfaction. 'Maurice will see Matilda and Mabel safely out of England, so we are left only with Bellême himself and Roger. And they will not remain in my realm for many more days now.'

'But what about Arnulf?' asked Geoffrey. 'You thought he was in Bridgnorth, but he is not. Are you willing to believe that he fled to Normandy after the fall of Arundel, as Matilda claims?'

'Arnulf is no longer a threat,' replied Henry enigmatically. Geoffrey glanced at a dark stain on his surcoat that had not been there when he had sold it, and wondered whether it was Arnulf's blood. It would certainly explain how they had managed to deprive him of a garment he had liked.

Beaumais came to inform the King that all was ready for the short ride from Bridgnorth to Shrewsbury, for what Geoffrey supposed would be the final confrontation between Henry and his most deadly enemy. Henry reached for his riding gloves and strode out of his tent. As he left, Geoffrey saw something flutter to the ground. It was a scrap of parchment. Aware that he should not meddle in matters that did not concern him, Geoffrey nevertheless leaned down to pick it up. It contained a crudely drawn body with a head toppling to one side. Geoffrey stared at it, and supposed it was the sign Matilda had passed Henry. It was certainly an appropriate one, given what Emma had been struggling to do with her mother.

Helbye was waiting with his horse, so Geoffrey climbed into his saddle and turned in the direction of Shrewsbury. Henry rode at the head of the cavalcade, flanked by his best knights, while Geoffrey was behind with Roger, Pantulf and Beaumais.

'It is almost over,' called Pantulf to Geoffrey, barely audible over the thundering of hoofs. 'My spies tell me that Arnulf fled to Normandy two weeks ago, where he will be safe from Henry, but not from his vengeful siblings.'

'Matilda,' said Geoffrey, glancing down to see his dog racing along at his side. Its tongue hung wetly from its mouth, and he wondered how long it would keep up with them before it decided this was not a good way to earn its daily meat. 'She is the only one who will join him. Roger and Bellême are still in England, and the others are dead.'

Pantulf gave a crafty smile. 'Roger is not here, either. The King ordered me to allow him to "escape" from Shrewsbury two days ago. This I did, and my men followed him to the coast, where he boarded a ship bound for Normandy. He is a vindictive man, and I doubt he will rest until he has meted out justice to Arnulf, who professed to be loyal while he feathered his own nest.'

Geoffrey was sure he was right, and understood exactly what the King had meant when he said he was satisfied that

Arnulf would not be a problem – assuming Matilda had not already acted, of course.

'No sign of Durand,' grumbled Roger, riding at his side. 'I am surprised he has travelled so far on his own. He is afraid of galloping, because he thinks he will be unseated and crushed under his pony's hoofs. Has he been lying to us all these months, and he is actually an accomplished rider?'

'I do not think so,' said Geoffrey, laughing at the notion.

'Then how long has he been a traitor? Carrying messages for Bellême?'

'If Durand was Bellême's man, then he would have been happy to remain inside Arundel. I suspect this is his first foray into treachery. But you are right: he is not a good horseman and we will catch him long before we reach Shrewsbury. Then we shall destroy the formula for Greek Fire.'

'Destroy it?' asked Roger in dismay. 'No, lad! We will sell it to the King for a handsome profit.'

'We will not!' exclaimed Geoffrey vehemently, glancing around uneasily to make sure no one had overheard. 'The King will not buy what he can take, and he is likely to accuse *you* of being a traitor for selling what he probably thinks should be given freely.'

Roger grumbled, but accepted that his friend was right. Geoffrey concentrated on the ride, enjoying the feel of his horse moving fast and sure along the road and the jangle and clink of armour. Then, in the distance, just breasting a hill, he caught sight of a familiar figure.

'There he is,' he shouted to Roger.

He spurred his horse faster, leaving the others behind, although Roger did his best to keep up. The distant rider heard the thunder of pursuing hoofs and looked behind him in panic. Geoffrey saw the pony rear, then dart forward. Durand was clearly under the impression that a hostile force was after him. With growing concern, Geoffrey saw that he might reach Shrewsbury after all. Durand was not encumbered with armour and his horse was able to make better time. Geoffrey charged on, determined to expend every last ounce of his strength to ensure that the message did not get to Bellême.

He breasted the hill Durand had laboured up, and saw the towers and roofs of Shrewsbury ahead, tucked into a bend of the meandering River Severn. He could make out the abbey, and the houses and buildings that clustered around its feet. Durand was almost at its gates, and Geoffrey urged his horse to run faster yet. The animal's flanks were heaving, and he knew it would not be able to travel much farther.

The city gate loomed ahead of him. Durand was already through, and the startled guards had not had time to close it. They saw a second horseman riding like the wind after the first and hesitated, not knowing what to do. In the end, they did what most civilian guards did when caught between forces controlled by the likes of the King and Robert de Bellême. They abandoned their posts and ran away, heading for the woods outside the city, where they would remain until there was a clear winner and they knew who to support.

Geoffrey reached the gate, and flew along the main street at a speed that was far from safe. People scattered as he thundered towards the castle, and he heard them cursing him for his vile Norman manners.

The castle was close, and Geoffrey could see Durand ahead of him, clattering up the road as fast as his winded nag would allow. Geoffrey's horse stumbled and almost threw him, but he held on and forced it forward. Durand flung himself from the saddle when he reached the barbican gate and started to hammer, thumping the oak doors with his puny little fists. He glanced behind him, saw Geoffrey and pounded harder.

The gate began to open, with Durand shoving desperately in an attempt to push it wide enough to squeeze through. But it was heavy and the guards were slow. Durand darted to the gap and wedged himself in it, wriggling desperately. Geoffrey was almost at the gate when arrows began to rain down from the archers who protected it. He raised his shield over his head, hearing the thud and rattle as missiles rained down on it.

He reached the gate and snatched a fistful of the squire's tunic with his sword arm, still holding the shield above his head. On the other side of the gate, hands reached out to haul Durand inside. The man's feet left the ground, and he howled in terror. Geoffrey's horse, unsettled by the furious ride and the hail of arrows, began to buck. Then something black and sticky dropped from the archers' gallery and on to Geoffrey and horse alike. It was Emma's runny Greek Fire.

With a massive surge of strength Geoffrey wrenched Durand from the guards' grip and hauled him across his saddle before turning and galloping away, feeling like a Viking kidnapping a woman. More missiles followed, and he heard a yelp of pain as one struck Durand's leg. Another hit Geoffrey's conical helmet with a resounding gong, while others bounced harmlessly off his mail. His horse screamed as an arrow grazed its flank. More black pitch slapped on to Geoffrey's armour, including some that stuck to his cheek, so the rank stench of it caught in his nostrils. But it did not ignite.

Then he was out of range of the castle's bombardment. Not wanting to meet any of Bellême's men, who might be stationed in the streets in readiness for an ambush, he cantered towards the city gate, and did not stop until he was some distance away. He left the main road and headed for a peaceful glade, where he hurled his squire to the ground like a sack of rubbish and tended his horse, soothing it with gentle words and running his hands down its legs to check for damage. It was in distress, and he knew he would not be riding it again that day. He decided Henry would have to do without him if he intended to fight Bellême at the castle.

The thump of hoofs grew closer, and he glanced across to the road to see Roger in the lead. He started to call out, to let him know that his desperate gallop had been successful, but knew he would not be heard. He turned back to his horse, noting that the scratch made by the arrow was not serious and, as long as it was properly washed and kept clean, it would heal well enough. Gradually, the faithful beast caught its breath, and Geoffrey used his spare shirt to wipe away some of the sweat that coursed down its flanks.

'It will take me ages to get that clean,' said Durand, watching him. He had not moved since Geoffrey had deposited him on the ground, although the knight knew he was unharmed.

329

'What makes you think you will have the chance?'

'I am your squire,' said Durand indignantly.

Geoffrey saw he was not in the slightest repentant for what he had done. 'You are Bellême's message boy,' he retorted in distaste. 'Give me the letter you were going to deliver from Sybilla.'

'Which one?' asked Durand. He scrambled quickly to his feet when he saw Geoffrey's murderous expression. 'There were two! Do not look at me like that. Which one do you want?'

'Both!' snapped Geoffrey, holding out his hand. 'And do not try to get the better of me. The King will have you hanged for this.'

'For delivering a message?' asked Durand, wide-eyed with innocence. 'I thought messengers were exempt from that sort of thing, and that it is considered poor form to punish them for ill tidings. Besides, Henry will not hang me.'

'What makes you so certain?' Geoffrey thought that if Henry did not order the man's execution, then he might do it himself. Durand had gone too far, and Tancred would just have to be disappointed that Geoffrey had not returned with a golden-haired warrior in tow.

'I tell him things,' said Durand. 'And he likes me.'

'You mean you are the King's spy, too?' Geoffrey was not sure whether to believe him.

'Why do you think he spoke in my defence earlier today?' asked Durand smugly. 'I am useful.'

Geoffrey supposed Henry might have ordered the squire to spy for him, just as he had recruited Hugh, whom most folk thought was weak-witted. Henry seemed to like agents with attributes that made them unlikely candidates for such work. He wondered whether Durand had been ordered to spy on Geoffrey himself, and the thought made him angry.

'Give me the letters,' he ordered, bringing his temper under control and fighting the urge to grab Durand and run him through before he could do any more damage.

Durand started to refuse, but tugged two parchments from his scrip when Geoffrey advanced on him with a black scowl. Something fell from his shirt as he did so. It was a plain

330

wooden cross. Something clicked into place in Geoffrey's mind.

'Petronus,' he said flatly. 'I should have known you are the kind of man who would choose strangulation as the means to dispense with a victim.'

'I did not kill Petronus,' said Durand, licking nervous lips. 'Whoever shot the archers did that.'

'Lies,' said Geoffrey, pointing to the cross. 'That belonged to Petronus, and I cannot imagine anyone else wanting to steal such a thing. But *you* still have a hankering for the Church, and were unable to resist such a token. You stole it after you murdered him.'

'He brought about that ambush,' said Durand sulkily. 'He ran away immediately afterwards, leaving you to deal with the chaos he had caused.'

'You admit it?' Geoffrey had not anticipated Durand would confess quite so easily.

'I did it for our own safety. He carried dangerous messages and it was obvious, even to the most stupid of men, that the attack was because of him.' He regarded Geoffrey defiantly, as though he included his master in the category of the 'most stupid'. 'It seemed the best thing to do. I am sorry, because Petronus seemed pleasant, but I would do the same again.'

'Durand!' exclaimed Geoffrey in disgust. 'You cannot go around choking people based on flawed interpretations of the facts – especially monks.'

'Why not?' demanded Durand. 'Roger is always telling me that I need to get out and slaughter more, so I decided to take him at his word. Besides, what makes monks any different from common men? I was one once, and I can tell you there is no difference at all.'

Geoffrey supposed that the rules quelling the murderous instincts of other men, who were concerned for their immortal souls, might not apply to someone like Durand. He struggled to understand.

'If Roger, Helbye and I had been obliged to escort Petronus to Westminster after you left us, we would have been killed, too,' insisted Durand. 'You were not there to help.'

'But strangulation!' Geoffrey was deeply repelled. It

331

seemed such an unmanly way to deal with a victim. 'Did you take the map he carried, as well as his cross? The document that the King's men and Bellême's agents have been at such pains to find?'

'Is that what it was?' asked Durand carelessly. 'A map? I could not tell.'

'Where is it now?'

'I lost it,' said Durand guilelessly. 'I *think* it dropped out of my scrip during the incident at London's public lavatory, but my scrip is always full, and I can never find anything in it, so who knows when the thing fell out?'

'God's teeth!' muttered Geoffrey, regarding his squire uneasily. 'I feel as though I am coming to know you for the first time.'

'I hope you like what you see,' said Durand with an impertinent wiggle of the hips. 'Bishop Maurice certainly did – at least, with the torches doused. I am not so sure what would have happened if he had insisted on lighting a candle.'

Geoffrey did not want to know. 'Tell me about this map. It is important and could be devastating in the wrong hands.'

Durand became serious. 'I honestly have no idea where it might be. I shoved it in my purse in the woods near Westminster, and then I simply forgot about it. I did not think about it again until I heard Henry telling you about it a couple of days ago. I immediately emptied my scrip to see if it was still there, but it had gone. I probably lost it months ago.'

Geoffrey regarded him in disbelief. 'Why did you not tell me all this back in March? That map may have allowed me to solve some of these mysteries weeks ago.'

'Because if I told you I had taken the map, you would have accused me of killing Petronus,' said Durand, not unreasonably. 'And I knew you would be angry. I was right: you are furious.'

'I am not furious!' snapped Geoffrey. He glared at Durand, and wondered whether the squire had learned such behaviour from him and Roger, or whether he was naturally the kind of fellow to throttle wounded clerics on forest floors. He

332

held up his hand to keep Durand away from him, and turned his attention to the parchments the squire had been about to deliver to Bellême.

He pulled them open and quickly scanned their contents. One was indeed a description of how to make Greek Fire, with an appended message stating that a condensed form of olive oil gave the best results. Geoffrey knew that edible oil – condensed or otherwise – had not been something the Crusaders had included in their experiments, and supposed Emma really had unravelled the mystery. He read on, and learned the original 'secret' ingredient was some kind of black oil that could be found only in the lands of the East, which collected in poisonous pools. It needed to be refined in a particular way before it was suitable for use in Greek Fire. Since Emma had not had access to the black oil, she had improvised, and had devised an alternative that was not perfect, but that had worked.

Geoffrey turned his attention to the second parchment. It was a letter from Sybilla to Bellême telling him that Matilda was the King's spy. She outlined a detailed plan of how Bellême could avenge himself on his treacherous siblings, leaving him and Sybilla to rule Normandy together in glorious harmony. Geoffrey doubted whether Bellême would have taken her advice. He crumpled the parchment in disgust.

'I believe those are addressed to me,' came a low voice from behind Geoffrey. Durand gave a squeal of alarm and darted away through the undergrowth, while Geoffrey spun around and found himself face to face with Robert de Bellême.

'I thought you were in Shrewsbury Castle,' was all Geoffrey could think of to say to the Earl, who stood in front of him in full battle gear. Bellême's dark eyes were flat and expressionless, and Geoffrey knew by now that this was a dangerous sign. He was angry and looking for spilled blood.

'That particular fortress is not a good place to be today,' said Bellême, regarding Geoffrey as intently as a cat would a mouse. 'My troops are spineless cowards, and have refused to fight. They heard about the fall of Bridgnorth and claim they cannot win at Shrewsbury if all my other strongholds have gone. I told them *I* ordered Bridgnorth to surrender, so that its army could come and relieve us, but they do not believe me.'

'They are right,' said Geoffrey. 'Bridgnorth's defenders are heading south, hoping to board a ship for Normandy before the King changes his mind.'

Bellême shrugged. 'It does not matter, if Shrewsbury is unwilling to fight. But I have not finished with England yet; I shall be back to claim what is mine. You will not be here to see it, though.'

'No,' agreed Geoffrey. 'I will be in the Holy Land with Tancred.'

'That is not what I meant,' said Bellême, tugging his monstrous sword from his belt.

'Not again,' groaned Geoffrey, backing away but declining to draw his own weapon. 'I do not want to fight you. Your rebellion is over, so why do you not follow the rest of your family and leave while you can?'

'Not as long as you are alive,' hissed Bellême. 'I knew Bishop Maurice was wrong when he said you were dead. I might have known I could not trust a cleric to tell the difference between a living man and a corpse.'

'You will not find me so easy to best today,' warned Geoffrey. 'This time we are more evenly matched in terms of armour and weapons. We could be circling and lunging at each other for hours, while your troops surrender and run away to save their lives.'

'You are afraid of me. That is why you will not fight.'

'I have never been afraid of you,' said Geoffrey coolly. 'Why should I be? I have never seen you kill a man in a fair fight – only when he is unarmed and defenceless, like that landlord in Winchester. How could I be afraid of a man like you?'

Bellême lunged, but it was an angry, clumsy blow, and Geoffrey had no trouble in evading it. He drew his own weapon and waited, determined that Bellême should do the attacking if he was so eager to fight, and tire himself first. Bellême swiped again, and their swords met with a loud clash that drew sparks. They pushed hard against each

334

other, and Bellême's greater strength showed when he almost shoved Geoffrey from his feet. Geoffrey pretended to stagger, and Bellême moved in to take advantage, while Geoffrey neatly stepped out of the way and struck hard to score a jagged wound in Bellême's hand. Bellême regarded it in astonishment, as though he could not believe it had happened. Then his surprise turned to fury, and he lunged again.

His hacking blow was so powerful that parrying it numbed Geoffrey's fingers. He almost dropped his weapon, and only just managed to block the second hacking sweep. Bellême gave one of his mirthless smiles and began to circle, while Geoffrey saw his relentless attack might well last until sunset, so determined was he to kill someone before he left England. Geoffrey knew he could not allow Bellême to defeat him, because then he would seize the secret of Greek Fire and Geoffrey knew he would use it. Knowledge of such a foul weapon might shift the balance of power in Normandy, and hundreds, perhaps thousands, of soldiers would die horribly at his hands. Geoffrey had to win.

The sun came out from behind a cloud, and Geoffrey was aware that he was sweating under his armour. His sword was slippery in his hand, and he was finding it difficult to clutch the thing. But he was used to fighting in the heat, and knew how to adapt. Bellême did not, and Geoffrey leapt forward to land a vicious stroke that saw the Earl's sword cartwheel from his hand and disappear into the bushes. Bellême drew his dagger, and gestured that Geoffrey should dispense with his sword and use his knife, so they would be equally armed.

'I do not think so,' said Geoffrey, who had no intention of yielding any kind of advantage to Bellême, who would not have done the same for him. 'Give yourself up, if you do not want to die.'

'You will not kill me,' jeered Bellême. 'You do not have the courage. King Henry wants me alive, so he can gloat over my defeat. It would be a hollow victory for him if I die at your hands.'

Geoffrey advanced relentlessly, with Bellême giving ground at every step. This time, he was determined that Bellême would not survive to continue his wicked, butchering life.

He intended to kill him, and did not care that it was no longer a fair fight.

'Enough!' came a voice from the edge of the clearing. 'I have been watching for some time, and it is obvious who will win this duel. Geoffrey, put up your weapon.'

It was Henry, with Durand cowering behind him. Durand gave his master a feeble smile, and the knight supposed he had not fled, as he tended to do when faced with violence, but had summoned the King, warning him that his enemy was not in the castle but in the woods. Roger stood to one side, and Geoffrey thought how good it was to see a friendly face. His dog was at Roger's side, and wagged its tail when it saw Geoffrey. Then it spotted Bellême, and its teeth bared in a snarl. Bellême heard it.

'That cur attacked me the last time we fought. You would be dead if it were not for him.'

He braced himself, and Geoffrey saw that he intended to hurl his dagger at the dog. Bellême was right: it had saved Geoffrey's life, and Geoffrey intended to do the same for the dog now. He gripped his sword and started towards the Earl, determined to bring the reign of Robert de Bellême to an end.

'Geoffrey!' came Henry's sharp command. 'I told you to disarm.'

But Geoffrey had no intention of putting up his weapon while Bellême held a knife. It was not just the dog Bellême had in his murderous sights: Henry was just as easy a target, and there would be little the King could do to avoid a powerfully flung blade. Geoffrey took another step towards the Earl.

'Geoffrey!' barked Henry. 'I ordered you—'

Bellême moved like lightning, and Geoffrey saw the King's jaw drop in horror as Bellême bent back his arm and prepared to hurl what could not fail to be a fatal weapon at such short range. Geoffrey lurched forward and crashed into him, so they both fell to the ground. He heard the breath rush out of Bellême, then felt himself grabbed by the arms and hauled away. Bellême was similarly secured, and stood struggling and spitting his hatred at both Geoffrey and Henry. One of

336

the King's men reeled back from Geoffrey with a sliced arm, and the other edged away when he saw he was likely to be next. No Crusader liked being manhandled.

'All right, leave him,' said Henry, seeing that Geoffrey was not going to surrender his weapons. 'He has just saved me from being skewered, so he means me no harm.'

'I was saving my dog,' said Geoffrey, somewhat imprudently. But he was angry: with Bellême and his ridiculous and unwanted feud, and with Henry for forcing him into affairs that were none of his concern.

'I almost killed the brute,' said Bellême, an amused smile playing at the corners of his mouth. Geoffrey was not sure whether he referred to the King or his dog, and supposed he would never know. Bellême was unlikely to confess to attempted regicide now he was the King's prisoner.

Meanwhile, the dog knew Bellême was not in a position to hurt it, so it ambled forward casually, nose to the ground, as if it were out for a pleasant walk. When it neared Bellême it darted forward and landed a vicious nip on the Earl's left ankle, before moving away to hide behind Geoffrey. Bellême screamed his outrage, and the soldiers holding him were hard-pressed to keep him under control. Henry laughed in startled surprise, while Geoffrey glanced down at the animal and saw it was pleased with itself.

Henry addressed Bellême. 'Shrewsbury has surrendered.'

'Already?' Bellême was shocked. 'I thought they would hold out until sunset, at least.'

'They handed me the keys of the castle as soon as I arrived,' said Henry, obviously enjoying the Earl's discomfort. 'Abbot Ralph obliged, because none of your regular soldiers were brave enough to do it.' He gestured behind him, and Geoffrey saw the gentle Benedictine who had befriended him at Arundel.

Bellême seemed to sag in his captors' arms. 'They did not even hold out for two hours,' he muttered. 'That was the extent of their loyalty to me.'

'You will be escorted from here to the nearest port,' proclaimed Henry in a loud voice. 'And you will never enter my kingdom again. If you do, you will be executed.

You shall forfeit all your English possessions, and all those of your family. There is no longer a place in England for any member of the House of Montgomery-Bellême. Now go.'

The Earl was hustled away, and Geoffrey saw the King had delegated a sizeable guard to travel with him. He was taking no chances with the man who had been a thorn in his side for so long. He was wise, Geoffrey thought. Bellême's troops at Shrewsbury might have disappointed him, but there would be others willing to rally to a rebellious noble if the price was right.

'You are wondering why I intervened,' said Henry to Geoffrey, tapping his arm and indicating that he should sheath his sword. 'You think I should have let you kill him.'

'It would be safer for you than having him in Normandy, allowing his hatred to fester and planning his next invasion,' Geoffrey pointed out. 'He will be your enemy for as long as he lives.'

'I know,' said Henry. 'But you are viewing the situation too simplistically. The truth is that I do not want my nobles to think I will resort to murdering any baron I cannot control. It would lead to even more rebellion, and I want my country to live in peace. The Bellême threat is gone, Geoffrey, and England is a better place for it.'

He turned and walked away, issuing orders as he went, while his courtiers hurried to follow him. The clearing was soon deserted, with only Roger slapping Geoffrey's shoulders in comradely affection, and the dog winding about his legs in the hope that its courage would be rewarded with something edible. Abbot Ralph lingered, too.

'It is over,' said Roger in satisfaction. 'Bellême will never befoul English shores again.'

'Perhaps not, but he will certainly despoil Normandy.'

'It is a pity you did not kill him,' said Ralph sadly. 'You are right: hundreds of innocents will perish by his hand before he is defeated or dies. It will weaken Normandy and make his domains dangerous and wretched places to live.'

'Yes,' agreed Geoffrey. 'But a weakened, wretched

Normandy can only be good for a King of England who has set his sights on ruling there, too. Henry knew what he was doing.'

'I am sure he did,' said Ralph softly.

Epilogue

Matilda smoothed out the crumpled parchment in front of her and stared at the uneven lines and words that were marked on it. The map had been through a good deal since it had been taken from the knight who had murdered her mother a quarter of a century earlier, and it had not benefited from being in the possession of the slippery Durand, either. Matilda had no illusions about Geoffrey Mappestone's squire. He had sold the map to the highest bidder, and since Emma and Sybilla were dead and no longer in a position to make good on their offers, and Bellême had been driven with unseemly haste from England, Durand had relinquished the map to Matilda. He now owned enough gold to keep him in silken shirts and scented pomanders for the rest of his life – which Matilda suspected might be a very short one if Geoffrey ever discovered what he had done.

She had wondered at first whether she had wasted her money, but Bishop Maurice had obligingly shown her how to interpret the wavy lines and marks, and how to relate them to specific geographical features. She told him the map was from an old hermit, and that she intended to build a chapel on the spot he had indicated. Maurice was not interested in why she wanted his help, only that she did not repel his sweaty-handed advances as they rode at a leisurely pace to the coast.

When she eventually reached Normandy, Matilda went to the castle at Bures, where Old Mabel had died. She walked along the River Dives for the distance specified on the map, and discovered the great oak tree that stood in a woodland glade fifty-seven paces from its muddy banks. Then she dug until she discovered what she was looking for. It was wrapped in a leather sack and was heavy with soil, but a quick glance inside showed her a mass of thick grey hair still attached to a skull. It looked so similar to Emma's that Matilda had almost dropped it, but she recovered herself and returned to where her brother Roger waited. Together they entered the castle and set about uniting head with body.

'Now she can be at peace,' said Roger, standing back from the wooden box and bowing his head as a mark of respect. 'We all knew she would never rest easy until she was whole again. We shall bury her in the churchyard tomorrow, and that will be an end to her wanderings.'

He went to make the arrangements – hiring a priest to speak the proper words and a carpenter to craft a better chest than the one in which Old Mabel had reclined headless for so many years. When he had gone, a shadow emerged from behind one of the wall hangings.

'Well?' asked Bellême softly. 'Can you do it, sister? Can you take up where Emma left off and see our mother walk the Earth once more?'

'Oh, yes,' said Matilda confidently. 'Our House will be strong again under her control, and we will take back what Henry stole.'

'Under *her* control?' asked Bellême warily. 'I have no intention of relinquishing the little power I have left to a corpse.'

'She will not be a corpse,' objected Matilda. 'Besides, she is our mother. Of course she will stand at the head of the family.'

'Not over me,' insisted Bellême. 'I will not agree to it. When she returns, it will be as my vassal, and she will do what I tell her.'

'She will not,' said Matilda, trying to remain patient with him. 'She is no longer human, and cannot be subject to human control. She will be more powerful than either of us. If you want your English estates back, then you must bow to her commands.'

'I will not!' shouted Bellême furiously. 'And if debasing

341

myself before a woman is the only way to reclaim my properties, then Henry can keep them.'

Before Matilda could stop him, he had reached into the box and snatched up the head by its matted grey mane. Dried dirt and the shells of long-dead insects scattered across the floor as he brandished it. Then he strode to the window and cast the object out, watching it arc as it fell down and down, until it landed with a splash in the deep, fast-running waters of the River Dives below.

Matilda gave a cry of horror and rushed to the window, but the deed was done, and Mabel de Bellême would remain headless into eternity. She watched her brother kick the box closed and storm from the room. She fought to control her temper, thinking about all that was lost. Then she wondered whether Old Mabel might answer her calls anyway, because head and body *had* been united, albeit briefly. She rummaged around in Emma's possessions until she found the scroll containing ancient words in a mysterious tongue. She laid it on the coffin, and surrounded it with lighted candles, as she had seen Emma do so many times. Then she stopped, listening intently.

Had she heard a faint knock from inside the box? Or had it been her imagination?

Historical Postscript

R oger was almost right in that Robert de Bellême, Earl of Shrewsbury, would never tread on English soil again. He came once more, at Christmas 1105, probably in an attempt to reconcile himself with Henry and have his lands back. Henry would not see him, and Bellême went home empty-handed.

After his expulsion at the end of summer 1102, Bellême retired to Normandy in a foul frame of mind. He immediately started to face trouble from his family. Arnulf thought Bellême should share his Normandy estates on the grounds that he had lost his own fighting his brother's cause, and when Bellême refused, Arnulf started to donate the disputed castles to the Duke of Normandy. Others also rose up against the unpopular Earl. Bellême reacted with characteristic savagery. He suppressed the rebellion brutally, and several vassals and high-ranking churchmen were obliged to flee to England. Among them was Abbot Ralph of Sées.

Bellême was excommunicated twice, then started to make trouble for King Henry's brother, the Duke of Normandy. Bellême met the Duke and King Henry in open combat at the Battle of Tinchebrai in 1106, where he was thoroughly routed. He asked for a pardon, which was granted, along with the return of some of his lands, although none in England. The final confrontation of Bellême and Henry came in 1112, when Bellême rebelled yet again. This time there was no pardon, and Bellême was imprisoned, first at Cherbourg and then at Wareham, where he died at an unknown date. Contemporary records do not mention him again, so he was probably kept in close confinement until he died.

The House of Montgomery-Bellême was powerful, and included Bellême's brothers Hugh (who died in 1098); Roger the Poitevin, Count of Marche; Philip the Grammarian (who died at the siege of Antioch – and who was a good deal more valiant than portrayed in this fictional account); and Arnulf, Earl of Pembroke (who later schemed to marry an Irish princess and died on his wedding day). All joined their older brother in rebelling against either King William Rufus or King Henry. They also had four sisters: Emma (abbess of Alménches, 1074–1113), Matilda de Mortain, Mabel (who I left out of this tale on the grounds that more than two Mabels would be confusing!) and Sybilla (or Sybil) fitzHaimo. It is thought that Sybilla had four daughters called Mabel (who later married King Henry's most famous illegitimate son, Robert of Gloucester), Haweis, Cecily and Amise.

Old Mabel de Bellême was as colourful and unpleasant as her offspring. She was short, said to be extremely vindictive and enjoyed a reputation as a poisoner. She had amassed a huge number of enemies when, probably around 1078, a man called Hugh of Saugei, who had suffered many injustices at her hands, burst into her castle at Bures with three of his brothers. Mabel had been bathing in the nearby River Dives, and was lying naked on her bed to dry off. Despite the fact that her son Hugh was in the castle with sixteen knights, the Saugei brothers reached her chamber and hacked her to pieces. One chopped off her head and took it with him, and it is said she was buried headless. The Saugei brothers were never punished for the crime.

Accounts vary as to whether Greek Fire was used during the First Crusade, although most scholars agree that it was deployed in later ones. However, a contemporary account by Crusade leader Raymond de Agiles reports Arabs firing incendiary devices such as pitch, wax, sulphur and tow during the siege of Jerusalem in 1100.

The Crusaders faced two problems in using Greek Fire. First, no one was quite sure what it was, and even today scholars argue about its consistency. Suffice to say it was a sort of medieval napalm, and that once it burned it was difficult to put out. The leading authority on the subject is the chemist J.R. Partington, who indicates that there were a number of substances under the loose name of 'Greek Fire'. He suggests that the 'secret ingredient', which made it so much more dreadful than mere pitch or quicklime, was some kind of refined oil. He goes on to say that the Arabs had probably already worked out how to refine petroleum jelly from natural oil, and the addition of this would give the right consistency for something that would burn and stick, and cause such terror.

The second problem with Greek Fire was actually propelling it into enemy lines. This was before the days of gunpowder, so it basically had to be hurled using catapult-like devices, which made it difficult and dangerous to handle. Misfires and accidents must have been commonplace.

Other characters mentioned in this book were real people, besides the Bellêmes. Bishop Maurice of London (died 1107) was famous for starting work on the great cathedral church of St Paul's in London (rebuilt by Sir Christopher Wren in a style Maurice would not have recognized) and for insisting that his rabid appetite for women was a medical necessity.

Richard Beaumais (or Belmeis; died 1128), who became Bishop of London when Maurice died, was a follower of Bellême until 1102, when he changed sides. Henry rewarded him by making him Sheriff of Shropshire, where he set about subduing this unruly area with a treachery and deceit that would have made Bellême proud. He enticed Prince Iorwerth to Shrewsbury and promptly imprisoned him, and kept the Welsh lords in tow by stirring up petty quarrels and intrigues to keep them divided. William Pantulf was another defector. He persuaded Iorwerth to change sides, thus helping to bring about Bellême's defeat. After Bellême's exile, Pantulf was rewarded with Stafford Castle.

Ralph d'Escures, Abbot of Sées (died 1122), is a more appealing character. In an age dominated by hard, aggressive and self-serving men, Ralph had a considerable degree of integrity, was pious (not always a given in twelfth-century monastics) and was generally liked. He was intelligent, but enjoyed a joke. He later became Archbishop of Canterbury. It was Ralph who handed King Henry the keys to Shrewsbury Castle, because it was said that Bellême could not bring himself to do it.